Indian Killer

Indian Killer

SHERMAN ALEXIE

Grove Press
New York

Published simultaneously in Canada
Printed in the United States of America

Library of Congress Cataloging-in-Publication Data

Alexie, Sherman, 1966–
     Indian killer / Sherman Alexie. — 1st ed.
        p. cm.
     ISBN-13: 978-0-8021-4357-0
        1. Indians of North America—Washington (State)—Seattle—
Fiction.
     I. Title.
     PS3551.L35774I56 1996
     813' .54—dc20   96-27996

Design by Laura Hammond Hough

Grove Press
an imprint of Grove/Atlantic, Inc.
841 Broadway
New York, NY 10003

Distributed by Publishers Group West
www.groveatlantic.com

12 13 14 15 16   10 9 8 7 6 5 4

to my mother and father, for staying

to Diane, for arriving

Acknowledgments

With thanks to Donna Brook, Dick Lourie, Alice Ducey, Morgan Entrekin, and Nancy Stauffer. I would also like to thank the Lila Wallace–Reader's Digest Fund for their valuable support.

We are what
We have lost

—Alex Kuo

I

Owl Dancing

I

Mythology

The sheets are dirty. An Indian Health Service hospital in the late sixties. On this reservation or that reservation. Any reservation, a particular reservation. Antiseptic, cinnamon, and danker odors. Anonymous cries up and down the hallways. Linoleum floors swabbed with gray water. Mop smelling like old sex. Walls painted white a decade earlier, now yellowed and peeling. Old Indian woman in a wheelchair singing traditional songs to herself, tapping a rhythm on her armrest, right index finger tapping, tapping. Pause. Tap, tap. A phone ringing loudly from behind a thin door marked PRIVATE. Twenty beds available, twenty beds occupied. Waiting room where a young Indian man sits on a couch and holds his head in his hands. Nurses' lounge, two doctor's offices, and a scorched coffee pot. Old Indian man, his hair bright white and unbraided, pushing his I.V. bottle down the hallway. He is barefoot and confused, searching for a pair of moccasins he lost when he was twelve years old. Donated newspapers and magazines stacked in bundles, months and years out of date, missing pages. In one of the examining rooms, an Indian family of four, mother, father, son, daughter, all coughing blood quietly into handkerchiefs. The phone still ringing behind the PRIVATE door. A cinderblock building, thick windows that distort the view, pine trees, flagpole. A 1957 Chevy parked haphazardly, back door flung open, engine still running, back seat damp and bloodstained. Empty now.

The Indian woman on the table in the delivery room is very young, just a child herself. She is beautiful, even in the pain of labor, the contractions, the sudden tearing. When John imagines his birth, his mother is sometimes Navajo. Other times she is Lakota. Often, she is from the same tribe as the last Indian woman he has seen on television. Her legs tied in stirrups. Loose knots threatening to unravel. The white doctor has his hands inside her. Blood everywhere. The nurses work at mysterious machines. John's mother is tearing her vocal cords with the force of her screams. Years later, she still speaks in painful whispers. But during his birth, she is so young, barely into her teens, and the sheets are dirty.

The white doctor is twenty-nine years old. He has grown up in Iowa or Illinois, never seeing an Indian in person until he arrives at the reservation. His parents are poor. Having taken a government scholarship to make his way through medical school, he now has to practice medicine on the reservation in exchange for the money. This is the third baby he has delivered here. One white, two Indians. All of the children are beautiful.

John's mother is Navajo or Lakota. She is Apache or Seminole. She is Yakama or Spokane. Her dark skin contrasts sharply with the white sheets, although they are dirty. She pushes when she should be pushing. She stops pushing when they tell her to stop. With clever hands, the doctor turns John's head to the correct position. He is a good doctor.

The doctor has fallen in love with Indians. He thinks them impossibly funny and irreverent. During the hospital staff meetings, all of the Indians sit together and whisper behind their hands. There are no Indian doctors, but a few of the nurses and most of the administrative staff are Indian. The white doctor often wishes he could sit with the Indians and whisper behind his hand. But he maintains a personable and professional distance. He misses his parents, who still live in Iowa or Illinois. He calls them often, sends postcards of beautiful, generic landscapes.

The doctor's hands are deep inside John's mother, who is only fourteen, and who is bleeding profusely where they have cut her to make room for John's head. But the sheets were dirty before the blood, and her vagina will heal. She is screaming in pain. The doctor could not give her painkillers because she had arrived at the hospital too far into labor. The Chevy is still running outside, rear door flung open, back seat red and damp. The driver is in the waiting room. He holds his head in his hands.

Are you the father?

No, I'm the driver. She was walking here when I picked her up. She was hitchhiking. I'm just her cousin. I'm just the driver.

The phone behind the PRIVATE door is still ringing. His mother pushes one last time and John slides into the good doctor's hands. Afterbirth. The doctor clears John's mouth. John inhales deeply, exhales, cries. The old Indian woman in the wheelchair stops singing. She hears a baby crying. She stops her tapping to listen. She forgets why she is listening, then returns to her own song and the tapping, tapping. Pause. Tap, tap. The doctor cuts the umbilical cord quickly. There is no time to waste. A nurse cleans John, washes away the blood, the remains of the placenta, the evidence. His mother is crying.

I want my baby. Give me my baby. I want to see my baby. Let me hold my baby.

The doctor tries to comfort John's mother. The nurse swaddles John in blankets and takes him from the delivery room, past the old Indian man dragging his I.V. down the hallway, looking for his long-lost moccasins. She carries John outside. A flag hangs uselessly on its

pole. No wind. The smell of pine. Inside the hospital, John's mother
has fainted. The doctor holds her hand, as if he were the loving husband and father. He remembers the family of four coughing blood into
handkerchiefs in the examining room. The doctor is afraid of them.

    With John in her arms, the nurse stands in the parking lot.
She is white or Indian. She watches the horizon. Blue sky, white
clouds, bright sun. The slight whine of a helicopter in the distance.
Then the violent *whomp-whomp* of its blades as it passes overhead,
hovers, and lands a hundred feet away. In the waiting room, the driver
lifts his head from his hands when he hears the helicopter. He wonders if there is a war beginning.

    A man in a white jumpsuit steps from the helicopter. Head
ducked and body bent, the man runs toward the nurse. His features
are hidden inside his white helmet. The nurse meets him halfway and
hands him the baby John. The jumpsuit man covers John's face completely, protecting him from the dust that the helicopter is kicking
up. The sky is very blue. Specific birds hurl away from the flying
machine. These birds are indigenous to this reservation. They do not
live anywhere else. They have purple-tipped wings and tremendous
eyes, or red bellies and small eyes. The nurse waves as the jumpsuit
man runs back to the helicopter. She shuts the rear door of the Chevy,
reaches through the driver's open window, and turns the ignition key.
The engine shudders to a stop.

    Suddenly this is a war. The jumpsuit man holds John close to
his chest as the helicopter rises. The helicopter gunman locks and
loads, strafes the reservation with explosive shells. Indians hit the
ground, drive their cars off roads, dive under flimsy kitchen tables.
A few Indians, two women and one young man, continue their slow
walk down the reservation road, unperturbed by the gunfire. They
have been through much worse. The *whomp-whomp* of the helicopter
blades. John is hungry and cries uselessly. He cannot be heard over
the roar of the gun, the chopper. He cries anyway. This is all he knows
how to do. Back at the clinic, his mother has been sedated. She sleeps

in the delivery room. The doctor holds her hand and finds he cannot move. He looks down at his hand wrapped around her hand. White fingers, brown fingers. He can see the blue veins running through his skin like rivers. The phone behind the PRIVATE door stops ringing. Gunfire in the distance. Nobody, not even the white doctor, is surprised by this.

The helicopter flies for hours, it could be days, crossing desert, mountain, freeway, finally a city. Skyscrapers, the Space Needle, water everywhere. Thin bridges stretched between islands. John crying. The gunner holds his fire, but his finger is lightly feathering the trigger. He is ready for the worst. John can feel the distance between the helicopter and the ground below. He stops crying. He loves the distance between the helicopter and the ground. He feels he could fall. He somehow loves this new fear. He wants to fall. He wants the jumpsuit man to release him, let him fall from the helicopter, down through the clouds, past the skyscrapers and the Space Needle. But the jumpsuit man holds him tight so John will not fall. John cries again.

The helicopter circles downtown Seattle, moves east past Lake Washington, Mercer Island, hovers over the city of Bellevue. The pilot searches for the landing area. Five acres of green, green grass. A large house. Swimming pool. A man and woman waving energetically. Home. The pilot lowers the chopper and sets down easily. Blades making a windstorm of grass particles and hard-shelled insects. The gunner's eyes are wide open, scanning the tree line. He is ready for anything. The jumpsuit man slides the door open with one arm and holds John in the other. Noise, heat. John cries, louder than before, trying to be heard. Home. The jumpsuit man steps down and runs across the lawn toward the man and woman, both white and handsome. He wears a gray suit and colorful tie. She wears a red dress with large, black buttons from throat to knee.

John cries as the jumpsuit man hands him to the white woman, Olivia Smith. She unbuttons the top of her dress, opens her bra, and offers John her large, pale breasts with pink nipples. John's birth mother had small, brown breasts and brown nipples, though he never suckled at them. Still, he knows there is a difference, and as John takes the white woman's right nipple into his mouth and pulls at her breast, he discovers it is empty. Daniel Smith wraps his left arm around his wife's shoulders. He grimaces briefly and then smiles. Olivia and Daniel Smith look at the jumpsuit man, who is holding a camera. Flash, flash. Click of the shutter. Whirr of advancing film. All of them wait for a photograph to form, for light to emerge from shadow, for an image to burn itself into paper.

2

The Last Skyscraper in Seattle

When no baby came after years of trying to conceive, Olivia and Daniel Smith wanted to adopt a baby, but the waiting list was so long. The adoption agency warned them that white babies, of course, were the most popular. Not that it was a popularity contest, they were assured. It was just that most of the couples interested in adopting a baby were white, so naturally, they wanted to adopt a white child, a child like them, but there were simply not enough white babies to go around.

"Listen," the adoption agent said. "Let's be honest. It's going to take at least a year to find a suitable white child for you. Frankly, it may take much longer than that. Up to eight years or more. But we can find you another kind of baby rather quickly."

"Another kind?" asked Olivia.

"Well, of course," said the agent. "There's always the handi-capped babies. Down's syndrome. Children missing arms and legs.

Mentally retarded. That kind of kid. To be honest, it's very difficult, nearly impossible, to find homes for those children. It's perfectly understandable. These children need special care, special attention. Lots of love. Not very many people can handle it."

"I don't think we want that," Daniel said. Olivia agreed.

"There are other options," said the agent. "We have other difficult-to-place children as well. Now, there's nothing wrong with these babies. They're perfectly healthy, but they're not white. Most are black. We also have an Indian baby. The mother is six months pregnant now."

"Indian?" asked Daniel. "As in American Indian?"

"Yes," said the agent. "The mother is very young, barely into her teens. She's making the right decision. She'll carry the baby to full term and give it up for adoption. Now, ideally, we'd place this baby with Indian parents, right? But that just isn't going to happen. The best place for this baby is with a white family. This child will be saved a lot of pain by growing up in a white family. It's the best thing, really."

Olivia and Daniel agreed to consider adopting the Indian baby. They went home that night, ate a simple dinner, and watched television. A sad movie-of-the-week about an incurable disease. Daniel kept clearing his throat during the movie. Olivia cried. When it was over, Daniel switched off the television. They undressed for bed, brushed their teeth, and lay down together.

"What do you think?" asked Olivia.

"I don't know," said Daniel.

They made love then, both secretly hoping this one would take. They wanted to believe that everything was possible. An egg would drop, be fertilized, and begin to grow. As he moved inside his wife, Daniel closed his eyes and concentrated on an image of a son. That son would be exactly half of him. He saw a son with his chin and hair. He saw a baseball glove, bicycle, tree house, barking dog. Olivia wrapped her arms around her husband, pressed her face to his shoulder. She could feel him inside her, but it was a vague, amorphous feeling. There was nothing specific about it. During the course of their married life, the sex had mostly felt good. Sometimes, it had been uncomfortable, once or twice painful. But she did not feel anything this time. She opened her eyes and stared at the ceiling.

Olivia knew she was beautiful. She had been a beautiful baby, little girl, teenager, woman. She had never noticed whether it was easy or hard to be that beautiful. It never really occurred to her to wonder about it. All her life, her decisions had been made for her. She was meant to graduate from high school, get into a good college, find a suitable young man, earn a B.A. in art history, marry, and never work. Somewhere between reading a biography of van Gogh and fixing dinner, she was supposed to have a baby. Except for producing that infant, she had done what was expected of her, had fulfilled the obligations of her social contract. She had graduated with honors, had married a handsome, successful architect, and loved sex in a guarded way. But the baby would not happen. The doctors had no explanations. Her husband's sperm were of average count and activity. "In a swimming race," their doctor had said, "your husband's sperm would get the bronze." She had a healthy uterus and her period was loyal to the moon's cycles. But it did not work. "Listen," the doctor had said. "There are some people who just cannot have babies together. We can't always explain it. Medicine isn't perfect."

Still staring at the ceiling, Olivia moved her hips in rhythm with her husband's. She wanted to ask him what he was thinking about, but did not want to interrupt their lovemaking. She lifted herself to her husband, listening to the patterns of his breathing until it was over.

"I love you," she whispered.

"I love you, too," Daniel said.

He lifted himself off her and rolled to his side of the bed. She reached out and took his hand. He was crying. She held him until they fell asleep. When they woke in the morning, both had decided to adopt the Indian baby.

Olivia was determined to be a good mother. She knew it was a complicated situation, that she would have to explain her baby's brown skin to any number of strangers. There was no chance that she would be able to keep her baby's adoption a secret. Two white parents, a brown baby. There was no other way to explain it. But she did not fool herself into thinking that her baby would somehow become white just because she and Daniel were white. After John arrived, she spent hours in the library. With John sleeping beside her, she would do research on Native American history and culture. The adoption agency refused to divulge John's tribal affiliation and sealed all of his birth records, revealing only that John's birth mother was fourteen years old. Olivia spent hours looking through books, searching the photographs for any face like her son's face. She read books about the Sioux, and Navajo, and Winnebago. Crazy Horse, Geronimo, and Sitting Bull rode horses through her imagination. She bought all the children's books about Indians and read them aloud to John. Daniel thought it was an obsessive thing to do, but he did not say anything. He had named the baby John after his grandfather and thought it ironic. His grandfather had been born in Germany and never really learned much English, even after years in the United States.

"Honey," Daniel whispered to his wife when John woke up crying. Three in the morning, the moon full and bright white. "Honey, it's the baby."

Olivia rose from bed, walked into the nursery, and picked up John. She carried him to the window.

"Look, sweetie," she said to John. "It's just the moon. See, it's pretty."

Daniel listened to his wife talking to their son.

"It's the moon," she said and then said the word in Navajo, Lakota, Apache. She had learned a few words in many Indian languages. From books, Western movies, documentaries. Once she saw an Indian woman at the supermarket and asked her a few questions that were answered with bemused tolerance.

"It's just the moon," whispered Olivia and then she softly sang it. "It's the moon. It's the moon."

Daniel listened for a few minutes before he rolled over and fell asleep. When he woke the next morning, Olivia was standing at that same window with John in her arms, as if she'd been there all night.

"We need to get John baptized," she said with a finality that Daniel didn't question.

Because the baby John was Indian, Olivia and Daniel Smith wanted him to be baptized by an Indian, and they searched for days and weeks for the only Indian Jesuit in the Pacific Northwest. Father Duncan, a Spokane Indian Jesuit, was a strange man. A huge man, an artist. He painted contemporary landscapes, portraits, and murals that were highlighted with traditional Spokane Indian images. His work was displayed in almost every Jesuit community in the country. He was a great teacher, a revered theologian, but an eccentric. He ate bread and soup at every meal. Whole grains and vegetable broth, sourdough and chicken stock. He talked to himself, laughed at inappropriate moments, sometimes read books backward, starting with the last page and working toward the beginning. An irony, an Indian in black robes, he took a special interest in John and, with Olivia and Daniel's heartfelt approval, often visited him. The Jesuit held the baby John in his arms, sang traditional Spokane songs and Catholic hymns, and rocked him to sleep. As John grew older, Father Duncan would tell him secrets and make him promise never to reveal them. John kept his promises.

On a gray day when John was six years old, Father Duncan took him to see the Chapel of the North American Martyrs in downtown Seattle. John found himself surrounded by vivid stained glass reproductions of Jesuits being martyred by Indians. Bright white Jesuits with bright white suns at their necks. A Jesuit, tied to a post, burning alive as Indians dance around him. Another pierced with dozens of arrows. A third, with his cassock torn from his body, crawling away from an especially evil-looking Indian. The fourth being drowned in a blue river. The fifth, sixth, and seventh being scalped. An eighth and ninth praying together as a small church burns behind them. And more and more. John stared up at so much red glass.

"Beautiful, isn't it?" asked Father Duncan.

John did not understand. He was not sure if Father Duncan thought the artwork was beautiful, or if the murder of the Jesuits was beautiful. Or both.

"There's a myth, a story, that the blood of those Jesuits was used to stain the glass," said Duncan. "But who knows if it's true. We Jesuits love to tell stories."

"Why did the Indians kill them?"

"They wanted to kick the white people out of America. Since the priests were the leaders, they were the first to be killed."

John looked up at the stained glass Jesuits, then at the Spokane Indian Jesuit.

"But you're a priest," said John.

"Yes, I am."

John did not have the vocabulary to express what he was feeling. But he understood there was something odd about the contrast between the slaughtered Jesuits and Father Duncan, and between the Indian Jesuit and the murderers.

"Did the white people leave?" asked John.

"Some of them did. But more came."

"It didn't work."

"No."

"Why didn't the Indians kill all the white people?"

"They didn't have the heart for it."

"But didn't white people kill most of the Indians?"

"Yes, they did."

John was confused. He stared up at the martyred Jesuits. Then he noticed the large crucifix hanging over the altar. A mortally wounded Jesus, blood pouring from his hands and feet, from the wound in his side. John saw the altar candles burning and followed the white smoke as it rose toward the ceiling of the chapel.

"Was Jesus an Indian?" asked John.

Duncan studied the crucifix, then looked down at John.

"He wasn't an Indian," said the Jesuit, "but he should have been."

John seemed to accept that answer. He could see the pain in Jesus's wooden eyes. At six, he already knew that a wooden Jesus could weep. He'd seen it on the television. Once every few years, a wooden Jesus wept and thousands of people made the pilgrimage to the place where the miracle happened. If miracles happened with such regularity when did they cease to be miracles? And simply become ordinary events, pedestrian proof of God? John knew that holy people sometimes bled from their hands and feet, just as Jesus had bled from his hands and feet when nailed to the cross. Such violence, such faith.

"Why did they do that to Jesus?" asked John.

"He died so that we may live forever."

"Forever?"

"Forever."

John looked up again at the windows filled with the dead and dying.

"Did those priests die like Jesus?" asked John.

Father Duncan did not reply. He knew that Jesus was killed because he was dangerous, because he wanted to change the world in a good way. He also knew that the Jesuits were killed because they were dangerous to the Indians who didn't want their world to change at all. Duncan knew those Jesuits thought they were changing the Indians in a good way.

"Did they die like Jesus?" John asked again.

Duncan was afraid to answer the question. As a Jesuit, he knew those priests were martyred just like Jesus. As a Spokane Indian, he knew those Jesuits deserved to die for their crimes against Indians.

"John," Duncan said after a long silence. "You see these windows? You see all of this? It's what is happening inside me right now."

John stared at Duncan, wondering if the Jesuit had a stained glass heart. Rain began to beat against the windows, creating an illusion of movement on the stained faces of the murderous Indians and martyred Jesuits, and on young John's face. And on Duncan's. The man and child stared up at the glass.

Father Duncan's visits continued until John was seven years old. Then, with no warning or explanation, Duncan was gone. When John asked his parents about Father Duncan's whereabouts, Olivia and Daniel told him that the Jesuit had retired and moved to Arizona. In fact, Duncan's eccentricities had become liabilities. After the strange Sunday when he had openly wept during Eucharist and run out of the church before the closing hymn, Duncan was summarily removed from active duty and shipped to a retreat in Arizona. He walked into the desert one week after he arrived at the retreat and was never seen again.

As he grew up, John kept reading the newspaper account of the disappearance, though it contained obvious errors. Anonymous sources insisted that Father Duncan had lost his faith in God. John knew that Duncan had never lost his faith, but had caused others to believe he did. His body was never found, though a search party followed Duncan's tracks miles into the desert, until they simply stopped.

For John, though, Father Duncan did not vanish completely. The Jesuit, exhausted and sunburned, often visited him in dreams. Duncan never spoke. He just brought the smell, sounds, and images of the desert into John's head. The wind pushing sand from dune to dune, the scorpions and spiders, the relentless yellow sun and deep blue sky, the stand of palm trees on the horizon. John always assumed it was a Catholic way to die, lost in the desert, no water, no food, the unforgiving heat. But the hallucinations must have been magical. John knew that real Indians climbed into the mountains to have vision quests. Stripped of their clothes, they ate and drank nothing. Naked and starved, they waited for a vision to arrive. Father Duncan must have been on a vision quest in the desert when he walked to the edge of the world and stepped off. Did it feel good to disappear? Perhaps Duncan, as Indian and Christian, had discovered a frightening secret and could not live with it. Perhaps Duncan knew what existed on the other side of the desert. Maybe he was looking for a new name for God.

John attended St. Francis Catholic School from the very beginning. His shoes always black topsiders polished clean. His black hair very short, nearly a crew cut, just like every other boy in school. He was the only Indian in the school, but he had friends, handsome white boys. And John had danced with a few pretty white girls in high school. Mary, Margaret, Stephanie. He had fumbled with their underwear in the back seats of cars. John knew their smell, a combination of perfume, baby powder, sweat, and sex. A clean smell on one level, a darker odor beneath. Their breasts were small and perfect. John was always uncomfortable during his time with the girls, and he was never sorry when it was over. He was impatient with them, unsure of their motives, and vaguely insulting. The girls expected it. It was high school and boys were supposed to act that way. The girls assumed the boys were much more complicated than they actually were. Inside, John knew that he was more simple and shallow than other boys, and less than real.

"What are you thinking?" the girls always asked John. But John knew the girls really wanted to tell him what they were thinking. John's thoughts were merely starting points for the girls to talk about mothers and fathers, girlfriends, ex-boyfriends, pets, clothes, and a thousand other details. John felt insignificant at those times and retreated into a small place inside of himself, until the girls confused his painful silence with rapt interest.

The girls' fathers were always uncomfortable when they first met John, and grew more irritated as he continued to date Mary, Margaret, or Stephanie. The relationships began and ended quickly. A dance or two, a movie, a hamburger, a few hours in a friend's basement with generic rock music playing softly on the radio, cold fingers on warm skin.

"I just don't think it's working out," she'd tell John, who understood. He could almost hear the conversations that had taken place.

"Hon," a father would say to his daughter. "What was that boy's name?"

"Which boy, daddy?"

"That dark one."

"Oh, you mean John. Isn't he cute?"

"Yes, he seems like a very nice young man. You say he's at St. Francis? Is he a scholarship student?"

"I don't know. I don't think so. Does it matter?"

"Well, no. I'm just curious, hon. By the way, what is he? I mean, where does he come from?"

"He's Indian, daddy."

"From India? He's a foreigner?"

"No, daddy, he's Indian from here. You know, American Indian. Like bows and arrows and stuff. Except he's not like that. His parents are white."

"I don't understand."

"Daddy, he's adopted."

"Oh. Are you going to see him again?"

"I hope so. Why?"

"Well, you know. I just think. Well, adopted kids have so many problems adjusting to things, you know. I've read about it. They have self-esteem problems. I just think, I mean, don't you think you should find somebody more appropriate?"

The door would shut with a loud and insistent click. Mary, Margaret, or Stephanie would come to school the next day and give John the news. The daughters would never mention their fathers. Of course, there were a few white girls who dated John precisely because they wanted to bring home a dark boy. Through all of it, John repeatedly promised himself he would never be angry. He didn't want to be angry. He wanted to be a real person. He wanted to control his emotions, so he would often swallow his anger. Once or twice a week, he felt the need to run and hide. In the middle of a math class or a history exam, he would get a bathroom pass and quickly leave the classroom. His teachers were always willing to give him a little slack. They knew he was adopted, an Indian orphan, and was leading a difficult life. His teachers gave him every opportunity and he responded well. If John happened to be a little fragile, well, that was perfectly understandable, considering his people's history. All that alcoholism and poverty, the lack of God in their lives. In the bathroom, John would lock himself inside a stall and fight against his anger. He'd bite his tongue, his lips, until sometimes they would bleed. He would hold himself tightly and feel his arms, legs, and lower back shake with the effort. His eyes would be shut. He'd grind his teeth. One minute, two, five, and he would be fine. He would flush the toilet to make his visit seem normal, slowly wash his hands and return to the classroom. His struggles with his anger increased in intensity and frequency until he was visiting the bathroom on a daily basis during his senior year. But nobody noticed. In truth, nobody mentioned any strange behavior they may have seen. John was a trailblazer, a nice trophy for St. Francis, a successfully integrated Indian boy.

There were three hundred and seventy-six students at St. Francis. Along with three black kids, John was one of the four non-white students in the school. He was neither widely popular nor widely disliked. He played varsity basketball for two years, but never started, and entered the game when the outcome, a win or loss, was already decided. He was on the varsity only because he was an upperclassman and over six feet tall. His teammates cheered wildly whenever he entered the game because teammates are taught to behave that way. John understood this. He cheered for his teammates, even during those games in which he never played. He never really cared if the team won or lost. But he was always embarrassed when he had to play, because he knew he was not very good. In fact, he only played because his father, Daniel, a St. Francis alumnus, had been a star player.

"You need to get your hand behind the ball when you shoot," Daniel Smith said to John during one of their driveway practices.

"Like this?" asked John, desperately trying to hold the basketball correctly.

"No," Daniel said, calmly, patiently. Daniel Smith never raised his voice, not once, in all the years. He would coach John for hours, trying to show him how to play defense, box out for rebounds, throw the bounce pass. No matter how poorly John played, and he was awful, Daniel never yelled.

One winter, when John was a sophomore, Daniel read about an all-Indian basketball tournament that was going to be held at Indian Heritage High School in North Seattle. Daniel and Olivia both looked for any news about Indians and shared the information with John. The sportswriter made the tournament into some kind of joke, but Daniel thought it was a wonderful opportunity. He had never seen Indians play basketball. Maybe John would improve if he saw other Indians play.

John had spent time at different Indian events. Olivia had made sure of that. But he had never seen so many Indians crammed into such a small space. The Indian Heritage gym was full of Indians. All shapes and sizes, tribes and temperaments. Daniel and John found seats in the bleachers and watched a game between a Sioux team and a local team of Yakama Indians. The game was fast-paced and vaguely out of control, with offenses that took the first open shot, from anywhere on the court, and defenses that constantly gambled for steals. Most of the players were tall and impossibly thin, although a few were actually fat. The best player on the court was a chubby guy named Arnold, a Yakama Indian. Daniel and John knew he was named Arnold because they heard his name announced over the loudspeaker.

"Arnold for two."

"Arnold with a three-pointer."

"Arnold with the steal, and a nice pass for two."

Daniel decided that Arnold was the best player he had ever seen. He could have played Division I basketball. God, Daniel thought, this Indian is fifty pounds overweight, closing in on forty years old, and still plays well.

"Watch," Daniel said to John.

John was watching Arnold, but he was watching the people around him too. So many Indians, so many tribes, many sharing similar features, but also differing in slight and important ways. The Makahs different than the Quinaults, the Lummi different from the Puyallup. There were Indians with dark skin and jet-black hair. There were Indians with brown hair and paler skin. Green-eyed Indians. Indians with black blood. Indians with Mexican blood. Indians with white blood. Indians with Asian blood. All of them laughing and carrying on. Many Indians barely paying attention to the game. They were talking, telling jokes, and laughing loudly. So much laughter. John wanted to own that laughter, never realizing that their laughter was a ceremony used to drive away personal and collective demons. The Indians who were watching the game reacted mightily to each basket or defensive stop. They moaned and groaned as if each mistake were fatal, as if each field goal meant the second coming of Christ. But always, they were laughing. John had never seen so many happy people. He did not share their happiness.

"Look at him," Daniel said. "Look at that guy play."

John watched Arnold shoot a thirty-five-foot jumper that hit nothing but the bottom of the net. A glorious three-pointer. The crowd cheered and laughed some more. Arnold was laughing, on the court, doubled over, holding his stomach. Laughing so hard that tears ran down his face. His teammates were smiling and playing defense. The other team worked the ball around, trying to shoot a long jumper of their own, wanting to match Arnold's feat. A big man caught the ball in the far corner, faked a dribble, then took the shot. An air ball, missing the basket and backboard completely, by two or three feet. The big man fell on his back, laughing. The crowd laughed and rolled all over the bleachers, pounding each other on the back, hugging each other tightly. One Yakama player grabbed the rebound and threw a long pass downcourt to Arnold. He caught the pass, fumbled the ball a bit, dribbled in for the layup, and missed it. So much laughter that the refs called an official timeout. John looked at his father. Daniel was laughing. John felt like crying. He did not recognize these Indians. They were nothing like the Indians he had read about. John felt betrayed.

John never did become a good basketball player, but he graduated from high school on time, in 1987. Since he was an Indian with respectable grades, John would have been admitted into almost any public university had he bothered to fill out even one application. His parents pushed him to at least try a community or technical college, but John refused. During his freshman year in high school, John had read an article about a group of Mohawk Indian steel workers who helped build the World Trade Center buildings in New York City. Ever since then, John had dreamed about working on a skyscraper. He figured it was the Indian thing to do. Since Daniel Smith was an architect, he sometimes flattered himself by thinking that John's interest in construction was somehow related. Despite John's refusal to go to college, his parents still supported him in his decision, and were sitting in the third row as he walked across the stage at St. Francis to accept his diploma. Polite applause, a few loud cheers from his friends, his mother and father now standing. John flipped his tassel from one side to the other, blinked in the glare of the flashbulbs, and tried to smile. He had practiced his smile, knew it was going to be needed for this moment. He smiled. The cameras flashed. John was finished with high school and would never attend college. He walked offstage and stepped onto the fortieth floor of an unfinished office building in downtown Seattle.

† † †

John Smith was now twenty-seven years old. He was six feet, six inches tall and heavily muscled, a young construction worker perfect for all of the heavy lifting. His black hair was long and tucked under his hard hat. When he had first started working, his co-workers used to give him grief about his hair, but half of the crew had long hair these days. Seattle was becoming a city dominated by young white men with tiny ponytails. John always had the urge to carry a pair of scissors and snip off those ponytails at every opportunity. He hated those ponytails, but he did not let them distract him at work. He was a good worker, quiet and efficient. He was eating lunch alone on the fortieth floor when he heard the voices again.

John swallowed the last of his cold coffee and gently set the thermos down. He cupped his hand to his ear. He knew he was alone on this floor, but the voices were clear and precise. During the quiet times, he could hear the soft *why-why-why* as Father Duncan's leather sandals brushed against the sand on his long walk through the desert. Once, just once, John had heard the bubble of the baptismal fountain as Father Duncan dipped him into the water. Sometimes there were sudden sirens and explosions, or the rumble of a large crowd in an empty room. John could remember when it first happened, this noise in his head. He was young, maybe ten years old, when he heard strange music. It happened as he ran from school, across the parking lot, toward the car where Olivia waited for him. He knew this music was written especially for him: violins, bass guitar, piano, harmonica, drums. Now, as he sat on the fortieth floor and listened to those voices, John felt a sharp pain in his lower back. His belly burned.

"Jesus," said John as he stood up, waving his arms in the air.

"Hey, chief, what you doing? Trying to land a plane?"

The foreman was standing in the elevator a few feet away. John liked to eat his lunch near the elevator so he could move quickly and easily between floors. He always liked mobility.

"Well," said the foreman. "What's up?"

John lowered his arms.

"On my break," John said. He could still hear voices speaking to him. They were so loud, but the foreman was oblivious. The foreman knew John always ate lunch alone, a strange one, that John. Never went for beers after work. Showed up five minutes early every day and left five minutes late. He could work on one little task all day, until it was done, and never complain. No one bothered him because he didn't bother anyone. No one knew a damn thing about John, except that he worked hard, the ultimate compliment. Not that the hard work mattered anymore, since there would be no more high-rise work in Seattle after they finished this job. They were building the last skyscraper in Seattle. Computers had made the big buildings obsolete. No need to shove that many workers into such a small space. After this last building was complete, the foreman would take a job for the state. He did not know what John had planned.

"Well," the foreman said. "Lunch is over. Get in. We need you down on thirty-three."

John was embarrassed. He felt the heat build in his stomach, rise through his back, and fill his head. It started that way. The heat came first, followed quickly by the music. A slow hum. A quiet drum. Then a symphony crashing through his spinal column. The foreman brought the heat and music. John looked at him, a short white man with a protruding belly and big arms. An ugly man with a bulbous nose and weak chin, though his eyes were a striking blue.

John knew if he were a real Indian, he could have called the wind. He could have called a crosscutting wind that would've sliced through the fortieth floor, pulled the foreman out of the elevator, and sent him over the edge of the building. But he's strong, that foreman, and he would catch himself. He'd be hanging from the edge by his fingertips.

In his head, John could see the foreman hanging from the fortieth floor.

"Help me!" the foreman would shout.

John saw himself plant his feet just inches from the edge, reach down, take the foreman's wrists in his hands, and hold him away from the building. John and the foreman would sway back and forth like a pendulum. Back and forth, back and forth.

"Jesus!" the foreman would shout. "Pull me up!"

John would look down to see the foreman's blue eyes wide with fear. That's what I need to see, that's what will feed me, thought John. Fear in blue eyes. He would hold onto the foreman as long as possible and stare down into those terrified blue eyes. Then he'd let him fall.

"Let's go, chief," the foreman said, loud and friendly. "We ain't got all day. We need you on thirty-three."

John stepped into the elevator. The foreman pulled the gate shut and pressed the button for the thirty-third floor. Neither talked on the way down. John could feel the tension in his stomach as the elevator made its short journey. He fought against the music.

"Chuck needs your help," the foreman said when they arrived.

John looked where the foreman pointed. The thirty-third floor was a controlled mess. Chuck, a white man with a huge moustache, was pounding a nail into place. He raised a hammer and brought it down on the head of the nail. He raised the hammer, brought it down again. Metal against metal. John saw sparks. Sparks. Sparks. He rubbed his eyes. The sparks were large enough and of long enough duration to turn to flame. The foreman didn't see it. The rest of the crew didn't see it. Chuck raised the hammer again and paused at the top of his swing. As the hammer began its next descent, John could see it happening in segments, as in a series of still photographs. In that last frozen moment, in that brief instant before the hammer struck again its explosion of flame, John knew exactly what to do with his life.

John needed to kill a white man.

3

Owl Dancing at the Beginning
of the End of the World

John sat alone on the fortieth floor. He could see a white man working at a small desk in an office across the street. A small man from
any distance. John knew he could kill a white man, but he was not
sure which white man was responsible for everything that had gone
wrong. He thought hard that day, could barely work, and often stared
off into space, trying to decide. Which white man had done the most
harm to the world? Was it the richest white man? Was it the poorest
white man? John believed that both the richest and poorest white men
in the country lived in Seattle.

    The richest man owned a toy company. No. He owned the
largest toy company in the world. It had thousands of employees. John
saw the rich man on television. In commercials. On talk shows. On
goofy game shows. His wedding was broadcast nationally. He had
married a movie star, one of those beautiful actresses whose name
John always forgot. Julie, Jennifer, Janine. The rich man's name was

short and masculine, a three-lettered name that was somehow smaller and still more important than John. Bob or Ted or Dan or something like that. A monosyllabic, triangular monument of a name. A name where every letter loudly shouted its meaning. John could not understand how a man named Bob or Ted became rich and famous by selling toys. How can a toy maker meet and marry a beautiful actress? John knew that Bob or Dan must have sold his soul, that slaves worked in his factories. Thousands of children. No. Indians. Thousands of Indians chained together in basements, sweating over stupid board games that were thinly disguised imitations of Scrabble and Monopoly, cheap stuffed monkeys, and primitive computer games where all the illegal space aliens were blasted into pieces. But John could not convince himself that the richest man in the world deserved to die. It was too easy. If he killed the richest white man in the world, then the second-richest white man would take his place. Nobody would even notice the difference. All the money would be switched from one account to another. All the slaves would stop making toys, move to another factory, and begin making car alarms, director's chairs, or toasters. John could kill a thousand rich white men and not change a thing.

The poorest white man in the world stole aluminum cans from John's garbage. Well, that was not exactly true. Every Monday, John set the cans outside his apartment building for the recycling truck to collect, but the poorest white man always arrived first. John watched him from his bedroom window. The poorest white man dressed in ragged clothes. His skin diseased, face deeply pockmarked, hair pulled back in a greasy ponytail. The poor man would pick up the aluminum cans one by one and drop them into his shopping cart. Empty Campbell's tomato soup cans, Pepsi cans, cans that once held stew or creamed corn, hash or pineapple chunks. One by one, carefully, as if the aluminum cans were fragile, priceless. John hoped the poorest white man sold the cans for cents on the pound, and then bought some food. The poorest man might have a family, a white wife, white kids, all starving in some city park. But John knew the poorest man sold the cans for booze money. He just drank and drank. Fortified wine, rubbing alcohol, Sterno. John hated poor white men, but he knew killing them was a waste. They were already dead. They were zombies. John could stick a bomb in one of his aluminum cans. A mercury switch. When the zombie picked up the can, the switch would move, and boom! But it would be a small gesture, little more than waving good-bye to somcone you had just met.

Rich man, poor man, beggarman, thief. Lawyer, doctor, architect, construction foreman. John knew this was the most important decision in his life. Which white man had done the most harm to Indians? He knew that priests had cut out the tongues of Indians who continued to speak their tribal languages. He had seen it happen. He had gathered the tongues in his backpack and buried them in the foundation of a bank building. He had held wakes and tried to sing like Indians sing for the dead. But Father Duncan was proof of something bigger, wasn't he? Father Duncan, an Indian, had walked into the desert like a holy man and disappeared. Whenever he closed his eyes, John could see the desert. The cacti, lizards, washes, and sand dunes, the lack of water. John knew what water meant to life. A man could have a camel loaded down with food, enough for weeks, but that same man would die without water. A man without water could last for two days, three days, four days at most. Father Duncan did not take any water into the desert with him. He left behind his paints and an empty canvas. He left behind his hat and shoes. But there was no water in the desert, not for miles and miles. How could Father Duncan have survived such a journey? How was he saved? How had he arrived in John's dreams, both awake and asleep? John could see the stand of palm trees at the horizon, either an illusion or a place of safety. Could see Duncan in his black robe staggering across the hot sand. If John concentrated hard, he could see Father Duncan's red-rimmed eyes, cracked lips, burned skin. So much thirst.

After quitting time, John rode the elevator down through the unfinished building. He rode with the foreman and a couple other co-workers named Jim and Jerry. Nobody knew the foreman's name.

He was simply known as the foreman. John knew these white men were mostly harmless and would live forever. They would leave work and have a few beers at the same tavern where they had been drinking together for years. They were regulars. Jim, Jerry, and the foreman would walk into the bar and all the patrons would loudly greet their arrival.

John stepped off the elevator, ignored offers to go for beers, and walked through the downtown Seattle streets. There were so many white men to choose from. Everybody was a white man in downtown Seattle. The heat and noise in his head were loud and painful. He wanted to run. He even started to run. But he stopped. He could not run. Everybody would notice. Everybody would know that he was thinking about killing white men. The police would come. John breathed deeply and started to walk slowly. He was walking in work boots and flannel shirt through Seattle, where men in work boots and flannel shirts were often seen walking. No one even noticed John. That is to say that a few people looked up from their books and a couple drivers looked away from the street long enough to notice John, then turned back to their novels and windshields. "There's an Indian walking," they said to themselves or companions, though Indians were often seen walking in downtown Seattle. John the Indian was walking and his audience was briefly interested, because Indians were briefly interesting. White people no longer feared Indians. Somehow, near the end of the twentieth century, Indians had become invisible, docile. John wanted to change that. He wanted to see fear in every pair of blue eyes. As John walked, his long, black hair was swept back by the same wind that watered his eyes. He walked north along the water, across the University Bridge, then east along the Burke-Gilman Trail until he was standing in a field of grass. He had made it to the wilderness. He was free. He could hunt and trap like a real Indian and grow his hair until it dragged along the ground. No. It was a manicured lawn on the University of Washington campus, and John could hear drums. He had been on the campus a few times before but had never heard drums there. He walked toward the source of the drums. At first, he thought it was Father Duncan. He was not sure why Father Duncan would be playing drums. Then he saw a crowd of Indians gathered outside a large auditorium, Hec Edmundson Pavilion. There were two drums, a few singers and dancers, and dozens of Indians watching the action. So many Indians in one place. There were white people watching, too, but John turned away from their faces. He stepped into the crowd, wanting to disappear into it. A small Indian woman was standing in front of John. She smiled.

"Hey," she said.

"Hey," he said.

"I'm Marie. Are you a new student here?"

"No."

"Oh," she said, disappointed. She was the activities coordinator for the Native American Students Alliance at the University and thought she'd found a recruit. A potential friendship or possible romance.

"What's your name?"

"John."

"What tribe you are?"

He could not, would not, tell her he had been adopted as a newborn by a white couple who could not have children of their own. Along with the clipping about Father Duncan's disappearance, John always carried the photograph of the day his parents had picked him up from the adoption agency. In the photograph, his father's left arm is draped carefully over his mother's shoulders, while she holds John tightly to her dry right breast. Both wear expensive, tasteful clothes. John had no idea who had taken the picture.

His adopted parents had never told him what kind of Indian he was. They did not know. They never told him anything at all about his natural parents, other than his birth mother's age, which was fourteen. John only knew that he was Indian in the most generic sense.

Black hair, brown skin and eyes, high cheekbones, the prominent nose. Tall and muscular, he looked like some cinematic warrior, and constantly intimidated people with his presence. When asked by white people, he said he was Sioux, because that was what they wanted him to be. When asked by Indian people, he said he was Navajo, because that was what he wanted to be.

"I'm Navajo," he said to Marie.

"Oh," she said, "I'm Spokane."

"Father Duncan," said John, thinking instantly of the Spokane Indian Jesuit.

"What?"

"Father Duncan was Spokane."

"Father Duncan?" asked Marie, trying to attach significance to the name, then remembering the brief fragment of a story her parents had told her. "Oh, you mean that one who disappeared, right?"

John nodded his head. Marie was the first person he'd met, besides the Jesuits at St. Francis, who knew about Father Duncan. John trembled.

"Did you know him?" asked Marie.

"He baptized me," said John. "He used to visit me. Then he disappeared."

"I'm sorry," said Marie, who was definitely not Christian. With disgust, she remembered when the Spokane Indian Assembly of God Church held a book burning on the reservation and reduced *Catcher in the Rye,* along with dozens of other books, to ash.

"I know a Hopi," said Marie, trying to change the subject. "Guy named Buddy who works at the U. He's a history teacher. Do you know him?"

"No."

"Oh, I thought you might. He hangs around with the Navajo bunch. Jeez, but they tease him something awful, too."

John barely made eye contact with Marie. Instead, he watched all of the Indians dancing in circles on the grass. It was an illegal powwow, not approved by the University. John could figure out that much when he noticed how the dancers were trampling on the well-kept lawn. Indians were always protesting something. Marie had organized the powwow as a protest against the University's refusal to allow a powwow. Only a few of the Indians had originally known that, but most everybody knew now, and danced all that much harder.

Marie had been organizing protests since her days on the Spokane Indian Reservation, though she had often been the only protestor. A bright child who read by age three, she had quickly passed her classmates by. When they had all been five and six years old, Marie had friends because she was smart. Everybody wanted to be smart. But as the years passed, many of Marie's reservation friends flunked classes, lost interest, were intimidated into silence by cruel, white teachers, or simply had no energy for school because of hunger. Marie felt more and more isolated. Some bright kids were more interested in Spokane Indian culture than in a public school education. Many of those kids skipped school so they could travel to powwows or attend various cultural events. During the summer, when powwow season was really in swing, those kids were too busy to pick up books. They could speak Spokane as fluently as many elders, but they could barely read English. They were intelligent and humorous, and never wanted to leave the reservation. They had chosen that life, and Marie both resented and envied them. Because she did not dance or sing traditionally, and because she could not speak Spokane, Marie was often thought of as being less than Indian. Her parents, who did speak Spokane, had refused to teach Marie because they felt it would be of no use to her in the world outside the reservation. Her mother, the speech therapist at the tribal school, and her father, the principal, knew their bright daughter belonged in that larger world. Instead of teaching her about Spokane culture, they bought her books by the pound at pawn shops, secondhand stores, and garage sales. She read those books and many others, studied hard at school, and endured constant bullying and taunting from many of her peers. Marie learned to fight, and her best friend, Sugar, a traditional dancer and accomplished street fighter, helped. Marie fought fiercely, without control or thought. She tackled people, bit and pinched, spat and kicked. She refused to accept beatings. She always wanted revenge, and would wait until the perfect moment, which could be months later, to ambush her enemies. In one memorable instance, she had stolen a knife from the high school cafeteria and chased Double Andy across the playground. Marie had really meant to stab Double Andy. Everybody had seen the crazy look in Marie's eyes that day and nobody bullied her for months after that. Still, her nose had been broken four times before she graduated high school.

After two years at tribal college, she was accepted into the University of Washington on a full scholarship. Through her intelligence and dedication, Marie had found a way to escape the reservation. Now she was so afraid the reservation would pull her back and drown her in its rivers that she only ventured home for surprise visits to her parents, usually arriving in the middle of the night. Even then, she felt like a stranger and would sometimes leave before her parents knew she was there. And she rarely spoke to any of her reservation friends. She was twenty-three, near the end of her final year as an English major, when she met John Smith.

"You live around here?" Marie asked John.

"No," he said.

"Man, you're breathing hard," she said, trying to make conversation. "What did you do, run here?"

"No, but I thought about it."

Marie laughed because she thought he was making a joke. John looked at her, not really sure why she was laughing.

"I can't believe the U wouldn't let us have a powwow in Hec Ed this year," Marie said.

"What's Hec Ed?"

"In the Hec Ed Pavilion," Marie said. "You know, the gym? Inside there? They wouldn't let us rent it this year, so we're messing up their nice lawn. I can't believe the cops haven't come yet."

"The cops? Really?"

"No, not really. We've got too many reporters here already. The U isn't going to stop us now. They'd look really bad. You know how white people are."

"Oh, yeah."

Expecting the usual Indian banter, Marie waited for him to say more. When he remained silent, she accepted that silence as being just as Indian as the banter, and turned away from him to watch the dancers. John knew that his silence was acceptable, but he also knew that he could have asked about her tribe, that Indians quizzed Indians about all the Indian friends, family, lovers, and acquaintances they might have in common. He was afraid she would discover that he was an Indian without a tribe.

Even though he had felt like a fraud at urban powwows, he had always loved them. Often, when he was a child, Olivia and Daniel had taken him. Through years of observation and practice, he had learned how an Indian was supposed to act at a powwow. When he got old enough to go without Daniel and Olivia, he could pretend to be a real Indian. He could sit in a huge crowd of Indians and be just another anonymous, silent Skin. That was what real Indians called each other. Skins. Other Indian men might give him that indigenous head nod, which confirmed a connection he did not feel. Indian women might give him that look which implied an interest he ignored. But he had always known that if he remained silent, he would receive a respectful silence in return. If he pursued conversation, the real Indians would be happy to talk. With Marie, he had chosen his usual silence.

She stood beside him. He could feel her there, but he continued to watch the dancers move in circles. A tall fancydancer caught his attention. The fancydancer cartwheeled across the grass, his brightly colored feathers nearly shocking in their clarity. Reds and blues, yellows and greens. The crowd gasped at the cartwheels. The fancydancer was bold, original, dangerous. Many Indian elders would surely disapprove of the cartwheels. Many elders dismissed any kind of fancydancing. It was too modern, too white, the dance of children who refused to grow up.

"Jeez," Marie said of the fancydancer. "He's good."

John turned his head to look at her. She smiled. She was a pretty, small-boned woman at least a foot shorter than he was. Her black hair was very long, hanging down below her waist. With her wire-rimmed glasses and black blazer, she looked scholarly and serious, even as she smiled. Her teeth were just a little crowded, as if there were one tooth too many. Her nose looked as if it had been broken once or twice. She had large, dark eyes magnified by her prescription.

"Do you dance?" she asked.

"No," he said.

"You don't talk much, do you?" she asked.

He shook his head.

"The strong silent type?" she asked. "All stoic and stuff, huh? How long you been working on that Tonto face? You should try out for the movies."

He swallowed hard and tried to concentrate on the dancers again. She stared at him. With his looks and stature, she thought, John could have been a wonderful traditional dancer. The old style, slow and dignified, a proud man's dance. John felt the power of her gaze, and was about to make an escape when the powwow's master of ceremonies called for an owl dance.

"It's ladies' choice," said the emcee. "Ladies, go snag yourself a warrior. If he says no, you bring him to me. Men, you know you can't refuse a woman who asks you to dance. You'll either pay up or tell everybody why you broke her heart."

"Hey," Marie said. "Do you want to dance?"

"I guess," he said. He had learned about owl dances, but feared them. John knew many Indian tribes believed the owl was a messenger of death. For those Indians, the owl was death itself. Yet, those same Indians who feared the owl still owl danced. John had always been confused by that. Were the Indians dancing out of spite? Were they challenging the owl? Or perhaps they were dancing to prove their courage. With Indians, death was always so close anyway. When Indians owl danced, their shadows were shaped like owls. What was one more owl in a room full of Indians dancing like owls?

She led him to the dance floor, where all the other couples had already formed a circle. There were old married couples, newlyweds, potential lovers, siblings, mothers and sons, a few reluctant teenagers, and a handful of preschoolers. Marie took John's left hand in her right, and placed her left hand on his right shoulder. He reluctantly placed his right hand on her left hip. Together like that, they waited for a few other stragglers to join the circle, all of the dancers waiting for the drums to begin.

"I'm not any good at this," he said. He had danced clumsy near-waltzes at high school dances with white girls, but had never danced with an Indian woman. He had never been close enough to an Indian woman to dance.

"Just like a foxtrot," she said as the drums began. "Two steps forward, one step back. With the beat. Twirl me around when everybody else does."

"Okay," he said. He did as he was told. He looked down at his feet, tried to stay in rhythm, failed miserably.

"You're a horrible dancer," she said with a laugh. He dropped her hand, stopped dancing, stepped back.

"I'm sorry," he said, wanting to run again.

"Jeez, it's okay," she said and smiled. "Just keep dancing. You can't quit."

It was a broom owl dance. One woman stood alone in the middle of the circle of dancers, holding a broom. She ran up to another dancing woman, gave her the broom, and they switched places. The displaced woman took the broom, ran around the circle, and gave the broom to a third woman. A kind of Indian musical chairs. There was much laughter. Friends chose friends. Sisters chose sisters. The broom passed from hand to hand. A tiny girl, barely able to lift the broom, dragged it around the circle, and gave it to her mother, who was dancing with the little girl's father. More laughter. The emcee encouraged everybody, told bad jokes, teased the young lovers. Everybody kept dancing, two steps forward, one step back. As John danced with Marie, he looked at the other dancers, men, women and children, all with dazzling eyes and bright smiles. So much happiness so close to him, but John could not touch it.

Marie saw the sadness in John's eyes. She had approached him because she thought he was a fellow student, another urban Indian, but now she felt his confusion and loss. He didn't know how to dance, didn't seem to recognize anybody at the powwow. Nobody shouted out his name in an effort to embarrass him as he danced. He was a stranger here, and Marie understood that isolation. Though she had blossomed in college and would be graduating with honors, her work for the Native American Students Alliance and her job at a downtown homeless shelter had led Marie to so many Indians who were, as John was, as she was, outcasts from their tribes. They were forced to create their own urban tribe. Some had been forced to leave their reservations because they were different, like Fawn, the Crow who would not talk about what had happened to her in Montana. Some had never lived on their reservations and had very little connection to their tribes. Nick, the son of a Ute doctor and Cheyenne nurse, had grown up upper-middle-class in St. Louis.

But, somehow, most every urban Indian still held closely to his or her birth tribe. Marie was Spokane, would always be Spokane. But she was also an urban Indian, an amalgamation that included over two hundred tribes in the same Seattle area where many white people wanted to have Indian blood. Marie was always careful to test people, to hear their stories, to ask about their tribes, their people, and their ties to the land from which they originated. The pretend Indians had no answers for these questions, while real Indians answered the questions easily, and had a few questions of their own for Marie. Indians were always placing one another on an identity spectrum, with the more traditional to the left and the less traditional Indians to the right. Marie knew she belonged somewhere in the middle of that spectrum and that her happiness depended on placing more Indians to her right. She wondered where John belonged.

"Hey," Marie said to him. "You're getting it now."

John listened carefully to the drums, which had drowned out all the other noises in his head. He concentrated on the music, his brow furrowed. Sweat, deep breaths.

"Jeez," Marie said. "Take it easy. You're supposed to be having fun."

A little girl handed Marie the broom. Suddenly, John was looking down at a new dance partner. She had huge brown eyes and short brown hair. She smiled with a mouthful of braces.

"I'm Kim," she said, laughed, and then ducked her head. She was playing at a courtship game, flirting and teasing with John as if she were ten years older than she was. This was all practice for her.

"I'm John."

The dance stopped, drums suddenly silent. The dancers clapped and thanked each other. The audience cheered. John looked for Marie. She was talking to a tall Indian man in traditional dance regalia. She stopped talking long enough to notice John. She smiled and waved. John raised his hand a little. He tried to smile, but could not make it happen. The traditional dancer with Marie turned toward John. He was fierce looking, all sharp feathers and angry beads, and seemed to be ten feet tall. John was not surprised that Indians had always terrified white people. He wondered what the early European settlers must have thought when they first encountered an Indian warrior in all of his finest regalia. Even in his flannel shirts and blue jeans, John knew he was intimidating. If I were dressed like a real Indian, John thought, I could rule the world.

"Thank you for the dance," said the little girl, Kim. She was still standing beside John, waiting for him to acknowledge her presence with a traditional politeness.

"Thank you," John said.

"You know," she said. "I'm a twin. My sister's name is Arlene. She's sick. That's why she's not here. Do you know her?"

"What? No, I don't know her," John said. "I'm sorry she's sick. Tell her I said so. Tell her to get well."

Kim giggled and ran away. John watched the little girl run back into the arms of an old Indian woman, her grandmother perhaps, and then he turned back toward Marie. But she was gone. John scanned the crowd. She had disappeared. He breathed deeply. Had she left with the traditional dancer? No. The dancer, standing with a group of other dancers, was drinking a Pepsi. Disappointed, John walked away. He turned his back and left the powwow. He wasn't even sure why he was disappointed, but he had overheard real Indian men talk to real Indian women. He could have mimicked their easy banter, their fluid conversation.

He could have said, "I'm not a dancer."

"I figured that one out," Marie might have said.

He could have been funny and self-deprecating. "I can't sing, either. When I dance and sing, I'm insulting thousands of years of tribal traditions. I've got to be careful, you know? I start dancing and they close the powwow. That's it. John has ruined it for everybody, the powwow's over." But John couldn't say anything. Not to the Indian woman who knew Father Duncan. Not to the beautiful Indian woman with the crooked front tooth.

Walking silently and quickly away from the powwow, John found himself on University Way, the heart of the University District, which everybody called simply the Ave. John could never understand things like that. Why did people change names as easily as they changed clothes? Though it was just another Monday night, dozens of people walked the Ave. Secondhand bookstores and a dozen Asian restaurants. Movie theaters and street performers. A black man in a wheelchair outside Tower Records calling out to everybody who passed him. Three dogs in red bandannas being walked by a twenty-something white woman wearing a blue bandanna. A teenage white couple kissing in a doorway. They were all so young and white, whiter, whitest. Three Asian-Americans, two African-Americans, but everybody else was white and whiter and younger than John. So many people. John was dizzy. He staggered as he walked and bumped into a knot of people who were bidding each other good night.

"Hey," said one of the young white men. "Watch your step, chief."

The white man wore faded clothes that were supposed to be old, but they were expensive new clothes designed to look old. A goatee and pierced ears, small gold hoops that looked good, blue flannel shirt, a black stocking cap, big brown leather boots. John stared at him.

"You okay, buddy?" asked the white man.

John was silent, carefully listening to the sounds of the street.

"Hey, chief," said the white man. "Had a few too many? You need some help?"

John did not respond. The white man was trying to be friendly. He was really not a man, John thought, just a boy dressed like a man. Though John was only a few years older, he felt ancient. He knew that Indians were supposed to feel ancient, old and wise. He concentrated on feeling old and wise, until the youth and relative innocence of this young white man infuriated him. John felt the rage he didn't like to feel.

"Hey," said the young man. "Hey, are you okay?"

"You're not as smart as you think you are," John said. "Not even close."

The young man smiled, confused and a little intimidated. "Calm down there, dude," he said.

"I'm older than the hills," said John, holding his hands out toward the white man. The young man looked at his friends, who shrugged their shoulders and smiled nervously. He turned back to John and flashed him the peace sign.

John was surprised by the gesture. He took a step back, momentarily disarmed. The young man finished his good-byes to his companions and walked away. John watched as the young white man crossed against the light, stopped briefly to look at himself in a store window, and then walked south down the Ave. Carefully and silently, John followed him.

4

How He Imagines
His Life on the Reservation

It is a good life, not like all the white people believe reservation life to be. There is enough food, plenty of books to read, and a devoted mother. She is very young, probably too young to have a son like John Smith, but it had happened and she has coped well. She had nearly given John up for adoption but changed her mind at the last minute. The social workers had tried to convince her otherwise, but John's mother refused to let him go.

"He's my son," she'd said. "He's always going to be my son."

They live with a large extended family group in a small house. John and his mother share a bedroom with two girl cousins. John's two uncles and two aunts share another bedroom. John's maternal grandparents share the third bedroom. One small boy cousin sleeps in a walk-in closet. Five or six transient relatives sleeping on the living room floor on any given night.

Everybody plays Scrabble.

It is not easy to explain why this particular group of Indians plays Scrabble. John's grandmother had bought their Scrabble game for a dollar at a secondhand store. For some reason, all the *E* tiles were missing when she brought it home. *E* is the most common letter in the alphabet, John knows, but that does not explain why all the tiles are gone. The family has always compensated by allowing any other tile to function as an *E*. It has worked well. It is diplomatic. Near the end of a game, when John's rack is filled with difficult letters, *Q*, *Z*, *K*, and he has nowhere to play them, he can always pretend they are all *E* tiles.

They eat well.

For breakfast, there is always corn flakes and milk, orange juice, whole wheat toast. John's grandparents love their coffee black and his mother mixes hers with lots of sugar. John's cousins eat quickly and run to school. They can all read and love their teachers, who are Indian. John is too young for school, but is smart enough to read books. He reads books all day, waiting to be old enough for kindergarten. His mother reads to him sometimes. They sit on the couch together and read books. John sometimes pretends that all of the difficult words, the big words with their amorphous ideas, are simpler and clear. A word like democracy can become rain instead. That changes everything. John can read a phrase from his history book and change it to "Our Founding Fathers believed in rain."

John's grandparents are very traditional people and are teaching John the ways of his tribe. Ancient ways. John is learning to speak his tribal language. Sometimes, the whole family plays Scrabble using the tribal language. This is much more difficult and John always loses, but he is learning. There are words and sounds in the tribal language that have no corresponding words or sounds in English. John feels the words in his heart, but it is hard to make his mouth work that way.

John is also learning to dance. His grandmother has made him a grassdancing outfit because he loves to dance.

"Listen to me," his grandmother says. "The grassdancers are special. You see, the grassdancers were always the first ones in the old ways. They're not first anymore, but before, they would dance in the tall grass and knock it down, make it flat enough for the other dancers. That's why the grassdancers move the way they do. Even if there's no grass, they have to pretend there is. Stomp the grass down when you dance. But remember, you have to fool the grass, too. You have to sneak up on it. You have to look like grass, move like grass, smell like grass. That's why grassdancers look like they do."

John is four years old when he dances at a powwow for the first time. His entire family is in the audience, cheering him on as loudly as tradition allows. He is nervous, waiting for the drums. Then they begin, and the singers, too, with their high-pitched wails. They are singing in a way that John feels in the center of himself, from his feet to his hair. The head dancer, a huge man in a traditional outfit, leads the dancers into the hall. This is the Grand Entry, the welcoming, the beginning of another powwow, John's first as a dancer.

He dances with the other grassdancers, young men mostly. There are a few middle-aged grassdancers, but grassdancing is mostly for the young. They dance in order of age. The oldest dancers enter first, followed by the next oldest, until, finally, the youngest, John. He turns in fast circles. He is the grass. He is the grass.

John's mother watches from the bleachers. She loves her son and cannot believe she almost gave him away. But that was so long ago, a million years ago, and she would never give him away now. Not for anything. Not for all the money in the world. She taps her feet in rhythm with the drums. She is a dancer, too, but wants this moment to be her son's. If she were dancing, she would not be able to see him make his first circle. He looks up into the crowd, looking for her. She waves her arms wildly. He sees her. He tries not to smile. Grassdancing is serious business. But he cannot help himself and grins with all of his teeth.

For lunch, when he is ten years old, John eats peanut butter sandwiches. The peanut butter is commodity food, government surplus, but it still tastes good. There are dozens of cans and boxes of commodity food in the house. John's mother uses them in wonderful and original ways. She makes the best commodity beef stew in Indian history.

She starts with the beef. She opens the can with a manual opener, a sharp and clever device. She barely has to work because the cutting is so easy. She pours the beef into a saucepan, seasons it with salt, pepper, paprika, cayenne, and brings it to a boil. In a separate pan, she combines vegetables from her garden—carrots, peas, celery, onions—and heats until tender. At the last possible moment, she combines beef and vegetables, stirring together. Stirring. When the vegetables are shiny with beef grease, his mother fills a bowl for each member of the family. They sit together to eat. Most every night, his cousins, grandparents, his entire family, all eat together. Then, of course, they have the fry bread. The fry bread! Water, flour, salt, rolled together and deep-fried. There is nothing like that smell, fry bread sizzling on the stove, a slight smoke filling the house. John can smell the fry bread smoke in his clothes. The scent rumbles his stomach. He loves this time, the dipping of fry bread into beef stew.

"So," says his mother. "What did you do today?"

"We were over to the pipes today," John says. He cannot lie.

"I told you not to go there," his mother says, a little angry. John knows her anger is because of love. The pipes are abandoned sewer pipes piled on a hillside near the old high school. Rusted metal, in fifty-foot sections, the pipes are magical, the reservation playground. Running water and soil erosion have created caves beneath the pipes, and certain pipes, propped up by others, rise at gentle angles in the air. It is a maze. One pipe, pinned between two others, is nearly vertical. Only the strongest of the boys and girls can climb inside that pipe, using its metal ribs for handholds. Crazy Randy climbs to the top of that pipe and hangs down from the rim, thirty feet above the ground. Everybody is jealous of Randy's strength and courage. They crowd around him to look at the cuts on his hands when he comes down. In the five years since the pipes were left there, no Indian child has ever been seriously hurt. There have been a few cuts and bruises, a couple of close calls, but the Indian children are safe in the pipes, a kind of safety that adults can never understand.

"It's okay, mom," John says. "Nobody gets hurt."

John smiles, beams really, and tries to hide his glee. Just that day, he had climbed into a cave beneath the pipes, a small cave with an even smaller entrance. When John climbed inside, he saw Dawn, the most beautiful Indian girl in the world, face smudged with dirt, stray grass in her hair, holes in her jeans.

"Shh," she said. "I'm hiding from Verla and them."

"Oh, okay."

They sat quietly, listening to the laughter and voices of other Indian kids. Somebody ran through the pipe directly above their cave. The echoes sounded like music. More kids ran through the pipe. The music was so loud that John worried the pipe was going to collapse. He was afraid. The fear felt wonderful.

"Do you like me?" asked Dawn, bold, as Indian girls and women always are.

"Yeah, sure," John said.

"Well, kiss me then. Now or never."

John kissed her then, quickly and dryly, chapped lips against chapped lips. He could feel her teeth clenched tightly behind her lips. His jaw ached with the effort. His heart sounded louder than the kids running through the pipes above his head. He wanted to sing a love song. The pipes were the best place in the history of the world.

"What are you smiling about?" asks his mother. John shakes his head. He fills his mouth with fry bread and stew, hoping his mother will not ask him any more questions. She smiles. She knows about Dawn. His whole family knows about Dawn and John.

No matter how much he enjoys breakfast and lunch, John knows that dinner is the best meal of all. No. After dinner is the best time. He is sixteen years old. His whole family sits in a circle in the living room and tells stories. His grandparents tell stories of the old times, before the white men came, when animals still talked. Coyote this, Coyote that. Raven flying around messing with everybody. Bear lumbering and rumbling across the grass. Mosquito mistaking urine for blood. His mother tells stories about other relatives, long since passed away. The uncle who was crushed beneath a falling tree. Another uncle who moved to the city and was never seen again. The aunt who went crazy. They are sad stories, but still filled with humor and hope, so the family is only half-sad. John knows that storytelling is a way of mourning the dead. His uncles and aunts, who are still alive and sharing the circle, tell stories about their travels. One uncle was in the Army, fought against Hitler, and came back with a medal. Another uncle built skyscrapers. A third fished for salmon in Alaska. The fourth fell in love with a Italian girl in Chicago, even though he only saw her a few times on a bus. So many stories to tell and songs to sing. John's cousins, the little girls, sing Christmas carols, the only songs they know, no matter the time of year. Ninety degrees outside and the girls singing "Winter Wonderland." John tells the longest stories, with many characters and changes of location. His stories are epic. They go long into the night. He invents ancestors. He speaks the truth about grandfathers and grandmothers. He convinces his family that Shakespeare was an Indian woman. The laughter and disbelief, the rubbing of bellies and contented sighs. His family listens to every word. His mother yawns once, twice, rubs her eyes, and listens some more. She can never get enough of her son. During his stories, John's family laughs in the right places and cries when tears are due.

5

How It Happened

The killer believed in the knife, a custom-made bowie with three small turquoise gems inlaid in the handle, heavy but well-balanced, nearly long enough to be considered a sword. A beautiful weapon, polished until the killer could see clear eyes, curve of cheek, and thin lips in the silver sheen of the blade. During those moments, with knife in hand, the killer felt powerful, invincible, as if the world could be changed with a single gesture. Snap of the fingers, one step forward, a hand closed into fist. With the knife, the killer became the single, dark center around which all other people revolved.

At home, the killer had sharpened the blade until it could cut away a thin layer of skin when just lightly run along a forearm. Everything had a purpose. The knife needed to be sharp. The killer wanted to carry the knife at all times, but its size and weight made it difficult to conceal. A special knife needed a special sheath. Since the killer could not sleep, there was plenty of time to build a sheath, fashioned from irregular leather pieces and nylon cord. With the knife resting comfortably in its sheath, hidden beneath a jacket, the killer could move freely. More importantly, the killer had quick access to the blade as it sat just above the left hip. For hours, the killer practiced pulling the knife from its sheath, then slashing, cutting, and thrusting the blade into imaginary enemies. Faster and faster. The killer practiced, as hands blistered and arms ached with pain, until exhaustion. Only then did the killer fall asleep.

At night, the killer dreamed of the knife. Of the search for a perfect knife. It had not been easy. There were many choices. Paring, chef's, boning knives. Bread, utility, carving knives. Wooden handles, plastic handles. So beautiful, the parts of a knife. Blade, bolster, tang, handle. Indestructible. Lifetime guarantees. Large sets. One knife at a time. Knife blocks with blade sharpeners included. Demonstration videos. County fairs. Mail order. Department stores and discount chains. Garage sales and secondhand stores. *A Short Guide to Cutlery.* In a large kitchen, the meat carver decided which piece of meat each guest received. The neck for the journalist, the breast for royalty. The killer had touched so many knives, studied their blades, tested their heft. The knife is the earliest tool used by humans, over two million years old. Knife, knifing, knives, to knife, to be knifed, knifelike. The killer sliced open test fruits and vegetables, ran fingers over the deep grooves cut into carving boards. Four thousand years ago, humans learned to separate elements, and discovered the power of iron. The killer shifted a knife from left to right hand, and then back again. How to hold a carving knife: last three fingers behind the bolster point, index finger on one side of the blade, thumb on the other side. The paring knife is an extension of the hand. The bread knife is perfect for cutting through objects with hard exteriors and soft interiors. Ancient and elemental, the knife. *The Illustrated History of Swords.* Blade against blade against blade. A knife must be sharp, clean, and stored properly. A blade should be sharpened before and after use. The mirror of a polished blade. The mirrors in a department store. The mirror of the sky visible between department stores. The Rockwell scale measured the hardness of steel. The higher the number, the sharper the blade. Steel tends to shrink back into itself after long periods of disuse.

Hiding that beautiful knife in the sheath beneath a jacket, the killer followed white men, selected at random. The killer simply picked any one of the men in gray suits and followed him from office building to cash machine, from lunchtime restaurant back to office building. Those gray suits were not happy, yet showed their unhappiness only during moments of weakness. Punching the buttons of a cash machine that refused to work. Yelling at a taxi that had come too close. Insulting the homeless people who begged for spare change. But the killer also saw the more subtle signs of unhappiness. A slight limp in uncomfortable shoes. Eyes closed, head thrown back while waiting for the traffic signal. The slight hesitation before opening a door. The men in gray suits wanted to escape, but their hatred and anger trapped them.

The killer first saw that particular white man in the University District. Confidently, arrogantly, the white man, Justin Summers, had brushed past the killer. With his head high and shoulders wide, Summers took up as much space as he possibly could. He strolled down the middle of the sidewalk, forcing others to walk around him. So when the arrogant white man rudely brushed past, the killer wanted to teach him a lesson. Nothing serious, just a simple and slightly painful lesson. Then, without reason or warning, the killer suddenly understood that the knife had a specific purpose. But the killer had to be careful. There were rules for hunting.

The killer knew that particular white man in the University District was all alone, and that was good. Men in a pack could protect each other. When threatened, they could scatter in many directions and confuse the killer. A solitary man was vulnerable. Easy to follow, that white man, so self-absorbed he failed to notice much of anything. Muttering to himself, looking down at the sidewalk, he

walked block after block. He ate Thai food by himself and read a
magazine. After he finished eating, the white man walked toward the
Burke-Gilman Trail. The killer followed him closely, and once stood
beside him as they waited for the walk signal. So close. At any time,
the killer could have reached inside the jacket and pulled out the knife.
The late evening streets were so quiet that the killer could have slid
the knife into the white man's kidney and then walked away. But the
moon was terribly bright and illuminating. There was a chance the
killer would be caught. Thrilled by the idea, the killer moved closer
to the white man, until they were almost touching. The white man
glanced at the killer. A superficial glance, nothing more important
than a wind blowing a newspaper down the street. The killer reached
inside the jacket and touched the knife.

The killer especially hated the white man's clothes and followed him as he walked south for a few blocks, then turned west on
the Burke-Gilman Trail. The killer could see and smell the white man.
Aftershave, leather jacket, Thai food. It was late, a few bicyclists
flashed by, but the trail was mostly deserted. The killer walked a few
feet behind the white man for a few minutes, then reached out and
tapped the white man on the shoulder.

"Whoa," said the white man. "You scared the shit out of me."

The killer was silent.

"Hey," said the white man. "Do I know you, man?"

The killer took a step back, knowing that anger would change
a face. The killer had seen other people do it. Other people could
change the shape of their faces at will. Through a trick of shadow and
moonlight, or through some undefined magic, the killer's face did
change.

"What's going on?" asked the white man, now really frightened by what he saw in the killer's face.

The killer saw the fear in the white man's blue eyes. The
man's fear inspired the killer's confidence. The killer slid a hand
beneath the jacket and felt for the knife. It was there in its home-

made sheath, blade sharp and beautiful. It would soak up all the moonlight. The white man was not stupid. When he saw the killer reach beneath the jacket, the white man began to desperately hope that somebody would walk along the trail soon. A dozen University cops were always breaking up unauthorized parties on campus, but very few ever patrolled the trail.

"What do you want?" asked the white man loudly, trying to inject anger into his voice. Be strong, he said to himself, don't show any fear.

"Hey, let's be cool about this. I don't want any problems," the white man said.

The killer moved quickly. With fingers wrapped around the handle, the killer snapped the knife out of its handmade sheath. The killer's feet moved forward, and the sharp blade forced its way into the white man's belly.

The killer had not necessarily meant for any of it to happen. The killer picked up the white man's body, carried it on a shoulder, and walked along the trail in a daze. A group of UW students staggered past, on their way home from some party, and laughed loudly at the killer. The killer stopped, ready to drop the body, and run.

"Shit, you're a strong one, huh?" one of the students slurred to the killer, and then tugged on the white man's leg. "Jesus, you got wasted, huh? Shit, wake up, wake up. The party's just starting."

The white man groaned and shifted. The killer was surprised that the man was still alive. His blood ran down the killer's back.

"Shit," said the student. "Don't you two be doing anything nasty now, huh?" Laughter. "You're both going to be hating it in the morning. Hangover City, you'll be hating it."

The students laughed and staggered away. The killer watched them go, breathed deeply, and kept walking down the trail. The killer wanted to drop the body and leave it where it landed, but felt responsible for the white man. Honestly, the killer had not necessarily meant to hurt him and wanted to make sure the man was buried properly.

There had to be a ceremony, a wake, silent prayers. That was how it was done. The killer had learned many ceremonies, but rarely practiced them.

The killer walked off the trail into a dark neighborhood. Silently singing an invisibility song learned from a dream, the killer carried the body to an empty house. A FOR SALE sign. Bare windows. A broken lock on the back door. The killer carried the body inside the house and gently set it on the living room floor. Kneeling beside the body, the killer cut the white man's scalp away and stuffed the bloody souvenir into a pocket. So much blood. The killer was drenched with blood, soaking shirt, jacket, and pants. The blood was beautiful but not enough. One dead man was not enough. The killer was disappointed. Disappointment grew quickly into anger, then rage, and the killer brought the knife down into the white man's chest again and again. Still not satiated, the killer knew there was more work to do. The dead man's blue eyes were open and still, pupils dilated. With hands curved into talons, the killer tore the white man's eyes from his face and swallowed them whole. The killer then pulled two white owl feathers out of another pocket, and set them on the white man's chest. Blood soon soaked into the feathers, staining them a dark red.

6

Truck Schultz

"Hello out there, folks, this is Truck Schultz on KWIZ, the Voice of Reason, and boy, do I have a problem!"

Schultz sat in the radio station, smoking a cigar, drinking coffee. A tall, muscular white man with a receding hairline, blue eyes, and large ears, he was the host of the most popular talk-radio show in the city and was ready to go national, sure that he would be more popular than Rush Limbaugh. Truck had started with a late-night jazz show on KWIZ a few years earlier. Not long after conservative radio hit it big, KWIZ changed its format to talk and Truck became a star. His promotional billboards were everywhere: KEEP ON TRUCKIN'! Now Truck had a hundred thousand listeners and a drive-time slot. He never played jazz anymore. Leaning close to his microphone, Truck exhaled a cloud of thick, gray smoke and spoke loudly and clearly.

"Through my sources in the Seattle Police Department, I've just learned that the body of a white man was discovered in a house in Fremont early this morning. My sources say that the man was scalped and ritually mutilated. That's right, folks. Scalped and ritually mutilated. My sources say certain evidence makes it clear that an American Indian might be reponsible for this crime. My sources would not reveal what that evidence was, but they did make it clear that only an Indian, or a person intimately familiar with Indian culture, would know to leave such evidence behind. What do you think, folks? Give me a call."

7

Introduction to Native American Literature

A few days after she met John Smith at the protest powwow, Marie Polatkin walked into the evening section of the Introduction to Native American Literature class for the first time. The professor had not yet arrived. The students were gossiping about the dead body that had been discovered in an empty house in Fremont.

"Yeah," said one older white woman. "I read he was scalped."

"Yeah," said a white man. "Like an Indian would do it."

"An Indian?"

"Yeah, Indians started that whole scalping business."

"Oh, that's spooky. And here we are, in an Indian class. I just got the shivers."

"You've got it all wrong," Marie said as she sat at a desk near the front. "The French were the first to scalp people in this country. Indians just copied them."

The white students all stared at Marie, saw that she was Indian, and then turned back to their conversation.

"I bet it was one of those serial killers," said another white woman.

"Yes," said a third white woman. "There's something in the water here. I mean, we've got the Green River Killer, Ted Bundy, the I-5 Killer. We, like, raise them here or something."

Marie tried to ignore the morbid discussion. She was more concerned about the professor. She'd signed up for the class because she'd heard that Dr. Clarence Mather, the white professor, supposedly loved Indians, or perhaps his idea of Indians, and gave them good grades. But he was also a Wannabe Indian, a white man who wanted to be Indian, and Marie wanted to challenge Mather's role as the official dispenser of "Indian education" at the University.

"He always wants to sweat with Indian students, or share the peace pipe, or sit at a drum and sing," Binky, a Yakama woman, had said. "He's kind of icky. He really fawns over the women, you know what I mean? Real Indian lover, that one."

Still, in spite of and because of Dr. Mather, Marie assumed she'd be one of many Indians in the class, all looking for an easy grade. But she'd been wrong in her assumptions. She was the only Indian in the class. When Mather walked into the class, he was wearing a turquoise bolo tie, and his gray hair was tied back in a ponytail.

While Marie was surprised by the demographics of the class, she was completely shocked by the course reading list. One of the books, *The Education of Little Tree*, was supposedly written by a Cherokee Indian named Forrest Carter. But Forrest Carter was actually the pseudonym for a former Grand Wizard of the Ku Klux Klan. Three of the other books, *Black Elk Speaks*, *Lame Deer: Seeker of Visions*, and *Lakota Woman*, were taught in almost every Native American Literature class in the country, and purported to be autobiographical, though all three were co-written by white men. Black Elk himself had disavowed his autobiography, a fact that was conveniently omitted in any discussion of the book. The other seven books included three anthologies of traditional

Indian stories edited by white men, two nonfiction studies of Indian spirituality written by white women, a book of traditional Indian poetry translations edited by a Polish-American Jewish man, and an Indian murder mystery written by some local white writer named Jack Wilson, who claimed he was a Shilshomish Indian. On the recommendation of a white classmate, Marie had read one of Wilson's novels a few months before the class. She'd hated the book and seriously doubted that its author was Indian, or much of a writer. She'd done some research on his background and found a lot of inconsistencies.

After seeing the reading list, Marie knew that Dr. Mather was full of shit.

"Excuse me, Dr. Mather," Marie said. "You've got this Little Tree book on your list. Don't you know it's a total fraud?"

"I'm aware that the origins of the book have been called into question," said Mather. "But I hardly believe that matters. *The Education of Little Tree* is a beautiful and touching book. If those rumors about Forrest Carter are true, perhaps we can learn there are beautiful things inside of everybody."

"Yeah, well, whatever was inside that man, it wasn't Cherokee blood." Marie's voice grew louder. "And there are only three Indians on this list, and their books were really written by white guys. Not exactly traditional or autobiographical. I mean, I think there's a whole lot more biography than auto in those books. And there aren't any Northwest Indian writers at all."

"Ah, yes," Dr. Mather said. "And your name is?"

"Marie. Marie Polatkin."

"By your appearance, Ms. Polatkin, I assume you're Native American."

"I'm Spokane."

"Ah, yes," Dr. Mather said. "I taught a Spokane named Reggie Polatkin. A relative of yours?"

"My cousin," said Marie suspiciously. She knew Reggie and Mather had been close at one time. But Reggie had been expelled

from the University after assaulting Mather for reasons that were
never clear. While Marie recognized that Mather was a pompous jerk,
she also knew that Reggie was no saint. In fact, he'd been involved in
more than a few fistfights in his life. And after he'd been expelled,
Reggie had simply disappeared. No member of their family had heard
from him in over a year. Marie didn't want Mather to give her a poor
grade simply because she was related to her crazy cousin. If she was
going to get a poor grade, she wanted to receive it because of her
own craziness.

"I trust you are aware that Reggie and I had, well, let's say it
was an academic conflict."

"Yeah," said Marie.

"Well," said Mather with a smile. "I hope you don't hold a
familial grudge against me, Ms. Polatkin?"

"Reggie is Reggie. I'm me."

"Fine, fine. Now, let's see, where were we? Ah, yes. The
Spokane Indians. Columbia Plateau, Interior Salish, closely related
to the Colville, Coeur d'Alene, Flathead, and others. A salmon tribe
whose reservation is bordered by the Columbia River to the north,
the Spokane River to the south, and Chimakum Creek to the east. A
veritable island of a reservation, is it not?"

"I guess," said Marie.

"Well, Ms. Polatkin, I understand your concerns. But I must
correct your math. We do have four Native American authors in this
course. Mr. Black Elk, Mr. Lame Deer, and Ms. Crow Dog did have
help transcribing their stories, but many people use professionals to
help write their books. And Mr. Wilson, as you can see by the sylla-
bus, is a Shilshomish Indian, which, unless I'm mistaken, is a Northwest tribe.

"You see, Ms. Polatkin, I envision this course as a compre-
hensive one, viewing the Native American world from both the interior and exterior. One would hope that we can all benefit from a
close reading of the assigned texts, and recognize the validity of a

Native American literature that is shaped by both Indian and white hands. In order to see that this premise is verifiable, we need only acknowledge that the imagination has no limits. That, in fact, to paraphrase Whitman, 'Every good story that belongs to Indians belongs to non-Indians, too.'"

Mather dismissed any further questions with a slight nod of his head, and proceeded to launch into a detailed lecture about the long tradition of European-Americans who were adopted into Indian tribes. A red-headed, green-eyed Irish and British mix, Mather proudly revealed that he'd been adopted into a Lakota Sioux family, an example of the modern extension of that long tradition.

"Dr. Mather," Marie said. "What about the long tradition of white guys who were killed by Indians? How about the white guy they found dead in Fremont? Can we talk about him, too? How about the modern extension of that long tradition?"

"Ms. Polatkin, I hardly see how the murder of one poor man has anything to do with the study of Native American literature."

Dr. Mather tried to ignore Marie, but she felt compelled to challenge him and constantly interrupted his first lecture. She was enjoying herself. She'd found an emotional outlet in the opportunity to harass a white professor who thought he knew what it meant to be Indian. For Marie, being Indian was mostly about survival, and she'd been fighting so hard for her survival that she didn't know if she could stop. She needed conflict and, in those situations where conflict was absent, she would do her best to create it. Of course, conflict with whites didn't need much creating. Her struggle with Dr. Mather, which started out as intellectual sparring, became personal, and intensified as that first class hour went along.

David Rogers, who had taken the class because of a specific sense of guilt and a vague curiosity, was fascinated by Marie. She seemed exotic and impossibly bold, speaking to a college professor with such disdain and disrespect. He had never known any woman who behaved in such a manner. David's mother had died when he was five years old, so he had only vague and completely pleasant memories of her. And most of the white girls in his hometown had been quietly conservative and unfailingly polite. David had not bothered to approach those few hometown white girls who had been even slightly rebellious. And he had never spoken to an Indian woman.

David had grown up on a farm near Marie's reservation. Throughout his life, his only real contact with Indians happened in the middle of the night when reservation Spokanes crept onto his family's farm to steal camas root, the spongy, pungent bulbs of indigenous lilies that had been a traditional and sacred food of the local Indians for thousands of years. The Spokanes arrived in the middle of the night because David's father, Buck, refused to allow them to gather camas, even though it grew on a few acres of their otherwise useless land.

On one particular night when he was twelve years old, David Rogers had been sitting for hours in the family hunting blind with his older brother Aaron and their father, Buck. Twenty feet off the ground, the blind, camouflaged by leaves and sod, had stretched between trees in a stand of windbreak pines. Ordinarily, the blind was used to hunt for the deer that often wandered through the open fields of the Rogers family farm. That night, however, Buck Rogers and his sons had been waiting for the Indians who came to steal camas root.

"Is that weapon clean?" Buck Rogers had asked Aaron.

"Yes, sir," Aaron had said and had given a smart salute. Though only a year older than David, Aaron had been much more experienced with weapons and held a vintage AK-47, semi-automatic, a full clip.

"How about yours?" Buck had asked David.

David had looked down at the small twenty-two-caliber rifle in his hands. Wood stock, metal trigger, smell of gunpowder. He'd looked back at his father and older brother.

"It's ready, sir," David had said, his voice breaking a little. He'd been scared.

Buck had heard the fear in his youngest son's voice. David had always been a strange one, and if left to himself, would have spent all of his time reading. Buck loved David, but thought he was probably queer. Buck had always know that Aaron Rogers was a whole different animal. He had been staring out into the camas fields, waiting for the Indians to appear. Wanting the Indians to appear.

"You see anything?" Buck had asked.

"No, sir," Aaron had said.

David had peered out of the blind. The fields brightly illuminated by the moon. Fallow fields reaching north to south. To the west, a dirt access road. David had swallowed hard when he saw the car, without headlights, appear over the horizon.

"There," Aaron had said, surprised by his own giddiness. He'd wondered if this was how the great Indian-fighters, like Custer, Sheridan, and Wright, had felt just before battle.

"Oh, we got them now," Buck had said. "We got them good."

The car had rattled down the access road and stopped beside a camas field. The engine had idled for a few moments before shuddering to a stop. Slowly and quietly, five, six, seven Indians had crawled out of the car. David had not understood how seven people could have fit into that small car. Four children, David saw, and a man and woman, perhaps the mother and father of the children, and, following behind them, an elderly woman.

"Tell me when, tell me when," Aaron had whispered to his father.

"Patience, patience."

The Indians had walked across the field until they were standing less than fifty feet away from the hunting blind. With his finger lightly feathering the trigger, Aaron had stared down the barrel of his rifle and sighted in on the Indian father.

"When? When?" Aaron had asked.

David had watched as the Indians, even the children, pulled out strange curved tools and began digging in the earth. Digging for camas root. David had wondered why the Indians loved the root so much. Why had they come in the middle of the night? After Buck had threatened them with physical violence? Even the Indian children, who David had always seen as wild and uncontrollable, quietly and respectfully dug for those roots. David had no idea the Indians had been root digging for thousands of years.

"Get ready," Buck had whispered. David, knowing what was expected of him, had reluctantly raised his rifle.

"They're just kids," David had whispered.

"Lice make nits," Buck had whispered as he raised his rifle.

The Indians dug for roots. As the old woman dug, she'd remembered when she had come here with her grandmother.

"Remember," Buck had whispered. "Shoot over their heads."

David had aimed his rifle at the moon, not wanting to even see the Indians as they ran away. He'd heard the soft laughter of the Indian mother. David had wondered if she was beautiful.

"Now," Buck had said and pulled the trigger. David had squeezed off a bullet and then had turned to look at his brother, who had not yet fired. David had seen the look in his older brother's eyes and had known Aaron was sighting in on the Indian father. Not above his head, but at his head.

"No!" David had shouted as Aaron pulled the trigger. The Indian man had fallen to the ground. He didn't move for a brief moment, long enough for David to cry out, but then the Indian man had jumped to his feet and, apparently unharmed, raced to the car. As the Indians drove away, Aaron and Buck had laughed and whooped loudly.

"You tried to shoot him," David had accused his brother.

"What are you talking about?" Aaron had asked.

"You aimed at him. You tried to kill him."

Buck had stared at his sons with recognition and love. Aaron, who had always wanted so much to be like his father that he wore the same shirts. And David, who had been scared of everything, but would fight Aaron for the slightest transgression.

"David," Buck had said. "Aaron wouldn't do something like that. We were just trying to scare them. Right, Aaron?"

"Right, Dad."

David had thought his big brother was lying.

"Did you see them Indians run?" Aaron had asked his father.

"I saw it," Buck had said.

"Just like the old days must have been, huh?" Aaron had asked. "Just like the old days!"

David had looked down at the rifle in his hands. He'd felt like crying.

"Hey," Buck had said to David. "What's wrong with you?"

David had looked at his father.

"Oh, Jesus," Buck had said. "You ain't going to cry?"

David had ducked his head.

"You look at me when I'm talking to you," Buck had said impatiently. He hated it when his son avoided eye contact. It showed fear. Buck had always hated fear.

"Yes, sir," David had whispered. With great effort, he'd looked into his father's blue eyes. David and Aaron had inherited the same color and shape of their father's eyes. Buck had seen a shadow of his face in his youngest son's. More important, he had also seen his late wife's fine features in David's face.

"Listen," Buck had said, softening. "I know this is a tough thing to do, shooting after people like this. But we ain't trying to hurt them. We're just trying to teach them a lesson. They're stealing from us, son. This is our land. My land. Your land. Your brother's land. This land has been in our family for over a hundred years. And those Indians are stealing from us. They're trying to steal our land. We just can't have that. Okay, son?"

"But they were kids," David said. "And an old woman."

"Indian is Indian," his father had said, close to losing his temper.

"Hey, Dad," Aaron had said, trying to divert attention away

from his little brother. "Let's go see if those Indians dropped anything. Maybe one of those weird digging sticks."

Buck had stared at David for a few seconds, trying to understand how this boy could have been his son. But there could be no
getting around it. David was his son, one of two. All the family he
had left in the world. Buck had shrugged his shoulders, mussed David's
hair, and then climbed down from the stand. Just before he'd followed, Aaron smiled at his brother.

"Hey, bro," Aaron had said. "Don't worry about it. You'll
get them next time."

Thinking about the camas field, David Rogers barely heard
Dr. Clarence Mather lecturing during that first session of the Native
literature class.

"Jack Wilson is much more than a mystery novelist," said
Mather. "He is a social realist. Unlike many other Native writers
whose work seems to exaggerate the amount of despair in the Indian
world, Wilson presents a more authentic and traditional view of the
Indian world."

"Oh, God," Marie blurted out.

"Do you have something to add, Ms. Polatkin?" asked Dr.
Mather. "Yet again?"

"How can Wilson present an authentic and traditional view
of the Indian world if he isn't authentic and traditional himself?" asked
Marie. "I mean, I've done some research on this guy. He isn't even
Indian at all. How would he know about the despair, or happiness, in
the Indian world?"

"Ms. Polatkin," said Dr. Mather, speaking very slowly. "Since
this is the first session of this class, perhaps you might let me actually
conduct the class? But, in answer to your questions, Mr. Wilson is,
in fact, a Shilshomish Indian."

"How do you know that?"

"Because he says so and I have no reason to doubt him."

"But the Shilshomish don't exist as a tribe anymore. There are no records of membership. Lots of people claim to be Indians, and Wilson's vague statements about his Shilshomish ancestors can't be verified."

"Are you going to blame Mr. Wilson for the shoddy book-keeping of others?"

"No, but don't you find it highly ironic that all of these so-called Indian writers claim membership in tribes with poor records of membership? Cherokee, Shilshomish? I mean, there's not a whole lot of people claiming to be Spokane. And do you know why? Because we're not glamorous and we keep damn good records."

"I fail to understand your point, Ms. Polatkin."

"There's more," Marie said. "I've been more and more curious about Wilson. I'm active in all the Indian organizations around here and I've asked around. Nobody at the Seattle Urban Indian Health Center has ever met Wilson, and nobody at the United Indians of All Tribes Foundation knows him. Nobody at Indian Heritage High School. And he's never been in contact with anybody at the Native American Students Alliance here at the University. I also called all of the local reservations and nobody has heard of him. Not the Lummi, Puyallup, Tulalip, or anybody else."

"Ms. Polatkin, please."

"And I called the American Indian College Fund and Wilson has never donated any time or money. About the only person who'd ever heard of Wilson was the owner of Big Heart's, the Indian bar over on Aurora Avenue. And the owner was white."

"Ms. Polatkin, will you please make your point."

"Well, for somebody who is supposed to be so authentic and traditional, Wilson sure doesn't have much to do with Indians. I mean, there are so many real Indians out there writing real Indian books. Simon Ortiz, Roberta Whiteman, Luci Tapahonso. And there's Indian writers from the Northwest, too. Like Elizabeth Woody, Ed Edmo. And just across the border in Canada, too. Like Jeannette

Armstrong. Why teach Wilson? It's like his books are killing Indian books."

"Are you finished now, Ms. Polatkin?" asked Dr. Mather.

"Yes."

"Fine, may we all continue with the study of literature?"

"If that's what you want to call it."

After class, David stopped Marie in the hallway. He wasn't sure what he wanted to say. He just knew he wanted to talk to the pretty Indian woman.

"Man," he said. "You've got a lot of guts, talking to a professor like that."

Marie looked at the short, stocky white man. He was a decent-looking guy, with pale blue eyes and sandy hair.

"It doesn't take guts to tell the truth," she said.

"Where I'm from, it does," he said.

"Where you from?"

"From Spokane. Well, from a farm outside of Spokane."

"You don't look much like a farm boy."

"Yeah, I know. That's what my dad tells me. My brother, too."

Marie laughed. David thought he was being charming.

"Hey," said David. "What do you think about the scalping of that guy? Do you think an Indian could do something like that?"

Marie gave him a cold, hard stare.

"Listen," he said, trying to change the subject. "You think maybe we could get together and study or something? I mean, I don't know much about Indians. Maybe you could help me?"

"Help you what?"

"You know. Help me get a good grade. I mean, I know about Hemingway, but I don't know anything about this Jack Wilson guy."

"I don't think so," said Marie. "I don't care much for study partners."

"Oh, well, how about lunch or something? Maybe a movie?"

"Are you asking me out? For a date?" asked Marie. She wasn't surprised. It had happened to her before. She thought David was just another white guy who wanted to rebel against his white middle-class childhood by dating a brown woman. He wouldn't have been the first white guy to do such a thing. She had watched quite a few white guys pursue brown female students, especially Asian nationals, with a missionary passion. Go to college, find a cute minority woman, preferably one with limited English, and colonize her by sleeping with her. David Rogers wanted a guilt fuck, Marie thought, something to ease his pain.

"Uh, yeah, I guess," said David. "Yeah, I'm asking you out."

"I don't date white men."

With that, Marie turned and left David standing alone in the hallway. Disappointed, he walked home to the place he shared with his brother, Aaron, a mechanical engineering major, and two other U of W engineering students, Sean Ward and Barry Church. Sean and Barry were studying upstairs while Aaron was watching television downstairs.

"So, how was your Indian class?" Aaron asked David. He had not wanted David to take the class especially since Aaron had heard Truck Schultz reveal that a white man had been killed by an Indian. David was always taking useless classes, like African American literature and women's literature. Yet, David had been the only male student in the women's literature class, and Aaron certainly appreciated those odds.

"It was okay," David said. "Only one Indian in there, though. A woman."

Aaron saw the interest in David's eyes.

"Is she fuckable?" Aaron asked.

David blushed.

"Oh, yeah, she must be a babe," said Aaron. "I hear Indian women like it up the ass. Like dogs, you know?"

"She isn't like that. She's smart. Besides, she said she didn't date white guys."

"Hey, bro, that's reverse discrimination," said Aaron and turned back to the television, where Robert De Niro and John Savage were playing a game of Russian roulette with some Viet Cong soldiers. De Niro held the pistol against his temple and pulled the trigger.

8

Testimony

"Mr. Russell, could you please tell us what you saw on the Burke-Gilman Trail that night?"

"I'm sorry, Officer, I was really drunk. I barely remember anything from that night."

"You were with a group of friends?"

"Yeah, we'd just come from one party and were headed for another."

"One of your friends said you all ran into, how did she say it, a shadow carrying a white guy on his shoulder. That sounds pretty memorable to me. She said you talked to this so-called shadow."

"I don't remember, Officer. I mean, I just don't remember."

"What did this shadow look like?"

"I don't remember. I remember long hair. But that's it. I don't think any of my friends remember much, do they?"

"It's pretty sketchy."

"Officer, can I be honest?"

"That's what we want you to be."

"Well, you see, there was this fog that night. Not like a real fog. But something else was happening, you know? It's like when you get real drunk and nothing seems real. You know how that feels? Well, it was like that, except worse. It was like everything was turned around. Up was down, left was right. I mean, I started looking at my friend Darren and thinking he was pretty damn cute. It was like everything went contrary, you know?"

"Did you take any drugs that night?"

"No, Officer. I was just drunk. And I know this sounds crazy. But you know what I think? I think I don't remember anything about that night because somebody wants me not to remember."

9

Building

John was walking in a cold, persistent rain. He was not sure where he walked, or how he came to arrive at his apartment building in Ballard, the Scandinavian neighborhood of Seattle north of downtown.

John lived in one of the few areas in Ballard with trees still left in the yards. The Scandinavian immigrants who'd settled Ballard had cut down most of the trees upon their arrival. The Danes, Swedes, and Norwegians had missed the monotonously flat landscapes of their own countries, and wanted their new country to remind them of home. Since the first days of their colonization of the Americas, European immigrants had strived to make the New World look exactly like the Old. They either found similar geographical or climatic locations, such as the Swedes had in Minnesota and the Germans in North Dakota, or they plowed, tunneled, clear-cut, and sculpted the land into something ethnically pleasing.

All John knew was that everything in this country had been changed, mutated. He kept walking. He had been walking for hours.

He was exhausted. He made his way upstairs to his apartment and, fully dressed, climbed into bed, but Father Duncan kept him awake. No. He had briefly fallen asleep, but Father Duncan shouted him awake. No. The phone was ringing and John refused to answer it. He knew it was his parents, trying to contact him. Then, a knocking on the door. His parents again. They always showed up in the middle of the night, hoping to catch John when his defenses were down.

"John, sweetheart," said Olivia. "Let us in. We've brought some food. Some breakfast. We've got oranges. Donuts. Wouldn't you like some breakfast?"

"Go away!" shouted John.

"John, it's your father. Let us in, champ. Let's talk."

"Go away! I don't know you! I don't know you!"

Sometimes, John opened the door and invited his parents into his apartment. Sometimes, he even telephoned his parents and invited them over. Once or twice, he had visited their home without their knowledge and stood over their bed as they slept. He talked to his parents every few days, just to be sure of their presence. However, he was never sure which Olivia and Daniel answered the phone, and he could never be sure which Olivia and Daniel came knocking at his door. He believed five different sets of Olivias and Daniels came to visit him, and he suspected there were many others, just waiting for him to weaken. One set of parents paid his rent, though John had plenty of money, and he had come to fear them most. They threatened him with words like "group home" and "medication." John had a cardboard box filled with medication in his closet. All of the Olivias and Daniels who visited him brought him pills, more pills, and still more pills. Vitamins, cough drops, and other circles, brighter and smaller, that quieted the voices in his head for a little while. But John knew those pills slowly poisoned him, too. He could take the pills and die young, or ignore the pills and live forever with the music in his head. John ignored Olivia and Daniel's knocking.

In his small, sparsely furnished apartment, John kept stacks of newspapers in all the corners, along with magazines, books, empty boxes, *TV Guide*, photo albums, a St. Francis yearbook. He slept on a twin bed with a red lamp, an apartment-warming gift from his mother, on the nightstand next to him. A tiny kitchen table ringed by more chairs than he needed. A refrigerator that held surprises, Tupperware containers filled with Olivia Smith's decomposing casseroles. A sink full of dirty dishes. There were no cockroaches in John's apartment. He had heard about cockroaches and feared them, though he had never seen one. He wondered if they carefully hid in the dark places of his apartment, and only came out when he was asleep. Cockroaches fear the light, and John understood that. He wondered if they talked to each other and whispered about him to the two other people who lived on the fourth floor with him. Though John rarely saw the human tenants, a Colombian woman who always seemed to be running off to play racquetball and an Irishman who played guitar long into the night, the roaches could have told them John's secrets. As a defense against the roaches, John constructed elaborate homemade roach traps with shoe boxes and honey, and carefully set them in every cupboard.

Olivia and Daniel knocked for hours, but John stayed in bed. After they went away, John could hear another knocking on the door, which became a different door. He briefly wondered if it was Marie, the Indian woman who had danced with him. But he closed his eyes and could see Father Duncan walking across the desert floor. Duncan's feet pounded so loudly that John covered his head with his pillow. Duncan was walking toward the stand of palm trees on the horizon. He looked disappointed and beaten, black robes coated with sand. His face sunburned, wrinkled. Duncan was a big bear of a man, half a foot taller than John and fifty pounds heavier, but with the most delicate hands. Those hands were completely contradictory placed at the ends of those huge, hairless arms. Those hands did not make sense, especially when Duncan was angry. Duncan would wave his arms in furious gestures, his beautiful hands floating like sails.

Still thinking of Father Duncan, John finally fell asleep and dreamed of the desert. He made it to work early that next morning.

He walked carefully along the girders. Just after the morning break, John saw an image of Duncan's hands so clear and startling that he nearly fell. John was attached to the building by a safety harness, but he knew that white men made the harnesses. It would only save white men. The leather, metal, and rope could tell the difference between white skin and Indian skin. But, despite his near fall, John kept working. As a good worker should be, he was always busy, but the foreman still watched him, and John knew he was being watched. He kept thinking of his mother, who had tried to visit him that morning. Olivia Smith was still exceptionally beautiful. Her few wrinkles just added a new regal quality. She had been absolutely stunning at thirty, thirty-five, forty. Clear pale skin and blue, blue eyes. She had been the object of many schoolboy crushes among John's friends. John walked along the girder and into the lunchroom at St. Francis High School ten years earlier.

"John, buddy," one friend whispered. "Your mom is a babe."

"No shit," a crass friend said. "If she was my mom, I would have never quit breast-feeding."

John felt the rage rise inside him, up from his stomach to the back of his throat. He wanted to strike out, to break that friend's nose, blacken another's eyes. He wanted to cause them so much pain. He could not believe his friends would talk about his mother in that way. But they also talked about their mothers in the same way.

"My mom's got a fat ass, all right," a boy said. "You should see her panties hanging up to dry in the bathroom. They look like sails. Jesus, it's like the goddamn America's Cup in there."

A huge jerk named Michael sat down beside John and started in.

"Smith," Michael said to him, "I saw your mom at the store last night. You are a lucky fucker."

Everybody at the table agreed and laughed, punched each other on the shoulders. John stared down at his sandwich. Sometimes he smiled and pretended to laugh when his friends teased him about his mother. He knew that was how he was supposed to react. Other times, he just ignored them and waited for the subject to change. A pretty girl would walk by and all his friends would launch into a long discussion of her alleged sexual history. But Michael would not leave it alone, even after John refused to acknowledge him.

"Smith," Michael said, because white boys always called each other by their last names. "I was just wondering. I mean, you're adopted, right? I mean, she's not even your real mother. Not really. You could get a little of that nookie and it wouldn't even be illegal, right? Not really."

John looked at Michael, who was smiling. Michael, with his swollen, bright-pink face. Michael, who would grow up to become an investment banker, a rich man with a wife, two sons, and a relatively clean life.

"I mean," Michael stage-whispered to John, so that everybody would be sure to listen closely. "Don't you ever want to sneak into her bed at night and give it to her?"

Everybody at the table was stunned. A few laughed nervously, wanting the good times to continue, hoping their laughter would lessen the tension. One or two smiled, enjoying the torment. Most had no idea how to react, but they all knew that Michael had taken it too far. They waited for John's reaction. When he sat frozen, Michael pushed further.

"Well," Michael continued. "She's a gorgeous white woman and you're an Indian, right? Don't you watch the movies? Don't Indians always want to fuck white women?"

John moved quickly, grabbing Michael around the neck and wrestling him to the ground. They rolled around the floor, throwing ineffective punches and kicks, fighting like people who have never been in a fistfight. The other boys quickly circled them, excited by the violence, but just as quickly the teachers broke it up, and John and Michael were sent to the principal's office. Michael went inside first, and came out with a forced smirk on his pimpled face.

"Now," said Mr. Taylor, the principal, when John was finally in his office. "What was this all about?"

Near tears, John breathed deeply and deliberately. He did not want to cry. His chest burned. He looked around the office. He saw the walnut desk, the bookshelves stacked thick with books that had not been touched in years. Various diplomas hung on the wall, a photograph of Mr. Taylor standing near the Pope.

"Are you hurt?" asked Mr. Taylor, a tall, chubby white man in an ugly sport coat. He was the first principal in St. Francis's history who was not a priest, although he frequently described himself as having been the best altar boy in the history of the Roman Catholic Church.

"John," said Mr. Taylor again. "Are you hurt?"

John shook his head.

"Well, then," said the principal. "Tell me what happened."

"Michael was," John began. "He was insulting my mother. He was saying ugly things."

Mr. Taylor knew how the boys saw Olivia Smith.

"John," the principal said, "I'm going to tell you something, but it cannot leave this office. Agreed?"

"Okay," John said. He was crying now.

"Michael is a jerk. Why did you listen to him? You're a good kid, John. You should just ignore him. He was trying to get a rise out of you."

John was shocked. Not just that this man knew Michael was wrong, but shocked at the same time that this offense could be trivialized.

"Don't act so surprised," said Mr. Taylor. "I'm not as out of it as all of you think I am. I know what goes on. Next time, you just walk away from him, okay?"

"Okay," John agreed, knowing that he could not walk away from any of it, but knowing that Father Duncan had walked away into the desert.

"Okay, then," said the principal and handed John a tissue. "Clean up your face and go back to class. I'll deal with Michael."

John stood to leave the office. Before he closed the door behind him, John turned back.

"Thanks," John said, always the polite student, wanting to push his anger into a small place.

"You're welcome."

John left the St. Francis principal's office and nearly stepped off the girder he was walking on ten years later. He looked at the ground thirty-seven floors below. Three hundred and seventy feet, give or take a few. The foreman was yelling at him.

"Quit your daydreaming and get to work."

John looked at the foreman, who had begun to speak a whole new language. All of his words sounded foreign. John spoke high school French and German, knew a few Spanish phrases, and had a decent Catholic student's knowledge of Latin, but the foreman's language was something else entirely. He had always been a good boss, even though he had never spoken at a volume that John could tolerate, but John did not trust him anymore. Whenever the foreman was close, John quickly evaluated his escape routes and identified potential weapons. He never allowed the foreman to stand between him and the elevator. This resulted in strange conversations. John pretended to talk to the foreman, who hardly ever said anything that made sense. But if the foreman blocked his path to the elevator, John grew more and more nervous. He kept moving and talking, talking and moving, until he was closer to the elevator than to the foreman. The foreman was not stupid. He knew that John was acting strangely.

"I don't know," the foreman would often say to his other workers. "That John is acting pretty damn strange lately."

"Lately?" somebody would usually ask. "He's always been a little off. How do you tell the difference?"

"But he's a good worker," another man would usually put in. "That's true," everybody would always agree. "He is that."

Whatever the other men felt, the foreman genuinely worried about John. They had never been friends, had never shared one moment of recognizable comraderie, but after years of working with him, the foreman had learned a few personal details about John. He knew that John was an Indian, that was obvious enough, but he had been raised by a white couple. The foreman did not know how that must have felt to son and parents. It did not make any emotional sense to him, but he knew that John barely spoke to his parents. He also knew that John never dated. At first, the foreman thought that John might be queer, but that was not it. John was just a loner, quiet and distant. It was only lately that he had become truly weird. John spent more and more break time alone on the fortieth floor, even spent work time there, and the foreman had had to go find him more than once.

After work that day, the foreman went home and ate two pork chops, five homemade biscuits, and canned green beans. His wife, Estelle, always had a good dinner waiting for him. They sat at their cheap table with four unmatched chairs in a kitchen whose walls had been a painful yellow when the paint was fresh, though now the glare had faded into a pale ugliness. They ate and watched the evening news on their thirty-one-inch television. While showing some homes to a potential buyer, a Century 21 salesman had discovered the body of the white man in an empty house in Fremont. The white man had been scalped and murdered. After hearing the bad news, the foreman pulled his wife closer and thought of John Smith. He loved his wife. She had gained a few pounds because of their three kids, but the foreman was no lightweight himself, and he knew it. He weighed himself every morning on the bathroom scale. He was getting to be a fat fuck. His pants did not fit right and his belly now hung over his belt. Everything seemed to be changing in his life, in the whole damn world. His kids were getting older, and wiser. They would know a lot more than he did pretty soon. Hell, he could barely remember their ages. Lately, when addressing a specific child, he ran though all of the possible combinations of their names before he found the correct one. Bobby, Dave, Cyndy, Robert, David, Cynthia, a group of strangers who could program a VCR. His wife had always been smarter. That did not bother him so much. She knew everything about him. She knew he had begun to hate work. He wanted to finish the lousy skyscraper and move on to his government job. He got a queasy feeling in his stomach every morning before work. Morning sickness, his wife teased him. But the foreman was beginning to wonder if he felt afraid of John.

"You know John, the Indian kid," the foreman said to Estelle. "He's been acting goofy. I'm wondering if he's got mental problems or something."

"What? Is he crazy?"

"Nah, he's not bug-eyed and slobbering. But still, he's . . . different."

"Different? He's always been different, hasn't he?"

"Yeah, but now he's really different."

"You think you should talk to him?"

"I've tried. But he hardly talks, and when he does, he sounds like a robot."

"Well, maybe you should talk to somebody else about him."

"Who? The union? The architects? That'll go over well. You see, gentlemen, we've got this Indian guy who doesn't talk and eats his lunch alone. He doesn't go for beers after work. He also arrives early, leaves late, does everything I tell him to do, and does it right. He's a really big problem. I mean, we've got a few guys about ready to flunk drug tests, a couple ex–Hell's Angels who ain't so ex, and a guy who knocked over a 7-Eleven, but I'm really worried about this Indian."

"Don't get smart with me. You're the one who brought it up."

The foreman apologized to his wife and hugged her tightly as they stood in the kitchen of their small house, their kids running and yelling in the yard. Maybe he could count everything good in his life on one hand, but that was more than most people could do.

That night, after he made love to his wife in his quick and clumsy fashion, the foreman fell asleep and dreamed. In that dream, a figure stood on the top floor of the last skyscraper in Seattle. It was dark in the dream, only a sliver of moon illuminating the building. The foreman approached the figure. With its back turned, the figure could have been a man or woman. The foreman was scared of the figure, but also very curious. The figure held an object in its hand. Something valuable, a gift for the foreman perhaps. The foreman stepped beside the figure, and both stared down at the street hundreds of feet below. Suddenly afraid of falling, the foreman woke with a sudden start and sat up in bed. His wife was soundly asleep beside him. He curled up close to her, fell back asleep, and remembered nothing of his dream by morning.

10

Confessions

"The establishment of gambling casinos on Indian reservations is very much an act of fiscal rebellion," said Dr. Clarence Mather during that second session of the Native American literature class. "However, I worry about the longtime cultural implications of such a rebellion. Are the Indians polluting their cultural purity by engaging in such a boldly capitalistic activity? As Jack Wilson writes in his latest novel, 'Indians are gambling with their futures.'"

"Dr. Mather," said Marie, raising her hand. Mather ignored her.

"Mr. Rogers," Mather said to David. "How do you feel about this?"

"Well," said David. "I've never been to a casino before. I don't know how I feel about it. But the state runs a lottery, doesn't it? Aren't the Indian casinos and the state lottery the same kind of thing?"

Marie was surprised by David's logic, but still suspicious. He tried to talk to her after that class, but she avoided him. Instead, she followed Dr. Mather back to his office. He was clueless, of course, as she tailed him through the dark campus, past quiet buildings and empty tennis courts. She could have closed her eyes and found her way. She had been negotiating the campus's maze of buildings and paths for a few years. At that late hour, the campus was surprisingly busy. A few students recognized Marie because she was a very vocal Indian student leader, but she ignored the friendly greetings of some and the hostile stares of others. Instead, she silently followed Mather into the Anthropology Building and up the stairs to his office. He was unlocking his office door, with his name stenciled in black on its gray-green opaque window, when Marie tapped him on the shoulder.

"Oh, Ms. Polatkin, you startled me."

Marie stared at the professor, who soon became very uncomfortable.

"Is there something I can do for you?" he asked.

"It's Wilson's book," Marie said and handed the mystery novel over to Mather. "I refuse to study it."

"Ms. Polatkin, Marie. Why do you insist on challenging everything I say?"

"I only challenge you when you're wrong. You just happen to be wrong about Wilson. I mean, we need the casinos. It's not like we're planning a rebellion. We're just putting food in our cupboards. If eating is rebellious, then I guess we're the biggest rebels out there. Indians are just plain hungry. Not for power. Not for money. For food, for breakfast, lunch, and dinner. Wilson doesn't know anything about that. You don't know anything about that."

Dr. Mather shook his head sadly.

"There you go again, creating an antagonistic situation. Don't you understand what I'm trying to teach? I'm trying to present a positive portrait of Indian peoples, of your people. Of you. I simply cannot do that if you insist on this kind of confrontational relationship. I mean, with all this negative publicity surrounding the murder of that white man, don't you understand I am trying to do a good thing here? People actually think an Indian killed and scalped that young man. Despite all the evidence to the contrary, people still think that Indians are savages. Don't you understand that I'm on your side?"

"On my side?"

"Yes, Ms. Polatkin, we, you and I, are on the same side of this battle."

Marie stared up at the tenured professor.

"What gives you the right to say that?" Marie asked him. "Who are you to tell me what battles I'm fighting?"

"Listen," said Mather. "I understand what you're going through, I really do. An Indian woman in college. I understand. I'm a Marxist."

"Really," said Marie. "I'm a Libra."

Unable to respond, Dr. Mather walked into his office and closed the door in her face. She heard Mather throw the deadbolt and Marie felt a sudden urge to smash the glass, break down the door, pull down the building. She wanted to tear apart the world. Mather would have never treated a white student that badly, nor would he have shut the door in the face of a man. At that moment, she wanted Dr. Mather to disappear. She wanted every white man to disappear. She wanted to burn them all down to ash and feast on their smoke. Hateful, powerful thoughts. She wondered what those hateful, powerful thoughts could create.

She was still fuming when she stepped into the QuickMart convenience store on the Ave. A penniless student, Marie usually had cereal for breakfast and dinner every day, and also for lunch on weekends. She was out of milk and QuickMart had the cheapest quart of nonfat in the University District. She was standing in the cashier's line when David and Aaron Rogers walked into the store.

"Hey, Marie," said David, obviously happy to see her. "How you doing?"

Marie was in no mood to talk to David, nor the big hulk with him. Aaron Rogers was a foot taller and a hundred pounds heavier than Marie. Aaron was more conventionally handsome than his younger brother, but Aaron's features seemed temporary, as if his blue eyes, aquiline nose, and strong jawline were simply borrowed from his parents' faces.

"Hey. What's your name again?" Marie asked David. She knew his name but wanted to offend him by pretending to forget it.

"It's David, David Rogers. And this is my brother Aaron."

With open disdain, Aaron stared down at Marie. She could smell the beer on his breath. She never drank, and absolutely hated its effect on people.

"So," Aaron said to Marie. "I hear you've been a pain in the ass."

Marie looked to David for an explanation.

"Hey, I never said that," David said to Marie. "I just said you were tough on the professor."

"Politically correct bullshit," said Aaron. "That's what I think."

Without a word, Marie turned away from the brothers, paid for her milk, and walked out of the store. She was halfway down the block when David caught up to her.

"Hey, hey," he said. "I'm sorry about that. Ignore him. He's kind of a jerk."

"He's your brother," said Marie. "Blood runs thick, enit?"

"Yeah, maybe. Listen, it's just Aaron, you know? He doesn't mean it. He just talks tough. He's really a nice guy. I mean, he's really good to me. He's kind of been taking care of me since our mother died."

"I'm sorry."

"It's okay. It was a long time ago. But Aaron just had to be tougher. He's not very good at showing his feelings and stuff."

"David," asked Marie. "Why are you trying so hard?"

"What do you mean?"

"I mean, why are you trying so hard to impress me? I'm really sorry your mother died, but it doesn't mean much to me. And I couldn't care less about your brother, you know? So, why are you telling me all of this?"

"I don't know. I guess, well, it's because I'm really sorry for what happened to Indians. It was a really bad deal."

"Yeah, you could say that."

"I just never got the chance to talk to a real Indian before. And you're real, so I wanted to tell you how I felt."

Marie looked at David. She knew he was hiding something.

"Listen," he said. "I heard about this casino up on the Tulalip Indian Reservation. I was wondering if you'd come with me. Kind of be my tour guide. Maybe Mather would give us extra credit. We could work on a paper together. Get the white boy's and Indian girl's take on it, you know?"

"David," Marie said. "I don't know what you're up to, but I'm not falling for it. Just leave me alone, okay?"

Marie left him standing there. David wanted to tell her about the camas fields back home. She was from the reservation. She must know about camas. He wanted to tell her about the Indian family that had come in the middle of the night to dig roots. Mother, father, four children, the old woman. Maybe Marie knew those Indians. Maybe Marie was one of those Indians. Maybe little Marie was running as David and Buck fired shots above her head. As Aaron shot at the Indian father. David wanted to tell Marie how he'd found one of those Indian root-digging sticks the morning after the shooting, and had buried it where his brother and father would never find it.

11

Cousins

After she'd left David Rogers standing in the street outside the convenience store, Marie walked home to her small apartment. As she
walked, her anger began to fade. She'd always had a quick temper,
was the first to shout obscenities or throw fists, but she was also the
first to laugh nervously and apologize. By the time she opened the
door of her apartment and saw Reggie Polatkin sitting at the shabby
kitchen table, Marie was calm. She'd neither seen nor heard from
Reggie in over a year, but she was not surprised to find him waiting
for her. Indian relatives had a way of just showing up at the doorstep.

"Hey, cousin," Reggie said to Marie.

"How'd you get in?" Marie asked as she placed her milk in
the refrigerator. Her apartment had one microscopic bedroom, a
bathroom with just enough room for toilet, sink, and small shower
stall, and a third room that functioned as living room, kitchen, din-
ing room, and study. Dozens of books were piled onto every free

space. Books served as furniture by propping up the black-and-white television, by supporting shelves that held yet other books, and by serving as impromptu coffee and end tables. Overpriced, depressingly cold, and battered by generations of student renters, the apartment felt like some tiny box of a reservation in the middle of a city. Marie had tried to brighten the place with flowers and colorful prints, but she still felt miserable whenever she came home.

"I got in by magic," said Reggie. "And I told the landlord I was your long lost brother."

"Long lost is right."

Reggie smiled. He was a very handsome man, with a strong nose, clear brown skin, and startling blue eyes that instantly revealed his half-breed status. In an attempt to look more traditionally Indian, he braided his long black hair into two thick ropes. He was just a few inches over five feet, which was pretty short even for a small people like the Spokanes. Like many short men, Indian and not, Reggie tried to compensate for his stature by growing a mustache. But he had an Indian mustache, meaning that ten or twelve thick black whiskers poked out from the corners of his mouth.

Reggie had grown up in Seattle with his white father, Bird, and his Spokane Indian mother, Martha. Though he'd visited the reservation a few times during his youth, Reggie had always been a stranger to Marie. Reggie was the mysterious urban Indian, the college student, the ambitious half-breed, the star basketball player, the Indian who would make a difference. On the reservation, among Marie's family, that was how Reggie had always been described, as the one who would make a difference. Reggie carried with him the collective dreams of the family. Marie had always been jealous of that, and when Reggie got himself kicked out of college because of an altercation with Dr. Clarence Mather, she'd felt a strange combination of relief and sadness. She'd felt sadness because she'd come to the University of Washington precisely because Reggie was enrolled there. She'd thought she would feel safer if she was near a relative, no matter how distant and aloof he was. And she'd felt relief because she'd hoped that Reggie's failure somehow made the possibility of her failure less likely, as if Reggie's expulsion from college had somehow paid in full her family's psychic debt.

Now, as Reggie Polatkin sat at her kitchen table, smiling and acting as if he were a regular visitor, Marie wondered how such an intelligent man could have sabotaged himself in such a profound way.

Reggie Polatkin, ten years old and little, had stared up at his white father, Bird Lawrence, a small man, barely taller than his son, but with huge arms and a coarsely featured face that made him appear larger than he was.

"Come on, you little shit," Bird had whispered. "You want to be a dirty Indian your whole life? What's the answer?"

"Dad, I don't know."

"What?"

"I don't know, I'm sorry."

Bird had slapped Reggie across the face.

"Okay, now for the second question. What year did the Pilgrims arrive in Massachusetts, and what was the name of the Indian who helped them survive?"

"Sixteen twenty," Reggie had whispered. "And his name was Squanto."

"And what happened to him?"

"He was sold into slavery in Europe. But he escaped and made his way back to his village. But everybody was dead from smallpox."

"And was the smallpox good or bad?"

"Bad."

"Wrong," Bird had said and slapped Reggie again. "The smallpox was God's revenge. It killed all the hostile Indians. You want to be a hostile Indian?"

"No," Reggie had said.

At that time, in the early seventies, Bird had been the area director for the Bureau of Indian Affairs, which was under siege by the American Indian Movement. All over the country, hostile AIM members had been attacking peaceful BIA Indians and non-Indians. Bird had known that the murder rate in Pine Ridge, South Dakota, was the highest in the country. All because of the hostiles. And those hostiles had been making it tough to help the good Indians. It had been happening since Europeans had first arrived in the United States. In the nineteenth century, while a peaceful and intelligent chief like Red Cloud had been trying to help his people, a hostile Indian like Crazy Horse had been making it worse for everybody. But Bird had always believed that Crazy Horse got what he deserved, a bayonet in his belly, while Red Cloud had lived a long life.

Martha Polatkin had married Bird because she was searching for a way off the reservation. She'd wanted to have a big house, a nice car, green grass, and, no matter how cruel Bird was, she'd known he could provide her with all of that. And because he had, in fact, provided her with all of that, she'd tried to ignore Bird's hatred of "hostile" Indians, even after he'd impregnated her and she'd given birth to Reggie. As for Bird Lawrence, he'd hated hostile Indians so much that he insisted Reggie use Polatkin, his Indian surname, until he'd earned the right to be a Lawrence, until he'd become the appropriate kind of Indian.

"Do you want to be a hostile?" Bird had asked Reggie again.

"No," Reggie had said.

"Good, good. What was the name of the Indian who lead the Pueblo Revolt of 1680 through 1692, and why did he begin the revolt?"

"His name was Pope. He was from San Juan Pueblo, and he said a spirit had told him to rid his homeland of the Spanish."

"What was the name of the Spanish commander who ended the revolt?"

"Uh, Diego. Diego."

"Diego what?"

"Diego . . . I don't remember."

Bird had punched Reggie in the stomach, knocking the wind out of him. When Reggie could speak again, Bird had continued the surprise quiz.

"You remember that crazy Indian's name, but not the name of the white man who saved thousands of lives? Why is that?"

"I don't know."

"You're hopeless. Can you explain why the Iroquois Confederacy fell apart from the years 1777 to 1783?"

"Because of the Revolutionary War."

"And?"

"Well, some Iroquois, like the Mohawks, wanted to fight with the British. But the Oneidas and the Tuscaroras wanted to fight with the United States. And the Seneca and the Onondaga didn't want to fight at all. Nobody could get along, so they broke apart from the Confederacy."

"And which Indians were right?"

"The Oneidas and Tuscaroras."

"Correct. Name the four Indian cowards who were indicted for the murder of two FBI agents on July twenty-sixth near Pine Ridge, South Dakota."

"Leonard Peltier, Bob Robideau, an Eagle, and, and . . ."

"I'll give you that one. Now, for the last question. What was the name of the Indian who helped raise the flag on Iwo Jima during World War Two?"

"Ira Hayes."

"And what happened to him?"

"He was a hero."

"No, you idiot. What really happened to him?"

"He died of exposure in the winter of 1955. Passed out in the snow."

"Why did he do that?"

"Because he was a dirty Indian."

"Exactly, and what tribe was he?"

"I don't remember."

Bird had slapped Reggie again and bloodied his nose.

"I want you to know I'm doing this for your own good," Bird had said. "I don't want you to end up like all the other Indians. I want you to be special. I don't want you to be running around with a gun. I want you to love your country. I want you to know your history." The white father gave his Indian son a handkerchief. "Here, clean your face."

Trying to avoid his father's beatings, Reggie had always studied hard and brought home excellent report cards. Bird would beam with pride and tape the reports to the refrigerator, that place of familial honor. On those rare occasions when Reggie had brought home a failed test or a flawed term paper, Bird would beat him.

"You stupid, dirty Indian," Bird would say, never above a whisper. "You'll never get into college this way. You want to be a drunk? You want to be one of those Indians staggering around downtown? What do you want to be, Reggie? What do you want to be?"

Over the years, Reggie had come to believe that he was successful because of his father's white blood, and that his Indian mother's blood was to blame for his failures. Throughout high school, he'd spent all of his time with white kids. He'd ignored his mother, Martha. He hadn't gone to local powwows. He hadn't danced or sang. He'd pretended to be white, and had thought his white friends accepted him as such. He'd buried his Indian identity so successfully that he'd become invisible.

Reggie had graduated from high school with honors and enrolled as a history major at the University of Washington. There he had met Dr. Clarence Mather.

"Hey," Marie said to Reggie as she sat at the table across from him. "I'm taking a class with your favorite teacher."

Reggie's eyes narrowed.

"Yeah," said Marie. "Dr. Clarence Mather."

"He's a fucking liar."

"Yes, he is."

Reggie was fuming. He'd never told Marie what had happened with Mather. She'd heard all kinds of stories from other Indian students. She'd heard Mather and Reggie had been lovers and that Reggie had threatened to kill Mather if he ever revealed it. She'd also heard that Reggie and Mather had fought because they'd fallen in love with the same Indian woman. She'd heard that Mather had stolen some of Reggie's academic research and claimed it as his own. So many stories, so many half-truths and outright lies. But since Indians used gossip as a form of literature, Marie knew she'd never heard the true story about Reggie and Mather. She knew the real story was probably something very pedestrian.

"Hey," said Marie, trying to be a good host. "You hungry or something? All I got is water and cereal."

"What kind of cereal?"

"Apple Jacks."

"Cool."

Marie poured two bowls of cereal. As they ate that simple dinner, Marie smiled at the small tragedy of it all. The two smartest Spokane Indians in tribal history were forced to eat Apple Jacks cereal for dinner.

"Quite the feast, huh?" asked Marie and laughed.

"Well, at least it's traditional," said Reggie, fighting back a smile.

"Yeah, don't mind us, we're indigenous."

They laughed together.

"So," said Reggie, more friendly now. "How is school going?"

"Ah, you know," said Marie. "It isn't easy."

Reggie knew.

"Are you working?" asked Marie.

"Mostly," said Reggie, who'd been running through a series of minimum wage jobs since he'd been kicked out of college. He mostly played basketball, especially at the all-Indian tournaments held nearly every weekend on the local reservations.

"How's your folks?" asked Marie.

"Mom's okay. Bird's got cancer."

Bird had recently been diagnosed with terminal prostate cancer and spent a lot of time in hospitals. Once, when Martha had called to say that Bird had asked for him, Reggie had promised to come home to the hospital, but had traveled to a basketball tournament in Montana instead.

"Oh, shit," Marie said. "I'm sorry. How is he? Really?"

"I don't know. Don't care much, either."

They ate the rest of their dinner in silence, then settled in to watch a bad movie on Marie's black-and-white television.

"Hey, cousin," said Reggie after the movie was over. "I hate to ask. But do you got any money I could borrow?"

Marie knew that Reggie had been building up the courage to ask for money.

"Reggie," she said. "If I had money, do you think we'd be eating Apple Jacks?"

Reggie smiled.

"Hey," he asked. "Have you heard about the scalping of that white man?"

"Yeah."

"What do you think?"

Marie shrugged her shoulders.

"Yeah, I agree," said Reggie.

He slept on the couch that night, and when Marie woke up early the next morning, he was already gone.

12

Seattle's Best Donuts

For the first time since he had started construction work, John asked for permission to leave early, and went straight home to sleep. He was tired and willing to admit it to the foreman. A little after ten that night, he woke from a nightmare he could not remember, but he felt its residual effects, the sweat, racing heart, tensed muscles. He rubbed his stomach, remembered how, when he was twenty years old, he thought he was pregnant. No one had believed him, so he had forced himself to throw up every morning to prove it. For nine months, he waited to give birth, surprised by how little his belly had grown.

"This is going to be the smallest baby ever," John had told Olivia. "You're going to be a huge grandmother. Gigantic. The biggest grandmother ever."

John had decided to have his baby at home because he hated hospitals and doctors, though he loved the nurses with their white nylons and long eyelashes. Using his latest paycheck, John made a list and then bought all the items he'd written down:

> towels, clean and hot
> hammer and nails
> baby blankets and toys
> bottle
> graham crackers and milk
> needle and thread
> radio
> sharp knife
> soup
> brand-new tool belt
> rent money
> newspapers with all the want ads cut out

On his delivery date, John lay naked on his bed, waiting for the baby. He watched the digital clock. 7:51. 7:52. 7:53. But the baby would not come. John felt his stomach, wished for labor pains, and heard the music growing louder and louder.

"No!" he'd shouted. "Don't cheat me! Don't cheat me again!"

But the baby never arrived, and John realized he had never been pregnant. He felt foolish. He had told everybody that he was pregnant, his mother and father, the woman who worked at the supermarket, his landlord. John packed up all his birthing supplies, the toys and blankets, knife and newspapers, and packed them into a box. He shoved the box under his bed and never looked at it. No. He opened it sometimes to take inventory, to make sure everything was still there. Criminals were everywhere these days, especially in his neighborhood. A girl had been shot and killed outside Ballard High School, just a few blocks away from his apartment. He was not going to take any chances with his possessions.

John smiled at the memory of his failed pregnancy. He was awake. He had to work the next day and he always tried to get plenty of sleep on work nights. The foreman liked to start early, so they would be done before that late afternoon sun took over. John thought this a strange belief, especially during winter in Seattle, when the skies were gray and rain fell constantly. John had seen one of his co-workers fall over with heat exhaustion a few summers earlier, but had never known it to happen since. Still, the foreman knew that an unconscious worker was an unproductive worker and made sure his men drank lots of water. John worried about what might have been in the water, but he usually drank it anyway.

John could not fall back to sleep. He crawled from bed, dressed in his work clothes, and walked to the all-hours donut shop on the corner. Seattle's Best Donuts. John liked their donuts well enough, but he was not sure if they were the best in Seattle. He had once asked if there had been some kind of contest, but the manager just laughed. The shop was small, simple, and passably clean, as if one wet rag had been used to clean the entire place. A large picture window fronted the store. A window display of donuts at the end of the counter and another display hanging on the wall behind the counter. The kitchen was dark and mysterious behind the swinging doors.

"Lookee here, lookee here," said Paul, the graveyard shift worker at the donut shop, when John walked in. Paul was a twenty-year-old black man, an art major at the University. He was handsome, with clear eyes and a strong chin. His hair was shaved close to his head. He worked the shift with Paul Too, an old black man whose great-great-grandmother had escaped slavery by marrying into the Seminole tribe. Paul Too sat at the counter, smoking a cigarette and reading the newspaper. He had a face like an old map, stained with age and folded incorrectly one too many times.

"Good morning, John," said Paul. "You having the usual?"

"Yeah," John said and sat beside Paul Too, who looked up from his newspaper and nodded. Paul set a jelly-filled donut and a cup of coffee in front of John. Paul Too picked up John's donut, took a bite, and set it back down. Then he sipped a little of John's coffee.

John watched Paul Too very carefully. One minute, two minutes went by. Paul Too had survived. The food had not been poisoned. John took a bite of his donut and washed it down with coffee.

"So, John," said Paul. "You couldn't sleep again?"

John shook his head.

"That's horrible. I hate it when I can't sleep. And I'll tell you, this graveyard shift messes with my sleeping. I never know what time it is. Never. Ain't that right, Paul Too?"

Paul Too sighed deeply and nodded his head in agreement, never lifting his eyes from the paper.

"How's your health been?" asked Paul. "Been quiet?"

John shrugged his shoulders.

"Yeah, I know how that goes. I hate it when things get loud. I need peace and quiet myself. Time to paint well, to let the colors in my head be the colors on the canvas, you know what I'm saying? A man doesn't need much in this world, does he, John? Just a little food, a little house, and a little peace and quiet. I once heard that a man needs a full stomach and a warm house before he'll listen to anybody's sermon."

Paul Too cleared his throat.

"I know, I know," said Paul. "I was going to give you credit, you grumpy old man."

John looked from Paul to Paul Too.

"You see, John," said Paul. "Old Paul Too told me that. He said every man needs a good meal, a big blanket, and some peace and quiet. He said it. I'm just paraphrasing."

Paul Too loudly turned a page, newsprint crinkling like a little bit of thunder.

"Okay, okay," Paul said. "So it was Bessie Smith who said it first. I was just paraphrasing Paul Too's paraphrase of Ms. Smith. Are you happy now, old man?"

John finished his donut, drank the last of his coffee. Paul swept them away and wiped the counter clean, leaving the rag for John to inspect. It was blue. John knew the blue rags were sterilized.

"So," said Paul. "How's your folks?"

John felt a little heat in his belly. Olivia and Daniel often came to the donut shop searching for John. Sometimes, they found him there. Other times, they just ate donuts and waited for John to arrive. John did not know if the donuts here were the best in Seattle, but his parents thought they were.

"I haven't seen them for a bit," Paul said. "I was just wondering." Then to change the subject: "Do you know who Bessie Smith was?"

John shook his head.

"She was a singer, a fine black woman, back in the twenties and thirties, sang like nobody can sing. Sang good enough to make you crazy, John. Just like what you hear in your head, except everybody could hear it. How's that for crazy? Drove the whole world insane and then she bled to death because they wouldn't let her in a white hospital."

Paul Too looked up at Paul.

"Yeah," said Paul to Paul Too, "I know you think it was murder. But you think everything is a conspiracy." Then to John. "Paul Too here thinks that Richard Nixon killed both Kennedys, Martin Luther King, and Malcolm X."

Paul Too wagged a finger at Paul.

"And," added Paul, "he thinks Mr. Nixon designed Pintos. You know what I'm saying? Those ugly little cars that looked like insects? You remember how they used to blow up? One little tap on the bumper and *boom*!"

Paul slapped his hands together loudly. John jumped up from his seat.

"Hey," Paul said. "I'm sorry there, John. Please, have a seat."

John sat down. Paul Too smoothed his pants and shirt, smoothed his hair with his left hand, picked up the local news section, and exhaled slowly.

"They found a white man's body," said Paul Too, reading from his newspaper.

"What man?" asked Paul.

"A dead man. They found his body in some empty house near Fremont. Houses all around there and nobody saw nothing. He was all messed up. What do they say here? Multiple stab wounds."

Paul whistled.

"How many is multiple?" asked Paul Too. "How do they say things like that? What do they do? Count them up and measure them? Well, this is a bunch of stab wounds, and this is a lot. But Jesus, this is multiple. I don't much care for it, you hear?"

"I hear," Paul said.

"What was his name?" John asked, surprising both Pauls. He rarely talked in the donut shop.

"Well," Paul said. "Tell the man what his name was."

"It says here his name was Justin Summers. Now, if that ain't the whitest white-guy name of all time, then I don't know what. It's just a damn shame."

John started to cry.

"What is it?" asked both Pauls, bracing for the worst. Olivia and Daniel's phone number was on a list near the telephone.

John covered his face with his hands.

"Did you know him?" asked Paul Too.

John shook his head furiously.

"Are you okay?" Paul asked. "Do you need anything?"

John put his face down on the counter, his shoulders and back heaving, loud sobs. No. Now he was laughing, deep belly laughs, his eyes still wet with tears. He laughed until he felt sick. Paul and Paul Too watched him. He might have laughed until he passed out, he had done it before, but another customer walked in the door and broke the spell.

"Well, hello there, Mr. Ruffatto," Paul said to the regular.

Paul Too placed a hand on John's shoulder. John stared at the hand, black skin, long fingers, wrinkled knuckles, a huge hand, callused and old. John eased out from under that hand, backed out of the shop, and started walking. He walked downtown and sat outside the building site. He stared up at the last skyscraper in Seattle. It was small, even by Seattle standards, and pointless. Why were they finishing this tall building when most of the skyscrapers in downtown Seattle were already in financial trouble? So many vacant spaces, so many failed businesses. None of the buildings in downtown Seattle were owned by the people who had originally financed their construction. Nothing was original. John watched his building. A few night people passed by, but John ignored them. He sat alone and quiet, wondering what would happen to him after the construction was complete.

13

Indian Gambling

David Rogers had never been to an Indian gambling casino before that night. He'd never been on an Indian reservation for that matter, despite the fact that there were at least a dozen in and around the Seattle area, and five within a few hours' drive from his family's farm. In fact, the city of Spokane was named after a local tribe, but David had never visited their reservation. He knew that Marie Polatkin was Spokane, but she had refused his offer to accompany him to the Tulalip Casino. He wasn't even sure why he wanted to go to the casino. He wanted to see Indians, he knew, but he didn't know what he would do after that.

His brother, Aaron, and his other housemates, Barry Church and Sean Ward, hadn't wanted to come with him.

"I'm not going on some reservation," Aaron had said. "You don't know what those Indians might do. Hell, they already killed one white guy. And you better not go either. What would Dad say if he knew you were going up there?"

So, with neither his brother's help nor his father's permission, David found himself alone and more than a little jumpy as he walked into the Tulalip Tribal Casino, just forty miles north of Seattle. David had expected to find something more illicit and foreign inside. From all the newspaper editorials, the public outcry, and his father's rantings, David had assumed the casino would be filled with drunk Indian men, half-naked Indian women, and Italian mobsters. Instead, on this weeknight, David saw a couple dozen white farmers losing money at the poker and blackjack tables while the farmers' wives dropped buckets of quarters into the slot machines. He was probably the youngest man in the casino, but he certainly wasn't the only white one. He looked like most of the other gamblers. All of the Indians, dressed formally in tuxedos and evening gowns, were working as dealers, cashiers, and waiters. David was vaguely disappointed. He'd come for some cheap, rebellious thrills, a white boy slumming it among the Indians, but he soon discovered that the most dangerous thing in the casino was the thick cloud of cigarette smoke.

Still, once he realized he was safe, David proceeded to have a great time. He'd brought only forty dollars with him and he intended to gamble until he was broke. He lost twenty bucks at blackjack, five at poker, spent five on a hamburger and french fries, and was down to his last ten when he decided to have a spin on the slot machines. There must have been a hundred machines lined up in a far corner of the casino. Most machines took quarters, but a few took silver dollars. Bright lights, flashing bulbs, sirens announcing wins. The *whirr-whirr-whirr* of the slots spinning, the *thuk-thuk-thuk* of the jackpot-jackpot-apple, a loser, falling into place. The housewives, with white buckets of quarters balanced in their laps, pumped money into the slots. It was all so loud, irritating, and irresistible. A few minutes before midnight, David sat at a one-dollar baseball-themed slot machine, beside a housewife who briefly glanced at him before turning back, with a loud sigh, to her own efforts. Her luck had been bad that night. With his no better, David soon lost nine dollars with nine spins of the slots.

"It's been that kind of night," the housewife announced.

"Yeah," David said, holding his last silver dollar. "This is it. Wish me luck."

"Luck."

David dropped the silver dollar into the machine, pulled the handle, and watched the Single-Single-Single drop into place. The housewife screamed as one hundred dollars' worth of silver dollars spilled onto the floor. A few other women jealously peered around corners as David scooped up his money. He'd won his money back! And then some.

"For luck," he said to the housewife as he handed her one of his silver dollars.

"You're not quitting, are you?" she asked.

"Well, maybe not. Maybe just one more."

He dropped one more dollar into the machine and pulled the handle, realizing this was exactly how casinos made their money. The slots spun, dropped. Home Run–Home Run–Home Run. The housewife was shrieking now and hugging David, who hugged her back. The sirens were deafening. Flashing red lights. The sudden appearance of two beefy Indian security guards. A crowd of white farm folk. Two thousand dollars! Two thousand dollars! Two thousand dollars!

After turning down management's attempts to give him a check, David walked out of the casino with two thousand dollars in small bills. He knew it was foolish, but he felt like a character in a Hemingway novel. Daring, masculine, without the slightest hint of fear. Or reveling in his fear, staring into the eyes of the charging beast. He wondered what Marie would say. What if she thought he was stealing from the Indians?

David, feeling wealthy and untouchable, walked past the Indian security guards, who were busy calming down a drunken farmer. David couldn't believe his luck. Aaron would go crazy. They'd party all night, skip class tomorrow, and drink through the weekend. Hell, they could go rent a hotel room and drink it up in style, paper the walls with twenty-dollar bills. David was laughing to himself, lost in fantasy, when he bumped into an Indian man standing near an advertising kiosk outside the casino.

"Excuse me," David said. He barely looked at the Indian, but noticed a funny sign on the kiosk. WELCOME TO THE SIXTH ANNUAL TULALIP INDIAN NATION ALL-INDIAN BASKETBALL TOURNAMENT.

"Hey," David said, pointing at the sign. "Gets pretty specific, doesn't it?"

The Indian didn't respond, which made David a little tense. He placed his hand on the large envelope of money in his coat pocket. He suddenly felt very white. The Indian, with a curious, canine twist of his head, looked at David. The Indian could smell the white boy's fear.

"Well," David said. "See you later."

David could see his pickup in the parking lot. About a hundred feet away. Twenty seconds to get there. Remain calm, he thought. As he walked toward the pickup, David dug through his pockets. He found the right key, and readied it for quick use. Then he glanced back toward the casino and saw that the Indian was gone. The parking lot was dark. No people. The hum of the freeway a few hundred feet to the east. Increasingly nervous now, David began to hurry. He reached his pickup and tried to insert the key, but his hands were shaking and he dropped it. Jesus, David asked himself, what are you so scared of? He bent down to pick up the keys, felt a sudden, sharp pain at the back of his head, and then felt nothing at all.

14

Testimony

"Mrs. Johnson, did you see anything or anybody suspicious in the casino?"

"No."

"Are you okay, Mrs. Johnson? Are you sure you want to do this?"

"Yes. It's just. I mean, he seemed like such a sweet boy. What was his name?"

"David. David Rogers."

"Yes, that's it. He give me a silver dollar. I have it right here. He said it was for luck and then he hit the jackpot. I guess he wasn't so lucky, was he?"

"No, ma'am."

"Do you know what happened to him? Do you know anything at all?"

"We're working on it, ma'am. Right now, we just know he left his pickup in the parking lot. That's all we know."

"It's like he just disappeared, isn't it?"

"Something like that."

"And all that's left of him is this silver dollar, isn't it?"

"Right now, it looks that way."

"But it's so small."

"Very small, ma'am."

"Does this have anything to do with that boy who was scalped down in Seattle?"

"We don't know, ma'am."

15

Variations

After Olivia heard the news about the young man who had disappeared from the Indian casino, she called Daniel at work.

"Daniel, have you heard about that boy who disappeared? From the reservation?"

"Yes," said Daniel impatiently.

"What do you think happened to him?"

"I don't know. It sounds like a robbery."

"I bet his family is worried sick," said Olivia, thinking about how John had often disappeared from her life, only to reappear at unexpected times. She wondered how she would feel if John disappeared forever. She thought about the white man who had been scalped and murdered. She wondered how his family felt about his death.

"Are you okay?" Daniel asked, hearing the worry in his wife's voice.

"I was just thinking about John. Have you heard from him?"

"No."

"Well, I was just thinking, you know, that maybe we could go see if he's at his apartment. I mean, he's not answering his phone. But maybe he's just ignoring it. Maybe he's hurt."

"If you want," Daniel said, not wanting to admit how much he wanted to go searching for John.

After work, Daniel drove from downtown Seattle east across the 520 bridge to Bellevue, picked up Olivia from her part-time job at the Bellevue Art Museum, and then headed back across the bridge. Heavy traffic. Daniel hated the two bridges, 520 to the north and I-90 to the south, that connected the eastern and western halves of the Seattle metropolitan area. Like most American cities, Seattle was a city of distinct and divided neighborhoods, and though it had a reputation for cultural diversity, there was actually a very small minority population, consisting primarily of Asian- and African-Americans. And the minority populations mostly lived, by choice and by economic circumstance, in the Central, International, and University Districts. The middle-class whites generally lived on the twin hills of Queen Anne and Magnolia, overlooking the rest of the city, while the rich white people mostly lived in Bellevue or on Mercer Island, a financial and geographical enclave that sat in the waters of Lake Washington, halfway between Bellevue and Seattle. Where water had once been a natural boundary, it now existed as an economic barrier. And in those places where natural boundaries between neighborhoods didn't exist, the engineers had quickly built waterways. So much water separating people.

Daniel knew that all the bridges and water were beautiful, but it was so hard to get from one place to another. Daniel hated traffic and constantly cursed other drivers. He took delays personally, as if each car were specifically placed to impede his progress. When John was young, Daniel had learned to control his tongue. But now that John was no longer a passenger, Daniel would fully vent his anger.

He honked his horn, yelled, and mumbled by turns, wanting to talk to his son, John, the boy who, despite all the water so close to home, had never learned to swim.

Olivia did not mind sitting in the car. The Lexus had a great stereo system. She could play a compact disc and compose herself in preparation for their visit with John. She loved classical music, especially Glenn Gould's rendition of the *Goldberg Variations*. For reasons she could not verbalize, Olivia had been immediately touched by his music. She was not a musical expert, had no scholarly vocabulary, but felt that she needed Gould's piano playing in order to feel more substantial. Each series of notes, played straight, inverted, repeated, became the reason she could get out of the bed some mornings. The music came to mean even more to her after she read about Gould's life, how he had quit performing publicly without the slightest warning. On that evening, he had signed an autograph for a backstage technician, told him that he was never going to perform again, and then played for the last time for an audience. It was wildly eccentric, Olivia thought, and impossibly romantic. It was the sort of rebellion that only a genius could have pulled off. Olivia wondered what Gould had felt that evening, how a weight must have lifted from his shoulders and drifted up into the rafters. As she and Daniel drove into Ballard in search of John, Olivia felt only sadness. While Gould had been very eccentric, quite probably mentally ill, he also managed to produce some of the greatest music of the twentieth century. Olivia wondered if her son, John, would ever be able to create anything of value.

John had left Olivia and Daniel's home shortly after high school graduation. Daniel had encouraged the move and preferred to view it as some sort of initiation into manhood. Secretly, though, Daniel hoped that the move would be good for John, who had become increasingly withdrawn and distant. Most teenagers were temperamental, but John's mood swings seemed to be too dramatic. Sometime during high school, he began to go immediately to his room after coming home. He would play one of the powwow music tapes he had bought, and not come out until morning. When Olivia brought John dinner in his room, Daniel felt that was being far too accommodating. But he knew he had been fairly lenient himself, due in large part, he thought, to John's status as an adopted child. Oh, there were lots of times when John was simply their son, with no need for any qualifiers, but the stark difference in their physical appearances was a nagging reminder of the truth. If Olivia and Daniel could not forget that John was adopted, then John must have carried that knowledge even closer to his skin. Daniel wondered if his worries about John were normal parental worries, or unfounded obsessions that somehow changed John's little teenage rebellions into full-scale wars. Maybe that was why John played his music so loudly, so he could not hear himself thinking about his mysterious origins. Sometimes, John would play his powwow music deep into the night.

"John!" Daniel would shout. "Turn that down!"

John would turn the music down for a few minutes, but then he would slowly increase the volume until it was as loud as it had been. Those drums filled the house. Midnight. One in the morning. Olivia seemed to sleep through it, but Daniel lay awake, a pillow over his head. Finally, after trying to shout the music down, Daniel would crawl from bed and storm down the hallway to John's bedroom. It was always dark but Daniel never bothered to switch on the light. The walk was so familiar he could have closed his eyes and found his way quickly. Daniel sensed that life was all about patterns, with humans, animals, and insects finding those patterns and holding onto them with all of their strength. God was a series of recurring images. Daniel had walked faithfully down the dark hallway to John's room without incident for eighteen years, bringing glasses of water and warm milk, comfort from nightmares and sleepy frustration, quiet discipline. Then, one evening when John was playing his powwow music at an exceptionally loud volume, Daniel tripped over a chair that had not been there before. As he hopped around and rubbed his bruised toe, Daniel did not stop to think about anything other than the pain and the music. He pounded on John's door, which was jammed shut. A few months earlier, Daniel had removed the lock from the door because John had taken to barricading himself in his room, but John then kept the door shut to outsiders with a butter knife inserted into the jamb.

"John!" Daniel shouted while pounding on the bedroom door. But the music only increased in volume until it sounded like a whole tribe was beating drums.

Daniel pounded on that bedroom door for hours, years, until he found himself pounding on John's apartment door in Ballard. Daniel wore a tailored suit, dark blue and tasteful, and a muted purple paisley tie, slightly out of style, his way of expressing his individuality. Olivia wore her favorite dress, red with large, black buttons. They both wore similar black overcoats. Daniel thought it vaguely embarrassing that he looked like his wife whenever it rained, without realizing how much he and Olivia always looked alike. Daniel pounded on the door. Olivia stood behind him. She had done this so often before, Daniel knocking and knocking, while John sat inside, ignoring them. Usually, if they stayed long enough, John would eventually answer the door. Once or twice, she had talked the landlord into opening the door, and then felt more like a trespassing thief than a mother. The landlord eventually gave her a key, but Olivia had never used it.

"He's not home," said Olivia.

"He's home," said Daniel, frustrated and slightly frightened because John had disappeared before.

Now, again, no answer as Daniel pounded on the door, as Olivia held her breath, as they tried to make contact with their son. The neighbors, Salgado in 401 and Heistand in 402, turned up their televisions. They had heard this knocking many times before. In the beginning, it had been touching and slightly irritating, the audible proof of parental love. But it had become desparate and lonely.

Olivia and Daniel were silent on the long drive back to Bellevue. As they drove over the 520 bridge, Olivia looked down and saw a man in a kayak, or actually the dark silhouette of a man in a kayak, passing beneath the bridge. A crazy man, thought Olivia, to be all alone, out there, on the dark water. Glenn Gould played his piano. Olivia did not say anything when Daniel switched off the CD player, silencing Gould, and turned on the radio.

"Hello out there, folks, this is Truck Schultz on KWIZ, the Voice of Reason. . . ."

16

Greek Chorus

". . . and boy, do I have a problem. You see, folks, I just got this newsletter from the Washington State Indian Tribes for Aboriginal Gambling. The W.S.I.T.A.G. How do you say that anyway? What do you think it means in Indian? Well, I think it means they want to turn our state into a nest of sin and debauchery.

"The W.S.I.T.A.G. wants to increase the number of full-scale gambling casinos in Washington. We're talking blackjack, poker, slot machines. We're talking roulette, keno, bingo, with absolutely no bet limits or state supervision. That's right, folks, the Indian tribes in this state want to subvert our constitution. They want to ignore the wishes of our government officials, of the voting public, and establish Vegas-style gambling casinos, complete with show girls, neon lights, and Wayne Newton.

"The Indian tribes insist that they have the legal right to establish casinos. They contend that the state has no say in these matters because of treaties that the tribes signed a century ago with the federal government. Can you believe this, folks? The Indian tribes believe that they are above the law. I wonder how far these Indians are willing to take this. What's going to happen next? When you wake up tomorrow morning, will there be an Indian tribe camped out on your front yard, demanding that your land revert back to them?

"Listen, folks, I admit that what was done to the Indians was wrong. But that was hundreds of years ago, and you and I were not the people who did it. We have offered our hands in friendship to the Indians, but they insist on their separation from normal society. They are an angry, bitter people, and treat the rest of us with disdain and arrogance. Maybe this whole Indian gambling thing is about revenge on the white man. They want to take all of our money. They want to corrupt our values. They want to teach our children that greed and avarice are good things.

"Let me give you an example of what Indian gambling has brought to our state. I want to tell you a little story about a young man named David Rogers. David is a student at the University of Washington. An upstanding young man, a good son, an English major who loved Hemingway. He shares a house with his brother, Aaron, who called me up this morning. Aaron told me all about his brother. You see, a couple days ago, David Rogers wanted to go gambling at the Tulalip Indian Casino just north of Seattle.

"Now, David didn't want to go alone, so he invited his brother to come along. But he refused. In fact, Aaron tried to discourage his little brother, but David was seduced by the easy money he thought he was going to make. Aaron kept telling his brother it was dangerous. He reminded his younger brother about the scalping and murder of Justin Summers. But David would not be denied.

"So, David went to the casino alone, and, lo and behold, he won two thousand dollars at the slot machines. Can you believe that? He must have thought he was the luckiest man alive. And you know what, he was lucky for a few minutes. He was also smart. Most people would have gambled their winnings away, thinking they were on a hot streak. But David, despite the protest of the casino management, collected his money and left the casino, anxious to celebrate with his brother. He left the casino and he has not been seen since.

"That's right, folks. David is missing. His pickup was found in the casino parking lot, but there is no trace of him. He's disappeared. Now, I don't want to jump to conclusions, but I can just imagine what happened."

Truck sipped at his coffee.

"The Indian tribes of Washington State have declared a cultural war on us, and the weapon they've chosen is the casino.

"What do you think, folks? Give me a call. . . ."

17

All the Indians in the World

In search of David Rogers, Aaron and Buck drove onto the Tulalip Indian Reservation. The Tulalip Tribal Casino was just a few hundred feet off the freeway, close to a Burger King restaurant and a 7-Eleven convenience store.

"Jeez," said Aaron, trying to ease the tension. "Long ways from camas root, don't you think?"

Buck didn't respond. He hadn't spoken much since he'd arrived in Seattle. On the short trip from Seattle to the Tulalip Reservation, Buck had driven with a calculated fury. He'd raced up on slower cars, flashing his lights and honking his horn. He'd changed lanes with sudden twists of the wheel. Aaron had been terrified.

Now, as he slowly pulled into the casino parking lot, Buck seemed to have calmed.

"Where was David's pickup?" asked Buck.

"Over there," said Aaron and pointed to the approximate place. The police had long since taken the pickup away.

Buck and Aaron stood in the parking lot, in the place where David's truck had been. In the very same air. Aaron breathed in deep. Unsure of what else to do, Aaron stared down at the ground, searching for evidence, some reason for David's disappearance. Aaron knew about the two thousand dollars David was carrying, but he also knew that David would have given it to a mugger in a second. He would have never fought back. David didn't work that way.

"Indians," whispered Buck as two large Indian men walked out of the casino. They looked like brothers, Aaron thought, although most Indians looked alike. The Indians were laughing loudly. Buck glowered at them. Aaron knew his father was carrying a pistol beneath his jacket. Aaron took a deep breath, ready for anything to happen. The Indians, still talking and laughing, walked past the two white men. Buck and Aaron turned to watch them as they climbed into a battered pickup and drove away.

"It could've been them," said Buck. "It could've been any of these Indians."

Inside the casino, more Indians. But no answers. Inside the Burger King and 7-Eleven, still more Indians. Indians driving by. Indians walking. Indians laughing. A world suddenly filled with Indians. But no answers.

"They took him," said Buck. "They've taken my David."

On the drive back to Seattle, Aaron stared at the trees beside the road. Tall, dark, and thin, they looked like Indians, ready to reach out and steal everything.

"Why'd you let him go there alone?" Buck asked Aaron.

"I told him not to go," said Aaron.

"You're his big brother. You're supposed to take care of him."

"I'm sorry."

Buck backhanded his son and bloodied his nose.

"No excuses," said Buck. "You let him down. You let me down."

Aaron, fighting back tears, wiped blood from his face. Buck passed a gasoline truck and two recreational vehicles. Aaron thought about his late mother, how she wasted away and died during one long summer.

"He's all we have," said Buck. "He's all we have left."

Aaron and Buck drove in silence after that. They didn't speak when Buck dropped Aaron off at his house. They didn't speak after Buck drove back to the family farm, sat at the kitchen table, and waited for his younger son to come home. He waited for a long time.

For Aaron, school simply ceased to be important. He felt a tremendous amount of guilt for letting David go alone to the casino. David had asked him to come along, but Aaron had refused. Their other roommates, Barry and Sean, had also passed on the offer, but Aaron felt a special responsibility for David. He was a weak, clumsy boy who had often needed protection from school bullies. Aaron had always provided that protection until the night that David disappeared.

Aaron designed a missing-person sign on his computer, printed hundreds of copies, and stapled them to telephone poles and advertising kiosks all over western Washington. Two or three times, he drove alone to the Tulalip Tribal Casino to look for any signs of David. Somewhere deep inside himself, Aaron realized it was probably hopeless, but it was all he knew to do. He could not cry, though he wanted to. He locked himself in the bathroom, stripped naked, sat on the floor, and prayed for tears. But it would not happen. After that, with only the faintest trace of emotion, he walked from store to store, asking each to place a missing-person flyer in the window. The store managers never turned him down. Everybody knew about the missing college student, the boy from Spokane who loved Hemingway. Aaron spent so much time searching for David that he just stopped attending classes. His other roommates, Barry and Sean, tried to comfort him in their clumsy ways, wanting to ease his pain, but Aaron refused all compassion. He needed some kind of ceremony in which to express his grief, but he was without ceremony. Without the ability to mourn properly, Aaron could only steep in his anger. Tapping a thirty-six-inch baseball bat against the floor, he spent hours alone in his dark bedroom, listening to Truck Schultz's radio show. Aaron made plans for revenge against the unknown. He stood and smashed the bat against the wall, punching a hole in the plaster. Then he swung the bat again.

18

In Search Of

On a bright and cold Saturday morning, John saw Father Duncan more clearly than he had ever seen him before. Duncan, that grizzly of a man, was kneeling in the sand. John could see his shoulders shaking with tears, or laughter, or passionate prayers. What does a priest pray for? For himself, for his own needs, for the same reasons that everybody else prays? John knew that priests also prayed for their congregations, for the Pope, for the blessing, for communion, for offering. Prayers for every occasion. Father Duncan kneeled in the sand and prayed, or laughed, or cried, or maybe he did all three simultaneously. Duncan, wanting to be heard by every version of God, prayed in English, Latin, and Spokane, a confusing and painful mix of syntax, grammar, and meaning. John could see that Father Duncan's black hair had grown so much that it reached the small of his back. Duncan's face was hidden behind those delicate hands, which were blistered, bruised, and trembling. The sun was so low that Father Duncan could have stood and touched it. Sand, scorpions testing the armor of enemy scorpions, tarantulas hiding in their self-made caves. That stand of palm trees still on the horizon. Storm clouds.

Feeling the need to run from that storm, John stuffed a few belongings into a backpack and hitchhiked down the coast. John often visited reservations searching for his mother, answers, some kind of family. Now, as he left, he didn't tell anyone where he was going. He planned on being back to work by Monday morning. He simply locked his apartment door behind him and walked out into the cold morning. In search of Bigfoot, he hitchhiked south to the Hupa Indian Reservation in northern California.

John had become obsessed with Bigfoot after watching an episode of *In Search Of*, the Leonard Nimoy–hosted television series about monsters and myths. John had learned about the cabin in Ape Canyon on Mount Saint Helens where a group of miners battled a small army of angry Bigfoot. John had been fascinated by the account, reenacted for television by bad actors, but had doubted it. Bigfoot were incredibly strong and intelligent. If an army of Bigfoot had angrily attacked a small group of miners in a thin-walled cabin, then John doubted that the miners would have survived. Instead, John believed that the Bigfoot had been having fun with the miners, those pale-skinned men who loudly crashed through the forest, announcing their presence to everybody, never burying their waste, leaving behind foul evidence of their passing. John could hear the Bigfoot laughing among themselves as they hoisted rock after rock against the roof of the cabin. He could hear the terrified screams of the miners as they cowered inside. When morning came, after the Bigfoot had tired of their game and gone, the miners quickly abandoned their camp. Ashamed of their cowardice, the miners had invented the story of their epic battle against the monsters who lived on the mountain. That was how it worked. John knew that white men did not know how to tell the truth. They lied constantly about women, money, monsters. White men made promises and did not keep them.

John had been mesmerized when Leonard Nimoy introduced the footage of the "most convincing evidence of Bigfoot's existence," and then screened Roger Patterson's famous film of his encounter with the monster on the Hupa Indian Reservation. John had kneeled down in front of his television as the Bigfoot stepped over the dead-fall in the middle of a clearing, and walked, with enormous, beautiful grace, from left to right across the screen. Patterson's horse, spooked by the monster, had thrown him, so the film was unsteady and dizzying. Despite the commotion, Patterson had kept filming as he fell, regained his footing, and ran after the Bigfoot. For effect, the frame was frozen just as the Bigfoot turned to look directly into the camera. Huge, brown, pendulous breasts; large chunks of muscle and fat carried at her hips and belly.

With his backpack and a few possessions, John hitchhiked to the Hupa Indian Reservation. It was a quick and uneventful journey. Over the course of fifteen hours, a long-haul trucker picked him up within the Seattle city limits and gave him a lift down Interstate 5 to Portland, Oregon, where John caught another ride, to the Hupa Reservation, with a salesman who leased movie videos to many of the small-town supermarkets, mom-and-pop rental stores, and obscure convenience stores in southern Oregon and northern California.

Once in Hoopa, on the reservation, John was unsure of what to do. He was confused by the spelling of Hupa, the tribe, and Hoopa, the town, and knew that something had been lost. And it appeared strange that this reservation town contained few Indians. It appeared to be a typical small town, with a grocery store, a gas station, a post office, a number of turn-of-the-century houses, a small clinic, and a few anonymous government buildings, though it was set down in the middle of a beautiful valley. The redwood trees filled the horizon. John walked around the town, attracting a lot of attention from the small number of Indians. The girls gossiped behind their hands, while the boys wondered if they could talk John into playing for their basketball teams. A tribal policeman with mirrored sunglasses and braids cruised by John. The Hupa Reservation was the kind of place where fugitives of all kinds came to disappear. John walked until he saw an old Hupa Indian woman sitting on a folding chair outside the local cafe. She was small and ancient, with a walnut face deeply lined with wrinkles. She wore a pair of blue jeans and a T-shirt that read BIGFOOT HUNTER. A handwritten sign at her feet said BIGFOOT HUNTER FOR HIRE.

"How much?" John asked her.

"How much for what?" she asked, smiling with a full set of dentures.

"Bigfoot," John said, pointing to the sign.

The old woman looked up at John. She saw a tall, handsome Indian man.

"What tribe you are?" she asked.

"Navajo."

"Ah, one of them, huh?" she asked and laughed loudly. John's face went hot. "Yeah, I knew a Navajo once. Laura was her name. Laura Tohe. You know her?"

John shook his head.

"Ah, she was a good one," said the old woman. "Haven't heard from her in a long time. A long time."

Thinking of Laura, the old woman sipped at her Pepsi.

"What's your name, anyways?" she asked after a moment or two.

"John."

The old woman studied John's face, trying to determine if the name fit his features. It did not.

"My name is Lu," she said. "But everybody calls me Sweet Lu."

She extended her hand and John shook it in the Indian way. He had learned some small things.

"You know," she said. "Most people call them Sasquatch these days. Makes it sound more Indian, don't it?"

John nodded his head.

"I'll take you to find ol' Sasquatch," she said. "And I'll give you the Indian discount, too, okay? How's twenty bucks sound?"

John handed her the money. Sweet Lu then packed up her folding chair and sign, threw them into the back of a rusty yellow pickup, and hopped into the driver's seat. John had to push a pile of newspapers and magazines to the floor before he could sit in the passenger seat.

"You better buckle in," she said. "It's a rough ride."

Sweet Lu drove that pickup deep into the woods, using logging roads and cattle trails. Once or twice, she simply imagined a path through the trees and followed it. They traveled for hours, mostly not speaking, though Sweet Lu would occasionally break the silence.

"You speak your language?" she asked John.

"No."

"Ah, too bad. That Navajo language is beautiful. Jeez, I remember when Laura Tohe would talk Navajo and all the Indian boys would come running. There was this one guy, named Phil something-or-other. Ah, he had it something fierce for her. Would ask her to speak in Navajo. Laura, say *chair*. Laura, say *horse*. Laura, say *desert*."

Sweet Lu laughed at the memory.

After a few hours, Sweet Lu dropped the pickup into low gear and chugged up a steep hill. She narrowly avoided a fallen tree, then stopped the pickup atop a rise. A small creek wound its way through the wash below. A few birds, which John could not identify, startled by the presence of humans, excitedly flew from tree to tree and chattered in their bird languages.

"Sasquatch fishes here, so keep your eyes open," said Sweet Lu, then promptly leaned back in her seat and fell asleep.

John waited and watched. Sweet Lu snored loudly. The creek water was green from that distance, and John knew that it must be cold, ice cold. A small doe gracefully stepped from the trees to sip water from the creek. The birds had quieted, finally accepting John and Sweet Lu's presence. A military jet, thousands of feet above them, left a vapor trail across the otherwise clear blue sky. John wondered if Sasquatch was out there in the woods, watching and waiting for the humans to leave. John knew he did not belong there or anywhere, but he never wanted to leave.

Near dark, Sweet Lu woke up with a sudden start. She had been dreaming about her late husband, a Hupa man who never did learn to speak English.

"You see him?" asked Sweet Lu.

John shook his head.

"Ah, too bad. I'll give you half your money back, okay?"

John shook his head.

"You sure?" asked Sweet Lu.

"Yes," said John.

Sweet Lu gave John a ride to the border of the reservation.

"I can't cross the border," she said with a laugh. "I don't have my passport."

John shook her hand again and waved as she pulled away. He stood there in the dark for a while, as cars filled with strangers passed him by, as the night sky became so clear that every constellation was visible. The Big and Little Dippers, Orion, Pegasus. John knew that stars were suns, that each was the center of its own solar system, with any number of planets dependent on its warmth and gravity. John, a falling star, brief and homeless, began the long walk back to Seattle, wondering what Olivia and Daniel would think of this adventure. Pragmatic people. When they swallowed the bread and wine at Mass, did they ever consider the magic of it all? There was magic in the world. John knew that real Indians felt it every day. He had only brief glimpses of it, small miracles happening at the edges of his peripheral vision, tiny wonders exploding while his back was turned.

John hitchhiked back to Seattle and made it to work that Monday morning. He was waiting when the foreman arrived early that morning, but John did not understood a word when the foreman tried to talk to him. All that morning, the foreman spoke a strange, unintelligible language. And worse than that, the foreman's face changed. Deep beneath the changes, he still looked like the foreman, but he resembled Daniel Smith, too. No. That wasn't quite right. The foreman could look like anybody. He could change his face at will. John knew that if he were a good Indian, he would have known the foreman was a shape changer, a loup-garou, a werewolf. Good Indians can always spot monsters. John also knew he could not stay on this job. He was frightened by the foreman and by all his co-workers. They were white men and he knew they talked about him. He knew they were plotting against him. There were too many of them and too few of John.

"Hey, John, you want to get a beer?" they always asked him, even after he had declined dozens of previous offers. Somewhere inside himself, John knew they just wanted him to be a part of the team. He understood what it meant to be a teammate. He'd been a teammate once. But he did not want to deal with the complications, the constant need to reassert his masculinity, the graphic talk about women. John could no longer stand such talk about women. Rain washed the windows of the building across the street, and John could see the blurry image of a woman talking on the telephone. She gestured wildly. From that distance, she was just a beautiful series of shapes and colors. Blond hair, a red dress, small hands, long fingers. He knew she was beautiful but, strangely enough, all he wanted was to watch her. He felt no need to touch her or even speak to her. His teammates and co-workers would have spoken of all the horrible things they might do to the beautiful white woman across the street. Or to a woman like Marie, the pretty Indian. John had heard such talk from the rich white men at his father's parties and from the working white men at the construction site. All poison and anger. John knew his co-workers wanted to poison him with their alcohol and mean words. They wanted to get him drunk and helpless. John had never taken a drink of alcohol in his whole life and he was not about to start now. He knew what alcohol did to Indians. Real Indians did not drink. John knew he could not stay in that place any longer. Father Duncan was praying in the desert. Perhaps he was praying for John's salvation. But John knew he needed to find his own salvation. He thought about the old woman, Sweet Lu, and wondered if she ever shared a salmon meal with Sasquatch. He thought about the beauty of myths and the power of lies, how myths told too often became lies, and how lies told too often became myths. He looked at the city's skyline, understanding the myth and lies of its construction, the myths and lies of its architects. John knew there was one white man who should die for all the lies that had been told to Indians. Understanding that, he set down his gear and walked away from the construction site without saying a word to anyone. The foreman watched John leave with no way of knowing if he would ever come back to work. As John walked away, the foreman remembered when the Indian had first appeared nine years earlier.

"Hello," he'd said, slowly and carefully, "I'm John Smith."

The foreman had offered his hand and John looked at it briefly, as if he were unsure of what to do. The foreman had figured that John was just nervous, especially after he refused to make any eye contact. John was always looking down at the floor, studying his hands, looking out the window.

"So," the foreman had said. "Why do you want to work construction?"

"I read about it," John had said. "In a magazine. Indians like to work construction. Mohawks. In New York City."

The foreman knew about the Mohawk construction workers, who had passed from ordinary story into outright myth. They were crazy bastards, walking across girders without safety harnesses, jumping from floor to floor like they were Spiderman's bastard sons. There were three or four generations of Mohawk steel workers. Old Mohawk grandfathers sat around Brooklyn brownstones and talked stories about working on the Empire State Building. They scared children with tales of relatives, buried alive in building foundations, who come back to haunt all of the white office workers.

"Are you Mohawk?" the foreman had asked.

"Uh, no."

"What are you? Snohomish? Puyallup?" the foreman had asked, running through his limited knowledge of the local tribes.

"No, I'm Lakota Sioux."

"Sioux, huh? Bad old buffalo hunter? The Plains are pretty damn flat. What makes you think you can climb up the side of a building?"

"I'm strong."

For no reason that he could verbalize, the foreman had hired John on the spot to do the grunt work, and John was strong, very strong. He carried scrap metal and garbage, pallets stacked with building supplies. He did every damn thing that you could want him to do, except talk much. But hell, the foreman had figured, good talkers are usually bad workers. The foreman had snuck John into the union, and pretty soon, John was climbing up the sides of buildings.

Things had been fine until John started talking to himself. Then he had stopped talking at all, stayed silent for a couple weeks, and now was walking off the job without permission, something he had never done.

"See you tomorrow, chief," the foreman said to himself as John disappeared into the lunch-hour crowd. The foreman was pissed that John had not bothered to officially clock out. But John had been so withdrawn and goofy this morning, the foreman had even thought John might try to take a dive off the building. Better to just let him walk away. The foreman wiped his face with a dirty handkerchief and turned back to work.

John kept walking. He was unsure of where to go and could not tell the difference between the noise of the lunch-hour crowd and the noise of the crowd in his head. Maybe they were the same people. He smelled the salt in the air and decided to walk to Elliott Bay. Maybe if he stood near the water, he could clear his head. But he was not sure how to get there. He knew he should carry a map because he was always getting lost, but he had just never bothered to buy one. Besides, maps were dangerous. If you were seen looking at a map, then everybody knew you were lost and vulnerable. You were easy prey. But John was strong. He looked for familiar landmarks, saw the neon lights of a porno shop and the huge sculpture outside the Seattle Art Museum. The Hammering Man. Fifty feet tall. Nothing abstract or confusing. Just a tall man with a hammer pounding the air. A moving sculpture that had received so many insults. A waste of tax money. No face, no hair, no sexual organs, no pores, no skin. Just the metal skeleton and the metal hammer. The Hammering Man was neither Indian nor white. He may have not been a man. What did it mean? John wasn't sure what the artist might have meant. But that didn't matter to John. The artist wasn't important anymore. The Hammering Man was simply all that John wanted to be. Important and powerful. Simple, unconcerned. The Hammering Man looked as if he could have stepped away from the museum, away from all the small details and painful reminders of his past, and walked into Elliott Bay. Walked until his head and hammer disappeared beneath the surface of the water. Kept walking. The hammer still pounding, still moving, back and forth, back and forth. The hammer was all that mattered. The tool and the use of the tool.

19

Native American Studies

Dr. Clarence Mather sat at a disorganized desk in the bowels of the Anthropology Building. He always came down here to relax, and he needed relaxation because his office was being bombarded with crank calls concerning the murder of Justin Summers and the disappearance of David Rogers, and because his Native American literature class had become a terrible power struggle with Marie Polatkin. Though fairly intelligent and physically attractive, she was rude and arrogant, thought Mather, hardly the qualities of a true Spokane. As if it ran in the family like some disease, Reggie Polatkin had also failed to behave like a true Spokane. Mather knew he could teach both of them a thing or two about being Indian if they would listen to him, but it seemed all of the Spokanes were destined to misunderstand his intentions.

Mather and Reggie Polatkin had been friends from the very beginning. Though Reggie couldn't have said as much, he'd immediately felt a strange kinship with the white man who wanted to be so completely Indian. Reggie was a half-Indian who wanted to be completely white, or failing that, to earn the respect of white men. Mather and Reggie were mirror opposites. Each had something the other wanted, and both had worked hard to obtain it.

Reggie and Mather traveled to men's gatherings and went into the sweathouse together. Reggie had usually been the only Indian at those gatherings and willingly played the part of shaman for the sad and lonely white men, many years his senior, who'd come to him for answers. For the first time in his life, Reggie felt as if being Indian meant something, as if he could obtain tangible reward from simply behaving as an Indian was supposed to behave, acting as an Indian was supposed to act. And the act became so convincing that Reggie began to believe it himself. His Indian act earned him the respect of white men and the sexual favors of white women.

Through Reggie, Mather was able to obtain entry into the Seattle urban Indian community. He went to parties where all the guests were Indian. He used a counterfeit tribal enrollment card to play in the all-Indian basketball tournaments. Together, Mather and Reggie went into Indian taverns and snagged Indian women. While Reggie went to bed with the most attractive woman of any pair of friends, Mather slept with the other, only slightly less attractive, half.

This had all continued until Mather found that box of recordings of traditional Indian stories. Mather had always enjoyed negotiating the narrow passageways, rummaging and foraging here and there. A few years earlier, he had found two boxes of reel-to-reel tapes filled with the voices of Pacific Northwest Indian elders. Recorded by a forgotten anthropologist during the summer of 1926, the tapes had just been collecting dust in a storage room when Dr. Mather stumbled upon them. Excited, but still protective of the discovery, Mather had decided to play the tapes for Reggie, one of the brightest Indians Mather had ever encountered.

The professor thought Reggie had a grasp of Indian history almost as strong as his own. And Reggie's knowledge of Spokane Indian history was probably a little more complete than Mather's. Mather thought the young Spokane might have been able to clarify some aspects of the story.

"Listen to this woman," Mather had said to Reggie as they listened to an Indian elder telling a story. "She's Spokane. Do you think you can identify her?"

Reggie didn't speak Spokane well, but he'd recognized that Spokane Indian elder's story.

"That's a family story. It belongs to the family. Not on some tape. It's not supposed to be told this way. You should erase that tape."

Mather had been shocked by the suggestion. Up until that point, Reggie had been a dedicated student. In fact, Mather had seen himself as a father figure for Reggie, and the young Indian had become something of a son. Mather had trusted Reggie, maybe even loved him, and had always assumed that Reggie felt the same about him. But Mather had felt only disappointment when Reggie said he wanted to erase the tapes. The professor had wanted to make them public and publish an article about them, but Reggie had heard the recorded voice of that old Spokane woman and had been suddenly ashamed of himself. He'd heard that ancient voice and wanted to destroy it. He'd wanted to erase the tapes because he had not wanted anybody else, especially a white man like Mather, to have them. He'd wanted to erase them because they'd never be his stories.

"This is a very valuable anthropological find," Mather had said. "I mean, nobody even tells these stories anymore. Not even Indians. We have to save them."

"Stories die because they're supposed to die," Reggie had said.

"But these stories aren't dead," Mather had said. "The elders must have wanted them to be saved. They allowed the anthropologist to record them."

"Look, I'm sure the elders definitely didn't understand how these stories were going to be used. Dr. Mather, you have to let these stories go. Burn the tapes. Or I'll burn them for you."

Reggie had stared at Mather with such startling anger that the professor had stepped backward and, frightened, had promised to burn the tapes. Later, angry at himself for having played the tapes for Reggie, Mather had hidden them in a dark corner of the basement instead. When Reggie had asked him later if the tapes had been destroyed, Mather denied that the tapes had ever existed. Mather had told that first lie because he believed he was protecting the recordings. He'd come to see those stories as his possessions, as *his* stories, as if it had been his voice on those tapes. He'd lied to preserve his idea of order. But with each successive lie Mather had told, he'd begun to lose track of the original reasons for lying. Layer after layer of lies. As an anthropologist, Mather could have dug into himself for years and not discovered the truth.

For Reggie, Mather's lie had become the breaking point after which he believed all white men were lying all the time. Reggie knew the history. Mather's friendship had simply become another broken treaty. Another beautiful series of promises that had been, in fact, a worthless stack of paper.

"I'm sure I don't know what you're talking about," Mather had lied to Reggie first, and then to Dr. Faulkner, the department chair, after Reggie had lodged a formal protest. All three men had been sitting in Faulkner's office, along with Bernice Zamora, the department secretary, who'd been taking notes.

"Why do you think Mr. Polatkin would make these kinds of accusations against you?" Dr. Faulkner had asked Mather.

"Frankly, I think it's because of Reggie's distrust of authority figures. In particular, Reggie has had an extremely difficult relationship with his father, a white man. I don't pretend to be a psychologist, but I believe Reggie is confusing his feelings about his father with his feelings for me."

"You liar," Reggie had said and left the office. He'd understood that Mather's lies would go undetected and unpunished. Later
that day, Reggie had cornered Mather in the Student Union Building.
"I trusted you," Reggie had said.

"It's you who violated my trust," Mather had replied. "You
certainly aren't behaving like a true Spokane."

Reggie had punched Mather then and wrestled him to the
ground, but a few other students had broken it up quickly. Naturally,
Reggie had been expelled from the University.

Now, as Mather sat in the Anthropology Building basement
and listened to his beloved secret tapes, he was professionally disappointed that he could never reveal their existence. Still, he was personally in love with the Indian elders' voices, men and women,
Snohomish, Makah, Yakama, Spokane, and he'd memorized all of the
stories. With those tapes, Mather owned twelve hours' worth of
magic. He listened to the magical recording of a Spokane Indian elder
telling a traditional story. A true Spokane. She spoke fractured
English, which Mather could barely understand, but her fluent Spokane was being translated by a Bureau of Indian Affairs agent. The
story was about Coyote, the trickster, and it echoed through the cluttered basement. Boxes of various artifacts were stacked in tall piles.
A maze of doors, small rooms, and hallways. Some rooms had not
been opened since the early part of the century, and exploring the
basement involved a contemporary sort of archaeology. The basement
even had its own mythology. Chief Seattle's bones were supposedly
lost somewhere in the labyrinth. And the bones of dozens of other
Indians were said to be stored in a hidden room.

As the Spokane Indian elder finished her trickster story, the
basement went dark. Mather smiled and thought of Coyote, assuming it was just a temporary power outage. But as five minutes passed,
then ten, Mather grew agitated. At least, he told himself he was
agitated. Actually he was becoming very frightened. The building

creaked and groaned. Other mysterious noises in the distance sounded like footsteps, whispers, a door slowly opening.

"Hello, this is Dr. Mather." His voice echoed loudly. "I'm in the northwest corner. By the furnace."

Dr. Mather listened for a response, heard nothing, and then realized he'd given away his exact position. If somebody was trying to hurt him, he'd know where Mather was. Nonsense, Mather thought, someone's coming to help me. But then he realized that nobody knew he was in the basement. It was late. Very late. Probably nobody was in the entire Anthropology Building except Mather. Or, nobody should be.

"Hello?" Mather asked, a question now.

He continued to sit at the desk and listen carefully. He heard somebody breathing, though he soon realized he was hearing his own inhalation and exhalation. Holding his breath, he listened, and heard a strange rattling. There, off to his right, that rattling again. Not like a snake, but like beads shaking, or sand in a shell, or bones rubbing together. Mather sat up straight in his chair. He thought of the Indian remains in that basement. The forgotten bones and fragments of clothing, Chief Seattle's bones. The rattling again. Mather was sweating, telling himself not to be such a child, a superstitious fool. Be analytical, he thought, decipher the sound. Wasn't it there before? Hadn't it been there all along? The total darkness had intensified other senses. You're hearing things you simply didn't notice before, Mather told himself. You hear better with your eyes closed. So what is it you're hearing? He listened. Bone moving against bone, ancient and forgotten. Calm yourself, Mather thought, and then something brushed against his face, and he panicked. The instinct for flight took over and Mather was up and running, tripping over boxes, smashing into shelves and closed doors. He could feel that something was chasing him, was right behind him, reaching for his neck. Mather ran for his life. He was still running when the lights suddenly flickered and brightened. Nearly blinded, he caught a brief glimpse of the low overhang ahead of him just before he ran into it, knocking himself unconscious.

"Dr. Mather?" asked the janitor as he came around the corner and saw the professor lying on the floor. "Is that you?"

20

The Sandwich Lady

John sat on a sidewalk in downtown Seattle beneath the Alaskan Way Viaduct. An ugly, gray monstrosity that would surely fall to pieces during a major earthquake, it served as a noisy barrier between downtown Seattle and the waters of Elliott Bay. However, as an unplanned benefit, the Viaduct also provided shelter for Seattle's homeless. Beneath the Viaduct, one could find cover from Seattle's rains, with the nearby waterfront and Pike Place Market attracting tourists who were sometimes willing to empty their pockets of loose change.

When he worked downtown, John visited the homeless Indians who congregated beneath the Viaduct and those in Occidental Park in Pioneer Square. But John was more often drawn to the Indians beneath the Viaduct. He'd walk down there during his lunch hours to spend time with them, though he never spoke more than a few words to anyone. Usually, he just walked by those real Indians, who sat in groups of three or four, nodding their heads when John walked past.

"Hey, cousin," the homeless Indians always called out to John. "You got any coins?"

John had come to know a few by their names, King, Agnes, and Joseph, and he recognized a few dozen by sight. Before he'd met them, John had shared the common assumption that all homeless Indians were drunks. But he had soon discovered that many of them didn't drink. John had been surprised by that discovery, and both relieved and saddened. He was relieved that many of the homeless Indians refused to surrender and drink themselves to death. He was saddened that so many Indians were homeless and had no simple reasons to offer for their condition.

On that evening, John sat by himself, apart from a group of Indians who were singing and telling jokes. More laughter. John watched those Indians, in dirty clothes and thirdhand shoes, miles and years from their reservations, estranged from their families and tribes, yet still able to laugh, to sing. John wondered where they found the strength to do such things. They were still joking and singing when Marie Polatkin drove up in a battered white delivery van. John recognized her from the powwow at the University. The Indian woman with crowded teeth. She haphazardly parked the truck and jumped out, talking fast and loud. The dozens of homeless women and men, Indian and otherwise, who lived beneath the Viaduct soon gathered around her.

"What is this?" John asked a white man in an old wheelchair. He wore an army surplus jacket and a dirty pair of blue jeans.

"It's Marie, the Sandwich Lady," said the wheelchair man.

"Sandwich Lady?"

"Yeah, man. You know? Sandwiches? Two pieces of bread with something between? When was the last time you ate?"

John thought about the lunch box he had left at work. Inside, a can of Pepsi, a convenience-store sub sandwich, an apple.

"Well," said the wheelchair man. "You better get in line if you're hungry. Her sandwiches go fast, man. I help her sometimes, you know? Making the sandwiches. Me and her are tight. Yeah, my name is Boo."

Boo offered his hand, but John ignored it. Shrugging his shoulders, Boo took his place in line, behind a woman talking to herself.

"Here's a ham and cheese, Bill," Marie said to the first man in line. She knew their names! "How you doing, Esther? You look good, Charles. Lillian, how's the tooth? Martha, where have you been? I've got a peanut butter and jelly for your son. Where is that boy?"

The wheelchair man and John stepped up next. John was embarrassed. He had nothing to give Marie, no gift, no blanket, no basket. He wanted to run, hoping to run away from everything, hoping he could run into a new skin, a new face, a new kind of music. He wanted to run into the desert. But he wanted to see Marie, wanted to hear her voice.

"Marie," he said.

"Yes," she said, not recognizing John for a brief moment, then visibly surprised when she did. John was homeless, she thought, an explanation for his strange behavior at the protest powwow.

"Marie," John said again.

"John, right?"

John nodded.

"How are you?" she asked.

"I wanted to see you."

"Well, it's good to see you. Are you hungry? Do you want a sandwich?"

John looked down at the sandwich in Marie's hand. He wondered if it was poisoned.

"No," John said. He struggled to speak. He wanted to tell Marie everything. He wanted to tell her about Father Duncan. He opened his mouth, closed it again, and then turned to run. He ran until he could no longer recognize anything around him.

"Who was that?" the wheelchair man asked Marie as John raced away.

"I'm not sure. A guy named John. Navajo."

"I think he likes you."

"Yeah, maybe, Boo. How've you been? How's the poetry coming along?"

"I wrote one for you," said Boo. He reached into his shirt pocket, pulled out a tightly folded wad of paper, and handed it to Marie. She took it, unfolded it, and read the poem.

"Thank you, Boo," she said. "That's very nice. Here's a turkey and Swiss."

"Thank you," he said and rolled himself away. Marie handed sandwiches out until her arms ached. For an hour, two. She talked to her friends, consoled, reprimanded, and touched them, her hand on their shoulders, her hand clasping their hands, fingers touching fingers, in greeting, in conversation, in departure. She ate a sandwich herself, washed it down with a Pepsi, and watched the night grow darker by degrees. She knew there were many men and women who waited for her to deliver those sandwiches. They waited for the food, for the company, for proof they were not invisible. For the mentally disturbed, Marie knew these sandwich visits might be the only dependable moment in their lives. She also knew she delivered the sandwiches for her own sanity. Something would crumble inside of her if she ever walked by a homeless person and pretended not to notice. Or simply didn't care. In a way, she believed that homeless people were treated as Indians had always been treated. Badly. The homeless were like an Indian tribe, nomadic and powerless, just filled with more than any tribe's share of crazy people and cripples. So, a homeless Indian belonged to two tribes, and was the lowest form of life in the city. The powerful white men of Seattle had created a law that made it illegal to sit on the sidewalk. That ordinance was crazier and much more evil than any homeless person. Sometimes Marie wondered if she worked so hard at everything only because she hated powerful white men. She wondered if she went to college and received good grades just because she was looking for revenge. She woke up at four in the morning to study before she went to class. She rushed from the University down to the shelter, to a protest, to the sandwich van. All to get back at white men? A police car rolled by. Officer Randy Peone. Marie knew him. She knew most of the cops who worked downtown. Patrols had been increased because the police knew something bad was happening. The officer waved to Marie. She waved back.

21

Killing the Dragon

On a cold morning, the killer walked through the park near home. The killer thought about the owl, the messenger of death for many tribes. The owl had night vision and could turn its head three hundred and sixty degrees without moving its body. The owl was silent, and wasted neither time nor emotion. The owl felt no guilt, no remorse. It lived to hunt, and hunted to live. One kill was no more important than the next, each successive murder replacing the preceding in the owl's memory. The owl kept no souvenirs, no mementos from the scene of the crime. The killer wanted so much to behave like an owl, to kill without emotion. But the killer felt incomplete, as if more needed to be done, as if the first hunt had only been partially successful, as if one dead body were not enough. The killer also needed trophies, the bloody scalp nailed to the wall, the shrine-in-progress. One beautiful knife, one beautiful scalp, and space enough for more. The killer knew that the next victim would have to be perfect and beautiful. The killer would have to send a message that would terrify the world.

The park was small and lovely. A few acres of perfectly manicured lawn, a softball diamond, a basketball court with chains on the hoops. A dozen picnic tables, pine trees, a man-made pond. A playground, with swing set, seesaw, and slide, where the killer sat and watched the neighborhood nannies congregate with their employers' children. With the babies in the nearby carriages and the older children climbing, swinging, and sliding through the playground, the nannies shared a morning conversation the killer could not hear. A majority of the nannies were black, a few were Latina, and one or two were young white women. The black and Latina women were older and most assuredly had their own children. Every morning, those brown women left their children behind and traveled to better neighborhoods to take care of their employers' children. Brown women spent more time with the white children than their own parents did. Brown children were left behind.

Anger growing, the killer thought of those rich, white children holding their arms out to strangers, not mothers, and about brown children holding their arms out to air. A simple and brilliant human connected two knives at a balance point and invented the scissors. And where were all the fathers? The brown fathers were killing themselves and each other. Like royalty, the white fathers crowded into stadiums to watch brown men kill each other. Kill, killed, killing.

The killer watched one little blond boy running across the playground. Mark Jones, six years old, though the killer had no way of knowing his name or age. The killer just saw a beautiful white boy. Blue eyes, blue stocking cap, white tennis shoes, Seattle Seahawks jacket buttoned tight. A perfect child who, through no fault of his own, might grow up into a monster. The killer felt the weight of the knife. Blade, bolster, tang, handle. Right now, the killer could run across the playground, pick up the white boy, and slash his throat before anybody could intercede. Killing the dragon before it could breathe flames. Working quickly and efficiently, the killer could probably kill a number of white boys before the nannies overcame their shock and reacted. One, two, three, the killer counted the white boys on the playground, seven, eight, nine. The killer watched the beautiful boy, Mark Jones, spinning on the merry-go-round. The meat carver held the most prestigious position on the kitchen staff.

The killer studied Mark and the other children, noting the hierarchy of playmates, the playground distribution of power. The boys and girls played together until they were seven years old, then separated by gender after that. The kids under five years old were treated with a general respect by the older children, but were definitely subject to the whims of their elders. Fat kids were ridiculed and left to play in their own groups. The one black child, a girl, played quietly with two white girls. Most of the kids were clumsy and weak and posed no threat to the killer, but there were two white boys with physical coordination beyond their years, and they fought for leadership of the playground. One of the boys, fairly short for his age, but stout and confident, was a conservative. When he was in charge, the group played games they'd played a thousand times before. Frozen Tag, King of the Hill, Double Dare. The other boy, Mark, the blond in the Seahawks jacket, was tall, thin, and fearless, a revolutionary. As the killer watched, Mark invented a game. During that game, all the kids piled onto the merry-go-round, then Mark and two or three of his favorites spun them around and around, as fast as possible. As the kids became sick or scared, they screamed for it to stop, but Mark ignored them as he continued to spin them. The only way to quit the game was to jump from the merry-go-round. Kids rapidly collected skinned knees and bruised faces as they worked up the courage and leapt into the dirt. When one last child was left on the merry-go-round, that one child most afraid to jump, Mark proclaimed that last child the winner. The kids played it again and again. Watching that game, the killer knew that Mark would grow into a powerful man.

So the killer waited until Mark Jones and Sarah, his young white nanny, walked out of the park. Holding the knife close, the killer trailed Mark and the nanny through a quiet neighborhood, past a 7-Eleven, a Safeway supermarket, Talkies Video, and dozens of anonymous apartment buildings to a two-story house partially hidden behind large trees. Silently singing an invisibility song, the killer ascended into one of the larger trees and looked into the kitchen and living room. Through the large windows, the killer watched the nanny feed Mark a bowl of tomato soup, a sandwich, and most of a bag of corn chips. Then the nanny and Mark settled down on the couch to watch television.

A little after six, Mark's mother, Erin Jones, a bank manager, pulled into the driveway. There was no sign of the father. The mother stepped into the house, received a warm greeting from the nanny and a brief nod of interest from Mark, and then walked into the kitchen to prepare her dinner. As she was cooking, the nanny gathered up her things and left the house without a word. She stood beneath the killer's tree and lit a cigarette. The exhaled smoke drifted up and past the killer, who could smell the boy's scent also wafting up from the nanny's clothes. The killer understood what needed to be done.

After dinner, Mark's mother got him ready for bed. Dressed in his favorite pajamas, the ones covered with the blind superhero Daredevil, Mark washed his face and brushed his teeth. His mother read him two stories before she turned out the light and left him alone in his bedroom. The killer saw the mother mix herself a drink and watch a movie. She was tall and skinny, with pinched features and very short, blond hair. A pretty woman, the killer thought, but obviously lonely. After the late news, the mother stripped naked and crawled into bed without washing her face or brushing her teeth. She read a magazine for a few minutes, then turned off the lamp, and quickly fell asleep.

The killer waited in that tree until midnight. The knife felt heavy and hot. With surprising grace, the killer stepped from the tree, walked up to the front door, and slipped the knife between the lock and jamb. The killer was soon standing inside a dark and quiet house, tastefully decorated in natural wood and pastel colors, with stylish prints hanging on the walls. With confidence, the killer explored the living room, bathroom, and study downstairs. Then the killer walked upstairs and into the master bedroom, where the mother slept alone. She had thrown off her covers, and the killer studied her naked body, pale white in the moonlight streaming in from the window. Small breasts, three dark moles just above the light brown pubic hair. She was almost too skinny, prominent ribcage, hipbones rising up sharply. The killer knelt down beside the bed as if to pray. Then the killer did pray.

Later, after that prayer was over, the killer walked down the hallway into the boy's room. Mark was curled up in a fetal position. An active dreamer, he was mumbling something the killer could not understand. The killer recognized the superhero on Mark's pajamas. Daredevil, the blind superhero, who used his other highly developed senses to fight crime. The killer's eyes closed. The killer wondered if the boy could be found by using other senses. The boy's smell, toothpaste, sleepy sweat, socks. By touch, warm and sticky skin. With eyes now open, the killer leaned over close to the boy and softly licked his face. Salt, something bitter, a slight sweetness. The boy stirred, opened his eyes, and stared at the killer's face, which shimmered and changed like a pond after a rock had been tossed into it. The killer set two owl feathers on the pillow beside Mark Jones's head and then gently lifted the boy from the bed.

2

Hunting Weather

I

The Aristotle Little Hawk Fan Club

Jack Wilson grew up white and orphaned in Seattle. Dreaming of being Indian, he'd read every book he could find about the First Americans and had been delighted to learn that they raised their children communally. An Indian child moved freely between tepees, between families. A child could be loved and disciplined by any adult in the tribe. During the long, cold nights, every campfire was a welcome sight for a lonely child. Wilson loved the idea, and tried to find some tribal connection with his eleven foster families, but could only advance a little beyond uncomfortable formality with one household before he was forced to pack up his meager belongings and move to another. Lying in strange beds, Wilson read about Indians and recreated himself in the image he found inside those books. He saw himself as a solitary warrior on horseback, crossing miles of empty plains, in search of his family.

Wilson's mother had died of cancer when he was a baby, and his father had died in a car wreck when he was ten, but something in

Wilson refused to believe in their deaths. He always expected a phone call from her, to see him come bursting through the front door with unexpected news. But it was a lie. Wilson knew about liars. And what the TV and movies said about Indians were lies. That they were evil. That they raped white women and ate white children. Indians were said to worship the devil. His teachers tried to tell him all these bad things about Indians, but Wilson had always fought them.

"So," said his high school principal when Wilson was sent in to see him yet again. "What about Indians this time?"

"I'm part Shilshomish Indian," Wilson said. "I looked it up. There was an old medicine man named Red Fox who lived in a shack on Bainbridge Island. Back in the 1920s or something. His Indian name was Red Fox, but his American name was Joe Wilson. My dad used to say that Joe Wilson was his great-uncle."

"Well, now, that's very interesting. How does it have anything to do with your visit to my office?"

"Mrs. Jorgenson said all the Indians were dead. I told her it wasn't true. I said I was Indian. She said I was a liar, and I said she was the liar. Then she sent me here."

"Are you lying?"

"No," Wilson said. "I promise. I looked it up. Well, my dad used to say he'd heard of a relative named Joe Wilson, who was a crazy old man. But that must be Red Fox, don't you think?"

Twelve years later, in 1977, when he was a rookie police officer in the Fourth Precinct of the Seattle Police Department, Jack Wilson still believed that Red Fox was a relative. He walked a beat downtown and knew the names of most of the homeless Indians who crowded together beneath the Alaskan Way Viaduct and in Pioneer Square. Lester, Old Joe, and Little Joe always together, Agnes and her old man, who was simply known as Old Man, the Android Brothers, who'd come here from Spokane years earlier and were collecting spare change for bus tickets back home. Beautiful Mary, who was still beautiful, even though a keloid scar ran from the corner of her left eye to her chin. She thought Wilson was handsome and called him by some word in her tribal language. She told him that it meant First Son, but it actually meant Shadow.

One evening, Beautiful Mary pushed Wilson into a dark doorway, unzipped his pants, pushed her hand inside, and stroked his penis. Wilson's knees went weak. He leaned against the door for support. He tried to kiss Mary but, still stroking him, she turned her face away. Then, without warning, she released Wilson and stepped back.

"What's wrong?" Wilson asked, his face red and sweaty.

Beautiful Mary shook her head. Wilson grabbed her arm with more force than he'd planned. He could see the pain in Mary's eyes. She twisted away from him and ran away.

Beautiful Mary was almost forty years old when she was murdered. Wedged between a Dumpster and the back wall of a parking garage beneath the Viaduct, she had been raped, then stabbed repeatedly with a broken bottle. Wilson had immediately emptied his stomach on the pavement. Then he had found a stray newspaper and covered her face. Her eyes were still open. He had called in quickly, but it took an hour for the ambulance to show up. While the attendants were loading Mary into the ambulance, one homicide detective arrived to investigate.

"You found her body, correct?" the detective asked Wilson.

"Yes, sir."

"And?"

"And what, sir?"

"And what did you notice? Any suspicious people? Witnesses? Evidence?"

"I didn't notice, sir. I, I knew her. Her name is Mary, sir. Beautiful Mary."

"She isn't so beautiful anymore," said the detective. He took a few notes, closed his book, and walked away. Wilson had assumed they would solve the case quickly. Beautiful Mary was a very visible member of the homeless community. Somebody must have seen something. Wilson read the newspaper the next day, looking for a story about Beautiful Mary. Nothing. No story the next morning, or during the next two weeks, either. He asked a few questions around the station house. Nothing. Three weeks after Mary's death, Wilson bumped into the police detective who was supposed to be investigating her murder.

"Excuse me, sir," said Wilson. "Have you learned anything more about Mary?"

"Mary?" asked the detective. "Who's Mary?"

"Don't you remember? Mary? Beautiful Mary? The Indian woman who was killed downtown? I found her body. A few weeks ago?"

"Oh, shit, of course. I remember you. The rookie. Lost your breakfast." Wilson blushed. "Shit, that case is low priority, rook. One dead Indian don't add up to much. Some other Indian guy killed her, you know. Happens all the time. Those people are like that. You ask me, it's pest control."

"Sir, I don't think so." Wilson fought the urge to punch the detective.

"You don't think what, rook?"

"I know those people, sir. The Indians. They're my people. They wouldn't hurt each other. We're not like that."

"How the hell are they your people?"

"I'm Indian, sir."

The detective looked at Wilson's blue eyes and blond hair. Wilson was tall, six foot, but slight of build. The detective laughed. Indian, my ass, he thought.

"Okay, Sitting Bull," said the detective, "I'm happy you're so proud of your people. But it's still low priority. You want to look into it, be my guest."

"I just might do that, sir."

The detective patted Wilson on the head, as if he were a dog, and walked away, laughing to himself. "Indian," he said and laughed some more.

Wilson tried to talk to the Pioneer Square Indians, Old Joe and Little Joe, Agnes and Old Man, the Android Brothers, but they refused to give him any answers about Beautiful Mary's murder.

Wilson eventually arrested a homeless white man named Stink and brought him in. The detective who had dismissed Wilson took over the case, led Stink into an interrogation room, and obtained a confession.

Stink hung himself in his cell that night, before he ever had a chance to go to trial, and Wilson was issued a small, vaguely insulting commendation for his "valuable assistance" in solving the crime. But Wilson had earned some respect, and he made detective in 1980. Working homicide, he quickly learned that monsters are real. He also knew that most of the monsters were white men. Plain, quiet men who raped and murdered children. Plain, quiet men who cut women into pieces. Ted Bundy, the Green River Killer, the I-5 Killer. Famous killers, obscure killers. The white man who grabbed his infant son by the ankles and smashed his head against the wall. The white man who doused his sleeping girlfriend with gasoline and then dropped a lit match on her face. While black and brown men were at war with each other, their automatic gunfire filling the urban night, the white men were hunting their own mothers, lovers, and daughters. Wilson never grew numb to any of it. Every Sunday, he knelt at a pew and confessed the sins of others. He worked hard, helped solve more than half of his cases, and slept poorly at night. His record was distinguished only by the small number of days he called in sick. While the other detectives had families and outside interests, Wilson had only his tribe of monsters. Wilson worked homicide for eight years before he injured his knee while on duty. He stepped out of his car near the end of his shift, slipped on oily pavement, and tore a couple of ligaments all to hell. He was desk-bound for a year, all the while in fruitless rehabilitation of his knee. Finally, he retired on a full disability pension. Since he had never married, or even been in love, he wound up alone in his little apartment on Capitol Hill.

A year into his retirement, after another boring Monday Night Football game, he was forced to weigh his options as a middle-aged, lonely ex-cop. Somehow, he found himself missing the monsters. He had no idea how that happened, but he knew he needed something to fill the hole that had opened inside himself. He could become a drunk, spend all his time in one of the cop bars, and get free beer and pity from active officers. He could sink into a deep depression, swallow the barrel of his revolver, and be buried with full honors. Or he could do something. He could, for example, sit down and write. Now, he had never written before, but he had always been good with a story, had always loved books. So he bought the most expensive typewriter he could find, because real writers didn't work on computers. He brought the typewriter back to his apartment and began to type.

His first book, titled *Little Hawk*, was published by a small local press. It received fairly decent reviews and sold a few thousand copies, so Wilson was hooked. Wilson's second book, *Rain Dance*, based on the murder of Beautiful Mary, was released a year later and became a regional best-seller. Both of Wilson's books starred Aristotle Little Hawk, the very last Shilshomish Indian, who was a practicing medicine man and private detective in Seattle. He was tall, so tall, according to the first paragraph of *Little Hawk*, that his long, black hair was taller than most people all by itself. Little Hawk was brutally handsome, of course, with a hawkish nose, walnut skin, and dark eyes.

A beautiful white woman fell in love with Little Hawk in each book, although he was emotionally distant and troubled. The beautiful white women fell in love with Little Hawk because he was emotionally distant and troubled. White women wrote letters to Wilson and confessed their secret love for Little Hawk. They wished they could find a man like Little Hawk, a quiet warrior with a good heart. Wilson knew it was all sort of ridiculous, but he loved the money and attention. Fan letters, small articles in the local newspapers, a three-minute interview on public radio. His fellow officers thought he had become rich and famous, so he went out and bought a brand-new 1994 Chevy pickup with a vanity license plate that read SHAMAN.

Lately, a New York literary agent had signed him up.

"Indians are big right now," said Rupert, the agent. "Publishers are looking for that shaman thing, you know? The New Age stuff, after-death experiences, the healing arts, talking animals, sacred vortexes, that kind of thing. And you've got all that, plus a murder mystery. That's perfect."

Rupert had gotten Wilson a deal with a New York publisher for his third book, which he had yet to write. His modest success had him struggling with writer's block. Every morning, he woke up early, ate his breakfast, and stared at the blank page in his typewriter. He had spent most of the advance money, and his agent and publisher were putting pressure on him to finish.

"How's the book coming along?" asked Rupert.

"It's going well," said Wilson, lying.

"They want to publish in the fall," said Rupert. "You think you can finish in time?"

"Sure," said Wilson. After he hung up the phone, he suddenly felt dizzy and nearly passed out. He needed help.

Trying to relax, Wilson drove over to the Seattle Police Department's Fourth Precinct on Second Avenue, his old haunt. He parked in a reserved space, but all the officers recognized his vanity plates and never had him towed. He limped into the precinct, still blue-eyed and blond, although he had put on forty pounds in the last couple of years. He was forty-seven years old, bulky, and working on an ulcer.

"Hey there, Mr. Mystery," said the desk sergeant, who often felt sorry for Wilson. The sergeant thought Wilson spent entirely too much time at the precinct, as if he were a twenty-two-year-old former high school football star who still went to games because he had nothing else to do. "How you doing?"

"Doing fine, doing fine," Wilson said. "What have you got?"

Wilson depended on the desk sergeant for inside information. The sergeant never gave him anything important, really, just interesting details that might find their way into his books. The first Little Hawk mystery was based on a true case of what some might put down to spontaneous combustion. An elderly woman had simply turned to ash while watching television in her apartment. There was no rational explanation for it, no hint of foul play. She had been sitting in a chair that also should have gone up in flames. But the chair was just a little charred, mostly intact, and covered with her ash. In the book, the victim was a gorgeous fashion model. In real life, the old lady's case was quietly filed away and never mentioned again. In the book, Little Hawk caught the murderer, an ex-fireman who'd been spurned by the model. The dead model's best friend, an even more beautiful and successful model, had fallen in love with Little Hawk.

"I've got a good one for you," said the desk sergeant, wanting to give Wilson something more substantial than he'd given him before. "But you've got to keep this one way under your hat."

"I don't wear a hat," said Wilson. It was an old joke between the two men.

"Well, then, keep it in your shorts," said the sergeant, finishing the joke.

"What is it?"

"You heard about that white guy they found dead the other day?"

"David Rogers?" asked Wilson, who knew about the white man's disappearance from the Tulalip Tribal Casino. Wilson kept a neat file of newspaper clippings about such crimes.

"No, not him," said the sergeant. "He's still missing. I'm talking about the other one. The one they found in that house in Fremont."

"Yeah, the Summers guy, what about him?"

"Well," said the sergeant, glancing around to make sure nobody could hear him. Everybody in the precinct knew he gave Wilson inside information, but he'd never before revealed details about an open case. "The killer left two feathers behind. Like a signature or something."

"Feathers?" Wilson blinked once or twice. "What do you mean?"

"What do you mean, what do I mean? Feathers. Like as in Indian feathers, you know? But I can't tell you what kind. We can't go public with that. The city would go crazy."

"Really?"

"Really. I thought that would interest you. Kind of right up your alley, ain't it?"

"Maybe," said Wilson.

"And that UW student, David Rogers, who disappeared from the Indian casino? I won't say the killer did that one, but we're looking real closely at it. And you know that kid, Mark Jones, the one who was kidnapped?"

"Yes."

"This killer took him."

"How do you know that?"

"The killer left behind two feathers on that little boy's bed. Hell, we haven't even told his parents what those feathers mean. What do you think they'd do if they knew about the killer?"

"Go crazy."

"Yeah. And this killer's got a name. You want to hear it?"

Wilson nodded. He knew that police officers and newspaper reporters loved to give clever names to the monsters.

"We're calling him the Indian Killer. Good, ain't it? Now get the hell out of here before I get in trouble."

Wilson smiled.

"See you, Sarge," said Wilson. As he left the precinct, Wilson could almost see Aristotle Little Hawk sitting on the passenger side as he climbed into his truck. Aristotle and the Indian Killer. Wilson could see the knife separating scalp from skull.

2

Testimony

"Mrs. Jones, I know this is a painful experience for you, but we need to go over it again."

"I've told you everything I can remember."

"Can we please reconstruct the events one more time?"

"I've told you. I came home from work."

"At what time?"

"A little after six. I usually get home a little after six. Then I walked into the house, and Mark and Sarah, the nanny, were watching television."

"What were they watching?"

"Some superhero show, I think. I just went right into the kitchen to make dinner and Sarah went home."

"And where was Mark at this time?"

"I told you, he was watching television."

"Now, what time did the nanny, Sarah, leave the house?"

"I don't know. Twenty after six, something like that."

"Okay, and what were you doing at that time?"

"I was making dinner."

"And what were you preparing?"

"Shit, I don't remember."

"Okay, okay, and then what happened?"

"I got Mark ready for bed, read him a couple stories, and then he went to sleep."

"And then what happened?"

"I went to sleep."

"Okay, and what do you sleep in?"

"What do you mean?"

"Do you sleep in a T-shirt, a nightgown, what?"

"Why is that important?"

"Well, there might be fiber evidence. Trace materials, you know?"

"Really? Well, I sleep in the nude."

"Naked?"

"Yes, you have a problem with that?"

"None at all. Does your husband sleep in the nude?"

"Sometimes. But since he was in Japan at the time, I have no idea what he was wearing."

"Okay, so you went to sleep. And then?"

"And then I was asleep."

"Where was Mark?"

"He was asleep in his bed."

"And then?"

"Shit, how many times do I have to tell you this? I woke up in the middle of the night and knew something was wrong. At first, I thought there must have been an earthquake. I mean, I used to live in southern California, so I know that feeling. But everything was still. And I was scared. So I went into Mark's bedroom to check on him."

"In the nude?"

"Of course not."

"And what did you find in Mark's bedroom."

"Nothing. He was gone. But I saw the feathers. Two of them."

"And what time was this?"

"I don't know. Do we have to keep going through this? I mean, are you trying to find my son or not? And what the hell were those feathers about?"

"Mrs. Jones, we're doing our best. Now, is it true that Mark has had some discipline problems at school?"

"Yes, but they have nothing to do with this."

"But he's been in a few altercations?"

"Yes, he has."

"Do you have any idea why?"

"He's a six-year-old boy. They have altercations."

"I'm sure. And how is your relationship with your husband?"

"It's fine."

"Fine?"

"Yes, fine."

"Is there any reason you can think of that Mark might have run away? Have you checked with all your friends and relatives who live in the area?"

"Mark didn't run away. Somebody took him."

"Mrs. Jones, do you know of anybody who might want to hurt Mark? Or take him?"

"No. Don't *you* know?"

"Well, there are certain other crimes that may be connected to your son's disappearance."

"Listen, I want to know: what kind of monster do you think would take somebody's child?"

3

The Learning Curve

John Smith stood in the darkness outside the UW Anthropology Building and stared at Marie Polatkin through the classroom windows. She was arguing with the professor, a white man wearing a gray ponytail and turquoise bolo tie. He also had a large bandage on his forehead, though John had no idea that the professor had injured himself by running into a low basement ceiling. John didn't know Dr. Clarence Mather, but he'd seen many other white men in Seattle who dressed that way. Those white men thought long hair and turquoise were rebellious, but John knew that, for white men, long hair and turquoise were simply another kind of military uniform. John wondered if Marie understood that. Perhaps she was telling the professor how she felt about his ponytail and turquoise bolo tie. Of course, John couldn't hear anything Marie was saying, but he could tell she was angry. She sat up straight in her seat, her finger jabbing the air as she made some point, one hand running nervously through her long, black hair. John thought she was beautiful.

After the class was over, as John followed Marie through the dark campus, he'd been surprised to learn that she was following the professor. She was good. She used trees and statues as cover, slipped into shadows and blind spots, stepped quietly across cement and gravel walkways. She was so good that John had lost sight of her a few times and, only by following the professor himself had he picked her back up again.

Dr. Mather, completely unaware of both Marie and John, walked to the faculty parking lot. A few cars were still left in the lot, which was faintly illuminated by two rows of streetlights. Mather set his briefcase on top of his car and began a methodical search for his keys, shoving his hands into every pocket. Marie crept so close to the professor that John was left breathless by her daring. She was just ten feet away from the professor when another white man called out. Marie disappeared behind a car as Mather turned toward the voice.

"Dr. Mather!" said the white man as he approached. "Dr. Mather, it's me. It's Dr. Faulkner."

Mather recognized Faulkner, the chair of the Anthropology Department.

"Good evening, Dr. Faulkner. How are you?"

"Fine, fine. How was your class?"

"Well, I'm having trouble with a student. An Indian student, actually. She is very disruptive."

"I'm sorry to hear that. What's her name?"

"Marie Polatkin."

"Polatkin? Polatkin? Why is that name familiar?"

"She's a cousin of Reggie Polatkin. You remember him, of course. He assaulted me in the Student Union Building."

"Of course. My God, Dr. Mather! You don't think there's some sort of conspiracy going on, do you?"

"No, no. Marie is a very bright girl, just confused. I'm sure things will work out. I mean, things are very tense in the class since David Rogers disappeared."

"He was your student?"

"And since that other man was scalped, my white students have been reluctant to express their opinions. Marie seems to be taking advantage of their fear."

"Listen, would you like to go for a drink? Perhaps we can discuss this."

"That would be fine."

Mather and Faulkner climbed into separate cars and drove out of the parking lot toward the same destination. John watched the cars pull away and wondered what Marie had thought of the white men's conversation. John stood at the edge of the parking lot and looked for Marie, but she had disappeared.

4

Chemistry

Walking down the Burke-Gilman Trail, Arthur Two Leaf thought about the evening chemistry class he'd just left. He was a carbon-based life-form. The chemistry professor, Dr. McMinn, was a carbon-based life-form. The plants on either side of the trail were carbon-based life-forms.

"We are all made of essentially the same DNA, the same genetic material," Dr. McMinn had said. "In fact, women and men share about ninety-nine percent of the same genetic material." She'd then looked at Arthur, who had a wild crush on the white professor. "And people of different races, such as Native Americans and European-Americans, also share about ninety-nine percent."

That might be true, Arthur had thought, but that one percent makes all the difference.

He was still thinking of Dr. McMinn's blue eyes, and speculating about her genetics, when three masked men stepped from the brush beside the trail. One man, wearing a white mask, was holding a baseball bat.

"Hey, prairie nigger," said white mask. "What the fuck you doing on our trail?"

Arthur suddenly understood the flight instinct. And he also understood how a deer could stare into the headlights of an approaching car and be unable to move.

"I don't want any trouble," said Arthur.

"You don't want any trouble?" asked white mask.

"No," said Arthur, his voice breaking.

"Oh, now, listen to him squeal," said white mask.

"Yeah, like a pig," said blue mask.

Purple mask was silent.

"Are you an Indian pig?" asked white mask.

"Whatever you say, man," said Arthur.

"Whatever I say?"

"Yeah, whatever."

"Well, Indian pig, I say this," said white mask as he punched the bat into Arthur's belly. Dazed, Arthur staggered and fell to the ground. As he fell, he could see the baseball bat in white mask's hands. Expecting a beating, Arthur reflexively curled into a fetal ball to protect himself. He wondered if he was going to die.

5

Big Heart's Soda and Juice Bar

Wilson's studio apartment was small but tidy. It was in an old building just east of downtown. He had lived in it forever even though he knew he could have moved into a larger place. He felt safe in this one. He liked his couch that folded out into a bed, the coffee table where he took many of his meals, the big-screen television filling up an entire wall, the clock radio, the chest of drawers with a black-and-white photograph of his birth parents set on top, the small desk with matching chair. His typewriter sat on his desk, along with a cup of pencils, some correcting fluid, and copies of his two published books. His kitchen was tucked into a corner: tiny refrigerator, stove, and sink. He had two plates, two settings of silverware, one cup, and one glass. Small stereo. A simple life, to be sure, but it was good camouflage from the monsters.

Wilson thought about the Indian Killer. A white man scalped, a white man disappeared, a white boy kidnapped. It was Biblical,

David versus Goliath. But Wilson was disturbed by that. He wondered if a real Indian was capable of such violence. He knew about
real Indians. He'd read the books, had spent long hours meditating,
listening to the voices from the past. From the confusing and complicated cornucopia of tribal influences that made up Wilson's idea
of ceremony came burned sage and tobacco, a medicine pouch worn
beneath his clothes, and a turquoise ring on his right hand. While
beating the drum he'd ordered from a catalog, Wilson played Southern and Northern style, often within the same song. Some nights,
Wilson would slip into the traditional dance outfit he'd bought at a
downtown pawn shop, drop a powwow tape into the stereo, and two-
step across the floor for hours. He dreamed of being the best traditional dancer in the world. Wilson saw himself inside a bright spotlight
in a huge arena while thousands of Indians cheered for him. Real
Indians.

Wilson sat down at the typewriter, cracked his knuckles,
typed the first word, and leaned back in his chair. He cleared his
throat, decided he was thirsty, and wondered if he had any milk left.
He drank gallons of one-percent.

He stood up, walked over to his refrigerator, opened it, and
discovered it was nearly empty. A pizza box, jar of mustard, and
unidentifiable lunch meat. Opening the refrigerator had made him
hungry, an automatic response, so he grabbed his apartment keys and
went for some dinner at Big Heart's Soda and Juice Bar on Aurora
and 110th. In light traffic, Big Heart's was at least a twenty-minute
drive from his Capitol Hill apartment, but Wilson never minded the
effort because Big Heart's was an Indian bar, meaning that Indians
frequented the place, although a white man owned it. Wilson spent
a lot of time at Big Heart's. The bar was a huge multilevel circus. On
the main floor, a twenty-seat bar, a jukebox, and a dozen tables. Two
pool tables on the lower level, a dance floor and bandstand on the
upper floor. Three or four hundred Indians shoved into the place on
a busy weekend night.

Despite all of the time he spent in Big Heart's, Wilson had never come to understand the social lives of Indians. He did not know that, in the Indian world, there is not much social difference between a rich Indian and a poor one. Generally speaking, Indian is Indian. A few who gain wealth and power as lawyers, businessmen, artists, or doctors may marry white people and keep only white friends, but generally Indians of different classes interact freely with one another. Most unemployed or working poor, some with good jobs and steady incomes, but all mixing together. Wilson also did not realize how tribal distinctions were much more important than economic ones. The rich and poor Spokanes may hang out together, but that doesn't necessarily mean the Spokanes are friendly with the Lakota or Navajo or any other tribe. The Sioux still distrust the Crow because they served as scouts for Custer. Hardly anybody likes the Pawnee. Most important, though, Wilson did not understand that the white people who pretend to be Indian are gently teased, ignored, plainly ridiculed, or beaten, depending on their degree of whiteness.

"Hey, there," said Mick, the bartender, who was also the owner, as Wilson took a seat facing him. "What'll you have? A hamburger and fries, a glass of milk, right?"

"I've been wondering," Wilson said to Mick after the food arrived. "How come so many Indians come here?"

Mick shrugged his shoulders.

"How long they been coming here?"

Mick looked around the bar. A few Indians were playing pool, a big Indian guy in a dirty raincoat was sitting quietly at the other end of the bar from Wilson, and one couple was slow dancing to a bad song on the jukebox. It was still early on a weeknight. Mick breathed in deep, tilted his head in thought, made clicking sounds with his tongue, counting that way.

"I guess it must be about five, six years now," said Mick. "A few Indians just showed up one night, you know, like they were scouts or something. Then there were a few more the next night. A couple weeks later and the whole place was Indian. You know, for a while, I used to have a lot of white customers, too, but the Indians drove them away. You're about the only white guy left."

Mick had always referred to Wilson as a fellow white guy. And that had always bothered Wilson, who was so proud of his Indian blood. He had told all of the Indians who would listen about Red Fox, his Indian ancestor. Wilson had not told them that he was a writer, though everybody knew anyway. He thought he was anonymous in this place, picking up bits of stray information for his novels, but Wilson wrongly assumed that the Indians who went to Big Heart's did not read any books, let alone his books. In blissful ignorance, he figured he fit in fine, though the Skins in Big Heart's knew that he was just another white guy trying to become Indian by hanging out in an Indian bar. Wilson thought he was charming, but he had just become an expected feature of Big Heart's, a cheap sort of entertainment, and all the Indians called him Casper the Friendly Ghost.

"Hey, Mick," said Wilson. "Have you ever had any serious trouble around here?"

"What do you mean?"

"I mean, have there been any killings, anything like that?"

"No way. Lot of fights, I guess, but nobody's been killed. Why you ask?"

"Just curious."

Mick nodded his head, then turned to wash a few glasses. There were only a few, just busy work, but he liked to stay on top of things. Mick had once come across one of Wilson's books and was surprised to see his face on the back cover. Mick was even more surprised when he read the book. It was pretty good, although Mick was kind of tired of hearing about Indians. Still, Mick thought, Aristotle Little Hawk was a good Indian, even if he was just some character in a book. He wished more Indians like Little Hawk hung out in the bar. He knew Wilson claimed he had some Indian blood, said so inside the book. But Mick did not buy that shit. Mick's great-grandmother was a little bit Indian, but that did not make him Indian. Besides, who the hell would want to be Indian when you could just as easily be white?

"I run a pretty tight ship here," Mick said to Wilson. "You can't let these people get anything started. You have to cut if off at the bud."

Wilson nodded his head and filled his mouth with fries. Mick was always complaining about Indians. Wilson thought it ironic, since Mick depended on Indians for business. If all of the Indians abandoned Big Heart's, Mick would go under in a few months. Big Heart's would become a ghost town. Once an Indian bar, always an Indian bar, and the white people would never come back.

Three Indian men in their early twenties walked into Big Heart's then, laughing and carrying on, having a good time. Wilson recognized them. One was Harley Tate, the Colville with the mashed nose who couldn't hear or talk. Another was Ty Williams, a chubby, light-skinned Coeur d'Alene. The third was Reggie Polatkin, the Spokane Indian with the startling blue eyes.

"Hey, Casper!" Reggie shouted to Jack Wilson. "How's it hanging?"

"Down to my knee," Wilson said, the expected response. He had learned some things in the bar.

"Hey," said Reggie. "Buy us a pop."

"Sure," said Wilson. "Three Pepsis, Mick."

"Jeez, you dumb-ass white guy," Reggie said, shaking his head. "Don't you ever get it right? The Colvilles drink Pepsi, but we Spokanes only drink Coke. And those damn Coeur d'Alenes drink 7UP, enit?"

"Never had it," said Ty, the Coeur d'Alene. "Never will."

"Well, then," Reggie said. "What do Coeur d'Alenes drink?"

"Blood," said Ty.

"Hey, Mick," said Wilson. "Make that one Pepsi, one Coke, and a tomato juice."

Reggie and his friends laughed.

"Good one, Casper, good one. Come sit with us."

Wilson received very few invitations to sit with the Indians in Big Heart's, so he jumped at the chance.

"Get some popcorn, too," Reggie said to Wilson, who filled up a couple of bowls and brought them to the table.

"You're a good man, Casper," said Ty. "I don't care what everybody else says."

Wilson blushed. These Indians could still make him blush. Harley the Colville made a few frantic hand gestures, sign language. Since they were frantic, Wilson figured he was telling a joke. Ty and Reggie, who had learned sign language, made a few signs in return. They all laughed again, Ty and Reggie loud and baritone, Harley high-pitched and slow.

"What did he say?" asked Wilson.

"Nothing important," said Reggie, still laughing a little.

They talked and laughed, signed and laughed, although Wilson understood few of the jokes, signed or spoken.

"Hey," Reggie asked Wilson. "Where are all the white women?"

There were a dozen or so white women who liked to sleep with the Indian men who frequented Big Heart's. Though Reggie generally preferred Indian women, he would fuck an Indian groupie now and again. He liked the power of it. He liked to come inside a white woman and then leave her lying naked on a hotel bed she'd paid for, or in the backseat of her car, or on a piece of cardboard in an alley outside Big Heart's.

During his senior year of high school, Reggie had been sitting with his white girlfriend and a few other white friends when a drunk Indian had staggered into the pizza place. Reggie had pretended not to see the Indian, who'd flopped into a seat, laid his head on the table, and passed out. The Indian smelled like he hadn't bathed in weeks. As if to tell a secret, Reggie's white girlfriend had leaned forward. Reggie and his white friends had leaned toward her.

"I hate Indians," she'd whispered.

Reggie had tried to laugh it off, but he'd felt as if he'd been torn in half. Later that night, his girlfriend had tearfully tried to apologize to him. They'd parked on a dirt road a few miles outside of Seattle.

"I'm sorry," she'd said. "I didn't mean you. I love you. You're not like those other Indians. You're not like them."

Reggie had not said anything. Without a word, he'd kissed her hard, stripped her naked, and fucked her for the first time. She'd cried out when he roughly penetrated her. She'd been a virgin, though Reggie hadn't asked and wouldn't have cared. Every night for a week, he'd picked her up from her house, driven her to that same dirt road, and fucked her. No condom, no birth control pills, no withdrawal. He came inside her and hoped he'd gotten her pregnant. He'd wanted her to give birth to a brown baby. He'd wanted to dilute his Indian blood. He'd wanted some kind of revenge. He'd wanted some place to spill his pain. After a week of painful and angry sex, his white girlfriend had broken up with him. She had not been impregnated. She would never speak to him again.

"Hey," Wilson said. "I heard something crazy."

"What?"

"I heard a white guy was scalped."

The Indians stopped laughing. They stared at Wilson.

"You're full of shit," said Reggie.

"No, really," said Wilson. "Somebody killed him and scalped him."

No laughter. Harley signed. Reggie signed back.

"What did he say?" asked Wilson.

"He thinks you're full of shit, too."

Wilson could see that Reggie was uncomfortable.

"You already knew about it, didn't you?" Wilson asked Reggie.

"Maybe. Maybe not," said Reggie, who had moved his chair away from Wilson. Harley and Ty signed back and forth.

Reggie stared angrily at Wilson, who could not think of anything to say. He knew he had crossed some line, had violated an invisible boundary. He was not being a good cop, it was all too obvious, but he could not help himself.

"How did *you* hear about it?" Reggie asked suspiciously.

"I heard some guys talking about it downtown," Wilson lied, still assuming the Indians didn't know he was an ex-cop. "And they were talking about that young boy, too. They think he was kidnapped by the same one who scalped the white guy."

Reggie nodded his head slowly, took a sip of his Coke. Ty and Harley exchanged nervous glances.

"Do you think an Indian would do something like that?" asked Wilson, leaning forward in his seat, ready to take mental notes.

Reggie stared at Wilson, a hard stare.

"What do you think?" asked Reggie.

Wilson sat back in his chair, drummed his fingers on the table.

"No way," said Wilson. "I don't think so. Not a real Indian."

"No, huh? Is that your answer?"

Wilson shrugged his shoulders.

"Well," said Reggie. "I think an Indian could do something like that. Maybe the question should be something different. Maybe you should be wondering which Indian wouldn't do it. Lots of real Indian men out there have plenty enough reasons to kill a white man. Three at this table right now."

"You're kidding, right?"

Reggie looked at his friends. Ty and Harley stood as if to leave.

"Wait, hey," said Wilson. "I was just talking. Come on, I'll buy you another round."

"No thanks."

"You sure?"

"Yeah, we're sure."

"Okay, then. I'll see you around, right?"

"Listen," said Reggie. "You know about Bigfoot? That Sioux Indian?"

"Yeah," said Wilson. "He died at the Wounded Knee massacre in 1890. He was Minneconjou Sioux, I think. He was killed because he was leading the Ghost Dance."

"The Ghost Dance?"

"Yeah, it was a dance that was supposed to destroy the white men and bring back the buffalo. Ghost Dancing was thought to be an act of warfare against white people."

"Yeah, and who killed Bigfoot?"

"The Seventh Cavalry."

"No, I mean, who killed him?"

"Some soldier, I guess. Nobody knows for sure."

"You're not paying attention. What color was the man who killed Bigfoot?"

"He would've been white."

"Exactly, Casper. Think about that."

The three Indians left the bar. A dozen other Indians walked in soon after and greeted Wilson. Reggie, Ty, and Harley bumped into a few friends in the parking lot. Ty and Harley were eager to talk about Wilson and the murders, but Reggie remained quiet. He knew that Wilson was probably trying to write some book about the scalping. And he'd get it wrong. Wilson didn't understand anything about Indians. Ty, with his voice, and Harley, with his hands, told other Indians about the scalping. The word spread quickly. Within a few hours, nearly every Indian in Seattle knew about the scalping. Most Indians believed it was all just racist paranoia, but a few felt a strange combination of relief and fear, as if an apocalyptic prophecy was just beginning to come true.

6

Testimony

"Mr. Two Leaf, how are you feeling?"

"My eye hurts."

"Yeah, that's a nasty black eye. Any other injuries?"

"A couple bumps and bruises. Nothing serious."

"Can you tell us anything about who did this to you?"

"Three guys in masks."

"Excuse me?"

"Three guys in masks jumped me on the Burke-Gilman Trail. I was coming back from class."

"You're a student at the University?"

"Yeah, a chemistry major."

"And can you tell me exactly what happened?"

"I was walking and these three guys jumped out of the bushes. One of them, the white mask, the leader, was talking smack at me."

"Talking smack?"

"You know, talking smack, talking trash, giving me shit about being Indian."

"And you are Native American?"

"Yeah, Makah."

"And then what did you do? Did you provoke the attack?"

"You mean, aside from being Indian, did I provoke the attack? No way. Three guys, one of them holding a baseball bat? They could've called me anything they wanted to call me."

"And what did they call you?"

"They called me an Indian pig. Oh, and they called me a prairie nigger. Pretty colorful, enit?"

"I suppose."

"That one pissed me off, though. I ain't no prairie Indian. I'm from a salmon tribe, man. If they were going to insult me, they should've called me salmon nigger."

"I'm surprised you can laugh about this."

"It's what Indians do."

"Weren't you afraid?"

"Yeah, I was afraid, but I'm afraid most of the time, you know? How would you feel if a white guy like you got dropped into the middle of a black neighborhood, like Compton, California, on a Saturday night?"

"I'd be very afraid."

"And that's exactly how I feel living in Seattle. Hell, I feel that way living in the United States. Indians are outnumbered, Officer. Those three guys scared me bad, but I've been scared for a long time. But, you know, I think something crazy is starting to happen."

"What do you mean?"

"Well, I've been hearing rumors, you know?"

"What kind of rumors?"

"That Indians are organizing. They're looking to get revenge."

"Revenge?"

"Yeah, Indians have been scared for a long time. Now they want to scare some white guys. Things are starting to get tense, you know? I mean, it's like fire and hydrogen. All by themselves, fire and hydrogen are fine. But you mix them up and *boom!* Volatile."

"Is there anything you can remember about the three men who attacked you?"

"The leader was the meanest one. The other two weren't angels, but that leader wanted to kill me, I think. If those joggers hadn't come along, he might have done it. He was plain crazy, you know? Crazy white guys."

"How can you be sure they were white?"

"Blue eyes, man, blue eyes."

7

Mark Jones

Mark Jones woke up in a very dark place but knew instantly that somebody was sitting near him. The frightened little boy tried to talk and
to move, but found he was gagged and his arms were tied behind his
back. He struggled against the ropes. The killer reached out and
touched him. Mark couldn't see the killer, but felt something familiar, and almost comforting, in the touch.

Mark closed his eyes against the sudden painful glare of a flashlight. At first, when he slowly opened his eyes, Mark could see only
that glare and the vague shadow of the killer. Then, as Mark's eyes
adjusted, the killer used the flashlight to illuminate the prized possessions. The beautiful knife, that silver blade with three turquoise
gems inlaid in the handle, hanging in a special place on the wall. Mark
started to cry, understanding the power of the knife. The killer then
illuminated a bloody scalp nailed to the wall, which made Mark scream
behind his gag. He wanted to go home, home, home. He coughed

and gagged around the cloth shoved roughly into his mouth. Fearing the boy might choke to death, the killer pulled the gag out and Mark breathed deeply. Fresh air, relief, a slight taste of hope. The killer held a juice box in front of him and the boy nodded.

Mark's hands were still bound, so the killer poked one end of the straw into the juice box and then put the other end of the straw into Mark's mouth. The boy drank greedily and quickly, broke into a spasm of coughs. After he regained his breath, Mark emptied the juice box. The killer let it drop to the floor. Then he put the gag back into Mark's mouth.

The boy started to cry again. The killer was lost in thought. By now, the killer had assumed the whole world would know about the power and beauty of the knife. But the police had managed to hide the truth. The newspapers knew nothing about the killer. The television knew nothing about the killer. And there was so much to know. Such as the fact that the scalping was just preparation, the prelude to something larger. The killer knew that the kidnapping of Mark Jones was the true beginning, the first song, the first dance of a powerful ceremony that would change the world. Killing a white man, no matter how brutally, was not enough to change the world. But the world would shudder when a white boy was sacrificed. A small, helpless boy. The killer, like a Christian plague, had swept into the Jones's house and stolen the first-born son of a white family.

The boy was frail, weeping himself into exhaustion, and the killer felt a shallow wave of compassion. But there was no time for that. The owl had no compassion for its prey. Without tears or hesitation, the owl ripped its prey apart to get at the eyes, at the heart, the sweetest meat of all. The owl hunted to eat. It had no message. But the killer wanted people to know about the message of the knife, and knew who would be the messenger. With a flutter of wings, the killer pulled the beautiful knife from its place on the wall, leaned over the boy, and began cutting.

8

The Messenger

Truck Schultz chewed on his cigar, leaned back in his chair, and closed his eyes. He was looking forward to a few days off. He was thinking about a fishing trip when his assistant walked into the studio with an open box.

"Truck," said Darla. "I think you better look at this."

Inside the box, a ragged piece of Mark Jones's Daredevil pajamas and two bloody owl feathers.

9

John Smith

At night, rain and fog invades the city of Seattle, an occupying force that pushes people inside homes, restaurants, and offices to escape it. One moment, bright moon and clear skies. The next moment, gray everywhere. At three in the morning the temperature drops, but not enough to frighten anybody but tourists. John was not a tourist. He was aboriginal. He stepped through this rain and fog without incident. He loved and needed the dark, feeling it contained more safety than the small circles of white light beneath each street lamp. He pulled his collar closer to his neck and marched through the slight cold. He walked across the Fremont Bridge, north of downtown, southeast of his Ballard apartment. There were no people, no cars. John was the last person left on earth. He wanted to be home alone, in his bed, quiet. This bridge was a bad place. Then the silence was broken. Twin headlights. Illumination. A pickup, filled with curses and Brut aftershave, rattled over the bridge.

"Fucking Indian!"

As the pickup left him behind, John raised his hand, fingers spread wide. He did not understand his own gesture. The pickup slowed, brake lights almost beautiful in the gray air, then stopped, still, reverse lights suddenly bright. John watched the pickup. He raised both hands in the air. He heard a man screaming, then realized he was screaming. As the pickup stopped short of him, the passenger door was flung open, and a big, black boot stepped down to pavement. John looked up into the night sky. The Aurora Bridge hung in the sky a couple hundred feet above the Fremont Bridge. Suicidal people jumped off the Aurora Bridge. Nobody jumped off the Fremont Bridge. More cars on the Aurora Bridge. Just the solitary pickup on the Fremont. John could hear every car and bridge in the city. So many cars and bridges in the city. John had lost count years before.

"Fuck you, Geronimo!"

A big white man in black boots. Driver's door open now. Two white men. No, two white boys, tall and skinny. Laughing and drinking at a safe distance from John. Seattle was a safe city. The news proved it every day because every murder, rape, and bank robbery made the papers.

"What the fuck you staring at?"

John was staring at the white boys. They were pale and beautiful. John pointed at them.

"What the fuck you pointing at?"

John knew these white boys. Not these two in particular, but white boys in general. He had been in high school with boys like these. He had sat in their pickups, showered with them after gym class, shared pizzas. He had leaned out the windows of their cars and screamed at downtown drunks. Sometimes he had leaned out the window and screamed at everybody they passed.

John was still screaming. He stood on the Fremont Bridge and screamed. The two white boys shouted curses at him, but they kept their distance, ready to jump into their pickup at the slightest provocation. John saw them as Catholic boys, in their junior year at private school. One played varsity basketball; the other played baseball. Both were class officers. They were the boys who forced their hands down the pants of girls who pretended to like it.

"She wanted it, you know? But I let her go, you know? I took pity on her."

John remembered how these boys talked. He had tried to talk that way himself. He had tried to lie as often as possible, understanding that lying was a valuable skill. High school taught white boys the value of lies, and John knew this. He knew these white boys intimately. He knew these two white boys standing on the Fremont Bridge were publicly loved and admired by their classmates and teachers. These were the boys who were secretly hated and envied, too. Their deaths could create a hurricane of grief and confusion.

During John's senior year in high school, one of his classmates had been killed in a car wreck on the Interstate. John had been sitting in his homeroom when the principal walked into the class with the news.

"I have some tragic, tragic news," said the principal without subtlety. "Scott O'Brien was killed last night."

John began to cry for reasons he could not understand. He had not liked Scott O'Brien. A few weeping girls huddled together in the corner. Scott's friends, all white boys, sat quietly and stoically, fighting back tears, sucking in their bottom lips, occasionally pounding their desks in imitation of the pointless, masculine methods of grief they saw on television. Sidney Bush, the only Jewish Catholic in Seattle, had his head down on his desk. His acned face was hidden, his fat shoulders were shaking. He might have been crying. But John knew better. Scott had been extremely cruel to Sidney.

"Kike!"

"Jewboy!"

"Fat ass!"

"Pizza face!"

John watched Sidney and knew that he was laughing quietly. Sidney had heard the news of Scott's death, thrown his face down on the desk, and couldn't help his joy. He was still laughing over there, in the far corner, near the tattered copies of Upton Sinclair's *The Jungle* and seventy-two editions of the St. Francis Catholic School Annual, dating back to the institution's early years.

"St. Francis, St. Francis, our trust in God for thee . . ."

Sidney Bush was laughing in the corner. John felt a single, hot tear sliding down his cheek and falling to the desk. John looked down at the tear, touched it with a fingertip. He knew that the next school annual would be dedicated to Scott O'Brien. A center spread filled with photographs and mementos, precious memories, and statistics. John knew there would be a prayer at graduation, a seat left empty in honor of the missing classmate. Yet, in the far corners of rooms, a few would be hiding their smiles.

"Fuck you, you fucking Indian!"

John remembered that he was still standing on the Fremont Bridge, still screaming, he believed, while the two white boys were getting bored, their curses losing volume and intensity. John felt the screams rattle his ribcage. His throat burned. He took a step forward, then another. The white boys were startled. The driver hopped into the pickup, ready to race away. The passenger threw his beer bottle in the general direction of John. The bottle revolved in the air as John watched its flight, its parabola, its sudden crash against the pavement at his feet. A close call. That white boy was an athlete.

"Fuck you!" from the departing pickup, squealing tires and laughter. John stood alone on the bridge. He needed a shower and shave. His whiskers had grown in clumsy patterns, thick at the chin and sideburns, barely visible at the cheeks and above his lip. His long hair was braided with a broken shoelace. John was quiet. He looked down at the pavement, stepped over the broken glass, and began walking. He walked up Aurora, past Big Heart's Soda and Juice Bar up on 110th and Aurora. He sometimes visited the bar, but he felt no such need that night. He walked past the graveyard where prostitutes laid down with customers, past Kmart and Burger King, the Aurora Cinemas. John kept walking past all of that. He could not find the courage to stop walking. He walked miles beyond any neighborhood that resembled his own. He walked until he found himself on a dead-end street, a cul-de-sac, a vanishing point. At the end of the street, a small Catholic church, painted white with blue shutters, had tiny, stained glass windows. A candle burned above the front door.

Inside the church, John found the usual pews, altar, confessional, more candles, wood carvings of Jesus crucified, Jesus entombed, Jesus rising again. John still believed in the mystery of his Catholic faith. He used to enjoy Mass, felt some comfort in the numbing repetition of word, symbol, and action. How, every Sunday, he knew exactly what the priest was going to say. There were no surprises, no sudden starts and stops, no need to interpret and understand. The priest told the congregation what to believe and the congregation believed him. But John had not been to Mass in years.

As John walked further into that small church, he saw a priest kneeling at the front. John knew who it was.

"Father Duncan," said John as he kneeled beside the priest, believing it was the same man who had baptized him years before. This was the priest who had walked into the desert and disappeared. This was the priest who knew everything.

"Father Duncan," John said again.

Father Phil, a tall Irishman with red hair and ruddy skin, turned from his prayers to look at John.

"Father Duncan," said John, desperately now, wanting recognition.

"No, it's Father Phil. Did you know Father Duncan?"

"Yes."

Father Phil had one of Duncan's paintings hanging in his study. He knew the story of the Indian Jesuit who'd walked into the Arizona desert and disappeared.

"He's gone," said John. "He disappeared."

"I know. I'm sorry."

John wept. Father Phil placed a hand on John's shoulder.

"I have sinned," said John.

"How long has it been since your last confession?"

"Years."

"What have you done?"

"I have had impure thoughts."

Father Phil closed his eyes, whispering prayers that John could not make out. John wanted to be forgiven. He felt the pain and rage rising in his throat.

"Father," said John, his voice rising, his hands gesturing wildly. "All the anger in the world has come to my house. It's there in my closet. In my refrigerator. In the water. In the sheets. It's in my clothes. Can you smell it? I can never run away from it. It's in my hair. I can feel it between my teeth. Can you taste it? I hear it all the time. All the time the anger is talking to me. It's the devil. I'm the devil. If I could I'd crawl into a hole if I knew God was in there. Where's the hole? You know, I just killed two white boys on the bridge. They were there on the bridge. They wanted to hurt me. They were the devil. I killed them. I threw them off the bridge into the water. They can't hurt me anymore. They hurt me. They wanted to steal my eyes. They wanted everything. What am I going to do? What am I going to do?"

Phil looked at John. He reached out and held John's hands. Phil wondered if the Indian was a killer, or lost, or both.

"My son," said Father Phil. "Tell me about your pain. I will listen."

John looked around the small chapel.

"Father, your church is empty."

"I know. Sometimes it feels empty even when it's full of people."

"How come?"

"Because people are lost."

John left that priest and his church and soon found himself standing outside his Ballard apartment. A note from his parents was taped to the door:

John—

Please call us when you get in.
We are worried about you. We love you.

Mom & Dad

John tore the note from the door, crumpled it into a ball, and shoved it into his pocket. He found the apartment key his mother had sewn into his pants. She had done the same for every pair of pants he owned. He opened his door and stepped inside.

10

Finding the Body

The blue van rolled slowly down a dirt road on the Tulalip Indian Reservation. Thick stands of trees flanked the road. The faint sounds of Interstate 5 could be heard in the distance, though the people inside the van, a Spokane Indian couple, were not comforted by those distant sounds of civilization.

"I think we're lost," she said.

"We're not that lost," he said. "You can hear the freeway. Listen."

She listened, could hear the big trucks hauling their cargo north to Canada and south to Seattle, quickly passing senior citizens leisurely touring in their recreational vehicles. She could hear the whine of a traffic helicopter. All those people so close and far away at the same time.

"Well," she said. "Unless I'm mistaken, we'd have to walk through the woods to get to the freeway. On foot, we'd know exactly where we are. But, unless I'm mistaken again, we're in the van. And since we can't drive through those woods, we are lost, enit? Listen, there were a couple houses back there. We could go back and ask for directions."

"We'll be fine," he said.

He drove five miles down the road until the asphalt turned into dirt and a sign proclaimed PRIMITIVE ROAD—NO WARNING SIGNS.

"Now," she said, "I think that is reason enough to turn around."

"Yeah, you're probably right."

"Hold on a second," she said. "I have to go pee."

She grabbed the roll of toilet paper they always kept in the glove compartment, jumped out of the van, and went searching for a good spot. She always felt like a dog when she had to go in the woods. Amusing herself, she pretended to sniff at a few trees, looked back at the blue van where her boyfriend waited, and then walked farther into the brush. She was wishing she had a temporary penis for outdoor urination use when she caught a whiff of something foul.

"Jeez," she whispered to herself, plugging her nose.

She tried to walk away from the smell, but it seemed to be everywhere. A dead animal, she thought. Then she wondered if it might be a dead porcupine. If the poker had not been dead too long, she might be able to salvage the quills and give them to some Indian grandmother. Indian grandmothers could always use more quills. She stood still and tried to discern the source of the smell. She could not tell in which direction she should go, but she knew it was close. She started walking in ever-widening circles, hoping to find the dead porcupine by stumbling over it. The smell grew more powerful as she walked closer to a stand of pines. When she stepped between two large trees, she saw the body sitting back against a stump.

"Holy Mary," she whispered and made the sign of the cross.

Dressed in a University of Washington sweatshirt and blue jeans, David Rogers almost looked as if he were resting after a long walk. His head fell against his left shoulder, a single bullet hole between his eyes. There was very little blood and no other wounds, though the body was well into its decomposition. For some reason, she noticed that the boy's tennis shoes were untied.

11

Fire Starter

"Truck," said the assistant over the intercom.

"Yeah," said Truck, without opening his eyes.

"You've got a call on line three, from Johnny Law."

Truck sat up quickly and took the call. Johnny Law was the pseudonym for Truck's source in the Washington State Patrol office. After Truck had received the piece of Mark Jones's pajamas and the two bloody owl feathers, he'd learned from Johnny Law that a serial murderer, dubbed the Indian Killer, was loose in the Seattle area. Leaving behind two owl feathers as a calling card, the Indian Killer had murdered and scalped Justin Summers, had kidnapped little Mark Jones, and was a suspect in the disappearance of David Rogers. Truck had been itching to broadcast the news, but the police had threatened to shut him down if he went public.

"What's up?" Truck asked Johnny Law.

"We found that college boy's body, David Rogers, up on the Tulalip Reservation about thirty minutes ago. He was murdered, shot in the head. The money he'd won was gone, of course."

"Is it an Indian Killer murder?"

"Doubtful. He was shot in the head. No signs of mutilation on the body. No feathers. Looks like a robbery. But we're not ruling anything out."

The caller hung up and Truck smiled. Fuck the police, he thought.

"When are we back on air?" asked Truck.

"Two minutes," said the assistant.

"Get me the file on that college kid who disappeared a couple weeks back."

The assistant raced to the filing room, pulled out the folder, and rushed it back to Truck. David Rogers. Twenty-one years old. A junior English major. Three point one grade-point average. He worked part-time in the computer lab.

"Thirty seconds to air," said the assistant.

"Free all the phone lines," said Truck. "I've got things to say. And try to get David's brother on the phone. Aaron, I think his name is. We've got his number around here somewhere. He called in a while back."

Truck continued to read. David's mother had died of cancer when he was five years old. His father, Buck, living on the family farm outside of Spokane, was distraught by his youngest son's disappearance. A good boy.

"Ten seconds to air," said the assistant.

Truck sipped at his coffee, wiped his face with his favorite handkerchief, and leaned toward the microphone.

"I've just received the disturbing news from my esteemed sources in the offices of the Washington State Patrol. It seems that the body of another white man has been discovered up on the Tulalip Indian Reservation forty miles north of Seattle. The details are sketchy, but authorities have identified the body as that of David Rogers, the University of Washington student who has been missing since he won two thousand dollars at a slot machine. The body was mutilated and dumped near the Tulalip Tribal Casino, the last place where David Rogers was seen alive. I know this is terrifying news, but I must inform you that the Seattle Police Department believes that a serial killer, known only as the Indian Killer, is responsible for David Rogers's murder, as well as the murder of Justin Summers, the bartender whose bloody body was found in Fremont. Both David Rogers and Justin Summers had been scalped.

"And there is more. The police insisted I keep this quiet, but the time for silence is over. Just a few days ago, the Indian Killer mailed me a special package. Inside the package were a piece of Mark Jones's pajamas and the Indian Killer's calling card. Now, I don't want to tell you what the killer sent me. But it's proof of the Indian Killer's existence. The Indian Killer has kidnapped and most likely murdered little Mark Jones.

"Citizens, I am deeply saddened by these murders. I extend my deepest sympathies to the family and friends of the murdered men. And most especially, to the mother and father of Mark Jones. I think we should have a moment of radio silence in their honor."

Truck pressed the mute button, sipped at his coffee, toked on his cigar, and watched the clock. A full minute passed.

"Citizens, I am outraged. What is our society coming to when good men cannot safely walk the streets of our cities? When a little boy can be taken from the safety of his own home? And you know these murdered men, this kidnapped little boy, were targets precisely because they were white. They were guilty of the crime of being white males.

"Yes, yes, citizens, I know, I know. What have I been telling you? Haven't I told you that our current political climate, with its constant vilification of white males, would prove to be disastrous? White males built this country. White males traveled here on the *Mayflower*, crossed the Great Plains on horseback, brought light to the darkness, tamed the wilderness. This country exists because of the constant vigilance and ingenuity of white males.

"And, now, through no fault of their own, two men are dead, and a little boy is missing, because they were white. If two black men had been killed because of their race, this city would be in a uproar. If a black child had been kidnapped by a white man, the city would be up in arms. Citizens, there would be a candlelight march. Our liberal black mayor would have appointed a task force by now. Of course, he would have. This whole country cares more about the lives of young black teenage hoodlums than it does about law-abiding, God-fearing white men.

"And now comes the news that an Indian savage is killing white men. Have we somehow traveled back to the nineteenth century? Has some Godless heathen been kept on ice on the reservation for a couple hundred years? Did they thaw that psycho warrior and send him into the city to scalp white men? Citizens, I'm happy I am balder than Kojak and Yul Brynner combined.

"Seriously, citizens, I'm deeply, deeply saddened. But, I have to tell you, I'm not surprised by this turn of events. I mean, what happens to a child that is given everything he wants? That child becomes an aggressive, domineering brat. Well, citizens, we keep giving Indians everything they want. We give them fishing rights, hunting lands. We allow them to have these illegal casinos on their land. They have rights that normal Americans do not enjoy. Indians have become super citizens, enjoying all the advantages of being Americans while reveling in the special privileges they receive just for being Indians.

"And we give all this to them because we supposedly stole their land from them. Indians are living a better life than they ever did before. They have jobs. They have electricity and running water. They have God. Citizens, and this is a fact, there are more Indians living now then there were when Columbus first landed on these shores. It's true, you can look it up.

"And despite all these special advantages, Indians still live in poverty. They live in filth, folks. Broken-down cars stacked in their yards. They have the highest infant-mortality rates. They have the highest rates of alcohol and drug abuse. Indians still get rickets, for God's sake. We give them everything, and yet they cannot take care of themselves.

"Would you give money to a four-year-old and tell her to feed herself, clothe herself, buy a house, pay bills? Of course not. Yet we give millions and millions of dollars to these Indians and expect them to know what to do with such wealth. Then when we, as tax-paying citizens, complain about such a waste of our tax dollars, the Indians call us racist. They whine about their treaty rights. They wave their flimsy little treaties around. Well, I've got a piece of paper to show those Indians. It's called the Bill of Rights and, citizens, it doesn't say one word about special rights for Indians. It's says that all men are created equal. All men, not just Indians.

"Calm down, citizens, calm down. I know how you feel. I know you're upset. You have every right to be upset. I'm upset. We have coddled Indians too long and we've created a monster. We share the responsibility.

"It's true, citizens, it's true. We should have terminated Indian tribes from the very beginning. Indians should have been assimilated into normal society long ago. We should have given them every chance to become fully productive members of our society. Yet we allowed them to remain separate. In fact, we encouraged their separation from the mainstream values and culture in this country. That separation created poverty. It created drug abuse and addiction. It created misery and anger. It created this Indian Killer. Now, I believe we should find this Indian Killer, give him a fair and speedy trial, and then hang him by the neck until he is dead.

"Yes, citizens, to paraphrase one of our great military leaders, Philip Sheridan, the only good Indian Killer is a dead Indian Killer."

12

The Battle of Queen Anne

Less than an hour after Truck Schlutz phoned Aaron Rogers and personally told him about the discovery of his brother's body, Aaron, Barry Church, and Sean Ward were cruising downtown Seattle, looking for Indians to attack. Aaron and Barry had both tossed baseball bats into the truck before they left the house. Each of the three had a ski mask shoved into his pocket.

"Let's do it for David," Aaron said to his housemates, pounding the steering wheel of his Toyota 4Runner as he cruised through downtown Seattle. On any given night, a couple dozen Indians usually staggered through the downtown streets. Aaron had often seen them. Homeless drunks. Men and women. Sitting in their own vomit. Rotten faces, greasy hair, shit-stained pants. Aaron had always been disgusted before. Now he felt a hate that made his chest ache. Sean and Barry scanned the streets. Other college kids on the street walked from bar to bar, laughter and conversation. A small crowd gathered outside the Elliott Bay Book Company. Couples slowly strolled past dark windows of stores.

"Where the fuck are they?" Aaron was screaming now, his face red with frustration.

"I've seen Indians up by the Seattle Center," said Barry. "On Queen Anne Hill."

Cornelius and Zera, homeless Indians, huddled together in a doorway across the street from a Blockbuster Video on lower Queen Anne Hill. The doorway was a good spot, kept warm by the furnace beneath it. Fairly safe, too, in a busy neighborhood. Cornelius and Zera had spent a year of nights in that doorway.

"You warm?" Cornelius asked Zera.

"Warm enough," she said. But she was shaking, and Cornelius pulled her closer. They'd been together for five years and had spent half of that time homeless. The other half, they'd shared and been evicted from three apartments. Money and jobs were seasonal. Cornelius, a Makah Indian, was a deep-sea fisherman, a job that would have kept him away for months at a time, and he just didn't want to leave Zera, a Puyallup. She was manic-depressive and simply couldn't take care of herself. So Cornelius worked as a manual laborer, losing the job whenever Zera showed up and terrorized customers and managers, or when he missed worked to search for her after her latest disappearance. She'd been hospitalized three times and Cornelius had always missed her so much he couldn't sleep. He would just walk around the hospital, one or two hundred times a day, until she was finally released.

"You warm now?" Cornelius asked.

She nodded her head, but he knew she was lying. He offered her a drink of coffee from the thermos. He'd always leave the empty thermos at the back door of the nearby McDonald's, and Doug, the redheaded night manager, would secretly fill it again with leftover coffee. Small kindnesses. Cornelius also had a loaf of bread he'd bought with money he'd made selling *Real Change*, the newspaper written and distributed by the homeless. He took out two slices, jammed them together, and offered it to Zera.

"Hey, look," he said. "A jam sandwich."

She laughed, took the sandwich, and swallowed it down.

As Aaron piloted his truck through lower Queen Anne in search of Indians, he brooded about David. Frail David Rogers with his lopsided grin. Always reading some damn book or another. Loved Hemingway's Nick Adams, the monosyllabic hero with the mono-syllabic name. Nick. The first man, the essential man, the genesis of man. Adams. Everything that David was not. In high school, David tried to play football and made the team as a fourth-string receiver. He cheered on Aaron, the toughest linebacker in the league. Aaron had wanted to play college football at the University of Washington, one of the best programs in the country, but they hadn't been inter-ested in him. He was too small for Division I, the recruiters told him. Junior college would be best, the coaches told him. But Aaron would not accept anything less than UW, so he enrolled anyway, and David had followed him. Aaron hadn't made it halfway through the first day of football tryouts when some behemoth knocked him unconscious and out of contention for a roster spot. After that, Aaron and David had grown even closer. More than brothers. They moved in with Sean and Barry, studied hard, and were well on their way to graduation when David disappeared. Aaron thought of his father, who was prob-ably driving to Seattle right now.

"Fuck," Aaron cursed while Barry held his baseball bat tightly. Sean was getting more nervous than angry. He'd never seen Aaron, who had quite a temper anyway, look so furious. Aaron had been on a short fuse since David had disappeared, and Sean could understood that. Hell, he missed David, too, but he was gone and there was nothing they could do about it. Maybe they thought they could do a lot about it, like beating the shit out of a few Indians with blunt in-

struments. Perhaps baseball bats. Sean shook his head. It was all getting out of control.

"They're hiding," Sean said. "We're not going to find them
now. Everybody must know about the Indian Killer."

"We'll find them," Aaron said.

"That's what I'm afraid of," said Sean.

Before Aaron could respond, Barry shouted and pointed up
the street at two Indians sleeping in a doorway. Aaron smiled. He
slipped a ski mask over his face, as Sean and Barry did the same.

Cornelius was watching Zera sleep. She spent most of her
waking hours in a struggle for emotional balance, and it showed in
her face. Deep wrinkles, haunted eyes, sudden gestures and unpre-
dictable movements. In sleep, she relaxed, sometimes smiled, and
Cornelius thought her beautiful. Sleep is a little piece of death, he
thought, and Zera found some peace in that temporary afterlife. He
was busy looking at her while she slept when the truck pulled up to
a sharp stop near the doorway.

"Hey, you fuckers!"

Three men in ski masks, white, purple, and blue, jumped out
of the pickup. Two of them, white mask and blue mask, held baseball bats. Purple mask was empty-handed.

"Wake up, wake up!" Cornelius yelled as he shook Zera
awake. They both struggled to their feet.

"Fucking drunks! Fuck you, fuck you!"

The man in the white mask advanced with his baseball bat.
He was obviously the leader. For some reason, Cornelius held out
the thermos as an offering. He looked down at his outstretched hand
and couldn't believe what he was doing.

"I don't want your booze!" shouted white mask as he swung
the bat and smashed the thermos out of Cornelius's hand.

"Home run! Home run!" shouted blue mask. He came forward, swinging his bat as if he were a baseball player warming up.
Purple mask stayed back.

"Come on, come on, you fucking Indian," said white mask. He jabbed his bat into Cornelius' belly. Zera was trembling beside him.

"We don't want no trouble," Cornelius said. "We'll leave."

"Go back to where you belong, man!" shouted blue mask. "Get the fuck out of our country, man!"

A crowd had gathered, though no one in it seemed eager to interfere. God, I hope somebody called the cops, thought Cornelius. When he flexed his hand, the pain told him white mask had broken it into pieces. Cornelius was still debating his options when Zera made her decision and tackled blue mask. Before Cornelius could react, white mask broke Cornelius's jaw with a wicked swing of his bat.

"Get her off me! Get her off me!" blue mask shouted as Zera tore at his face. As purple mask tried to pull her off, white mask savagely beat Cornelius. Five, ten, twenty swings of the bat. Four cracked ribs, punctured lung, various contusions and abrasions, concussion.

Purple mask had pulled Zera off blue mask, who had smashed her across the face with his bat. The amount of blood shocked blue mask. He stepped back.

"Payback, motherfucker, payback!" shouted white mask. He kept swinging the bat at Cornelius, might have beaten the life out of the Indian, if purple mask had not pulled him away.

"We got to go!" shouted purple mask. Blue mask was already in the driver's seat, ready to roll. White mask smashed Cornelius one last time, jumped into the 4Runner with the other two, and screamed triumphantly as they sped from the scene.

13

Night Terrors

As Olivia and Daniel ate breakfast, the radio announced that Mark Jones had been kidnapped by the Indian Killer. A homeless Indian couple had been assaulted by three masked men. Olivia had wanted to talk, but Daniel excused himself from the table. A few minutes before seven in the morning, Daniel Smith left home, saying he had extra work at the architecture firm.

As Daniel drove away, Olivia knew that he was really going to look for John. As he drove from Bellevue over the 520 bridge west to Seattle, Daniel could see a few sailboats out for an early cruise on Lake Washington. A man and woman, dressed warmly, were aboard a large one with a red and white sail, just a hundred feet or so from the bridge. As Daniel imagined he heard their laughter, he felt jealous. Man, woman, boat, water, freedom. Everything so simple for them. The shadow of Mount Rainier rose on the southern horizon. On a slightly overcast day, the mountain was just a ghost, a subtle reminder of itself, a brief memory. With unlimited visibility, the mountain was spectacular and surreal, rising as it did over the urban landscape of Seattle. Daniel knew that accidents had occurred on Seattle freeways because of drivers who were distracted by Rainier's beauty. Local Indians had always believed that Rainier was a sacred place, not to be climbed or trivialized. Daniel wondered if any Indians had wrecked their cars because of a view of the mountain.

He parked the car downtown in a lot near the firm and walked the streets. Little traffic, a few cars and out-of-season tourists. A heavy rain had fallen, leaving behind that particular odor which so many people associate with fresh air and nature, though that smell rises out of the damp, musty places in a city. Still, Daniel had always loved the rain and what it left behind. As Daniel wandered, he felt no love for the rain or the city. He felt lost and hopeless, searching for his son, who had become a stranger. Daniel had never done anything this desperate. He had no idea what he was doing, only that he would not find John by sitting inside, just waiting. He was shocked by the number of homeless people, especially the dozens of Indians, who were living in downtown Seattle. He was intimidated, but he soon found the courage to talk to them. Outside the Elliott Bay Book Company, which had not yet opened, Daniel saw a homeless Indian man in a wheelchair.

"Hello," Daniel ventured. The Indian was about forty years old, with long, greasy hair. He wore a U.S. Army jacket and a red beret.

"Hey," replied the Indian. "You got any change?"

Daniel dug in his empty pockets. Then he pulled a couple dollars from his wallet and handed them over.

"Thanks." The Indian quickly pocketed the money.

"Listen, could I ask you something? I'm looking for my son. He's Indian. A big guy. Talks to himself."

"Hey, partner, most everybody down here talks to himself. How'd you get an Indian son anyways? Marry you some dark meat, enit?"

"No, no. He's adopted."

"What's his name?" asked the Indian.

"John. John Smith."

"You adopted an Indian kid and named him John Smith? No wonder he talks to himself. What's your name?"

"Daniel."

"Hey, Daniel, I've got to say I don't know one Indian named John Smith. I know King and Agnes. I know Marie the Sandwich Lady and Robert. But I don't know a John Smith. Ain't nobody knows any Indian named John Smith. Ain't no such thing. You must have dreamed him up."

The Indian laughed, slapped his own face, twirled around in his chair.

"You know," drawled the wheelchair Indian. "I bet you're a cop, enit? You're just a cop looking for that Indian Killer, right?"

"No, no. I'm really looking for my son. This Indian Killer thing has me worried about him."

"All the cops been through here a million times already," said the Indian. "Asking me this, asking me that. I'll tell you what I told the others. I know who killed those white people."

"You know who did it?"

"Damn right, I know," said the Indian. He laughed loudly, rolling his chair away from Daniel.

"Wait," Daniel called after him, caught in the surprise of the moment. "Who did it?"

"It was Crazy Horse," shouted the Indian, who stopped and looked back over his shoulder. "You know Crazy Horse?"

"Of course," said Daniel, who'd read most every Indian book that Olivia had set in front of him. "He's Oglala Sioux, right?"

"Oh, yeah, he's Oglala." The Indian, slowly wheeling back, closer and closer to Daniel, kept speaking. "And he's more. This Indian Killer, you see, he's got Crazy Horse's magic. He's got Chief Joseph's brains. He's got Geronimo's heart. He's got Wovoka's vision. He's all those badass Indians rolled up into one."

The wheelchair Indian dug through his pockets, pulled out a series of wrinkled news clippings, and waved them in the air.

"See," said the Indian, "I'm keeping track. We all are. Every Indian is keeping score. What? This Killer's got himself two white guys? And that little white boy, enit? That makes the score about ten million to three, in favor of the white guys, enit? This Killer's got a long ways to go. Man, he's the underdog."

The Indian laughed loudly, slapping his still legs. He began to roll away from Daniel.

"But who is he?" asked Daniel.

"It's me," said the Indian, his laughter getting louder as he rolled farther away. Then, still laughing, he stepped out of his chair, pushed it quickly down the street, and disappeared.

Though unnerved, Daniel could not stop searching for John. He spent most of the day in downtown Seattle, but never found anybody, white or Indian, who had ever heard of an Indian named John Smith, though they all knew a dozen homeless Indian men.

"Yeah, there's that Blackfeet guy, Loney."

"Oh, yeah, enit? And that Laguna guy, what's his name? Tayo?"

"And Abel, that Kiowa."

After searching for hours, Daniel returned to his car and made it back to Bellevue for an early dinner.

"How was your day?" asked Olivia, hoping that he'd tell her about his search for John.

"Okay," said Daniel.

John's parents ate the rest of their meal in silence.

That night, Olivia Smith dreamed: Father Duncan dipping baby John into the baptismal; four-year-old John heaving a basketball toward the hoop as Daniel laughs and claps his hands; Daniel kissing down her belly; John's naked body, bloody and brown, dumped on a snow plain. Olivia dreamed: a red tricycle; lightning illuminating a stranger standing at a window; pine trees on fire; an abandoned hound mournfully howling beside a country road. Olivia dreamed: John standing alone on the last skyscraper in Seattle as wind whips his hair across his face; Daniel holding her head under water at Lake Sammamish until she panics; the moon rising above the Space Needle; Father Duncan dipping the adult John into the baptismal.

With a sudden start, Olivia sat up in bed, awake, unsure of her surroundings. Slowly, she recognized her bedroom, maple bureau, huge closet door ajar, Daniel snoring lightly beside her. Knowing she would not sleep now, she crawled from bed and walked into the bathroom. Without turning on the light, she pulled down her pajamas and sat on the toilet. She could not go, though there was a slight pressure in her bladder. She briefly wondered if she had an infection. She held her head in her hands and waited. She thought about the Indian Killer murders, how the news was filled with photographs of the white men who had been killed. Of the little white boy, helpless and small, as John had once been. She wondered if John was safe. She wanted to pray, but felt embarrassed by her position. Then she prayed anyway as her legs fell asleep.

As Olivia prayed, Daniel dreamed: his secretary leaning over his desk with papers to sign; the Bainbridge Island ferry crossing rough waters. Daniel dreamed: young John running across a field; a stranger hammering nails into a joist. Daniel dreamed: a red truck breaking through a guardrail; a pistol firing. Daniel dreamed: a man screaming; John standing over the bed.

Frightened, Daniel sat up in bed, sure that John was there. Daniel could almost smell his son. Smoke and sweat, sweet and dank. Then Daniel could smell his son, could feel him there.

"John?" asked Daniel.

Olivia heard her husband, quickly pulled up her pajamas and stepped into the bedroom.

"Daniel," she said. "Who are you talking to?"

"It's John," he said. "He's here."

Olivia looked around the bedroom. The windows were locked tight. The bedroom door was shut. Since the closet door was slightly ajar, she opened it and turned on the light. Daniel's suits on one side, her dresses and blouses on the other. On both sides, above their clothes, boxes were stacked from shelf to ceiling. A dozen pairs of Daniel's shoes scattered on the floor; ten pairs of Olivia's. No John. She switched off the closet light.

"He's not here," Olivia said to Daniel, to herself. "You're dreaming."

"No," said Daniel. "He's here. I can smell him."

Olivia sniffed the air. She knew her son's smell. Was confident of that. Knew she could've been blind and still picked him out of a crowd. She'd held his clothes to her face and breathed in deeply. She'd held him close in her arms and buried her face in his thick black hair. When he was young, he smelled of cut grass and pine trees, band-aids and hydrogen peroxide, strawberry Kool-Aid and Ivory soap. As he grew older, he smelled of Old Spice and dirty tennis shoes, sec-ondhand smoke and ocean, pepperoni pizza and musty libraries.

"He's here," Daniel said, nearly pleading now. "I know it."

Olivia heard the obvious fear and confusion in her husband's voice. She had not often heard him sound so defenseless. She went to his side, touched his face.

"It's okay, it's okay," she whispered. "Go back to sleep."

Daniel pointed at the place where John had been standing.

"Right there," Daniel said. "He was right there."

Olivia looked at the spot. She wanted to see John standing there. She wanted it so much that he almost appeared. As if John was struggling to step from another world into this one, a sliver of light floated there at the foot of the bed. Olivia could see it, and knew that it was an illusion, an odd moment of moonlight, the afterimage of the closet's bright lamp. But she wanted to believe in it.

"Right there," Daniel whispered as Olivia gently pushed him onto his back.

"I know, I know," she said as Daniel closed his eyes and fell back to sleep.

Wide awake now, she walked downstairs into the kitchen for a glass of milk. She opened the fridge and saw that the leftover roast had been cut into. She then saw the carving knife dropped carelessly into the sink. Daniel's midnight snack. No wonder he was dreaming, Olivia thought as she washed the knife and replaced it in the cutting block.

14

Blank Pages

Wilson woke slowly, keeping his eyes closed even as he drifted into consciousness. The clock radio beside the bed was playing a song about fire and rain. Sunlight filtered softly through his closed eyelids, creating a fireworks display. The next-door neighbor's dog barked through the thin walls of the apartment complex. No pets allowed, but Wilson did not mind the dog. He had often considered getting a dog himself. The garbage truck two blocks away rumbled through gears. The smell of eggs and hamburger from the apartment below him. A mother and father, two boys, down there in such a small space, a one-bedroom only a little larger than Wilson's studio. They were never loud, never bothersome. Wilson heard only the faint metallic music of the boys' video game, Nintendo or some such thing. The mother, Janice, picked up Wilson's mail when he was away, though he rarely was. She would deliver it to him neatly wrapped in one of those huge rubber bands that seem to have no other use than wrapping up large bundles of mail. He wondered how Janice fit her husband, two sons, all the eggs and hamburger, and those huge rubber bands into that little apartment.

He remembered other mornings, waking up, wondering which foster parents were keeping him, surrounding him with their space. He often forgot. One day the O'Gradys' large house, and then he was in the Smith's tiny place the next morning, waking up in the same bed with Stuart Smith, who wet the bed. No. Wilson wet the bed but always blamed it on Stuart. After he moved from the Smith house, Wilson slept alone and could not blame it on anybody else. The Johnsons were kind and considerate about Wilson's bed-wetting. Mrs. Johnson slipped a shower curtain between the sheets and mattress when she made the bed, and washed the soiled sheets without saying a word. The Sheldons were cruel. Mr. Sheldon shamed him. Mrs. Sheldon made him wash the sheets himself by hand. Some nights, he was forced to sleep in the bathtub, without blankets, sheets, or pillow, because he had ruined so many. The Hawkinses simply made him sleep in the same wet sheets night after night. The Crowleys locked him in a dark closet for hours at a time.

As a teenager, Wilson had learned to control his bladder on most nights. But when he did wet his bed, he woke up early and washed the sheets. During sleep-overs with friends, he stayed awake all night, terrified to fall asleep. While living with the Lambeers, he'd once fallen asleep on the floor during an overnight birthday party and stained a shag carpet. His new friends had promptly and completely ostracized him after that. Alone and frightened, he made friends with family pets, and if those family pets sometimes ignored him, Wilson kicked them. Their yelps of pain made him feel better. Or he led the dogs and cats miles away from the houses, tied them to traffic signs, and walked away. They came back, or they didn't. Wilson had once set a bowl of antifreeze in front of a family dog and watched happily as the dog lapped it up.

Now, as an adult, Wilson tried to forget all that, but once in a while he still woke up with a start, worried that he'd wet the bed yet again. He'd woken up that morning, touched his crotch and the sheets beneath him, and breathed a sigh of relief. He'd been up late working on his novel, *Indian Killer*. With his other novels, he usually wrote about five pages a day, but he had managed to fill only a single page of *Indian Killer* before he forced himself to bed at 3 A.M. He'd only written ten very rough pages since he had talked to the desk sergeant about the killings. Up late every night, trying to finish. So much pressure, so many monsters. Wilson wondered about a woman, a wife, calling him to bed. Would she have let him stay up until three in the morning? He was frightened by the thought, by a woman. He thought of Beautiful Mary pushing him into that doorway, how she held his penis with her callused hand. He saw her scarred face and her dead eyes. He trembled at the memory and wondered if he would sleep. As it was, Wilson crawled into cold sheets and lay there wide awake for hours before sleep surprised him and dragged him off into the dark. He had never remembered his dreams very well, but last night, he knew he had fought off a variety of faceless monsters. Then he had dreamed about the murders. To his surprise, Wilson had dreamed of David Rogers's face as a bullet passed through his brain, had seen the blood fountain from Justin Summers's belly, had heard the muffled cries of Mark Jones. Now Wilson's arms and legs felt sore.

Wilson kept his eyes closed. He ran his hands over his body, searching for strange bumps and growths. He was getting to be that age and had to be more careful. Any change, however slight, was cause for concern. No pain, nothing new there, no growths, no tumors, no chemotherapy, no hair falling out, no funeral with his fellow officers in their dress blues telling funny stories and outright lies about his worth as a human being.

Wilson opened his eyes. He was hungry. He slid out of bed, stepped into clean blue slippers, went to the bathroom, and washed his face. The newspaper was waiting for him just outside his front door. The delivery guy always folded it strangely. It must have something to do with the union, Wilson thought. He thought that every

morning. He read the front-page headlines about the Indian Killer as
he walked over to the little kitchen area, poured Grape-Nuts and one-
percent into one of his two bowls, pulled one of his spoons from the
drawer, and sat down to eat.

Along with speculation about the identity of the Indian Killer
came the disturbing news of several racially motivated attacks. An
Indian man had been attacked on the Burke-Gilman Trail by three
masked men swinging baseball bats. An Indian couple had been brutally beaten by those masked men and were now in the hospital with
fractured skulls and other injuries.

Wilson finished the newspaper and breakfast, washed the
bowl and spoon, and dressed. He had work to do. He combed his
hair, brushed his teeth, locked the apartment door behind him, and
caught a bus downtown to Occidental Park in Pioneer Square. It had
been more than ten years since he'd walked a beat in the Square. But
he knew the street where the homeless Indians still hung out, and
they could have some answers.

He stepped off the bus a couple blocks away from Occidental Park and heard the music. It was a Thursday. Wilson remembered
that the Pioneer Square Business Owners Committee had decided,
whatever the weather, to hold outdoor concerts in Occidental Park
every Thursday at noon. It was not much of a park, one city block
filled with benches and bad publicly funded sculpture. No grass and
no flowers, just red brick pavement covered with cigarette butts and
graffiti. Skinny trees grew at regular intervals. The merchants had
convinced the city that holding concerts in the park would attract
more tourists to the downtown area, but there was a problem. Occidental Park was a gathering place for dozens of homeless people.
So every Thursday morning around ten, the Seattle Police Department quietly drove the homeless out of the park. By noon, it would
be filled with tourists. Around one in the afternoon, the homeless
would begin filtering back in. By five, the park would once again
belong to the street people.

Wilson walked into the park just as the street people were starting to return. Due to the Indian Killer threat, police patrols had been increased, and five cops walked through the park. Some band played an unidentifiable mix of trumpets, piano, strange-looking guitars, and voices. Everybody in the band was white. One homeless white guy in a wheelchair had rolled himself right next to the stage. He was loudly singing along with the band. The musicians gave him angry looks, but the homeless guy was probably a better singer than any of them. Wilson watched that scene for a while, but he was looking for Indians. A few dozen Indians were regulars in and around Pioneer Square, as Indians had been when Wilson was a rookie cop. Some of those walking slowly in the Square were the sons and daughters of Indians from Wilson's youth.

A local phone company had set up a promotional display at the south end of the park. Anyone could make a free three-minute long-distance call to anywhere in the country. All people had to do was to leave their names and current phone numbers, so they could be subjected to dozens of calls from minimum-wage telephone solicitors. There were six telephones and a pile of directories. A smiling woman answered questions.

Wilson sat on a bench near the telephones. For a while, he watched tourists surprising people back home. One vacationing man made an anonymous semi-obscene phone call to his boss back in Wisconsin. Amused and bored at the same time, Wilson was about to leave when he noticed an Indian man leaning against a tree about twenty feet from the phones. He was obviously homeless. Dressed in dirty clothes, shoes taped together, broken veins and deep creases crossing his face. The Indian might have been twenty or fifty. There was no way of knowing for sure. Slowly, the Indian man made his way closer to the phones. Wilson watched him. The Indian stood next to a traveling salesman making a call home to his wife. Wilson stood up and carefully walked closer. He did not want to scare the Indian guy away. Wilson felt he still looked like a cop.

"Yeah, it's been fun," said the salesman into the telephone. "It's been raining a little, but not like they say. I could see the mountains. Yeah, this Indian Killer thing is going on. No, I'm not worried. You know how it is."

As the businessman talked, the Indian moved closer to the phone. Wilson moved closer, too. The Indian smelled bad. The businessman wrinkled his nose, finished his conversation, hung up the phone. He looked at the Indian with disdain, and then quickly walked away. The Indian picked up the phone and held it to his ear.

"Can I help you, sir?" asked the telephone woman. She looked at the Indian as if he were contagious. She said "sir" like anybody else would have said "asshole." She wondered if he was the Indian Killer, but decided this man couldn't have hurt anyone in his condition.

"I want to make a call," said the Indian.

"And where might you be calling?" asked the telephone woman.

"Home," said the Indian. "My reservation."

"And where, precisely, is your reservation, sir?"

"Montana."

The telephone woman assessed him. This promotion was certainly not targeted at him. But she was just a temporary employee anyway, and who wants to get into an argument with a homeless Indian in downtown Seattle? She read from her list of questions.

"Sir, who's your current long-distance carrier?"

"What?" asked the Indian.

"Who's your current long-distance carrier?"

"Oh. The Moccasin Telegraph."

"Are you happy with their service?"

"You bet. They're loud and proud."

"And what other long-distance carriers have you had?"

"Oh. You mean like smoke signals?"

"Sure, like smoke signals."

"Well, then, I had smoke signals."

"And were you happy with their service?"

"Damn right I was."

"Have you ever employed Pacific Sun as your long-distance carrier?"

"No, who's that?"

"We're Pacific Sun, sir. Would you ever consider using our service?"

"Sure."

"Okay, then," said the telephone woman as she handed the Indian a clipboard and pen. "Sign here and fill in your address and current phone number here."

"No problem," said the Indian as he filled out the form with bogus information.

"Use that phone there," the telephone woman said. "You've got three minutes."

Amazed, Wilson watched as the Indian dialed the telephone, surprised the telephone woman had played along. The Indian closed his eyes in concentration, slowly pulling each digit from some phone number in his past. Wilson wanted to know who the Indian was calling. A grandmother? Parents? Lover?

As Wilson edged closer and eavesdropped on the conversation, Marie Polatkin watched it all from across the street. She was sitting in her sandwich van, waiting for the concert to end. The ten-year-old van was white, with "Seattle Open Heart Mission" painted crudely on both sides. Inside the van, there was a driver's seat, a passenger seat, and a dozen bakery racks, enough to hold hundreds of sandwiches.

Marie had been watching Wilson since he first walked into the park. She had recognized him from the author photograph on the back of his book she'd been forced to study in her Native American literature class. Dr. Mather had told the class that Wilson was going to be giving a public reading at the Elliott Bay Book Company soon, and he was giving extra credit to anybody who attended. Marie planned to go, but she certainly wasn't going to sit quietly and listen to Wilson tell lies. She had read some interview where Wilson had proudly revealed that his great-grandfather or uncle or somebody had a little Indian blood. She couldn't understand the gall of such people. After all, she had a little bit of white blood, but that damn sure did not make her white. She looked in the rearview mirror of the van and saw what anyone would see reflected, an Indian woman. Dark eyes and hair, brown skin. She could not be white if she wanted to be white. And she had wanted to be white more than once. When she was nine years old, sitting on the front porch, she had rubbed her face with a piece of her dad's sandpaper, trying to get rid of her color. Her skin was raw and bloody when she quit, still Indian. Now she was proud of being Indian, but it wasn't a simple feeling. In the eyes of the white world, any Indian woman was the same as all other Indian women. Only white people got to be individuals. They could be anybody they wanted to be. White people, especially those with the most minute amount of tribal blood, thought they became Indian just by saying they were Indian. A number of those pretend Indians called themselves mixed-bloods and wrote books about the pain of living in both the Indian and white worlds. Those mixed-blood writers never admitted their pale skin was a luxury. After all, Marie couldn't dress up like a white woman when she went to job interviews. But a mixed-blood writer could put on a buckskin jacket, a few turquoise rings, braid his hair, and he'd suddenly be an Indian. Those mixed-bloods could choose to be Indian or white, depending on the social or business situation. Marie never had the opportunity to make that choice. She was a brown baby at birth, born to a brown mother and brown father.

"Vulture," Marie said to herself as she watched Wilson inch closer to the Indian man on the phone. Marie knew he was King, a Flathead from Arlee, Montana. Jesus, Marie thought, if that white guy gets any closer to King, they're going to be dancing.

"Nah, I'm okay," King said to the person on the other end of the phone line. "Yeah, been saving up some coins. Thinking about coming back home, you know?"

King had left the reservation in 1980 to attend college and become a teacher. He had made it through one semester before he ran out of money. Too ashamed to return to the reservation, he'd worked on a fishing boat for a few years, then was struck by a hit-and-run driver while on shore leave. Too injured to work, without access to disability or workers' compensation, King had been homeless for most of the last ten years.

"Sir," said the telephone woman. "Your three minutes are up. We have to close up shop."

"Okay, okay," King told the woman, then said a few more words into the phone and quietly hung up. He cleared his throat, blinked back tears, and walked away.

Wilson began to picture the Indian Killer using the free telephones. But who would he call? An ancient ancestor, somebody from the sixteenth or seventeenth century, a wise old medicine man? Maybe a medicine man who was murdered by white people. The medicine man wants the Indian Killer to get revenge. Wilson cursed himself for not bringing along a notebook. Walking north out of the park, he hoped he could catch the next bus home to write this down.

With head low and shoulders hunched, King walked south across the street toward the sandwich van. His telephone call had been a failure. He had talked to a stranger, a young boy, maybe fourteen. An Indian stranger, but still a stranger. King had dialed that number hoping to hear his sister on the other end of the line, but it was some other Indian. It was a number on the Flathead Reservation, King's rez, but it wasn't his family's number. A Flathead boy answered but did not know if any of King's relatives still lived on the reservation. Maybe all of his relatives had left. Disappeared, or died. The Indian boy had been polite and had listened to King rattle on for three minutes. The boy had even asked about King's health. Somebody had taught that little Flathead boy how to be a good Indian.

"Hey, King," said Marie. She was leaning out the window of her van, holding a couple of sandwiches. Her glasses were slipping off the bridge of her nose, but she couldn't do much about it with sandwiches in one hand, the other hand clutching the steering wheel as she leaned out the window.

"Marie," said King. "What kind you got?"

"Ham and cheese, turkey and Swiss. And peanut butter and jelly."

"Jeez, ain't had P.B. and J. in a long time."

"How long?"

"A long time," said King, stretching out the vowel sounds.

"Well," said Marie. "Come sit in the truck with me. I can't feed anybody until the band leaves anyhow. Give me some company, enit?"

"Enit," said King. He climbed into the cab. He smelled bad, but Marie was almost used to it. The band played horrible music for another hour, as the tourists left the park by twos and threes. Marie gave sandwiches to a few men and women who recognized the van. Clouds arrived. Rain fell. A light rain. Enough to make you consider a heavier coat, but not enough to make you wear one. The tourists were gone; the homeless had returned. Marie wanted, just once, to have enough sandwiches. There were never enough sandwiches. King kept telling her stories about his reservation and she kept smiling.

15

Mark Jones

Mark Jones was sure he was alone in the dark place. He listened for the killer, and heard only his own breathing. Mark was very young, only six years old, but he was smart. He knew the killer would never let him leave.

A few hours, or days, or weeks earlier, the killer had cut a piece from Mark's pajamas. When the killer had first started cutting, Mark had screamed, thinking he was going to die. But the killer hadn't hurt him at all, had just taken the pajama piece and left Mark alone in the dark place. Mark had cried at the damage to his Daredevil pajamas. The blind superhero who didn't need light to see. Mark wished he could see in the dark.

As frightened as he was, Mark somehow found the strength and courage to stand. With his hands bound and his mouth gagged, Mark shuffled through the room, trying to find a door, an escape. He didn't want to make any noise. He wanted to be as silent as the killer. Mark searched. He stumbled, staggered, and finally fell. As he fell, he screamed through his gag.

16

The Last Precinct

Wilson drank only milk at The Last Precinct, a cop hangout in downtown Seattle. It was a small place, one room with ten tables, forty chairs, and a jukebox. Nobody ever sat at the bar. The men's and women's bathrooms were used interchangeably, since the patrons were rarely women. The cops tended to segregate themselves by beat, homicide detectives sharing one table, narcs another. The vice squad took up half the place, and a few patrol cops sat in a corner. But whatever their beats, the men were loud and drunk. The drinks were cheap and strong. Wilson felt no need to sit with a certain group, or to get drunk. Let the others drink themselves stupid. Wilson understood that need, but would not allow himself to lose control.

This evening, Wilson sat with Randy Peone, a patrol cop from downtown, who was seriously considering a change of careers; Bobby, a SWAT sharpshooter with ulcers; and Terrible Ted, an especially drunk and belligerent homicide detective.

"Look at us," said Ted, waving his huge arms to show surprise at the group around the table. "We got a Mick, a Wop, a Kraut, and a fucking Indian."

"Indian?" asked Bobby. "Who's Indian?"

"Wilson's a fucking Indian," said Ted. "What? Apache or something, right, Wilson?"

Smiling, Wilson shook his head.

Bobby studied Wilson's features in the dark of the bar.

"Jesus," said Bobby. "You don't look Injun. You look like an American to me."

"He's got some Indian blood in the woodpile, don't you?" asked Ted. "Yeah, his grandmother liked her some dark meat."

Wilson just smiled.

"You know about that scalping?" asked Ted. He leaned awkwardly over the table.

Wilson stopped smiling and said, "Yeah, you working on it?"

"Nah, George has got it," said Ted. "Why? You hear anything?"

"Not much," said Wilson.

"I thought you might have," said Ted. "You being an Indian and all. I hear you fuckers tell each other everything."

"Hey, Wilson," said Peone, trying to change the subject. "You're going to be appearing at some bookstore?"

"Yeah," said Wilson. "At Elliott Bay Book Company tomorrow night. You should come."

Peone laughed.

"No thanks," said Peone. "I ain't into that stuff. You working on a new book these days?"

Bobby and Peone waited for Wilson's answer. Ted snorted dismissively. Wilson sipped at his milk before he spoke.

"Yeah, it's about the Indian Killer."

"No shit," said Peone.

Terrible Ted was suddenly interested.

"Where you getting your information?" he asked, leaning forward. His beer nearly tipped over but Bobby reached out and saved it.

"Here and there. Just been talking to some Indians, you know? It's all fiction."

"What are you trying to find?" asked Ted.

"Shit," said Peone. "What you getting so testy for, Ted? You think Wilson killed those people?"

Everybody laughed, except Terrible Ted.

"He's messing with a current investigation," said Ted. "He ain't no cop anymore. He wasn't much of a cop when he was a cop. He's just a goddamn writer."

Wilson and Ted glared across the table at each other. Peone ordered another round in an attempt to calm everybody down.

"Hey," said Bobby. "Did you hear the joke about how the Indian boy got his name?"

"Listen," Wilson said to Ted. "I'm not messing with your investigation. I'm just talking to Indians a little bit. It doesn't mean anything."

"It means something," said Ted. "An Indian is out there killing people and you're talking to Indians. That means something."

"How do you know an Indian did it?" asked Wilson. "Because of the scalping? Shit, anybody who ever watched Western movies knows about scalping."

"It's more than that," said Ted. "We know it's an Indian."

"You sure?" asked Wilson. "How do you know it isn't somebody pretending to be Indian."

"We know, we know," said Ted.

"Yeah," said Bobby, continuing his joke. "So this Indian boy says to his mom, 'Mom, how do Indians get their names?' His mother says, 'Indians are named after the first thing their mothers see after giving birth. Like with your brother, I looked outside the tepee after giving birth to him, and saw three antelope running. That's why your brother is named Running Antelope.'"

The waitress, Chloe, arrived with drinks. She was tall and beautiful and hated cops.

"Hey, Chloe," said Ted. "You ever fucked an Indian?"

Chloe looked at Ted with as much boredom as she could manage.

"No, really," said Ted. "I want to know. I mean, are they animals or what? Were you ever scared they was going to kill you?"

Chloe silently took five dollars from the pile of money in front of Ted and walked away.

"She wants me," said Ted, smiling. He stared hard at Wilson, who was getting very nervous. Peone shoved a new beer at Ted.

"Hey, Ted," said Peone. "Drink up."

"And then," said Bobby, desperately trying to finish his joke. "His mother said, 'When I gave birth to your sister, I saw an eagle flying near the sun, so I named her Burning Eagle. That's how Indians name their children. Why do you ask such questions, Two Dogs Fucking?'"

Bobby laughed loudly at his own joke. Terrible Ted and Wilson continued to stare at each other. Peone felt his stomach burning. He figured he was going to have to break up a fight soon. But Wilson and Ted were both forty pounds overweight, so the match wouldn't take long. It would be just two more fat cops slugging it out in The Last Precinct. They would bruise up their knuckles a bit and then be arm-in-arm an hour later. Best friends. Just like grade-school boys after a tussle at recess.

"You know," said Ted. "I hate Indians."

Peone forced a laugh and slapped Ted on the back. Ted ignored him.

"They smell," continued Ted. "They're fucking drunks and welfare cheats. They ain't got no jobs. They're lazy as shit."

Wilson was suddenly angry and scared at the same time.

"You don't know anything about Indians," said Wilson.

"I know what some Indian did to that kid. Just about cut off the top of his head. And left two bloody owl feathers."

"An owl?" asked Wilson.

"Yeah, an owl!" shouted Ted, standing and spilling beer everywhere. "You think I'm stupid? You think I don't know about Indians? You don't believe me?"

Wilson leaned back in his chair, out of Ted's reach. He slid his hand inside his jacket, kept it there.

"What?" screamed Ted, noticing Wilson's move. "You going to pull your piece on me? Go for it, you fucker!"

Peone and Bobby both stood and held Ted back.

"Hey, hey," said Peone. "Take it easy, Ted, take it easy."

Wilson stood up and stared at Ted.

"You fucking Indian lover!" shouted Ted. The whole bar watched, eager for a fight, a violent release of stress.

"Hey," Peone said to Wilson. "Why don't you just go on home?"

Wilson nodded his head and headed for the door. Ted, wanting to chase Wilson down, fought against Peone and Bobby.

"Fucker!" shouted Ted as Wilson left the bar and walked into a foggy evening. It was cold. Wilson shoved his hands deep into his pockets and walked to his truck. His hands were shaking with anger as he unlocked the door and hopped inside.

"Shit," he whispered to himself and leaned his head against the steering wheel. He never understood why people hated Indians as much as they did. Terrible Ted had probably never talked to any Indians he wasn't arresting at the time. Wilson remembered Beautiful Mary, who had been almost forgotten because she was an Indian. He remembered how she had lain behind the Dumpster beneath the Viaduct. Blood everywhere. A broken bottle tossed in the Dumpster. Her eyes still open. Nobody in the police department cared when an Indian was killed, but everybody cared now that an Indian might be killing white men. Wilson wondered what would happen when the press found out more about the murders.

Wilson started his pickup and pulled away from the curb. He drove up Denny Way to Broadway on Capitol Hill. On Broadway, runaway kids huddled in doorways, smoking cigarette butts. Aspiring rock stars strummed air guitars in front of Mexican restaurants. A couple of homeless men sat in front of the all-night supermarket. Gay and lesbian couples strolled together, safer in this neighborhood than in any other in Seattle. An illegal firework lit up the sky, a traffic signal blinked yellow. A German shepherd with a red bandanna tied around its neck yawned. A drunk man tried to parallel park his Honda. How many people knew that an Indian might be killing white men?

Wilson thought about the Indian Killer, the owl and feathers. The owl was a messenger of death, of evil. Wilson had read about Native American perceptions of the owl. If you were visited by an owl, that meant you were going to die soon. Wilson had always been fascinated by owls. He often visited the owls in the Woodland Park Zoo, and they often came to visit him in his dreams.

In one recurring dream, Wilson is riding with his real parents in a big car. They are all quiet and content. Hank Williams on the radio. Wilson looks up at his father, who is driving and smoking a cigar. Wilson's father looks back and smiles around the cigar. It is a beautiful moment. Wilson's mother is humming along with the radio. She is small and pale, ethereal in the darkness of the car. Then the family looks ahead, headlights illuminating the dark road. Wilson's father inhales and exhales smoke. Suddenly, an owl floats directly in front of the car. Wilson's father has no time to hit the brakes. Wilson can only begin the first note of a scream when the owl crashes through the windshield. Wilson always wakes up at that moment in the dream.

Wilson drove slowly down Broadway. He still missed his father, who had never smoked a cigar in his life. He missed his mother.

Wilson turned on the radio. Truck Schultz, the homegrown conservative talk-show host, was pontificating.

"Citizens, we need to do something about this illegitimacy rate," said Truck. "This country is full of welfare babies giving birth to welfare babies. Citizens, we need to stop this cycle of poverty. And believe me, I've got the solution. You see, it's all about education. The smart kids aren't getting pregnant. How many honor students are getting pregnant? None. Well, citizens, I propose that we sterilize any girl whose I.Q. is below one hundred.

"Now, seriously, citizens. I think this program is going to work. Not only will we decrease the illegitimacy rate, but we'll also stop the dumbing down of America. Dumb girls will not give birth to dumb babies. Evil girls will not give birth to evil babies. Indian women will not give birth to Indian Killers. What do you think, citizens? Why don't you give me a call at 1-800-555-TRUK and tell me how much you agree with me."

17

Deconstruction

"The Indian Killer," began Dr. Mather, "is an inevitable creation of capitalism. A capitalistic society will necessarily create an underclass of powerless workers and an overclass of powerful elite. As the economic and social distance between the worker and elite increases, the possibility of an underclass revolution increases proportionally. The Indian Killer is, in fact, a revolutionary construct."

Dr. Mather was wearing a huge bandage on his forehead. A few of the students wondered aloud if he'd been attacked by the Indian Killer, but Marie Polatkin knew that wasn't true. None of them knew that Mather had knocked himself silly by running into a low overhang in the Anthropology Building basement.

"The kidnapping of Mark Jones is actually a bold, albeit cowardly, metaphor for the Indian condition. Indian people have had their culture, their children, metaphorically stolen by European-American colonization. And now, this Indian Killer has physically and metaphorically stolen a European-American child."

Marie raised her hand. She had been tolerating Dr. Clarence Mather's babble for far too long. There were only ten students in the Introduction to Native American Literature class that evening. The news of the Indian Killer had scared the rest of them away, Marie supposed. Just like white people, worried that some killer Indian was going to storm a university classroom.

"Now," continued Dr. Mather, ignoring Marie's raised hand. "If we compare the construct of the Indian Killer with Jack Wilson's fictional alter ego, Aristotle Little Hawk, we can begin to more fully understand the revolutionary nature of Mr. Wilson's mystery novels. The Indian Killer and Little Hawk are twentieth-century manifestations of the classic Indian warrior. One, the Indian Killer, is wild and untamed, à la Geronimo, while the other, Little Hawk, is apparently tamed and civilized, a hangs-around-the-fort Indian, if you will, but is, in fact, actually working within the system in his efforts to disrupt it."

"That's bull!" shouted Marie.

"I take it that you have something to add to our discussion, Ms. Polatkin."

"Yeah, I'm wondering why you think you know so much about Indians."

"I hardly think I have to prove myself to you, Ms. Polatkin."

"Have you ever lived on a reservation?"

"I have spent time on many reservations."

"Yeah, but have you ever *lived* on a reservation?"

"I lived on the Navajo Indian Reservation for three months."

"Three months, huh? You must have learned so much. You must know so much about our revolutionary tendencies."

"Ms. Polatkin, I'll have you know that I was actively involved with the American Indian Movement during the late sixties and early seventies. I smuggled food to the Indians at Wounded Knee."

"Yeah, and you had the money to buy the food that you smuggled in there, didn't you?"

"Could I ask you what you're trying to accomplish, Ms. Polatkin?"

"Well, I'm just sick and tired of people like you. You think you know more about being Indian than Indians do, don't you? Just because you read all those books about Indians, most of them written by white people. By guys like Jack Wilson."

"Jack Wilson is a Shilshomish Indian, Ms. Polatkin."

"Sure he is. He's quite the Indian warrior, isn't he? Just like the Indian Killer, huh? A big buck of an Indian man, right? I mean, what makes you think the Indian Killer is Indian anyway?"

"The scalping, of course."

"You think Indians are the only ones who know how to use a knife? And do you think Indian *men* are the only ones who know how to use a knife? I'm pretty good with a knife. I bet even you, the adopted Lakota that you are, can wield a pretty fair blade yourself, enit? Who's to say I'm not the Indian Killer? Who's to say you're not the Indian Killer?

"I mean, calling him the Indian Killer doesn't make any sense, does it? If it was an Indian doing the killing, then wouldn't he be called the Killer Indian? I mean, Custer was an Indian killer, not a killer Indian. How, about you, Doc, are you an Indian killer?"

"Ms. Polatkin, I beg your pardon." Dr. Mather laughed nervously. "I am certainly no murderer."

"Are you scared of me, Dr. Mather?"

"Of course not."

"Oh, I think you are. I'm not quite the revolutionary construct you had in mind, am I?"

"Ms. Polatkin, I wish . . . I wish you'd take your . . . your seat," he stammered. "So we may continue with our class."

"I'm not an Indian warrior chief. I'm not some demure little Indian woman healer talking spider this, spider that, am I? I'm not babbling about the four directions. Or the two-legged, four-legged, and winged. I'm talking like a twentieth-century Indian woman.

Hell, a twenty-first-century Indian, and you can't handle it, you wimp."

"Ms. Polatkin, I'm going to have to ask you to leave the classroom. In fact, I strongly suggest that you drop this class entirely."

Marie turned away from Dr. Mather, gathered her books, and headed for the door.

"Dr. Mather," she said before she left. "An Indian man is not doing these killings."

18

Cousins

John knew the darkness provided safety for Indians now. But long ago, Indians had been afraid of the darkness. During the long, moonless nights, they had huddled together inside dark caves and had trembled when terrible animals waged war on each other outside. Often, those horrible creatures would find the cave and carry off one of the weakest members of the tribe. Indians had been prey. This had gone on, night after night, for centuries. Then some primitive genius had discovered the power of fire, that bright, white flame. Fire pushed back the darkness and kept the animals at bay. During the night, Indians still huddled together in their caves, but a fire constantly burned at the cave's mouth. At first, those small white flames were a part of the tribe. Neither male nor female, neither old nor young. Neither completely utilitarian nor absolutely sacred. Still, despite the Indians' best efforts, the flames began to rebel. At first, in small ways, by refusing to burn. Then, by scorching a finger or hand. And finally,

by pulling a careless child into their white-hot mouths and swallow-
ing it whole. And always, always, the flames were growing in number and size. John knew they became candles, then lamps, then cities
of lamps. Those white flames re-created themselves in the image of
Indians. They grew arms and legs, eyes and hair, but they could never
make themselves dark. They built dams that sucked white light from
the rivers, and wires, crackling with white light, that connected
houses, and houses filled with thousands of white lights. Those white
flames could build anything. They tore everything down and rebuilt
it in their image. Bright lights everywhere, cities casting their lights
upward until the dark sky could not be seen, animals with neon in
their eyes. But those white lights could not make themselves into
Indians. And those white lights envied the Indians' darkness. Their
white-hot jealously grew into hatred; hatred grew into rage. The
Indians became prey again, and now, for hundreds of years, the Indians have been burned, then dropped to the ground as piles of smol-
dering rags. Reduced to red ash that floats in the wind.

　　Now, as John walked through downtown Seattle, as white
people walked wide circles around him, as they crossed busy streets
to avoid him, as they pointed at him and whispered behind their hands,
he began to see them as they truly were. White flames. A family of
white flames, mother, father, daughter, son. A flame riding a bicycle.
Flames crowding onto the Bainbridge Island ferry. A flame playing a
battered guitar. Flames sitting in the cars passing by. One flame leaning out a pickup window, shouting obscenities at John. He wondered
if Father Duncan, before he disappeared in the desert, had begun to
see people as they truly were. Had Father Duncan, in his beautiful
black robe, looked into the mirror and seen the white flame dancing
at his neck? There were flames everywhere in downtown Seattle.
Three large white flames surrounding a tiny, old Indian woman beneath the Alaskan Way Viaduct.

　　"Hey, Indian Killer," the brightest flame taunted the old
woman, who wore dark sunglasses and carried a white cane. "Come

on, Indian Killer, come on. Show me how tough you are. Kill me, kill me."

The old woman had no escape. Painfully skinny, her elbows and knees larger than her arm and leg muscles, her head and feet large and out of proportion, she looked more manufactured than human. She raised her fists to the three white flames surrounding her.

"Get away from me!" shouted the old woman. "I ain't done nothing to you!"

John easily pushed aside the three flames and stood beside the old woman. John faced the three flames. John, feeling as strong as water. The flames wavered in his presence. A small crowd had gathered to watch. Other flames. A few of them shouting protests.

The flame that burned brightest had to smile, raise his empty hands and clap them together. The old woman was startled, but John didn't react. The flame laughed. He pointed at John, and then all three flames piled into a pickup and drove away. The crowd of white flames that had gathered to watch soon dissipated.

"Hey, cousin," the old woman said to John. "You showed up just in time. I was about ready to hurt somebody."

"They're gone," John said.

"What tribe you are?" asked the old woman.

"Navajo."

"Ah, Nah-vee-joe, huh? N-a-v-a-j-o, " the old woman spelled. She sniffed at John. "Yeah, you do smell like the desert. You a long ways from home, enit?"

John didn't reply.

"You got some place to stay, Mr. Nah-vee-joe? Me, I've got lots of places to stay around here. All these white people think I'm homeless. But I ain't homeless. I'm Duwamish Indian. You see all this land around here." The old woman waved her arms around. "All of this, the city, the water, the mountains, it's all Duwamish land. Has been for thousands of years. I belong here, cousin. I'm the land-lady. And all these white people, even the rich ones living up in those penthouses, they're the homeless ones. Those white people are a long way from home, don't you think? Long way from E-u-r-o-p-e."

John looked at the white flames around them. Just a few now. It was getting late. He saw flames crossing an ocean of gasoline.

"Hey, cousin, what's your name?"

"John. John Smith."

"Well, John-John, you want a drink?"

John looked at the bottle wrapped in a brown paper bag. He was disappointed in the old woman.

"I don't drink," John said.

"Heck, John-John, it ain't a-l-c-o-h-o-l. It's water. Bottled water at that. You can't tell anymore what they put in the tap water, you know?"

John knew they could put poison in bottled as well as tap water, but he didn't want to scare the old woman.

"What's your name?" John asked.

"Can you keep a secret?"

"Yes."

"Well," she whispered. "My Christian name is Carlotta Lott, but my real name, my Indian name is . . ." The old woman sniffed the air to make sure nobody was close enough to hear. "My Indian name is . . . are you sure you can keep a secret?"

John nodded.

"Okay. My real name is Carlotta Lott."

John was confused. The old woman was laughing loudly. She clapped her hands, slapped her belly with unmitigated glee. John reached out and touched Carlotta's shoulder.

"John-John," said Carlotta, suddenly serious. "There's a big difference between what those white people think about Indians and what we know about us. A big d-i-f-f-e-r-e-n-c-e. And there's even a bigger difference between what Indians think about each other, and what you and I know about ourselves."

John released Carlotta's shoulder. She took off her sunglasses and John stared at her dead eyes that were as white as salt.

"You see, John-John, I think I know a little about you. I think I know a little of what you want. I can feel it in here." Carlotta touched her chest. "You got something special about you, enit?" Then lower and deeper, as if her voice were coming from a different place inside of her. "Real special."

John nodded. Carlotta reached into her pocket and pulled out a small, rusty knife. Just a small paring knife rescued from a restaurant Dumpster. The old woman found John's hand and folded his fingers around the knife handle.

"This is my magic," said Carlotta. "And I think you know about magic. There's good magic and there's bad magic. This knife is both."

John held the knife. It was small and pitiful.

"I think you know about the knife, don't you? K-n-i-f-e. Silent K, John-John, silent K."

John tried to give the knife back to the old woman. He didn't think he needed it.

"No, no, Mr. Nah-vee-joe, it's my gift to you. From a Duwamish Indian to a guest, a visitor." Carlotta bowed deeply. "You honor me with your presence. H-o-n-o-r."

"I have nothing for you," said John.

"Yes, yes, you do, your ears, John-John, your ears."

John touched both of his ears, one and then the other.

"Listen to me, John-John. I used to see. I have seen many things. Things that were good. Things that were bad. Things I wasn't supposed to see. We've been good to white people, enit? When they first came here, we was good to them, wasn't we? We taught them how to grow food. We taught them to keep warm. We was good hosts, enit? And then what did they do? They killed us.

"But we'll get back at them, John-John. I've got me a time machine. And I can show you how to use it. You can go back to that beach where Columbus first landed, you know? You can wait there for him, hidden in the sand or something. C-a-m-o-u-f-l-a-g-e. And when he gets on the sand, you can jump out of hiding and show him some magic, enit? Good magic, bad magic, it's all the same."

The old woman pointed in the general direction of the puny knife in John's hand.

"Magic, magic, magic," chanted the old woman. "You want to go back? You want to know how to use the time machine?"

"Yes."

The old woman stuck her right hand in her pocket. She wiggled it around as if searching for something.

"You want to see the time machine?" asked the old woman. "I got it in my pocket."

"Yes."

"You sure you want to see it? It's powerful. And once you see it, there ain't no going back. N-o."

"Yes."

The old woman whipped her hand out of her pocket and held it out to John. It was empty. John could see the dirty, brown skin, the four fingers and opposable thumb. John stared at Carlotta's empty hand, and then at the knife in his own hand, and understood.

19

The Aurora Avenue Massacre

"What's my name?" asked Reggie. He held a tape recorder in front of the white man.

"I don't know," sobbed the white man. He was on his knees while Ty and Harley held his arms at painful angles behind his back. They were all on the Indian Heritage High School football field, just a few blocks from Big Heart's Soda and Juice Bar. It was late. Loud traffic on Aurora Avenue to the west and Interstate 5 to the east. Reggie was recording all of it.

The white man had been camping on the football field, after having hitchhiked into town. He'd dropped out of college a few months earlier and had been exploring the country ever since. He had one hundred dollars in cash, two hundred in traveler's checks, three ripe bananas, a Jim Harrison novel, and various articles of clothing. Also, a sleeping bag, small one-man tent, first-aid kit, flashlight, portable radio, and an Eddie Bauer backpack.

"What's my name?" Reggie asked again.

"I don't know."

Reggie kicked the white man in the stomach. Hard enough to bruise, but not enough to cause permanent damage. Reggie was good at this. He looked down at the kneeling white man.

"Hurt him," Reggie signed to Harley.

Harley nodded and twisted the white man's arm. Howls of pain that Harley could not hear. Howls of pain that Reggie recorded and would listen to later.

"Now," Reggie said. "What the fuck is my name?"

"Please. Please stop. I don't know. I don't know."

"My name is Ira Hayes," Reggie said.

"Okay, okay," said the white man. "Your name is Ira Hayes."

"Yeah, you know I was one of those guys who raised the flag at Iwo Jima?"

"Iwo what?"

Reggie kicked the white man.

"Iwo Jima, asshole. An island in the Pacific. During World War Two. One of the bloodiest military exercises of all time. Thousands and thousands died. But I survived, man. I climbed to the top of Iwo Jima and helped plant that flag. I was a hero. And now I'm dead. You know how I died?"

"No."

Reggie kicked the white man again.

"You know how I died?"

"How?"

"Exposure. I fucking froze to death in a snowbank."

The white man looked up at Reggie, who then slapped him hard across the face. Reggie held the recorder close to the sobbing man.

"Why'd you let me freeze?" Reggie asked.

"I . . . I didn't."

Reggie slapped him again.

"Why'd you let me freeze?"

The white man shook his head. Reggie grabbed him by the hair.

"What's my name?"

"Ira Hayes."

Another slap.

"Wrong. What's my name?"

"Ira Hayes, Ira Hayes." The white man pleading now. Reggie slapped him twice.

"What's my name?"

"I don't know."

"Do it," Reggie said to Ty, and he twisted the white man's arm until something popped. The white man screamed into the tape recorder.

"Somebody's going to hear us," Ty said to Reggie, who then took a handkerchief out of his back pocket and shoved it into the white man's mouth.

"What's my name?" Reggie asked the white man, who could not respond intelligibly. Reggie slapped him.

"Shit, when you going to learn," Reggie spoke directly into the tape recorder. "My name is Black Kettle. And I'm alive right?"

The white man nodded agreement.

"Wrong," Reggie said and kicked him. "I'm dead."

The white man wept.

"Because you white bastards murdered me. You killed me on the Washita River in Oklahoma. You and that fucker Custer, remember?"

No response.

"Yeah, we were flying a U.S. flag above our village, remember? We saw you coming, your Seventh Cavalry, and my wife and I rode out to meet you, to ask for peace. And you shot us before we even spoke. Do you remember?

"And do you remember my camp on Sand Creek in Colorado four years earlier? Do you remember when you and Colonel John

Chivington rode on our camp. Once again, we were flying a U.S. flag, and a white flag. We had no weapons, none, not one rifle. We were mostly women, children, and old people. And you rode in on us and killed three hundred. Do you remember? What's my name?"

The white man wearily shook his head.

"It's Black Kettle, you fucker," said Reggie and punched the white man in the face, knocking him unconscious.

"Oh, shit," Reggie said into the tape recorder. "He's out."

"That's enough," signed Harley. "Let's get out of here."

Ty agreed.

"Listen," signed Reggie. "It's over when I say it's over."

Reggie shook the white man until he came to.

"What's your name?" Reggie asked him and he grunted something through his gag.

"No, that ain't it," said Reggie. "Your name is Truck Schultz."

The white man was skinny, with an unkempt goatee. He was extremely near-sighted but had lost his glasses somewhere during the struggle with Reggie, Ty, and Harley.

"Aren't you a white-trash asshole named Truck Schultz?" Reggie asked. "What do you think? You like that name?"

The white man shook his head.

"Really? You don't like that name? You are positive that's not your name? You sure?"

The white man nodded.

"Damn, you white guys look alike." He signed to Ty and Harley. "Don't they look alike?"

Ty and Harley nodded. Reggie kneeled down beside the white man.

"You ain't Truck Schultz, huh?" said Reggie. "Well, you look like one of those professor types. Are you a professor? I mean, with that fucking goatee, you look like a professor. Are you sure you're not? Speak into the mike, man."

The white man grunted and nodded his head.

"I'm really sorry," Reggie whispered. "I guess I confused you with someone else. Can you ever forgive me?"

The white man nodded.

"Really? That's so kind of you," said Reggie. "I mean, we're all human, right? And we make mistakes, don't we? I mean, we were looking for a white-trash asshole named Truck Schultz, and it looks like we got ourselves a whole different white-trash asshole, right?"

The white man vigorously nodded his head.

"Well, then," said Reggie. "Let's say we make a deal. How about I promise to let you go if you promise to keep all this between us. Does that sound okay?"

"Hm-huh, hmn-huh," the white man agreed through the hand-kerchief in his mouth.

"You promise?" Reggie asked as he dropped the tape recorder into a pocket. He then placed his hands on either side of the white man's face, leaned in close as if he was going to kiss him, and forced his thumbs into the white man's eyes. The white man screamed as Reggie dug into his eyes, searching for whatever existed behind them. The white man fainted from shock and pain. Stunned, Harley and Ty let go of the white man's arms and stepped back. The white man flopped facedown into the grass and did not move.

"What did you do?" Ty asked.

"I took his eyes," Reggie said, genuinely surprised by Ty's question.

Harley looked down at the white man's body, then at Ty and Reggie, and ran away. Ty soon followed, and Reggie kicked the white man once more before chasing after his friends.

20

The Elliott Bay Book Company

Wilson was excited about his reading, and worried that news of the Indian Killer would make the bookstore cancel. But Ray Simmons, the readings coordinator, who somehow found the time and energy to schedule over three hundred readings a year, had assured Wilson that it was going to happen. The Elliott Bay Book Company was a beautiful store in the heart of Pioneer Square, just a few blocks from the Alaskan Way Viaduct and the waters of Elliott Bay itself.

There was another side to the coin, though. Because of the proximity of the water, and because the Elliott Bay's basement was actually below sea level, rats had often been seen darting through the store. Wilson had never laid eyes on the rats but had heard rumors that they were often mistaken for small dogs. It was said that Elliott Bay's owners had once bought a small battalion of cats to take care of the rats. One night, after closing, they had released the cats into the store. When the store had opened early the next morning, the cats had disappeared. It was a wonderful rumor and, if true, more proof that Elliott Bay was a great bookstore. Wilson certainly would have hated it if rats lived in his building. Yet he believed the rats, or the rumors of rats, belonged at Elliott Bay, and gave the place mystery as well as beauty.

Wilson decided to take a taxi to the bookstore for his reading. It would save time and energy, he told himself, an excuse for arriving in as formal a manner as he could afford. Wilson, waiting outside his building when the cab pulled up, immediately recognized the driver, Eric. As an ex-cop, Wilson knew a lot of cab drivers, all kinds of emergency room doctors, and many bar owners.

"Hey, Wilson!" shouted Eric, who apparently had no control over the volume of his voice or any idea that he always yelled.

"Hey, Eric," said Wilson as he climbed into the cab.

"Where to?"

"Elliott Bay bookstore."

"So, you got a reading, huh?" asked Eric. He was a frustrated writer himself who found Wilson particularly interesting, although he had never told Wilson that. "You going to read from one of your old books or something new?"

"I don't know."

Eric and Wilson lapsed into silence for five dollars' worth of city streets, down Capitol Hill to Pioneer Square.

"Hey!" shouted Eric. "You hear about that Indian Killer?"

Wilson nodded.

"Three's the number, I guess! Two white guys and a little white boy! Indian Killer got them all!" shouted Eric. "It's about time!"

"The police don't think David Rogers was murdered by the Indian Killer."

"Well, whatever, it's about time!"

"What do you mean?"

"I mean, those Indians always get the raw end of the deal! It's about time for some payback, don't you think? I mean, there's all sort of stuff going on! One Indian guy got jumped by white guys with baseball bats! And an Indian couple were about killed by the same guys on Queen Anne Hill! They're in the hospital. One white guy got beat up by three Indians up on some football field!"

Wilson leaned back heavily in his seat.

"Hey!" said Eric. "You got some Indian blood, right?"

"Yes."

"Well!" said Eric. "Aren't you happy about this? I mean, it'll teach white people not to mess with Indians anymore! I mean, I'm a white guy and I'm not about to mess with Indians now! Not that I ever did to begin with! I mean, Indians are cool, don't you think?"

Wilson did not respond.

"Hey, Wilson!" said Eric after a long while. "You okay?"

Wilson did not even hear Eric's question. He was lost in his thoughts, wondering if he could finish his Indian Killer novel before some hack wrote a cheap paperback. Wilson could just imagine the cover of that hack book: an obscenely muscular Indian, bloody knife in his hand; a beautiful white woman in a ripped dress; a horse. It would be called *Savage Revenge* or *Apache Vengeance*. Whatever the hack book was called, Wilson knew it wouldn't be as serious as his.

Wilson was still thinking about his book when Eric pulled up in front of the Elliott Bay Book Company. A crowd of Indians was milling about at the entrance.

"Hey!" said Eric. "Looks like you're being protested!"

A dozen Indians marched in a circle. They carried picket signs that said things like WILSON IS A FRAUD and ONLY INDIANS SHOULD TELL INDIAN STORIES. A handful of non-Indian spectators had gathered to watch the protest. A few people crossed the picket line and entered the bookstore. A local news reporter was interviewing one particularly vocal Indian woman.

"Why exactly do you dislike Wilson's work?" asked the reporter, a generically handsome white man.

"Wilson is a fraud," said Marie Polatkin. "He claims to be Indian, yet has no documentation to prove it. His novels are dangerous and violent."

"Do you think his novels might have an influence on the Indian Killer?"

"I don't know," said Marie. "But I do think books like Wilson's actually commit violence against Indians."

Wilson paid Eric, stepped out of the cab, and walked toward the bookstore. He wanted to ignore the whole situation, but the reporter abandoned Marie and deftly intercepted him.

"Mr. Wilson," said the reporter. "Many people in the Indian community dispute your claim of being Indian. In fact, some think that your books may encourage violence. They say your books might be a prime motivating factor for the Indian Killer. How do you respond to that?"

"That's ridiculous," said Wilson. "I'm an ex-cop and I happen to be a member of the Indian community. I am a Shilshomish Indian."

"Bullshit, bullshit!" chanted the protesters.

Wilson tried to enter the store, but the reporter grabbed his elbow.

"Mr. Wilson," said the reporter. "These protestors have presented a petition signed by two hundred Indians that asks you to quit writing books about Indians. How do you feel about that?"

Wilson blinked, stunned by the petition.

"Well," he said, searching for words. "I don't really know. I mean, nobody has the right to tell me what I can or cannot write."

"There are two hundred Indians who disagree with that, and Marie Polatkin insists she can get hundreds more to sign her petition. How many signatures would be enough to make you quit, Mr. Wilson?"

"I have no comment," stammered Wilson as he broke free of the reporter and stumbled into the bookstore. He was reeling. How many would be enough? A hundred thousand? A million? What if every Indian in the country asked him to quit? He was a real Indian himself and had done all he could to help other real Indians. He was on their side. Wilson was dizzy with confusion as Ray Simmons escorted him downstairs, where ten fans waited for him.

Outside, the protest continued. Marie, pounding a drum, led the chants. Her voice was hoarse. Her shoulders and hands ached. She could not hit the drum any longer. As she handed it over to another protester, she noticed John Smith standing all by himself. Huge and obviously Indian, he was automatically a frightening part of the protest, even though he had no idea what was happening.

"John," said Marie and raised her hand.

He was wearing a clean T-shirt, blue jeans, and a black coat. He was clean-shaven and his hair was combed into careful braids. It was a good day for John.

"John," Marie said again as she walked up to him.

"It's me, Marie," she said.

"I know," he said. "You're protesting again."

"Yeah," said Marie, smiling. "Protesting this, protesting that."

The crowd swirled around them. John felt threatened.

"What are you protesting now?" asked John.

"Don't you know? This writer, Wilson, pretending to be an Indian? Writes mystery novels?"

John nodded, remembering that Olivia Smith had given him one of Wilson's books as a birthday gift. John had never read it. The book sat in one of the neat piles in John's room. Now, as Marie talked about Wilson, John saw the anger in her brown eyes.

"Wilson is a fraud! Wilson is a fraud!" chanted the crowd. When Marie raised a fist into the air and jointed the chant, John became fascinated. She was wearing red gloves, and he reached out and touched her clenched hand with his fingertip. Her fist felt hot. Marie grabbed John's hand and formed it into a fist. Suddenly, John's arm shot up, his fist above his head. He began to chant along.

"Wilson is a fraud! Wilson is a fraud!"

The protest lasted until the Indians got hungry. They drifted off in pairs, in groups of four or five. The spectators and news crew had left long before. Meanwhile, Wilson's reading had drawn a decent audience, mainly of people who wanted to see what the fuss was all about. Marie and John were sitting in her sandwich van outside the bookstore when Wilson poked his head out the door, looking for Eric, the taxi driver.

Marie spotted Wilson when the taxi pulled up and he jumped in, eager to get home. Marie decided to follow the cab. John didn't say a word.

"So!" Eric asked Wilson. "How did it go?"

"It was an adventure," said Wilson. His audience had peppered him with questions about the so-called Indian Killer: "Mr. Wilson, since you see so clearly into the Indian mind, I was wondering if you might know what this Indian Killer might be thinking?" "Don't you think the Indian Killer is just another sign that the American culture is spiritually bankrupt? Don't you think we all need to turn to the Indian religions in order to save our country?" "Are you going to write about the Indian Killer?"

The people had applauded when Wilson revealed that his next novel was going to be about the murders, and he had smiled at the applause. Then he realized that he should have kept his mouth shut. Now that his secret was out, other authors and publishers would surely confirm his worst fear and rush books into production.

Inside the sandwich van, Marie and John rode in silence. She was intent on following the taxi. She wanted to know where Wilson lived. She wanted to protest right outside his house. The police would come for sure, especially in light of this whole Indian Killer thing. That could be a big scene, all three local networks might show. John watched the taillights of the taxi. They reminded him of something he could not remember. It was a nagging feeling that hurt his head. His stomach growled loudly.

"You hungry?" asked Marie. "There might be a few sandwiches in the back. Help yourself."

John looked behind him and saw the metal racks that held the sandwiches. Other than the racks, the van was bare. John spotted a sandwich on the floor and picked it up. He worried that it might be poisoned.

"Did you make this?" John asked Marie.

"Yes."

John knew then that it could not be dangerous. He was hungry and wanted to eat it, but felt guilty because he had nothing to offer Marie in return.

"Go ahead," she said.

The sandwich tasted like smoke.

"Man," Marie said. "I hate this guy."

"Who?" asked John with a mouth full of bread and bologna.

"Wilson. He's a cannibal. No, he's not even eating his own kind. He's a scavenger. He's a maggot."

The sandwich suddenly tasted like anger.

"And there's this other guy, Dr. Clarence Mather. He's teaching my Native lit class, you know? He's one of those kind who thinks he knows everything about Indians. An Indian expert. Arrogant asshole."

John nodded. He remembered the night he had followed Marie as she had been following Mather.

"You were following your teacher," John said.

Marie stared at the taxi ahead of them.

"How do you know that?" she asked.

"I was following you."

"Why?"

"I don't know."

Marie seemed to accept that answer as being honest and decided she'd have to be more careful in the future.

"If you ask me," said Marie. "The wrong white guys are dying."

The sandwich soured. John quickly finished it and licked his fingers. He thought about Jack Wilson and Clarence Mather, and wondered how their fear would taste.

The taxi pulled up in front of Wilson's, and Marie pulled up right behind the taxi, her headlights filling the cab.

"Hey!" shouted Eric as he noticed the van. "I think we've got company!"

Wilson turned around in his seat. He could not see who was in the van because of its headlights. Eric reached under his seat and pulled out a sawed-off golf club, a one-iron. Wilson and Eric stepped out of the taxi at the same time. When Marie turned off her headlights, Wilson recognized her as the leader of the protest, Marla or Maria or something like that, but he couldn't quite see who was with her.

"What do you want?" screamed Eric, waving his golf club.

"It's those protesters," said Wilson.

"Come on out of there!" shouted Eric, "I'll give you something to protest!"

Marie smiled at the cab driver's bravado. He did not look like much of a fighter, or a golfer. John saw the club and closed his hands into fists. Just two white men. John knew he could hurt them.

"Come on!" shouted Eric.

John stepped out of the truck.

"No," said Marie, but John was already marching toward Wilson and Eric. The cab driver quickly backpedaled, but John saw that Wilson held his ground with a surprising lack of fear. Actually, Wilson was too shocked by John's obvious resemblance to his own hero, Aristotle Little Hawk, to be afraid. Wilson felt as if he'd brought Little Hawk to life through some kind of magic. Wilson had always felt magical, but he'd had no idea how much power he really possessed.

"Aristotle," said Wilson.

John knew about Aristotle. The philosopher was required knowledge for Catholic schoolboys. But he had no idea why this white man was talking about an ancient Greek while a crazy cab driver was swinging a tiny golf club. It was very confusing. John wondered if these white men were real.

So John reached out to touch Wilson, to test his reality. Eric suddenly found his courage and, screaming like a television Indian, charged John. Wilson heard the screams and reflexively fell to the ground. Eric swung his one-iron blindly at John, who snatched the club out of the air and took it away. Disarmed and terrified, Eric fell to the ground beside Wilson. John raised the club above his head and stepped toward the men. Wilson reached inside his jacket and John wondered if the white man had a weapon. Then Wilson relaxed and showed John both hands.

"John!" shouted Marie. For a brief moment, she thought that John was going to smash the men's brains with the golf club, but John just screamed and threw the strange weapon toward the apartment building. Glass shattered. Windows lit up. Marie dropped the van into drive and pulled up beside John. Wilson and Eric scrambled out of the way.

"Get in! Get in!" shouted Marie. John looked at her. He wondered if she was real. He turned away from her, ran away, disappeared. Marie watched him running, then she quickly drove away.

"I'm glad you saw them," said Eric. "You can tell the cops who it was! Those damn protesters!"

"No," said Wilson, firm in his belief that the big Indian would have valuable answers. "We don't need the cops. I was mistaken. I don't know who they were."

"But you said you recognized them?"

"No, I was mistaken."

"Jeez, it's a good thing that wasn't the Indian Killer, huh? We'd both be dead!"

"Maybe. Maybe not."

Eric shrugged his shoulders. He was sure Wilson was lying, but not sure why. It didn't much matter since no one had been hurt. Wilson was already unaware of Eric, of Marie, of everything but John. Wilson was enchanted with John. Wilson thought that a man who looked like that could be Little Hawk. Wilson wanted John all to himself.

21

Testimony

"Mr. Harris, can I have a few words with you?"

"Hey, dude, are you, like, a cop?"

"Homicide detective, actually."

"Well, I haven't been homicided. At least, not yet. No thanks to those Indians, though. They blinded me, man."

"The doctors think you'll be able to regain some of your vision. Maybe all of it."

"That's what they tell me. But I don't know, man. I'm scared. I can't believe what those Indians did."

"Yes, well, that's what I'd like to talk to you about. Are you sure they were Indian?"

"Positive. Braids and all. Just like the movies."

"Do you think you could identify them? Perhaps work with one of our sketch artists to come up with a composite? I know it will be hard without your eyes. But we've got to try."

"Just like the movies, huh?"

"Just like the movies."

"Yeah, man, I'll do my best. Like I said, they were some right-eously angry dudes."

"Can you tell me exactly what happened that night?"

"Yeah. You see, man, I've been hitching across the country, trying to find myself, you know? Out there in the open spaces, man, you can see some powerful shit, I mean, some powerful stuff. But anyway, I was on my way to Canada. I, like, met these Canadian dudes down in Arizona a few weeks back and they said I could visit them anytime I was in Canada."

"And that's why you were camped on the Indian Heritage High School football field."

"Yeah, but I didn't know it was an Indian school. It was some righteous grass to me. I mean, I knew it was a football field, but I don't believe in football, you know? I was rolled up in my sleeping bag, sleeping, when these three guys pulled me out and started beating me up."

"And you're sure there were three of them?"

"Uno, dos, tres."

"And did they say anything? Mention any names or places?"

"Hey, man, they were recording me."

"Recording?"

"Yeah, with a tape recorder, you know, like it was an inter-view or something, like they wanted to keep a sound track or some-thing. And they kept calling me weird names."

"Can you remember what they called you?"

"No chance, man. I was out of it by then. I was all dizzy and everything was moving in circles. Everything spinning, and then one dude shoved his fingers into my eyes and here I am in the hospital."

"Is there anything else you can remember?"

"I think one of them was deaf."

"Deaf?"

"Yeah, all three were talking with their fingers, you know? Sign language. And one of them had blue eyes. A blue-eyed Indian."

"You're positive about that?"

"Yeah, yeah. You know, I was listening to the boob tube and heard something about this Indian Killer. You think these guys have something to do with that?"

"We're looking into that possibility."

"It's so strange. It's, like, those Indians guys hurt me just because I'm white. But I haven't done anything bad to Indians. I like Indians, man. I even visited a couple of reservations. The Navajo, the Hopi. Beautiful. And this Indian Killer is killing white guys just because they're white, right? And he kidnapped that little boy because he was white?"

"That seems to be the motive."

"And that little dude, what's his name, Mark?"

"Yes, Mark Jones."

"Yeah, well, he certainly didn't do anything bad to Indians. I mean, not every white guy is an evil dude, you know?"

22

Slow Dancing with the Most Beautiful Indian Woman on Earth

If a white stranger, completely unaware of the year, happened to stumble into Big Heart's Soda and Juice Bar and heard the music blasting from the jukebox, he might assume that he was living in 1966. Or 1972. Perhaps as late as 1978. The white stranger would see over two hundred Indians dancing. A white stranger might have assumed the Indians were celebrating something special, and they were. Mick had opened the bar, despite the Indian Killer scare, and was pulling in the dough. The Indians were dancing to Hank Williams, Patsy Cline, Roy Orbison, Johnny Cash, Chuck Berry, early Stones, earlier Beatles. Disco had been outlawed by the patrons of Big Heart's. Black music was rare. World music never made it through the door. Lou Reed and Kiss were favorites, though. Blood, Sweat, and Tears, Three Dog Night, and Creedence Clearwater Revival were revered. But there were no white strangers in Big Heart's that night, though a few dozen Indians were new in town, just visiting, playing in a basketball tournament, looking for love, lost. All thinking about the Indian Killer. John was there too, neither stranger nor tourist. He had no definition for what he was. Drinking his Pepsi, he sat at the bar.

He felt guilty for having left Marie alone with Wilson and the cab driver, but John had been frightened by his anger. He stood over those two white men and wanted to kill them both. He wanted to smash their faces, break their bones, and crush their blue eyes. The only thing that stopped him was the thought of Marie, who would have witnessed it. She should not be subjected to such things. She was special and deserved something better. John had wanted to trust her, the woman who gave sandwiches away, but her thick glasses were frightening. Her crooked front teeth were absolutely terrifying. John could feel the heat spreading in his belly when he thought of her, the Indian woman with small breasts and thick hips. He wanted to tell of his plan, his need to kill the white man who was responsible for everything that had gone wrong. But she might misunderstand. John could not risk that. He had not meant to leave her behind, but he had to protect himself. He could have crushed the writer and cab driver, but that would ruin everything. There were too many eyes watching. John had to sacrifice his time with Marie so that he could live. He had to have priorities, make schedules, budget his time and energy. He had found his way to Big Heart's because he knew he would be safe there. So many Indians. Though he knew he wasn't a real Indian, John knew he looked like one. His face was his mask. John knew all of this to be true.

If John had happened to look at the Big Heart's dance floor right then, he would have seen two Indian women, tired of waiting to be asked, dancing all by themselves. He would have seen dozens of other dancing couples, and large groups of single Indian men. Too shy to dance, they sat in large groups, whispering about their romantic intentions.

"Hey, you see that one?"

"Yeah."

"I'm going to ask her to dance."

"When?"

"Pretty soon. I'm taking my time."

Those discussions went on for hours while the women waited, or danced with each other, or left the bar. When an Indian man finally found the courage to dance, he usually stood in place, shuffled his feet back and forth, snapped his fingers in time with the music. The only Indian men who danced with abandon were the same ones who danced traditionally during the powwows. Whenever a fancydancer or a grassdancer took the floor at Big Heart's, he was the object of much curiosity.

John never danced. He barely talked. Indian women often approached him because he was a big, handsome buck with long, black hair. The women sat in dark corners and watched John.

"You see that big one over there? He looks like he just got off a horse."

"Oh, yeah, enit? I think he's Navajo. You know I'd comb his hair every night."

The Indian women would laugh. They were always laughing. John wanted to laugh. He knew his laughter would make him feel more like a real Indian. He listened closely to the laughter, tried to memorize it. A booming belly laugh from a fat Lummi Indian. A low chuckle from Jim the Colville. A poke-to-the-rib-cage giggle from Lillian, a Makah. All kinds of laughter. All kinds of Indians. John would practice at home, stretch his mouth into those strange shapes called smiles, and laugh loudly enough to make his neighbors nervous.

John sat at the bar and laughed. Nobody paid much attention. It was not unusual for an Indian to sit alone at a bar and laugh.

"Hey." A woman's voice. John ignored it.

"Hey." The woman again. John closed his eyes.

"Hey," said the woman as she touched John's shoulder. Frightened, he whirled in his seat. The Indian woman stepped back. John studied her for any signs of danger. She was tall and dark, her black hair cut into a stylish bob. Beautiful and confident. She wore a red shirt and blue jeans.

"You want to dance?" she asked.

John shook his head, turned back to his soda.

"Come on," she said. "Shock me."

She took John's hand and led him onto the dance floor. He did not recognize the song, but it was too fast.

"My name is Fawn. I'm Crow," she said, dancing a circle around John. She spun, shook her hips and hair. She put her hands around John's waist and danced in closer.

"Who do you love?" she asked. It was more a step in her dance than a question or invitation. John raised his fist in the air the way that Marie had taught him. Fawn looked at his fist, at the ceiling. She laughed, raised her fist to the ceiling. Other dancers watched this happening. They raised their fists to the ceiling. Nobody knew why they were doing this. It just happened. One song blended smoothly into another, then another. John raised both fists. He pumped them into the air. One white guy was singing on the jukebox, then another, and a third. Song after song. Indians dropped quarters into the jukebox, punched the buttons, and waited for their songs to play. There were so many quarters in the machine, so many songs requested, that the jukebox would still be playing a few hours after closing time.

Fawn and John danced. Jealous Indian men watched closely. Fawn was a beautiful woman who never went home with anyone, but most of the men liked to assume they would be the first. John was taking that opportunity away from them. Ty, the Coeur d'Alene, Reggie, the blue-eyed Spokane, and Harley, the deaf Colville, watched and simmered.

"Who's he think he is?" signed Harley.

"Sitting Bull," signed Ty.

"No," said Reggie. "He's just bullshit."

Reggie had been pursuing Fawn, without success, for a couple years.

"Hey," Fawn shouted to John over the music. "I seen you in here before, enit?"

John nodded his head. He wondered if she was listening to the same music he heard.

"Yeah, I thought so," she said. "You're that shy one. What's your name?"

"John."

"What tribe you are?"

"Navajo," said John.

"Hey, hey, a sheep eater!" Fawn laughed and slapped John playfully on the cheek. He touched his face. "Kind of tall for a Navajo, ain't you?"

"I don't eat sheep," said John.

"I was kidding," said Fawn, amused by John's seriousness.

"I don't eat sheep," John said again.

Fawn laughed, hugged him close for a brief moment, then danced a little further away. He could not understand why this woman thought he ate sheep.

"I don't eat sheep," John said for the third time. The sheep were singing in his ear. The voices, which had descended to whispers for a while, began to grow in volume again. Greg Allman was singing somewhere in the distance. But he sounded more and more like Father Duncan. He was singing to John, trying to convince him that Fawn was the devil.

John turned away from Fawn, from the noise and music. She reached for him, but John shrugged her off. He walked off the dance floor and pushed past Reggie, spilling Reggie's Pepsi. Reggie cussed and wiped at his suddenly wet and sticky shirt, but John just stormed out of the bar. Reggie, Ty, and Harley followed him. John staggered into the parking lot, hands pressed against his ears, trying to quiet the noise. There were a dozen cars parked under the dim lights. A steady stream of cars flowing up and down Aurora Avenue. A few Indians in the parking lot. Inside, most danced to Deep Purple and "Smoke on the Water." John fell against a blue van.

"Hey!" shouted Reggie. "That's my rig!"

Reggie did not own a car, but he was looking for a reason to fight. John looked at Reggie, Ty, and Harley. He recognized Harley, the deaf one. He'd seen him in the bar many times before. John had always been fascinated by Harley's signing, his fingers forming words and sentences almost without effort. John stepped away from the van and stared at Harley's hands. Harley gave him the finger.

"You were dancing with my woman," said Reggie.

"Fawn?" asked John.

"Yeah, she's my woman."

Reggie stepped closer. He was much shorter than John and sixty pounds lighter, but Reggie was a veteran bar fighter backed by two friends.

"I don't want you near my woman," said Reggie. He poked a finger into John's chest. John recoiled at the touch. Reggie assumed he was afraid. He shoved John back into the van.

"Oh, man," said Reggie, pretending that John had dented the door panel of the van he did not own. "Look what you did to my van. Can you believe that, Ty?"

Ty shook his head.

"Can you believe what he did to my van, Harley?" signed Reggie.

Harley shook his head.

"I've seen you around, you know," Reggie said to John. Reggie pointed a finger at him. "You're Navajo, enit?"

John could barely hear Reggie now. The noise in his head was deafening. He wanted to tell these Indians everything. Maybe they could help him. He wanted to tell them he was not Navajo. He had no idea what kind of Indian he was. These Indian men, these warriors, would know how to be Indian. John was lost, trying to sign, twisting his hands into shapes that approximated words.

"Look at that," said Reggie. "Now he's making fun of Harley."

Harley closed his hands into fists.

"Man, you Navajos think you own the world, don't you?" asked Reggie. "Well, this ain't Navajo land, cousin. Ain't no sheep around here. You're in the land of the salmon people." Reggie slapped his chest. "I'm a salmon man. Ty and Harley here are salmon men. What do you think of that?"

John covered his ears with his hands and fell to his knees. Tears, whimpers, head bobbing in time with the music in his head.

"Look at you," said Reggie. "You Navajos are supposed to be the toughest Indians in the world and look at you now. You ain't tough. You ain't nothing. Your people would be ashamed of you."

John whimpered. Reggie, Ty, and Harley laughed, confident, though somewhat surprised by their easy victory. Reggie leaned down beside John to whisper in his ear.

"Hey, Sheep Boy," whispered Reggie. "You don't belong here. You ain't Indian. If you don't eat salmon, you ain't shit."

Reggie was feeling very tough.

"You're lucky I don't kill you," whispered Reggie. "I eat Navajos for lunch. Then I eat white men for dessert."

John looked up at Reggie.

"You don't believe me?"

John kept shaking his head, sure that Reggie was lying.

"Thing is," said Reggie, "I'm not Chief Joseph, man. None of that 'I will fight no more forever' crap. I'm going to keep fighting, Sheep Boy. I'm going to fight forever."

"You're the devil," John said to Reggie.

"No, I'm not. I'm God."

Reggie stood and kicked John in the ribs. John grunted with pain, closed his eyes, and searched his mind for a better place to be. Ty and Harley stared at Reggie.

"What the hell you doing?" signed Harley, genuinely afraid.

"Just giving him shit," signed Reggie and winked.

John opened his eyes and slowly stood. He towered over his tormentors. He raised a fist in the air. Ty, Harley, and Reggie, laughing loudly, all did the same. They were still laughing as John staggered out of the parking lot. He stepped onto Aurora Avenue, turned south, and walked away from Big Heart's. With the police patrols increased, two black-and-whites slowly cruised by John. He walked past the Oak Tree Cinemas, the World's Greatest Sushi, Chubby & Tubby's sporting goods and home supply store. Green Lake to the east, the ocean to the west. Water everywhere. So many places to drown.

23

A Conversation

"Aaron, son, what's happening over there?"

"I don't know, Dad. Things are getting pretty crazy."

"I read some Indians got jumped by three guys with baseball bats. You wouldn't know anything about that, would you, son?"

"No, sir."

"Are you telling me the truth? You know how much I hate liars."

"Dad."

"Tell me the truth, son."

"Yeah, it's me."

"And Barry and Sean?"

"Yeah."

"Why, Aaron?"

"For David. It's all for David."

"You've got to stop this, son. You're going to get caught. Or hurt. I don't want to lose you, too."

"Dad, I miss him."

"I miss him, too. But those Indians aren't worth it. They're not worth anything."

"Dad?"

"Yeah?"

"Do you remember that night when we shot at those Indians in the camas field?"

"Of course. We scared the crap out of them."

"Remember how you told us to shoot above their heads?"

"Yeah."

"I aimed for that Indian guy. I aimed right for him. And when he fell down, I thought I got him. And I was happy."

"Why are you telling me this?"

"What if I caused all of this? What if David is dead because I tried to shoot that Indian?"

"That's nonsense, Aaron. You were just a kid. You didn't know any better."

24

Mark Jones

The killer watched Mark sleeping in the dark place. The little boy had been sleeping constantly. It was getting harder and harder to wake him, and then he wouldn't eat or drink much when he was awake.

The killer knew that a decision had to be made. The world now knew of the killer's power and beauty. The newspapers were filled with interviews with the mother and father of Justin Summers, the first murder victim. Justin's parents wept, and the killer loved their pain. Mark's parents were subdued, in shock, too numb to show much emotion.

I just want the person who kidnapped Mark to know this, said Mrs. Jones in the largest article. *Mark is a very special boy. He's got a mother and a father who love him very much. He's got a grandmother and two aunts. His nanny, Sarah, loves him like a son. He's just a little boy. Please give Mark back to us.*

The killer looked at the sleeping boy, dirty, smudged with dust from the dark room. His face was stained with juice and food.

The killer sat in the dark and thought about the future, the ceremony. The killer left the dark place, filled a bucket with warm, soapy water, grabbed a hand towel from the bathroom, and went back inside to clean Mark. The killer was gentle. Mark didn't wake as the killer carefully undressed him, removing the filthy Daredevil pajamas. Mark didn't wake as the killer washed his face and body, his arms and genitals, his legs and feet. Mark didn't wake as the killer dressed him in a large T-shirt.

The killer took the special knife down from the wall, slid it into the handmade sheath, and looked down at the sleeping boy. The killer picked up Mark Jones and, holding the boy as a parent would hold a child, left that dark place, and went out to finish the ceremony.

25

How He Imagines His Life
on the Reservation

John sees the sadness in his mother's eyes as he prepares to leave the reservation for college. She wears a simple dress, something she sewed herself late at night. Lately, she has not slept well because she constantly worries about her son. She had given birth to him when she was very young, fourteen years old, and had greeted his arrival with a combination of fear, love, and ignorance. Her own mother had died while giving birth to her, and her father had been killed in Korea. Raised by a series of cousins and near-relatives, an orphan, she was not sure she knew how to be somebody's daughter, let alone somebody's mother. When John was born, the result of a random powwow encounter, he might as well have been an alien. Brown-skinned and bloody, twisted with the shock of birth, John screamed. But was he screaming out of rage, hunger, terror, or something more? She held him to her chest and prayed. Please, she whispered to him, stop. Ever since his birth, she has expected those screams, even now

as she stands on the porch and watches John pack the car with his last
piece of luggage. He is leaving her, leaving for college, and she is
terrified of the life that awaits him in the white world.

"Are you sure about the car?" he asks.

"Yes, yes," she says. "I don't need it. I can use the tribal van.
Or I can walk if I need to go to town. It's not far."

"But what about winter?"

"I'll walk faster," she says, and they both laugh.

She looks at her son. He has grown into a handsome man, tall
and strong. But more than that, he is smart and generous, good to children and the tribal elders. For ten years, she has driven the tribal lunch
van, which delivers meals to the elders, and John has often helped her.
That was the way they both learned to speak the tribal language.

"*Etigsgren*," said the elders upon their arrival.

"*Etigsgren*," said John, perfectly mimicking the elder's guttural
stops and singsong accent.

"*Ua soor loe neay. Reliw yerr uo hove?*" asked the elders.

John smiled and shook his head. He did not have a girlfriend.
He spent most of his free time with the elders. He vacuumed their
carpets. He chased down rogue spiders in their bathtubs. He never
killed the spiders; the elders had taught him that was bad luck. But
the elders didn't want little monsters slinking around their houses
either. So John would gently scoop the spiders into his hands and carry
them outside. He could feel the spiders' legs wildly kicking and tick-
ling his palm. He had always felt guilty about taking the spiders from
their familiar surroundings and abandoning them in the wilds of a
reservation backyard. John was not sure what spiders had to fear, but
he was sure it was out there somewhere, waiting and watching. While
the elders watched from their kitchen windows, John would kneel
in the grass, set his hand close to the ground, open his fingers, and let
the spiders loose. In their panic, the spiders would blindly scramble
away, somehow convinced that they had broken free of their prisons
and needed to quickly hide. John studied the grass as the spiders

climbed over leaves and twigs, small stones and broken glass, until they disappeared into the small shadows.

"*Ua roob gey da yoo,*" said the elders when he returned.

"Not so good," said John, feeling guilty and privileged.

"Ah," said the elders in halting English. "You'd feel better if you had a girlfriend, yes?"

John had been too busy with school, basketball, and his work for the children and elders to worry about girlfriends. John had always been good in mathematics and science and had become an excellent teacher. The little Indian girls were the quickest learners, and they were beautiful. Much taller than the boys and more mature, the girls publicly recognized the magic of mathematics and science, how they proved the existence of God.

John had read about a species of South American ants that raised aphids like cattle. He had described this to Indian boys, who made a conspicuous display of their feigned skepticism, and to Indian girls who believed it wholeheartedly.

"Listen," John had said. "The aphids, these small insects that suck the juice from plants, well, they eat this one kind of plant that the ants cannot eat. The aphids eat it all up and clear it out of the way, you know? Then as the aphids digest this plant, some chemical process inside the stomach changes the plant into a sugar. The aphids secrete this sugar, which the ants harvest to feed to their larvae. Really. The ants keep the aphids in little stockyards inside their nests. Isn't that great? The ants collect this plant, carry it back inside the nest, and feed the aphids in the little stockyards. Isn't that amazing?"

The Indian girls would laugh and write long essays about ordinary magic, about their grandmothers, who could make stews out of anything. They would remember beautiful stews crafted from a single potato, a can of tomato soup, and deer jerky.

"Remember that?" the Indian girls would ask themselves and other girls, and they would all remember the stories, and would laugh at the memories. Then they would hand in their essays, shyly smile

at John, and run outside to the basketball court. Meanwhile, the Indian boys would sulk in the back of the room. They would answer
questions in rough monosyllables, all the while drawing amazing landscapes filled with impossible animals: the buffalo with intelligent blue
eyes; the salmon with arms and delicate hands; the deer driving a
pickup; the bear dribbling a basketball down the court. When John
came around to check on the boys, they would hurriedly cover their
drawings, both ashamed and proud of their artistic impulses.

"What do you have there?" John would ask.

"Nothing," the Indian boys would whisper.

"You can't go to recess until you show me," John would say.

The Indian boys would stare out the classroom window and
watch the Indian girls run up and down the basketball court.

"Here," the Indian boys would say and reveal their drawings.
"It ain't no good."

"It's very good," John would say, which always made the Indian boys shrug their shoulders. "Go to recess."

The boys would run to join the girls on the basketball court.
John loved the children's laughter, the way those stoic, silent boys
became so loud and excited, those bright, talkative girls so intense
and competitive on a basketball court. Basketball was all math and
science.

John had studied hard in high school. His grades and basketball had won him a scholarship from the state university and he now
was heading off to college to be a pre-medicine major. He would be
only a hundred miles away, but it might as well have been a thousand
miles.

"I'll come back every weekend," he says to his mother as he
slams the trunk shut.

"Don't do that," she says. "You need to make friends."

John smiles at his mother. He would have come back every
weekend if she had wanted that, but she has released him. John
breathes deeply, fighting back tears. He has always wanted to go to

college. He has dreamed of it, dreamed of walking through the hallways with serious purpose, his backpack filled with complicated books and reams of paper. Drinking coffee and arguing important points with other students. Finding the professor who would be a father figure, who would guide him carefully toward his future. An Indian man, or a black man, or maybe a Chinese man. Yes, a tall Chinese man with a passion for the Pittsburgh Pirates. College would transform John. He would become a doctor and return to the reservation to practice. It is all he has ever wanted. To help his tribe.

John had known he wanted to go to college when he was three years old. He had learned to read then, and reading taught him everything he needed to know about life outside the reservation. He picked up a book before he could read, when the words were still a mess of ink and implications, and somehow understood the purpose of a paragraph. The paragraph was a fence that held words. All the words inside a paragraph had a reason for being together. They shared a common history. John began to see the entire world in paragraphs. He knew the United States was a paragraph within the world. He knew his reservation was a paragraph within the United States. His house was a paragraph distinct from the houses to the west and north. Inside the house, his mother was a paragraph, completely separate from the paragraph of John. But he also knew that he shared genetics and common experiences with his mother, that they were paragraphs that belonged next to each other. John saw his tribe as a series of paragraphs that all had the same theme. They all belonged to the same tribe, shared the same blood. John could step into his classroom and see his features in his classmates. The wide face and brown skin, the high cheekbones and strong jawline, the large ears and long eyelashes. No matter their heights, they all had long bodies and short legs. Girls and boys, men and women, everyone had narrow hips and a flat ass.

John looks at his mother crying on the porch and sees himself in her features. She is a beautiful woman, somehow more beautiful as she cries. John does not quite understand why this is true. He cannot understand why he likes to see those tears on his mother's face. It is proof of her love, certainly, but it touches something else inside of him so strongly that he takes a step backward.

"Don't cry," he says to his mother, but they both know she is going to cry for hours. John feels a single, hot tear roll down his face.

"You're going to be somebody important," she says.

John tries to smile. He goes to his mother and takes her in his arms. She is a small woman, but John can feel the strength in her arms and back when he hugs her.

"Don't let them hurt you," she whispers.

John holds his mother.

"They're going to try to stop you," she says. "They're going to try to humiliate you. They're going to call you names. They'll want you to fail."

"I'm going to be fine," says John.

She looks up at her son, takes his face in her hands.

"Listen to me," she says. "Don't let them change you."

John kisses his mother and turns away from her. He climbs into the car and starts it. He drops it into drive and pulls away from their small house. His mother stands still and quiet on the porch, watching him leave the reservation. She closes her eyes and listens to the sounds of the car fading into the distance. Then all is quiet.

26

Hunting Weather

At five that foggy morning, Truck Schultz stood at the back door of
the KWIZ studio. On a cigar break, he was thinking about how the
Indian Killer, that sick bastard, had actually made Truck's show the
highest-rated radio program in the Pacific Northwest. Truck smiled,
tossed his cigar away, and tried to open the door. It was locked. Truck
pounded on it—the buzzer was broken—but there was no response.
He knew the janitor and a neurotic producer or two were inside.
Darla, his assistant, was in her office. Truck pounded on the door
until his hand hurt.

"Shit," he said and stared into the fog surrounding him. He'd
have to walk to the front, through the parking lot and a dark alley.
The fog was thick, the sun had not yet risen, the air cold and heavy.
Vernon Schultz, Truck's father, would have called it good hunting
weather. A garbage truck rumbled down a street in the distance.

"Double shit," Truck said and stepped away from the back
door. He was immediately surrounded by a strangely dark and dense

fog. Fucking Hound of the Baskervilles, Truck thought as he walked
through the parking lot. He could make out the dim shapes of cars.
Shrouded in fog, the cars looked like large animals, monsters even,
ready to pounce. Truck laughed nervously, and heard his laughter
echo loudly across the parking lot. His own pickup sat in the best
space. He briefly thought about driving the truck to the front, but
then remembered he'd left his keys inside the studio.

"Triple shit," he said as he thought about the Indian Killer and
perfect hunting weather. Truck wondered how it felt to kill a man.
Truck himself had never been able to kill a deer, let alone a man.

"There," Vernon Schultz had whispered to his son as they
sat together in the hunting blind. A doe had emerged from the fog
just fifty feet away. The twelve-year-old Truck took aim, watching
the deer daintily step across the cold ground, but could not pull the
trigger.

"Now," whispered Vernon, but Truck couldn't shoot.

"Now," Vernon said, much louder, and the doe, suddenly
aware of their presence, bounded back into the fog.

"Oh, damn," said Vernon and gave his son a gentle nudge.
"Couldn't do it, huh?"

With tears in his eyes, Truck looked up at his father.

"Next time," Vernon said.

"Next time," Truck said as he made his way through the foggy
parking lot outside the KWIZ studio. He wondered how the Indian
Killer had found the courage to cut a man's throat. Truck shivered
out of fear, though he told himself it was because of the cold. He knew
the alley was close because he could smell the garbage Dumpster.
Something made a noise out there in the fog, and Truck had to resist
the urge to run. The flight instinct.

"Darla?" Truck asked, wondering if his assistant had realized
he hadn't come back from his smoke break. No response, but he had
heard footsteps, then a painful scratching noise, as if two pieces of
metal were being rubbed together. Truck walked faster, stepped into

the alley, and felt a powerful claustrophobia. He couldn't see the walls of the alley, but he knew they were there, just beyond his reach. He could see neither the parking lot behind him nor the street ahead of him. He realized he'd blundered into an enclosed space. Panicked prey, he thought, a hunter's dream.

A large bang caused Truck to drop to one knee. He couldn't tell whether it had come from behind or in front of him. The fucking fog has never been this bad, thought Truck, never, not once. He'd always thought fog was a minor nuisance, at worst potentially dangerous, but this fog felt specific and alive. This fog had sharp teeth. Truck slowly rose and stepped toward an alley wall. He touched the damp stone with one hand and felt some relief. He'd begun to wonder if the world had ceased to exist outside the fog. But he knew that wall and trusted there was another wall on the opposite side of the alley. He'd driven and walked between these walls for years. He could smell the Dumpster, and he knew there was a NO PARKING sign on the opposite wall. Truck was afraid.

"You got to kill them with one shot," Vernon Schultz had explained. "If you just wound them, all their fear rushes through their bodies, gets into the meat. All that good meat will get filled up with fear, son, and that just tastes awful."

With one hand on the wall, Truck walked down the alley. His fear rushed into his muscles. His legs and arms ached. His head felt heavy and full. He knew he could just lie down in the alley right there and fall asleep. He kept walking, and each step seemed to take forever, as if the street beyond the alley was hundreds of miles away.

A sudden flutter of wings above him. Truck wondered what kind of birds flew in the cold and fog. Bats? Owls? He knew the Indian Killer had sent him two owl feathers, along with a piece of Mark Jones's pajamas, but the police had refused to tell him what these things meant. He knew it was more than just a signature. It was some kind of Indian voodoo. Truck didn't believe in magic, but he believed in evil. The Indian Killer was out there somewhere, perhaps in that alley with him, and Truck wished he were carrying a pistol. He knelt down on the ground and searched for a weapon: broken bottle, stick, stray pipe, rock, anything. He found only newspaper and paper sacks.

"I know you're there," Truck shouted into the fog. "And I've got a gun."

No response.

"I'm walking through," Truck shouted. "You better just get out of my way. I'll blow your fucking head off."

Silence.

"Here I come," Truck shouted as he walked down the alley.

"You got to hang the deer meat up high," Vernon Schultz had said. "The bears will get at it, or the dogs, or the wolves. You got to hang it high, and you got to camp upwind from it. A half mile away, at least. You don't want to be between that meat and some hungry bear, son. Hang it up there high."

Truck held his head high as he walked down that alley, deeper and deeper into the fog.

3

Last Call

1

Mark Jones

Silently singing an invisibility song, the killer walked past the police car parked outside the Jones's house. The officer was reading a Tony Hillerman novel and never looked up as the killer passed within two feet of him. Carrying the sleeping child, the killer stepped through the front door and into the living room. Fully clothed, Mr. Jones was asleep on the couch. A stack of beer cans on the end table next to him. An infomercial soundlessly playing on the television. Tall and muscular, but weak and vulnerable in sleep, Mr. Jones was an easy target. The killer could have torn his eyes and heart out and eaten them.

Mrs. Jones was asleep in the master bedroom. Wearing pajama bottoms, her breasts bare, she was curled into a ball. She was sucking on her thumb, her face drawn and crossed with new lines. Even as he slept in the killer's arms, Mark Jones must have known his mother was close. He must have smelled her, heard her breathing, felt her presence. The restless little boy dreamed of his mother and twisted in the killer's arms. Mrs. Jones stirred, but didn't wake.

Carefully, the killer leaned over the bed and set Mark down beside his mother. In her sleep, Mrs. Jones draped an arm over her son. Perhaps she thought it was her husband. Perhaps she was dreaming of Mark. The boy nestled into his mother's arms. The killer could barely breathe, and wanted to lie down with the mother and child. The killer wanted to press against the mother's breast and suckle. Then, ever so gently, the killer leaned over the mother, and kissed her cheek. She smiled in her sleep.

The killer quickly left the room, walked past Mr. Jones in the living room, and out to the patrol car. The killer had plans. The officer had fallen asleep with his mystery novel dropped into his lap. Though the window was closed and the door locked, the killer could have broken through the glass. A shotgun, radio, pistol in the holster. The officer was young, inexperienced, on a rookie's detail, babysitting a house. Standing beside the patrol car, the killer stared back at the house. The killer took two owl feathers out of a pocket and fastened them beneath the patrol car's windshield wipers. Then the killer ascended into a tall tree to wait and watch.

First, the mother woke and found her son in her arms. She screamed with joy. Then came the fear as she realized the killer had been inside her house again. And a whole different kind of scream. That scream woke the young officer. He saw the owl feathers beneath his wipers and assumed the worst. He called in for backup before he bravely entered the house by himself. He climbed the stairs and saw the mother, father, and baby wrapped up together. He saw the mother's bare breasts and had an uncomfortably erotic thought, at the same time suddenly realizing that he was pointing his pistol at the family he'd been assigned to protect.

The last day was just beginning. The killer had counted coup, had won a battle without drawing blood. The killer knew there was more work to be done before evening came. Silently singing, the killer descended from the tree and floated away from the Jones's home.

2

Testimony

"Mr. Schultz, we can't find any trace that anybody was in that alley with you. Nothing in the parking lot, either. There's nothing. None of your co-workers saw or heard anything suspicious. All they heard was you screaming. Blubbering, somebody said."

"You listen to me, smart ass. I know there was somebody out there. I could hear him. He was after me. It was that goddamn Indian Killer. First he sends me a piece of that dead kid's pajamas, and then he comes to kill me."

"Listen, don't talk to me about the Indian Killer. You're the one starting up all this trouble. You're the one broadcasting lies. And that dead kid is alive."

"What?"

"Yeah, we just heard it. The Indian Killer brought the kid back to his house."

"What?"

"Yeah, took some balls, didn't it? Put that kid in his momma's arms while she was sleeping. She woke up screaming bloody murder, I guess."

"Well, that's good news. The kid is alive."

"You don't sound so enthused about it."

"Well, pardon me if I'm not dancing. But that Indian Killer tried to kill me tonight. And here you are calling me a liar."

"I'm not calling you anything, Mr. Schultz. There's just no evidence that anybody was in that alley except you. You know what I'm thinking? I'm thinking that your co-workers played some kind of joke on you. Make the big shot Truck Schultz wet his pants."

"I didn't wet my pants."

"Whatever. Now, I advise you to stay out of dark alleys and parking lots until we catch this Indian Killer, okay? Maybe there was somebody in that alley with you, so let's not take any chances, okay? And you stay off the radio."

"If that Indian Killer comes near me again, I'll kill him."

3

Seattle's Best Donuts

At two in the morning on that last day, John Smith was softly singing a Catholic hymn that Father Duncan must have sung before he went to the desert. A song about water and forgiveness. John sat in his customary chair at the long counter, which carried three chairs, or four, sometimes even five. But John recognized his chair because strange chairs were dangerous for John. They shifted shape, became unrecognizable. Once he learned to trust a chair, it stayed a chair. People worked that way, too. If John learned to trust somebody, like Paul and Paul Too in the donut shop, then those people became chairs. Comfortable, predictable. A safe chair and safe people were the most valuable things in the world. Rain fell outside, on the pavement brightly lit by neon and streetlights, where there were no chairs. John knew that Father Duncan would welcome this rain as he walked through the desert, as he tripped, fell to his knees, and began an accidental prayer. John could see Duncan with his delicate hands clasped tightly together, fingernails grotesquely long and dirty. Those nails would cut into Duncan's palms if he made a fist. Duncan made a fist with his right hand. A few drops of blood fell to the sand.

Paul was flipping through the latest issue of *Artforum*. Paul Too sat in his favorite chair, reading the newspaper. Both men understood John's need for repetition, the ceremony of a donut and coffee at two in the morning. Paul Too had already sipped at John's coffee and nibbled on his donut to prove they were not poisoned. Both noticed that John was in an especially bad state. His face was bruised and dirty. He smelled like a week of bad weather. He was talking to himself.

"How are you, John?" Paul asked.

"I met a woman."

Paul and Paul Too exchanged a quick glance.

"Really?" asked Paul casually. "And what's her name?"

"Marie. She's the Sandwich Lady."

Paul and Paul Too were relieved this woman existed only in John's head. They were frightened at the thought of a woman who might be interested in John.

"So," Paul humored John. "What does the Sandwich Lady do?"

"She gives out sandwiches." John was irritated at Paul's ignorance. "What else would the Sandwich Lady do?"

"Oh, of course. What kind of sandwiches?"

"All kinds. I don't want to talk about it anymore."

Paul raised his hands in surrender. John was definitely in a bad mood. Olivia and Daniel had visited the shop a few times lately looking for John. They had been frightened, although Daniel tried to hide it. Paul wanted to call John's parents; their number was written beside the telephone, but he knew that John would panic if he did. Paul looked to Paul Too for help.

"Hey, John," said Paul Too. "When was the last time you were home?"

John ignored him.

"Your mom and dad been looking for you," said Paul Too. "Have you talked to them?"

John shook his head.

"They must be worried about you," said Paul Too. "With all this Indian Killer stuff floating around, you know?"

"I didn't do anything," said John.

"That ain't what I'm saying," said Paul Too. "You looked at the news lately? Indians in the hospital, Indians in jail. It's ugly out there. Makes me happy I'm black."

John looked at Paul Too, then down at his hands. They were dark, smudged with sugar, flour, and maple. John figured he was as black as Paul, if not as dark as Paul Too. John understood slavery, how the masters whipped the darker ones more than they whipped the lighter ones. A dark Indian was better than a light Indian, John knew. For black men, it was best to be lighter, more like whites, to look like a cup of coffee with cream. A dark black man was the most dangerous kind. Indians wanted to be darker; black men wanted to be lighter. Was that how it worked?

John was five years old when he first realized his parents were white and he was brown, and understood that the difference in skin color was important. He had walked into his parents' bedroom without knocking. He was supposed to knock. His father, with just a towel wrapped around his waist, was standing at the foot of the bed. His mother sat on the edge of the bed. She wore just a pair of black panties and a bra. His father was thinner then, with a hairless chest and flat stomach. His skin was so pale that John imagined he could see through it. Olivia was beautiful as milk. Large breasts, long legs, wide hips all creamy. Only the small mole, a few inches above her belly button, was dark. She was drying her hair with a blue towel.

"John," said Olivia, surprised and embarrassed. John was supposed to be napping. She and Daniel had just made love, then showered together. John had no way of knowing this, but Olivia somehow assumed he did.

"Hey, buddy," said Daniel. "You're supposed to knock, remember?"

John slowly nodded his head and turned to leave the room.

"Wait," said Olivia. She rose from the bed and walked across the room toward John. Her bare feet on the hardwood floor. John remembered that. She kneeled in front of John. Her skin still pink from the hot water, the soft towel. John expected punishment.

"It's okay," she said and gave him a kiss on the cheek. "You go and play now."

John ran from the room. His body rebelled. He felt heat and cold, excitement and embarrassment. All that pale skin. Outside, he sat in his favorite tree and studied his own skin. The pale brown of his palms, the dark brown of his arms, his legs. He did not look like his parents, especially when they were naked. They were even more pale in their nudity. A pink shirt, tan pants, navy blue shoes could make his mother look like a rainbow, but underneath, she was a snow-bank, a bolt of lightning, a blank piece of paper. John understood he was not only darker without clothes, but he was different shades of darkness. His penis was very dark, the darkest part about him. John felt disturbed by all this knowledge. He wanted to look like his parents. He rubbed at his face, wanting to wipe the brown away.

Inside the donut shop, John rubbed his face against the counter. Paul and Paul Too watched with curiosity and concern. They had learned to let these episodes run their course. Sometimes, John would come back. Sometimes, he would fall further into his own little world. There was nothing to do but watch. John rubbed his face against the counter for ten minutes. His face had changed when he looked up at Paul and Paul Too.

"I could be famous if I wanted to be," said John.

"Sure you could," said Paul.

"You don't believe me?" asked John, sensing Paul's condescension.

"We believe you," said Paul. "Don't we believe him?"

"Damn straight we believe you," said Paul Too.

John stood. He raised his right fist above his head. This gesture, he had learned, forced people to react. It frightened Paul and Paul Too.

"I could kill somebody," said John. "Then I'd be famous. They'd put me in the newspapers, wouldn't they?"

John stepped up onto his chair, then up onto the counter, his fist still raised above his head. Paul Too carefully moved the coffee and donuts away from John's feet, then he stepped back.

"What would you do if I killed a white man?" John asked Paul Too.

"No," said Paul Too. "I don't want anybody to die."

"You liar," said John. "You'd kill white people if you could."

John looked out the window and saw the rain. It was a light, constant rain, like many Seattle rains, which mistook persistency for power. If Father Duncan were here, he would be dancing in the rain. The priest was crazy. If God decided to send a lightning bolt, Duncan would be a perfect target. Bare feet in rain puddles. A priest who wanted to be closer to God. A priest who walked into the desert without telling a soul. A priest who never came back. Or John could be wrong. Maybe Duncan was the lightning.

"Do you believe in lightning?" John asked Paul Too.

"Hey, John," said Paul Too. "Why don't you come down off that counter? Your coffee is getting cold."

John jumped off the counter, stumbled, then regained his balance. He leaned in close to Paul Too. Paul grabbed the smelly mop from behind the counter and stepped closer to the pair, ready to defend the old man. John had always kept his distance from people before. He had always maintained an invisible barrier around himself. If anybody stepped inside that barrier, John would immediately move away. But now John had his face in Paul Too's face. He was a foot taller than the small black man, but Paul Too never blinked. John's breath smelled of coffee, donut, and smoke, like something was burning inside of him.

"Can you hear him praying?" John asked Paul Too.

"Who?"

"Father Duncan. He's outside."

Paul and Paul Too looked out into the empty street.

"You're a nigger," John blurted out. "You're both niggers."

Paul tightened his grip on the mop, moved a little closer to John, who growled at Paul's approach. Paul Too motioned for Paul to back off.

"Now," said Paul Too. "That ain't a nice thing to say."

Paul was ready to smack John over the head. He was scared. John's face looked like he had just stepped out of a late Picasso.

"What would happen if I killed you?" John asked.

"I'd be dead," said Paul Too.

"Nobody would even care," said John in a new strange sing-song voice. "I watch the news. I read the papers. Nobody cares about you. Black people get killed every day and nobody cares. It wouldn't even matter. Killing a black man wouldn't get me famous, would it? Killing a black man wouldn't solve a thing, would it?"

As he spoke, John could hear Father Duncan's sandals scratching against the sand. A soft shuffle in the rain. A whisper. Nothing makes sense. If you kill a black man, the world is silent. You can hear a garage door opening from twenty blocks away. You can pick up a pay phone and hear only the dial tone. Shooting stars sound exactly like the soft laughter of a little girl in Gas Works Park. If you kill a white man, the world erupts with noise: fireworks, sirens, a gavel pounding a desk, the slamming of doors. John could not understand the economics of it. Read the newspapers if you can ignore the paper cuts. Watch television if you can avoid the heat emanating from the screen, which is meant to cook your brain. Nothing made sense.

John closed his eyes, rubbed his head. He could not understand. He needed help. Marie. She would help him if only he had something to give her in return.

"Hey, John," said Paul Too. "Look at me. It's your friend. It's me, Paul Too."

John opened his eyes, stared at Paul Too.

"I'm sorry," said John. "I can't help it. Any of it."

Paul Too patted John's shoulder, which caused the big Indian to recoil. He backed away from Paul Too. John looked at Paul, who was holding the flimsy mop like a broadsword.

"You could be the devil," John screamed at both men and ran out of the donut shop. Paul and Paul Too, weak with relief, fell into chairs.

"Shit," said Paul. "What the hell was that about?"

"It ain't looking good. It ain't looking good at all."

Paul Too shook his head, picked up a donut, thought about taking a bite, but realized he probably couldn't swallow.

"That's it," said Paul. "I hate this job. I'm quitting."

"He's worse than I ever seen him," said Paul Too. "And he's been coming in here for years. Since before you got here."

"You don't think he's the one doing that killing, do you?" asked Paul.

"What? John? Oh, no. Don't be saying that."

Paul Too threw the donut down with disgust.

"Lord," he said. "I hate donuts."

Paul was looking down at the mop in his hands.

"Shit," said Paul Too. "What were you going to do? Disinfect him?"

4

Higher Education

Marie sat in an uncomfortable chair in the office of Dr. Faulkner, the department chair. Faulkner and Dr. Clarence Mather sat opposite her, while Bernice Zamora, the department secretary, was busy taking notes. A replay of Reggie's meeting, except this time Marie was the hostile Indian.

"Well, since it is your class, Dr. Mather," said Faulkner, "and since you did file the complaint against Ms. Polatkin, we'd like you to start."

Mather sat up straight, adjusted his bolo tie, and cleared his throat.

"Well, first of all, I'd like to point out that I have the highest respect for Ms. Polatkin. She is an extremely intelligent girl. And certainly ambitious. But I think her ambitions outweigh her intellect. She is very much like a relative of hers, Reggie Polatkin, who we have some experience with."

"I don't know Reggie Polatkin," said Marie. "I mean, he's my cousin, but I've only met him once or twice. I don't know anything about him."

"As you know," continued Mather, "I am teaching the evening course of the Introduction to Native American Literature class this semester. As a tenured full professor, I certainly don't have to be teaching an evening class, and as an anthropology professor, I certainly don't have to be teaching a literature class. But I felt there was a need the University simply wasn't meeting. I took it upon myself to fill that need. Ms. Polatkin obviously had a need for such a class, and enrolled in my section."

"Excuse me," said Marie.

"Yes," said Faulkner.

"Why isn't an Indian teaching the class?"

"Why would you ask that?" asked Faulkner.

"Well, when I take a chemistry course, I certainly hope the teacher is a chemist. Women teach women's lit at this university, don't they? And I hope that African-Americans teach African-American lit."

"Do you understand why I have problems with her?" Mather said. "She is incapable of reasoned discussion. I simply will not have her questioning my authority in my class. She must be forced to drop it."

"Ms. Polatkin," said Faulkner. "Dr. Mather is an expert in Native American studies. He has published many books and countless articles. He has worked with dozens of Indian tribes. He has been teaching for twenty years."

"I have been involved with Native Americans longer than you've been alive," Mather said to Marie.

"Listen," said Marie. "As long as I've been alive, I've been an Indian."

"I hardly think this is appropriate," said Mather with a dismissive wave of his hand. "Why should I have to prove myself to a student, and an undergraduate at that?"

"You really think you know about Indians, don't you? You're such an arrogant jerk."

"Ms. Polatkin, I fail to see where this is getting us," said Faulkner. "I mean, in light of the tension this Indian Killer situation is causing, I think we should reschedule this meeting for a more appropriate time."

"I've been adopted into a Lakota Sioux family," protested Mather.

"That just proves some Indians have no taste."

"Ms. Polatkin, please!" said Faulkner.

"You really think you know about Indians, don't you?" Marie asked Mather. "You think you know about the Indian Killer, huh? Well, do you know about the Ghost Dance?"

"Of course."

"Yeah, and you know that Wovoka said if all Indians Ghost Danced, then all the Europeans would disappear, right?"

"Yes, it was a beautiful, and ultimately desperate, act."

"Yeah, you don't believe in the Ghost Dance, do you? Oh, you like its symbolism. You admire its metaphorical beauty, enit? You just love Indians so much. You love Indians so much you think you're excluded from our hatred. Don't you see? If the Ghost Dance had worked, you wouldn't be here. You'd be dust."

"Dr. Faulkner," Mather said. "Please put an end to this ridiculous digression."

But Faulkner, fascinated by Marie now, was silent.

"So maybe this Indian Killer is a product of the Ghost Dance. Maybe ten Indians are Ghost Dancing. Maybe a hundred. It's just a theory. How many Indians would have to dance to create the Indian Killer? A thousand? Ten thousand? Maybe this is how the Ghost Dance works."

"Ms. Polatkin, the Ghost Dance was not about violence or murder. It was about peace and beauty."

"Peace and beauty? You think Indians are worried about peace and beauty? You really think that? You're so full of shit. If Wovoka came back to life, he'd be so pissed off. If the real Pocahontas came back, you think she'd be happy about being a cartoon? If Crazy Horse, or Geronimo, or Sitting Bull came back, they'd see what you white people have done to Indians, and they would start a war. They'd see the homeless Indians staggering around downtown. They'd see the fetal-alcohol-syndrome babies. They'd see the sorry-ass reservations. They'd learn about Indian suicide and infant-mortality rates. They'd listen to some dumb-shit Disney song and feel like hurting somebody. They'd read books by assholes like Wilson, and they would start killing themselves some white people, and then kill some asshole Indians, too.

"Dr. Mather, if the Ghost Dance worked, there would be no exceptions. All you white people would disappear. All of you. If those dead Indians came back to life, they wouldn't crawl into a sweathouse with you. They wouldn't smoke the pipe with you. They wouldn't go to the movies and munch popcorn with you. They'd kill you. They'd gut you and eat your heart."

5

Olivia and Daniel

Olivia watched her silent husband eat his food so quickly he could not have said what he had eaten. Then, without a word, he left the table and continued his isolation in his study. He pulled an atlas from a shelf. A map of Korea, of Vietnam. Wars, wars, wars. One inch equals one hundred miles. One inch equals ten miles. The scales were always different. Nothing was ever the same as it was before. He fixed himself a vodka Collins, sat down at the desk with his atlas, and switched on the radio. For reasons he could never explain to himself or anyone else, Daniel had been a fan of Truck Schultz's since the early days. Daniel listened.

In the study, a leather couch, an oak desk and chair, maple bookcases filled with unread books and dog-eared atlases. Daniel loved maps. He would study them for hours, dreaming of places he had never been. Daniel replaced the Southeast Asia atlas on the shelf and pulled down a Montana state map. He studied Montana as he listened to Truck talk about the Indian Killer. For a brief moment, Daniel wondered if John could be capable of such violence. Then he dismissed the thought and worried about John's safety. If people thought some crazy Indian was committing the crimes, then John would be a likely target for revenge. Daniel, unaware that Olivia was eavesdropping outside the study, sipped at his vodka.

Olivia Smith hated Truck. Right now, she hated her husband for listening to Truck. And her hatred for Truck was growing rapidly. He was talking about Indians as if they were animals. It had been weeks since John had quit his job and disappeared.

"Daniel!" said Olivia and walked into his study. "Did you hear that? Nobody knows if an Indian is doing this killing. This is just evil."

"Calm down," said Daniel. "I'm just listening. Besides, he isn't serious."

"I'm tired of you apologizing for that man. He's going to get somebody hurt. Maybe John."

"Look, it's just Truck."

"But what about John?"

"He'll be all right," Daniel said and turned off the radio.

He leaned over his map of Montana. Billings, Bozeman, Butte. Poplar, Wolf Point, Glendive. There were so many places to go. Olivia watched her husband ignore her and immerse himself in the Montana map. He silently read his way across the whole state. Missoula, Harlem, Crow Agency. Little Bighorn, Yellowstone, Glacier Park. He tried not to think of his son, who could be dead, or lost, without a map, a legend.

"Daniel," Olivia said softly, knowing he would pretend not to hear. If she said his name louder, he would look up with feigned surprise. If she touched his shoulder, he would jump in his seat, turn on her with anger. He hated to be scared. She thought of her options and left the room.

Olivia walked into John's old bedroom. It was decorated with photographs of brightly lit fancydancers. R. C. Gorman's and T. C.

Cannon's prints. A Laguna pot, a miniature totem pole, a Navajo rug stapled to the wall. A gigantic dreamcatcher, which was supposed to entrap nightmares, was suspended over the bed.

Olivia thought back to John's nightmares. How the child often screamed himself awake. Night terrors, the doctor said, he'll grow out of them. Olivia became an insomniac, unable to sleep for more than a few minutes at a time because she constantly waited for those screams. When she rushed to John's bedside, he would be sitting upright, eyes and mouth open wide. John, she would say, it's okay, it's okay, it's Mom. But he could not be comforted. Some nights he did not even recognize Olivia. His eyes would be locked on some distant, invisible object: a monster, a raging river, flames. He would punch and kick Olivia when she tried to hug him. This happened a few times a week from the time John was a toddler until he was twelve years old.

Still, during waking hours, John was a bright and happy boy, if somewhat quiet. He was affectionate, laughed easily, smiled more often than not. The doctor who measured the spaces between his bones said that John had so much room to grow. He was going to be tall and handsome.

The change in John happened quickly. Or perhaps the change was happening all along and Olivia had simply failed to notice. Perhaps it was so subtle as to create an illusion of speed. However it happened, John had changed.

Olivia stood in John's old bedroom and prayed. She had watched her son, a stranger when he was first put into her arms, become a stranger again. Now, she listened for the sounds of her husband in his study. It was quiet. She could hear cars passing by their house. One, then two close together, then a long pause before another, and a fourth not long after. She could hear the dull hum of the refrigerator and the slow ticking of the grandfather clock. Neither worked well. She left the bedroom and quietly walked into Daniel's study. He was asleep at the desk, his face pressed against a map of

Alaska, the last frontier. She wondered how many vodkas he had finished. His face was damp. She touched his cheek, briefly wondered if he had been crying. Perhaps. Probably. Daniel Smith was a decent man. He worked hard for his family, brought home more than enough money, and loved his wife and son.

Olivia stared at her husband as he slept at his desk. She thought about waking him and taking him to their bed. But she did not want to talk to him. She thought about John, all alone in the world. Then she made a decision. Olivia slipped on a jacket and a pair of tennis shoes, found her car keys, locked the front door behind her, and stepped away from the house.

6

The Searchers

Reggie's apartment was small but surprisingly clean, with a huge stereo and television, a small bookcase holding college textbooks and a few novels, including both of Jack Wilson's. Reggie, Ty, and Harley were watching John Ford's classic western, *The Searchers*, starring John Wayne and Natalie Wood. Both Reggie and Ty tried to translate for Harley, who couldn't read John Wayne's lips all that well. Still, with his friends' help, Harley understood the plot of the movie. Natalie Wood had been kidnapped by Indians, and her uncle John Wayne had spent years searching for her. He planned on killing her if he ever found her, because she'd been soiled by the Indians.

"What would you do if some Indians took your niece or your child?" Harley signed the question to Ty.

"I'd wonder which powwow they were going to," signed Ty.

"Seriously."

"Seriously, I don't have a child. I don't know."

"I'd kill her," signed Reggie. "I understand what John Wayne is feeling. How would you feel if some white people kidnapped an Indian kid? I'd cut them all into pieces."

Reggie slashed the air with his empty hand. He thought of Bird, that brutal stranger who pretended to be Reggie's father. Reggie wondered if he'd been stolen away from his real family. Maybe there was an Indian family out there who was missing a son. Maybe Reggie belonged to them.

"Hey, Reggie, you got to calm down," Ty said.

Reggie glared at him.

"Who the fuck are you to tell me what to do?" asked Reggie.

"Now, listen," said Ty. "Me and Harley talked it over, man. I mean, you're just taking it too far. Beating up that white guy was one thing. Fucking up his eyes was something else. We got to stop this. People are going to think we scalped that guy. And then you recorded it, man. That's just sick."

Reggie, thinking of Dr. Mather's precious tapes of traditional stories, had listened to the recording a number of times. Who can say which story is more traditional than any other?

"And now we're beating up Indians. We ain't supposed to be hurting our own kind, are we?"

"And how do you feel about this?" Reggie signed the question to Harley.

"You're going to get us in trouble," signed Harley.

Reggie leaned close to Harley's face.

"Hey, Reggie, leave him alone," said Ty.

"There you go," Reggie signed to Harley. "Are you afraid?"

Harley shook his head.

"Yeah, you're scared," Reggie spoke now. "Read my lips, chickenshit. You know the name of the Cavalry soldier who killed Crazy Horse?"

Harley shook his head.

"Well, I don't know either, but I know the name of the Indian who was holding Crazy Horse's arms behind his back when that soldier bayoneted him. You know his name?"

Harley shook his head.

"His name was Little Big Man. You understand what I'm getting at?"

Reggie touched Harley's nose with the tip of his finger. A single drop of blood rolled from Harley's nostril. Ty jumped to his feet in shock. Harley pushed Reggie away and stood, signing so furiously that neither Reggie nor Ty knew what he was saying.

"Slow down," Ty said.

"I'm leaving," Harley signed to Ty. Then to Reggie. "You get yourself caught, but I'm not going to get caught with you."

Harley grabbed his jacket and slammed out of the apartment.

"Chickenshit!" Reggie screamed after him. "Pussy!"

"Reggie," Ty said. "You know he can't hear you."

"Fuck you."

Shaking his head, Ty sat back down and turned up the television volume. John Wayne riding down on an Indian village. Yet again.

"What the hell are you doing now?" asked Reggie.

"I want to know how this ends."

7

Testimony

"Mark? Mark, can we talk to you?"

"Do I have to?"

"You could really help us. We need you to talk, okay?"

"Okay."

"Can you tell us about the man who kidnapped you?"

"It wasn't a man."

"Was it a woman?"

"No."

"We don't understand, Mark. Was it a man or a woman?"

"It was dark there."

"Yes, we know it was dark, but did you see anything? Did you see the person who took you? Did he talk to you? Did you see his house? Anything?"

"I saw what it shone with the light. Hair on the wall."

"Yes, Mark, and anything else? Maybe feathers?"

"Yes, feathers."

"Owl feathers?"

"I don't know. Lots of feathers."

"And where did you see the feathers, Mark?"

"On the wings."

"What wings? Was there an owl there? Did the kidnapper have a bird?"

"No, it was a bird."

"I don't understand, Mark. What was a bird?"

"It."

"Mark . . ."

"It was the bird that was there."

"And where was the man who kidnapped you?"

"It could fly, I bet."

"The bird could fly?"

"No, no. It could."

"Mark, I know this is difficult. But I need to know what you're trying to tell me."

"I think it could fly because it had wings."

8

How It Happened

The killer watched the businessman park his car. A magical moment, really, a bolt of lightning. No sleight of hand, no mirrors, no dark closets, no playing cards, no scarves, no rings, no doves appearing from flames. Just real magic. Just a white man appearing as the killer was coming down the street. Edward Letterman, businessman, pulling up in his rental car. Short, overweight, and white, Edward dropped a few quarters into the parking meter, though he didn't have to at that time of night, and walked away.

The killer followed Edward two blocks into the pornographic bookstore. The lights were bright and irritating. Inside the bookstore, the smell of ammonia was strong, but something stranger and thicker lurked beneath, a smell almost like blood. There were rows and rows of pornographic magazines and videos. Dildos and artificial vaginas sat on one shelf, while blow-up dolls sat right below them. Everything was loudly bright. There were ten or twelve white men milling about, all studiously avoiding any eye contact. The killer watched Edward work a cash machine. There was a twenty-four-hour cash machine in the porno bookstore. That was a dangerous sign, the killer knew. Edward pulled a handful of bills from the machine and smiled.

The killer watched Edward waddle over to another machine, a change machine. Edward slid a few dollars into the machine and quarters dropped out. The whirr of the change machine sickened the killer. Edward walked over to a door, opened it, and stepped in. He was gone. The killer walked over to the door beside Edward's and opened it. There was a stool and a television screen inside a small booth, little more than a closet.

The killer stepped inside the booth, shut the door, and sat down. The killer saw the slots for change and inserted a few quarters into the machine. When the television screen came to life, a white man and brown-skinned woman were having sex. He was doing her from behind, like a dog would. The killer was both fascinated and repelled. A collage of enormous breasts and huge penises, frightening and blurry, trying to make the killer believe that people did these things to each other. The screen flickered, then went dark. There were so many things in the world the killer could not understand, how a white man fit himself inside a brown woman in such ways. Rage made the killer push against the walls of the booth. The world, even the tiny part of it contained in that dark cubicle, was too large. Shame washed over the killer in waves, each one larger than the last.

Without a word, the killer walked out of the store, crossed the street with the light, and sat at the bus stop, waiting.

While the killer waited, Edward enjoyed a number of short subjects. He knew he had parked the rental car in a great spot on a side street. He only had to walk two blocks to his car, and then drive ten minutes uptown to the Quality Inn. Simple stuff. He stepped outside the porno shop and checked his watch. He started to walk. It was a warm night, the cloud cover was low, light traffic.

The killer reached inside between jacket and shirt and felt the handle of the beautiful knife with three turquoise gems inlaid in it. A powerful weapon. The killer sat on the bench and watched Edward leave the porno shop, jaywalk across the street to within five feet of the bench, and head north toward his car. The killer waited a few moments, then stood slowly and followed him. As the businessman unlocked his car he heard footsteps behind him. He was mildly curious about the footsteps, but was more concerned about getting back to the hotel in time to call his wife. He sat down inside the car and was just about to close the door when the killer reached inside and set the knife gently against Edward's throat. Edward's heart stopped for a moment, then began to beat wildly.

Edward was pushed into the passenger seat as the killer sat in the driver's seat. Edward didn't want to see the killer, but the killer grabbed Edward's face and looked into his eyes. Edward tried to reason with the killer.

I have money. Credit cards, cash. You can have this car. It's just a rental.

Edward could feel nothing but the knife at his throat. The hand holding the knife was not shaking. Edward wanted it to shake. He wanted the killer holding the knife to be afraid. If the killer in the driver's seat felt scared, then Edward thought he had a chance. It was early evening. There should have been any number of people passing by. But there was nobody. Edward pleaded for his life.

What do you want?

The killer drew a very shallow cut across Edward's throat. A small trickle of blood ran down his neck. Edward was crying now.

Please, I'm scared. Please. Don't hurt me.

The killer pushed the blade a little deeper into Edward's skin, drawing a few drops of blood.

I'm sorry. Please. I'm married. I have two sons. I'll show you.

Edward reached for his wallet too quickly and the killer dug the blade into his throat. Slowly now, Edward pulled the wallet out and held it up. With one hand, he flipped it open and the pictures fell out accordion-style. Edward held the photographs up. His wife in her garden. She planted tomatoes every year, but she hated tomatoes, and gave them all away. His wife reading a John Grisham novel. His wife in close-up smiling, a slight gap between her front teeth. His sons as babies, one walking, the other lying on his back reaching for his own toes. His older son as quarterback, ball held tightly in his right hand, arm cocked back as if to throw a long pass. His younger son as middle linebacker, knees bent, face partially hidden beneath his helmet.

Oh, God, don't hurt me. I have a family. Don't hurt me.

The killer took a long, deep breath, tightened the grip on the knife, and pulled the blade across Edward's throat. The blood fanned out in an arterial spray. The killer stabbed again and again. Paused briefly to stare at the white man's body. Then stabbed until arms and back ached from the stabbing. Stabbed and cut, sliced and hacked. Stabbed until the dark blood absorbed all the available light, until the nearby traffic signals flared and then went dark. The killer leaned over close to Edward's chest and feasted on his heart. Then, feeling depleted but unfulfilled, the killer cut the white man's scalp away. The killer tucked the scalp into a pocket, dropped two owl feathers on the man's lap, stepped out of the car, and disappeared.

9

Marie

Marie knocked on the back door of the homeless shelter in Belltown, a downtown Seattle neighborhood that was a strange combination of gentrified apartment buildings and dive bars, trendy restaurants and detox centers. Marie knocked again. No answer. Impatiently, she kicked the door with her boot. She was in a bad mood because she'd been forced out of Dr. Mather's Native American literature class. He was a liar and she was being punished, if not seeing or hearing his rubbish could be called punishment. Still, she had been in class long enough to let the other students know the real story, and no matter what those white men said or did, she would never retreat. She'd contradict them. She'd get her degree and make them eat it. She'd beat them at all of their games.

Rumor had it that the Indian students were going to be asked to keep a lower profile until the Indian Killer was captured. Marie had no idea how Indian students could have kept any lower profile at the University without leaving it altogether. The whole situation infuriated her. She kicked at the shelter door again, was about to go around to the front when the door swung open. Boo sat in his wheelchair with a loaf of bread in his lap and a smear of mayonnaise on his forehead. He had obviously been constructing sandwiches for the van.

"Mayo?" she asked. "We can't use mayo. We can't afford it, and it goes bad."

"It's good to see you, too," said Boo, smiling.

Marie had to smile back. Boo was a nice white guy, not intimidated by her in the least. He obviously had a crush on her, and had written poems for her. He had been helping her make sandwiches for a few months, though he was not all that dependable. When she hadn't seen him for a couple of days, she knew she would find him later, drunk or drugged, with a sheepish look on his face. But he knew a thousand jokes and was the fastest sandwich maker in the world when he was sober. Marie had once bought him a T-shirt that gave him that title, and Boo had hidden it away in a special place.

"How we doing?" asked Marie.

"I don't know how you've been, but I'm doing fine. Just a couple dozen sandwiches to go."

Marie rolled Boo into the kitchen, a relatively small space for the number of meals that were prepared there. Industrial sinks and ovens, stand-up freezer and two large refrigerators, a small door that led to the large pantry. A big table in the center of the kitchen was stacked high with sandwiches and sandwiches-to-be. For the thousandth time, Marie wondered why she kept returning to this depressing place.

"Hey," said Boo. "Earth to Little Dove. You having a vision or something?"

"What did you say?" Marie was startled back to the kitchen.

"Are you communing with the Great Spirit?"

Boo often teased Marie about her supposedly genetic connection to Mother Earth and Father Sky. And she did enjoy a walk in the woods as much as anybody else. But the earth could take care of itself. She had learned that, every once in a while, the earth would cram a hurricane or earthquake down people's throats as a little reminder. Other people, Indians and not, could run around on the weekends pretending to be what they thought was Indian, dancing half-naked and pounding drums, but Marie knew there were hungry people waiting to be fed. Dancing and singing were valuable and important. Speaking your tribal language was important. Trees were terrific. But nothing good happens to a person with an empty stomach. Suddenly, she laughed, pushed Boo's chair into a corner between boxes, and left him stranded.

"Hey, hey," he said. "No fair."

Marie picked up a loaf of bread and lay down a row of slices. She quickly set a slice of bologna on each piece of bread, then threw another piece of bread on top of that. A very simple sandwich.

"Man," said Boo after he finally managed to free himself and roll up beside her. "I don't know how you expect us to choke down those dry sandwiches."

"No mayo!" shouted Marie, surprised by the anger in her own voice.

"Listen to you," said Boo, just as surprised. "You sound like that Indian Killer or something."

"That's not funny," she said sharply.

Boo had been trying to lighten the mood but he realized his mistake. He tried to make up for it.

"I was just kidding. I mean, it's not like you're the Indian Killer, right?"

Marie stared at Boo. He swallowed hard.

"You're not the Indian Killer, are you?"

Marie wanted to scream at him. She felt the anger in her belly and hands. But she could not lose her temper.

"I mean," said Boo, "it's not like a woman could have done those killings. A woman wouldn't have kidnapped that kid."

"Why not?" asked Marie.

"A knife just ain't a woman's weapon of choice."

"Of course it is. Men kill with guns. Women kill with knifes. It all goes back to the beginning of time, Boo. Men hunted and women cooked. We use what we've been taught to use."

"But these are men being killed. It would've taken a big man to kill them."

"Or a magical woman," said Marie, as she picked up a butter knife and waved it in the air. She turned toward Boo with a crazy look in her eyes. She vaguely threatened him with the knife. Boo feigned, and felt, fear. He rolled back in his chair.

"You know what I'll turn you into, don't you?" asked Marie as she tossed the knife from hand to hand.

"Yeah," said Boo, at last. "Toast."

Boo helped Marie with the last few sandwiches. As they loaded them into the delivery truck, Marie kept thinking about what Boo had said about the knife. Marie thought about John Smith. He was huge and had easily disarmed that cab driver outside Wilson's apartment building. When he had towered over Wilson and the cabbie in the sandwich truck's headlights, Marie had briefly wondered if John was going to kill the white men. No. No, that was not it at all. She had wondered if John was going to hurt them, maybe rough them up a little. She had never worried that he was going to kill them. John was a little strange and quiet, but most Indian men were kind of strange and quiet. Besides, John had not hurt either of the men. He threatened them with that sawed-off golf club and then ran off. After all, that golf club was the cabbie's weapon, and Wilson was a vulture. She remembered being a little disappointed that John had not hurt them.

"Hey," Marie said to Boo. "Come to think of it, what makes you think this Indian Killer is an Indian man? How many Indian serial killers do you read about?"

Boo shook his head.

"None is right," said Marie. "Everybody is talking Indian Killer this, Indian Killer that. Reporters all over the place. What if the Indian Killer isn't an Indian guy? What if this Indian Killer is just trying to make people think an Indian guy did it?"

Marie picked up a bologna sandwich that had fallen to the floor and threw it at Boo, who fielded it cleanly and tossed it into the back of the truck. Marie rolled Boo into the back of the truck, secured his chair, and then climbed into the driver's seat. She started the truck, let it warm up for a few minutes, and pulled out of the shelter's parking lot.

10

Truck

Truck was smoking his fifth cigar of the day and receiving dozens of phone calls, as he did every hour that he was on the air. The police had told him not to tell the public about his experience in the back alley.

"Listen," the detective had said. "I don't think there was anybody in that alley with you, but psycho bastards like the Indian Killer thrive on this kind of attention. They feed on it, breathe it. Don't give him what he wants."

Truck agreed not to talk about it, though he did so mainly because he was ashamed that he'd been so frightened. Truck watched the red lights on his phone blinking. George on line one knows who the Indian Killer is. Ronnie on line two is worried about the Indian Killer. Helen on line three wants to put all Indians in jail.

"Helen," said Truck. "You're on the air. What's your problem?"

"Well, Truck, it's about this Indian Killer. You see, I just don't think we should take any chances. We should lock up all the

Indians, just like we locked up the Japs during World War Two. I mean, it's for our own safety. Once we catch the Indian Killer, we can let the other Indians go."

"And where do you think we should keep these Indians?"

"Oh, I don't know. Maybe on some island somewhere."

"Well, Helen, that's a very interesting idea, but it wouldn't work very well. Indians are damn good swimmers. Folks, we have to take time out for some commercial messages. Stay with us. We'll be back in a few."

Truck dropped off the air, toked on his cigar.

"Truck," said his assistant over the intercom. "It's Johnny Law."

Truck sat up quickly to take the call from his source in the Washington State Patrol office.

"What's up?" Truck asked.

"They just found another body. Downtown. A white businessman. A guy named Edward Letterman."

"Indian Killer?"

"Indian Killer, for sure. He was scalped. Two owl feathers left behind. And the fucking sick bastard ate his heart."

"Ate his heart?"

"Like a fucking sandwich."

Truck whooped. He turned to his microphone.

"Folks," he said. "The Indian Killer has struck again."

II

Wilson

Wilson felt tied to a dying typewriter. The writing had always come easy to him before, but he could barely manage to write a few paragraphs of *Indian Killer* before he had to stand up, stretch, read a magazine, watch television. Any excuse not to write. He knew he had to finish the book, but he was somehow afraid of it. His agent and publisher were waiting. But he had to find the ending, had to write the book that was more true than any of the other Indian Killer books he knew would be published. He dreamed constantly about the murders. He saw the face of that man in Fremont when the knife slid across his throat, and felt the weight of that little boy's body. After those dreams, Wilson would lie awake for hours, staring at the walls.

Wilson looked at the blank page in his typewriter and at the *Indian Killer* manuscript stacked haphazardly on the table beside it. His manuscripts were always a disorganized mess, in stark contrast to his tidy apartment, balanced checking account, and simple eating habits. He supposed it was easy to be well-organized when you lived alone. Roommates, wives, kids, pets—they all added an element of randomness that Wilson could never have tolerated. That was probably why Wilson's dreams troubled him so much. They were beyond his control. Still, he knew that Indians were supposed to listen carefully to their dreams. Aristotle Little Hawk had solved more than one crime by using information he had obtained in dreams. Wilson felt he'd been chosen for a special task. Maybe that was the reason for his dreams. People were dying horribly for reasons he alone understood, and he was the only one who could truly talk about the Indian Killer. Wilson knew that he was writing more than a novel. He would write the book that would finally reveal to the world what it truly meant to be Indian.

Obsessed with all of it, Wilson knew that more people were going to be hurt, and killed, and he also knew his book would be ignored when it was published. He was positive a dozen knockoffs were already on their way to the printers. Wilson picked up the ringing telephone.

"Hey, Wilson," said Rupert, his agent in New York. "What the hell is going on out there? I thought you people gave up that cowboys-and-Indians shit."

"Jesus," said Wilson. "You wouldn't believe the mess. Cameras everywhere. It's a race war."

"Yeah, well, I hope you're getting it all down. It's great material."

"I've almost finished a first draft," Wilson lied.

Rupert whistled.

"Hot damn, you should send me the pages. You got my Fed Ex number?"

"Yeah, but I'm not sure what to do."

"Well, you stick the pages in an envelope and then mail them to me."

"No, that's not what I meant. I mean, there must be a dozen books coming out of this thing, right?"

"Listen up. You're writing a novel, champ. That's fiction. You get to make up shit. Besides, you know how this will turn out in real life. In the third act, they'll find some white guy in eagle feathers is doing the killing. White guys are always the serial killers. Think about it. Bundy, Gacy, Gilmore. Where's the drama in that? It's been done. You get to tell a new story. You're the Indian writer. This belongs to you, Wilson."

Wilson hung up the phone. His little apartment seemed so much smaller with all the uncertainty shoved into it. He wanted the world to know about the real Indian Killer, and not just somebody else's invention.

It was past eight in the evening on that last day when he grabbed his keys off the hook near the door, walked quickly to his truck, and drove down Capitol Hill to the Fourth Precinct. A number of television vans were parked at haphazard angles outside. It seemed like half of the reporters in the city had converged on his source of information. After parking in his usual spot, Wilson walked into the lobby and saw a large number of reporters and cameramen milling about. The bright lights of the television cameras were painful to the eyes. The desk sergeant who always supplied Wilson with inside information was using his usual methods to maintain some sense of order.

"All of you, get the fuck out of here!" yelled the sergeant.

Nobody paid much attention. Wilson saw a white man standing alone in the corner between the water fountain and the pay phone. A short, stocky guy, big belly, strong arms, a red flannel shirt, looking confused. Wilson wondered if he knew what was happening.

"Hey," said Wilson.

"Hey," said the man.

"Kind of crazy in here, isn't it?" asked Wilson.

"Yeah, they told me to pick a number a couple of hours ago. I got number three. I figured it wouldn't take long. I ain't heard much since then."

"Maybe they start at a hundred and work backwards." Wilson laughed at his own weak joke, that sort of short, loud, staccato laugh that men use in social situations. The man smiled and studied the number in his hand.

"So," asked Wilson. "What is going on anyhow?"

"You a reporter?" asked the man, studying Wilson carefully.

"No," said Wilson, lying only a little.

"I guess they found a body downtown."

"A white guy?" asked Wilson.

"Yeah, I heard it on the radio coming over here. On the Truck Schultz show. Do you listen to him?"

"No," Wilson lied.

"Well, you should. Truck heard about the body and went live with it. I guess it was some visiting businessman. He was all cut to hell, I guess, just butchered."

"Do they think the Indian Killer did it?"

"That's what Truck said. All I know is this place was empty when I first got here. And now it's a zoo. All these reporters are just trying to catch up with Truck now."

"Life is crazy," Wilson said to the man, who promptly agreed.

"And you know what else?" asked the man. "I came here because I thought I might know who the Indian Killer is. There was this Indian used to work for me. I was his foreman, you know? Working on the last skyscraper in Seattle. The last one. Guy's name was John Smith. Kind of a funny name for an Indian, don't you think?"

Wilson nodded his head.

"Anyways, he was a great big kid. Always kind of goofy, you know? Talking to himself all the time. Don't get me wrong. He was a good worker and all, but he was just plain weird. He never talked to anybody but himself."

Wilson was fascinated. A weird Indian climbing through the skyscrapers of Seattle. The foreman noticed the faraway expression on Wilson's face and was suddenly uncomfortable.

"I know it don't sound like much," said the foreman. "I mean, John was a good worker, but there was something wrong with him.

Really wrong. He just up and quit on me a while back. I didn't think much of it at the time. But with these murders happening, it just kept nagging at me."

As much as Wilson liked the foreman's story, he didn't believe it. Every Indian in the city was probably suspected by his neighbors and co-workers. Wilson needed to talk to the desk sergeant, who was still trying to control the crowd. Finally, Wilson caught his friend's eye, and the sergeant waved at him.

"You a cop?" asked the foreman, noticing the exchange.

"Yeah," said Wilson, another half lie.

"Listen," said the foreman, nearly pleading now. "I know I sound goofy. But I mean it. There was something really strange about John. I feel it in my gut. I think he's the one. Here, look at him."

The foreman handed Wilson a photograph taken at the construction site. Wilson studied it carefully. In the foreground, a group of workers were eating lunch together. One worker held a hammer above his head, like he was going to drive a nail into his own skull. Everybody laughing. In the background, a tall Indian man sat apart from the others. He stared into the camera with obvious anger. He had eyes like the eyes of all those old-time warrior Indians who were forced to sit still for Army photographers. Those defeated warriors always had smooth faces and flat expressions, but their eyes were dark and filled with a feral, kinetic hate. The foreman's photograph was color, but the Indian looked like he might have been photographed in sepia tones.

Wilson studied the Indian's face for a few moments longer and felt a faint sense of familiarity. Then it came to him. The Indian in the photograph was the same Indian who had attacked him outside his apartment. Wilson remembered the Indian's eyes, how odd they looked when he had taken the golf club away from Eric the cabbie and then towered over Wilson. Out of habit, Wilson had reached into his jacket, ready to pull his weapon. The Indian had come with that Indian woman protester. She was quite the nuisance at his reading. What was her name? Marla? Maria?

"What did you say his name is?" Wilson asked the foreman.

"John. John Smith."

Wilson stared at the photograph of John Smith, remembered how he'd thought the Indian was Aristotle Little Hawk come to life. Wilson had really thought he saw Aristotle for the first time when he saw John, but it had been so dark and confusing. Later, Wilson just assumed he had seen what he wanted to see, his hero, conjured by a frightening moment. Now he was unsure of what he had seen.

"Can I keep this?" asked Wilson. "For the investigation."

The foreman was hesitant.

"Listen," said Wilson. "Why don't I just sign this into evidence, okay? Just leave me your phone number and somebody will contact you tomorrow. You don't want to wait around here all night, do you?"

"Not really."

"Well, then, let's do it," said Wilson. "By the way, you wouldn't happen to have a home address for John Smith, would you?"

"Sure I do."

The foreman gave Wilson his phone number and John's address and then left, feeling that he had performed his civic duty. As soon as the foreman drove away, Wilson dodged a reporter, pushed the precinct door open, and walked toward his pickup.

12

Truck

"Citizens," Truck said. "The Indian Killer has done it again.

"Folks, I'm tired.

"I'm tired of witnessing the downward spiral of this country. Its culture, its history, its hopes, its dreams. The first Europeans sailed to this country with the hopes of building a new civilization, a better civilization. We dreamed of a country where every man was equal, where we were all given the opportunity to live, love, and die as free men. We didn't come here to suckle at the morally bankrupt teat of the government. Oh, sure, we made some mistakes along the way, but we learned from those mistakes and put them behind us. Together, we have created the greatest civilization that man has ever known. All along the way, there were many naysayers and cynics. There were traitors and subversives. There were beggars and sycophants. There were those who would have us cater to the lowest common denominator. There were communists and socialists. There were atheists and nonbelievers. My fellow Americans, five hundred years ago, we came to this untamed land as God-fearing individuals who wanted to live individual lives.

"And now, the dreams of one individual, Edward Letterman, have been murdered. The dreams of a young boy, Mark Jones, have been slaughtered. The dreams of a young man, Justin Summers, have been destroyed.

"And yes, the dreams of David Rogers have also been murdered. What were his dreams? He dreamed of being an English teacher. He dreamed of marrying. He dreamed of having children, of watching them grow into capable young adults. He dreamed of a nice house, two cars in the garage, and a dog named Fido. He had the same dreams as you and I, folks, the same dreams, and the Indian Killer has taken them away. And who is this Indian Killer?

"He's a coward, obviously. But he's more than that, much more. I want to tell you a story, folks. It's about Marcus and Narcissa Whitman, two of the first missionaries who ever brought God's word to the Indians. You see, the Whitmans worked with some of the tribes over in the eastern part of the state. Tribes like the Yakama and the Spokane, the Palouse and the Cayuse. But it all seemed to be such a hopeless task. The Indians were Godless people. They were savages, folks. Let's not deny it. Let's not pretend to be politically correct. Oh, sure, a few enlightened Indians did convert to Christianity and lived full lives, but their fellow tribal members often butchered them. Most of the Indians refused to listen to the Whitmans. They refused to attend church. In fact, in a combined effort to save the Indians from themselves, the Whitmans and the U.S. Army sent Indian children away from their parents to attend missionary boarding school.

"Now, I know this could sound like a cruel act, but we must remember that the Whitmans were good people with a good purpose. Yet, even though Indian children were given the benefit of a wonderful religious education, they refused to learn. This is a fact, folks. The Indian children would often turn their desks away from the Whitmans and face the back of the room. The Indian children refused to speak English. They refused to give up their superstitions. They continued to practice their primitive religions. What were the Whitmans to do?

"Well, if you remember your history, you will recall that many Indians died of smallpox epidemics in the early days of this country. Smallpox was new to the Indians and they didn't have any natural immunity. That's a tragic fact, folks. But many revisionist historians would have you believe that we gave smallpox to the Indians on purpose. Many liberals would have you believe that we used smallpox as a weapon against the Indians. What trash! That's like saying I'm guilty of assault if you catch a cold after shaking my hand. Am I right or am I right?

"But, back to the point: the Whitmans knew about the Indians' terrible ordeal with smallpox. They knew about the Indians' mortal fear of smallpox. For Indian children, smallpox was like the bogeyman. Now, I don't fully agree with the Whitmans' next move, but they were desperate. All of their efforts to help the Indians had been foiled time and time again. What the Whitmans did was this: they built a box from scrap wood and painted it black. Now this box was about the size of a hat box. Not too big, not too small. The Whitmans set this box in front of a class full of Indian children and told them it was filled with smallpox. The Whitmans told the Indian children the box would be opened if they refused to pay attention to their lessons.

"Yes, I know it was a hard thing for the Whitmans to do. They must have been tortured by their decision to use the box in that manner. But it provided much-needed discipline. The Indian children began to learn. They paid attention. If we only had such discipline today, we might not be graduating kids who cannot read, count to ten, or dissect a frog. Of course, the Indian children were not terribly bright, but the Whitmans persevered. Soon, the Indian children had learned enough valuable lessons to go back to their tepees and try to teach their parents, too. This is where the trouble started. The Indian parents were shocked by their children's knowledge. The Indian children were growing beyond their parents, and their parents couldn't stand it. They rose up against the Whitmans and slaughtered them. Marcus Whitman was tied to a tree and burned alive. Narcissa Whitman was raped by hundreds of Indian warriors before she died of fright.

"It's all true, folks, you can look it up. Now, what does this all mean? I know you want to know, and you know that I have the answers. You see, those Indians refused to be helped, even when evidence of their children's progress was placed in front of them. Those Indians responded in the only way they knew how to respond: with violence. And now it's happening again. Despite all that we have done to help the Indians, they have refused to recognize it. They have refused to recognize how well we have educated them, how well have we fed them, how well we have treated them. To this day, they have responded to our positive efforts in the only way they know: violence.

"This Indian Killer is merely the distillation of their rage. He is pure evil, pure violence, pure rage. He has come to kill us because we have tried to help him. He has come to kill us because his children have moved beyond him. He has come to burn us at the stake. He has come to violate our women. When the Indians attacked the Whitmans, that missionary couple refused to fight back because they were pacifists. They died as honorably as they lived. But no matter how honorable they were, they died horrible deaths. We cannot allow this to continue. We must defend ourselves, our families, our homes. We must arm ourselves and repel further attacks on our great country. I regret to say that many white people stood back and did nothing when Marcus and Narcissa Whitman died. Ten years from now, when people ask you what you did when the Indian Killer was attacking, what will you say? A hundred years from now, when your grandchildren read about the Indian Killer, what will the history books say about you?"

13

Anger

Aaron flopped on the living room couch and screamed loudly.

"What the hell was that about?" asked Sean, trying to study at the desk in the living room. In the secondhand recliner, Barry sat and read the latest Tom Clancy novel.

"Let's go fuck somebody up," said Aaron.

His roommates ignored him. He got up from the couch and turned the radio up to a painful volume.

"I'm trying to study," said Sean, whose soft, serious face contrasted sharply with his muscular body.

"It's Truck time," said Aaron as he tuned the radio to KWIZ. Sean pretended not to hear Aaron, but Barry threw his paperback across the room. Truck spoke. That was how David Rogers's brother and roommates learned about the latest murder. Less than twenty minutes after they heard the news, Aaron and Barry were in downtown Seattle beating an old Indian named Lester, while Sean sat in the back seat of Aaron's Toyota 4Runner and watched it happen. The old man wrapped his arms around his head and lay on the ground while Barry kicked him. The three white boys hadn't even bothered to wear their ski masks this time. But Aaron's face was so contorted with rage he looked like a different person.

"Get up, you fucking squaw!" shouted Aaron. He had a bloody nose from a wild haymaker. Lester, who had won quite a few bar fights in his youth, had managed to land that first punch. After that, Aaron kicked Lester in the groin so hard that he lifted the old Indian out of his shoes. With all the fight kicked out of him, Lester had just fallen to the ground and covered up, hoping they would not send him to the hospital. Living on the streets, he had been beaten quite a few times. It was part of the territory. The cops would be along eventually to break it up. Sometimes a few bystanders jumped into the action and stopped it. With this Indian Killer thing happening, Lester was surprised that this was the first bunch of white guys to jump him. He was also surprised that he had somehow lost his shoes.

"Get up! Get up!" shouted Aaron, totally out of control. Barry had stopped kicking the old man, but Aaron was now trying to pick him up to deliver more punishment.

"He's had enough," said Barry. "We've got to go. The cops will be here soon."

Barry dragged Aaron away from the old man. They hustled into the 4Runner and raced away from the scene. They pulled into a parking lot near Pike Place Market a few blocks away.

"Fuck, yeah," said Aaron. "That felt good."

"Your nose is bleeding," Sean said to Aaron.

"What?" Aaron wiped his face and saw blood on his hand. "Fucking squaw got lucky with the first punch, didn't he?"

Barry laughed nervously. Sean felt sick to his stomach.

"Let's go get us some more," said Aaron.

"Maybe that's enough," said Sean.

"Are you talking to me, you pussy?" Aaron bellowed at Sean, who looked shocked. "Yeah, you pussy. I want to go kick some more Indian ass."

"Hey, Aaron," said Barry. "Maybe that is enough? I mean, we're going to get caught. We're not even wearing our masks."

"I'm not going to do it anymore," Sean announced. "We put those other Indians in the hospital. And this sure isn't helping David anyway."

Barry also wanted to stop, but he was afraid of Aaron's reaction.

"Fuck that," said Aaron. "The police aren't going to do anything. Hell, the police are probably beating the shit out of Indians, too. And David would've wanted us to do this, man. It's for him."

"Listen to yourself," said Sean. "Do you believe what you're saying?"

Aaron leaned over and punched Sean in the forehead. Barry shrank back in fear.

"Do you hear me?" asked Aaron. "Do you hear me, you pussy? I'm saying those fucking Indians killed David."

Sean was crying.

"I always thought you were a pussy," said Aaron. "Look at you. Big as a fucking house, but you're just a pussy. All fucking righteous now, aren't you? You weren't so righteous when we started this, were you? Now, you decide. We're going to go kick some more ass, aren't we?"

Aaron looked at Barry, who hesitated briefly before agreeing.

"See," Aaron said to Sean. "Barry's with the program. Now, are you with us or are you against us?"

"That old man didn't do anything," said Sean.

"He's Indian," said Aaron. "That's enough. Now, I'll ask you one more time. Are you with us or against us?"

Sean looked at Barry, who avoided eye contact, then back to
Aaron, who made a fist.

"Get the fuck out of my truck," Aaron said. "You're done.
You hear me? You're done."

Sean opened his door and stepped out. As the 4Runner pulled
out of the parking lot, Sean touched his bruised forehead. He found
a pay phone and called a cab, which took him to the Fourth Precinct.

14

A Conversation

"Mom, it's me, Reggie."

"Oh, my God, are you okay?"

"Yeah, I'm fine. How's Bird?"

"He's in chemo. It's not going well."

"I'm sorry."

"Me, too. He's asked about you. He watches television. He worries about you with this Indian Killer running around. He's really sorry for everything."

"Listen, I hate to ask, but do you got any money?"

"Reggie, aren't you scared? Has anybody tried to hurt you?"

"Nobody can hurt me, Mom."

"That's not true."

"Yeah, Bird would know about that, wouldn't he?"

"He's changed, Reggie, he really has."

"Sure, sure. Hey, Mom, you know about the Battle of Steptoe Butte?"

"What about it?"

"Yeah, you remember how all those Spokane Indians had those Cavalry soldiers surrounded? Trapped up on Steptoe Butte? It was, what, 1858?"

"There were other tribes besides the Spokane there."

"Yeah, well, we Indians had them white guys trapped. Had them surrounded and what did we do? Those white guys were completely and totally helpless. And we let them go."

"What are you trying to say, Reggie?"

"I don't know, Mom. Maybe Indians are better people than most. I just need to know if you got any money."

"I'm broke, Reggie. You could ask Bird. He'd like to talk to you."

"That's okay, Mom. Listen, I got to go. See you."

"Wait, Reggie. Wait. Reggie? Reggie?"

15

Mother

Wilson sat in his pickup outside John Smith's apartment building in Ballard. There were too many shadows. A man could hide in a dozen different places on this block and not be seen until it was too late. Wilson was excited. He could feel John Smith's presence.

According to the foreman, John Smith lived on the top floor. Wilson looked up and saw only one lit window in a top-floor apartment. Wilson checked the mailboxes. John Smith in 403. Hiestand in 402, Salgado in 401. Wilson tested the front door of the apartment building. Unlocked. A nonsecure building. Wilson took a deep breath. Wilson had no idea what John Smith would do when confronted.

Wilson slowly climbed the stairs, his bad knee aching with the effort. As a cop, he had been in many situations like this. A dark building, a potentially dangerous suspect somewhere up the stairs. It was never as dramatic as the movies or books. No cats springing into the frame as a false scare. No extras scrambling for cover. Only the cop, the dark stairs, and the suspect. Wilson had always enjoyed the hunt.

Wilson reached the fourth floor. He passed by 401 and 402. At 403, he stood close and listened. He could hear vague noises from inside the apartment. Smith was home. Wilson debated his options. He could bust down the door with weapon drawn. He could stand away from the door and shout orders to Smith. *Come out with your hands up!* But what would he do after Smith came out? Wilson thought hard, then he shrugged his shoulders, and knocked politely on the door.

"John!" cried the woman who threw open the door, an action that caused Wilson to jump back and reach inside his coat. He stopped himself when he noticed the white woman standing in the doorway.

"Oh," said Wilson, embarrassed at his obvious error. "I'm sorry. I was looking for John Smith."

"This is John's apartment," said Olivia Smith. "He's my son."

Wilson was confused. This beautiful blond, blue-eyed white woman could not be the mother of an Indian man.

"My name is Olivia Smith." Wilson's confusion was familiar to Olivia from so many faces. She was always forced to offer explanations. "And he's adopted."

"Oh, I see," said Wilson. "Is John home?" He noticed how her face was drawn and pale. She looked like she'd been crying.

"No, no. Are you a friend of his?"

"Uh, not really, no."

Olivia, suddenly nervous, took a small step back into the apartment. She had her hand on the door, ready to close it quickly.

"What do you want with my son?" asked Olivia.

"Well, ma'am, my name is Jack Wilson. I just wanted to ask him a few questions about a book I'm working on."

"Jack Wilson?" asked Olivia. She recognized the name because she still read every book about Indians she could find. "You write those murder mysteries, don't you?"

"Yes, ma'am, I do."

"Aristotle Little Hawk, right?"

"Yeah, that's right," said Wilson, flushing with pride.

"I like your books. You really get it right."

"Thank you."

Olivia invited Wilson into the apartment, feeling as if she somehow knew him simply because she'd read his books. She offered him a donut from a box sitting on the kitchen table. They were Seattle's Best Donuts, but Wilson declined. He stood awkwardly in the middle of the room, while Olivia sat at the table.

"What kind of book are you writing, Mr. Wilson?" asked Olivia, falling back on politeness.

"It's about the Indian Killer," said Wilson.

"You can't think John has anything to do with that?" asked Olivia, alarmed now.

"No, no. I was just doing some research when I heard about this Indian guy, your son, a high-rise construction worker. I thought it was interesting."

"It's the last skyscraper they're going to build in Seattle."

"Yeah, I heard."

"Can you imagine that? When we think of cities, don't we think of tall buildings? Now we have all these computers and things. People can work from anywhere. They don't need to be bunched up in the same big buildings anymore. They don't even need to be in the same country to work together anymore. Things change, don't they?"

"Yes, they do."

Olivia picked up a donut, nibbled at it, then studied it.

"John loves these things," said Olivia.

Wilson looked around the room. It was spare and cluttered at the same time. Prints with Indian themes hung at strange angles on the walls. The bed was made haphazardly. Boxes of assorted junk were stacked neatly in every corner.

"Where is John?" asked Wilson.

"I don't know," said Olivia. "We've been looking for him for a long time."

Wilson looked at Olivia's left hand. Married to a rich man, judging by the size of the diamond. She wore the standard casual outfit for middle-aged white women in Seattle: a white T-shirt, blue jeans, black blazer.

"Do you have a family, Mr. Wilson?"

"No."

"No wife?"

"No, never."

Surprised, Olivia quickly studied Wilson's features. He wasn't a bad-looking man, middle-aged, a writer, probably intelligent. He should have been married a couple times by now. Then Olivia remembered that he had been a cop, and changed her mind. He must have lots of problems. She thought about asking him to leave, but decided that it did not matter. She couldn't see how her troubles could get much worse.

"My son doesn't even know I'm here, Mr. Wilson. He'd be angry if he knew I had a key to his place. He's got some real problems, with me, and his father. He's got problems with everybody. I'm not sure he'd even talk to you."

"What kind of problems?" asked Wilson.

Olivia hesitated for a moment, then continued, too tired to maintain secrets.

"He's got everything and nothing," she said. "Every time we took him to a new doctor, there was something else wrong with him. But hey, he doesn't drink or do drugs. He doesn't even take the drugs that are supposed to help him."

Olivia started to cry, got angry at herself for breaking down, and then cried even harder. Wilson took a step toward her, raised his hand as some sort of clumsy offering, and stopped.

"I'm sorry," said Olivia, wiping her face with her hands. "I'm just so tired. I can't sleep. I'm so scared. I keep thinking about this Indian Killer. Sometimes, I wonder. I think, maybe . . ."

Olivia closed her eyes, swallowed hard, trying to maintain her composure. When she had visited the donut shop just before trying John's apartment, Paul and Paul Too had told her about John's wild behavior.

"John was such a gentle boy," said Olivia. "He wouldn't even kill bugs. Really. Me, I'm terrified of spiders. Just phobic. I remember this one time, John couldn't have been more than five or six years old, and I was cleaning the upstairs bathroom. I can remember it like it was yesterday, you know?"

Wilson nodded his head, and glanced at his watch.

"I even remember the song on the radio. The Beatles. That strawberry song, remember? I was singing with the radio, cleaning the bathtub, when this huge spider came out of the drain. I screamed like crazy. Daniel, my husband, was at work. It must have been summer because John was home. He heard my screaming and he came running, you know, to save Mommy. I was trying to smash that spider with my shoe when John came into the bathroom. He just screamed at me, 'No, no!' and then I smashed that spider flat."

Wilson walked a few steps closer to Olivia, who seemed lost in the memory.

"Oh, God, he cried over that spider. Just bawled. Made me bury it in the backyard. We even had a funeral. Isn't that funny?"

Olivia looked up at Wilson and smiled. He smiled and nodded his head.

"Mrs. Smith," said Wilson. "He sounds like a good boy."

"He was," said Olivia. "He was."

"You don't have any idea where he is?"

Olivia sat up in the chair, wiped her face again, sensing Wilson's impatience.

"No, Mr. Wilson, I have no idea."

Wilson took the foreman's photograph out of his pocket and showed it to Olivia.

"Is this your son?"

Olivia stared at the photograph of her son, his face empty and dark.

"That's John," she said.

Wilson tucked the photograph back into his pocket and turned to leave.

"Thank you, Mrs. Smith," said Wilson as he opened the door.

"Mr. Wilson," said Olivia just before he closed the door behind him.

"Yes."

"If you see John, tell him to come home."

Wilson left Olivia alone at the table. He raced down the stairs and jumped into his pickup. He figured he could find John or somebody who knew John at Big Heart's. As he drove away, Olivia watched him from the apartment window. She knew that everything was going wrong, but she felt powerless to stop it. Her husband was probably asleep on the couch in his study. That's how it must be. He had been too tired to walk up the stairs to bed, so he slipped off his shoes and pants, loosened his tie, and then curled up on the couch. He had probably called out to her, had not received a response, and had assumed she was asleep. That was how it must be. He was asleep on the couch, wearing a nice shirt and loosened tie. A decent man, he was probably dreaming about his son. Daniel twisting and turning in his sleep. All of it quickly becoming a nightmare. Olivia loved her husband. She watched Wilson's pickup until it disappeared into the rest of the city. He drove north. Olivia looked south toward downtown Seattle and counted the number of streetlights. One, two, three, then ten, then more. She counted until there were none left to be counted, and then she began again.

16

Marie

Marie and Boo set out to deliver their sandwiches on that last night. They drove from the Belltown shelter south toward Pioneer Square. A white van. Three traffic signals. Red light, stop. Green light, go. A stop sign that was mostly ignored. Intermittent wipers sweeping against the windshield every few seconds.

"You know," Boo said. "You're like the ice cream man in this truck. Remember how they used to play that music? Man, you could hear those trucks from miles away. We should hook some music up to this rig, don't you think? We'd have homeless folks just chasing us down the street."

Marie laughed. She stopped when she saw King staggering across the street. His face bloody. Marie helped King into the truck and saw that his wounds were not that serious. She bandaged him up with the first-aid kit. King told her that two white guys in a pickup had jumped him.

"Jeez," King had said. "They would've killed me, I think. But some other white guys broke it up."

Marie looked at King. She saw that blood and recognized it, knew that Indian blood had often spilled on American soil. She knew there were people to blame for that bloodshed. She felt a beautiful kind of anger. On the Spokane Indian Reservation, an old Indian woman grew violently red roses in the same ground where five Indian women were slaughtered by United States Cavalry soldiers.

17

Catholicism

Seattle Police Officer Randy Peone turned from Denny onto Third in downtown Seattle and saw a barefoot old Indian man staggering down the street.

"Officer, Officer," the old man slurred. "I want to report a crime."

"What crime?" asked Peone.

"I've been assaulted."

The old man's face was a mess of cuts and bruises. His left eye would be swollen shut in the morning.

"Who assaulted you?" asked Peone.

"A bunch of white kids," said the old man. "They stole my shoes."

The officer looked down at the old man's bare feet. They were stained with years of dirt and fungus. Peone figured the old man was delusional. Who would want to steal the shoes that had covered those

feet? But the old man was in a bad state, and there had been a number of racial attacks since the Indian Killer case became public, and
especially since that white kid had been kidnapped. Though the child
was safely home now, the Indian Killer was still at large.

"What's your name?" Peone asked the old man.

"Lester," he said.

Peone climbed out of the cruiser, tucked the old man into
the back seat, jumped back into the car, and radioed the dispatcher.

"Dispatch," said Peone. "This is unit twelve. I've got me a
drunk who needs a band-aid and bath. I'm taking him to detox."

Peone was on his way when he passed John Smith kneeling
on the sidewalk farther north on Third. John was singing loudly and
had attracted a small crowd. He was also holding a pair of shoes that
could barely be defined as shoes. Peone figured he had found the man
who had beaten up the old guy and stolen his shoes. These two Indians were probably buddies and had fought over the last drink in the
jug. He pulled up close to John and turned his flashing lights on. The
red and blue distracted John from his singing. Peone looked at John.
A big guy, thought the officer, who only briefly considered calling
for backup.

"Hey, there," Peone said as he walked up to John, who was
still entranced by the flashing lights.

"He's crazy," said a guy from the crowd that had gathered.
"He's singing church songs."

The crowd laughed. Officer Peone looked at John and wondered which mental illness he had. The Seattle streets were filled
with the mostly crazy, half-crazy, nearly crazy, and soon-to-be-crazy.
Indian, white, Chicano, Asian, men, women, children. The social
workers did not have anywhere near enough money, training, or time
to help them. The city government hated the crazies because they
were a threat to the public image of the urban core. Private citizens
ignored them at all times of the year except for the few charitable
days leading up to and following Christmas. In the end, the police

had to do most of the work. Police did crisis counseling, transporting them howling to detox, the dangerous to jail, racing the sick to the hospitals, to a safer place. At the academy, Officer Peone figured he would be fighting bad guys. He did not imagine he would spend most of his time taking care of the refuse of the world. Peone found it easier when the refuse were all nuts or dumb-ass drunks, harder when they were just regular folks struggling to find their way off the streets.

"Okay, okay," Peone said to the crowd. "The show's over. Let's clear it out."

Since it was Seattle, the crowd obeyed the officer's orders and dispersed. John had forgotten about the flashing lights and was singing again, in Latin. Peone had been an accomplished altar boy way back when and recognized the tune. He could almost smell the smoke from the thousands of altar candles he had lit.

"Hey, chief," said Peone. "You okay?"

John stopped singing and noticed Peone for the first time. He saw the blue eyes and blue uniform, the pistol and badge. Blue sword, scabbard, white horse. The bugle playing.

"He's gone."

"No, he's not gone. He's in the back of my car."

John stood, walked over to the car, and looked inside. He saw the old Indian man. He threw the Indian's shoes at the window. They bounced off the glass and landed on the sidewalk.

"That's not Father Duncan," said John.

"Who?" asked Peone.

"Father Duncan. He's gone."

Peone could see the terrible sadness in John's eyes. The officer wondered where the Indian thought he was, and who he thought he might be. Probably a schizophrenic. He was big and strong enough to hurt a man, but Peone, through years of applied psychology lessons taken on the streets, knew that most schizophrenics rarely hurt anybody except themselves.

"Hey, big guy," said Peone. "You been taking your medicine?"

"No," said John. "They're trying to poison me."

"Is that why you hurt your friend?" asked Peone, pointing toward the old man in the back of the car.

"He's not my friend. I don't know him."

"Really?" asked the officer. "Well, then, what happened to his face?"

"I don't know," said John.

Officer Peone knew he would have to take John to the hospital. He was obviously sick and needed help. He began to wonder if John might be dangerous, might be the Indian Killer. Why hadn't he called for backup?

"Hey, chief," said Peone. "Let's you and me go for a ride."

John, suddenly frightened, took a step back.

"You could be the devil," John said to Peone.

"I could be," said Peone. "But I'm not. Come on, why don't I take you and your friend to the hospital. Get you both fixed up, okay?"

"I'm afraid," John whispered, then he kneeled and began to pray. "Our Father who art in Heaven, hallowed by thy name, thy Kingdom come, thy will be done . . . "

"On Earth as it is in Heaven," continued Peone.

Surprised, John stared at Peone.

"Give us this day our daily bread . . . ," said Peone.

"And forgive us our trespasses," said John, "as we forgive those who trespass against us. And lead us not into temptation . . ."

"But deliver us from evil . . ."

"For thine is the kingdom and the power and the glory, forever and ever."

"Amen," said John and Peone together.

John closed his eyes and pressed his head against his clasped hands. He was praying. Peone reached for his handcuffs. John heard the jangle of the cuffs and keys, opened his eyes, and panicked. He leapt to his feet and ran into an alley. Peone ran a few feet after John before he came to his senses. He climbed back into his car, told the dispatcher what had happened, and then shook his head.

"Indians," whispered Peone.

"Yeah, Indians," said Lester, the old man in the back seat. He laughed.

"What's so funny?" asked Peone.

"Catholic cops are funny," said Lester.

"You were listening?"

"Yeah."

"Yeah? Catholic Indians are funny."

"There's lots of Catholic Indians."

"There's lots of Catholic cops."

The old man started laughing again. Peone had to laugh a little with him.

"So, tell me the truth," said Peone. "Why did your friend beat you up? I thought you Indians took care of each other."

"We do take care of each other," said Lester. "But I don't know that Indian and he didn't beat me up. I told you. Some white guys did it. And stole my goddamn shoes."

Peone stepped out of the car, grabbed the shoes, and threw them into the back seat with the old man.

"There's your shoes," said Peone when he was back in the car. He wondered how he would fill out the paperwork on this encounter. After his fellow officers heard about this, they would probably give him a nickname. Something like Altar Boy or Shoes. Peone smiled. He liked nicknames.

18

Last Call at Big Heart's

Wilson walked into Big Heart's Soda and Juice Bar. There was a small crowd of forty or fifty Indians. They all stared at Wilson as he sat at the bar, where Mick had a glass of milk waiting for him.

"Slow night?" Wilson asked Mick.

"With Indians," said Mick, "it's never slow."

Wilson sipped at his milk and looked around the bar. It felt changed. He studied the patrons as they studied him.

"Hey, Casper," said Reggie, the Spokane. Ty stood behind him. "How Indian are you tonight?"

"Indian enough," said Wilson. "Where's Harley?"

"He's missing in action," said Reggie. "Tell me again, how Indian are you?"

"Indian enough."

"Sure you are. How much Indian blood you got anyways? Maybe a thimble's worth?"

"The blood don't matter. It's the heart that matters."

Ty and Reggie laughed.

"What's so funny?" asked Wilson.

"You know," Reggie said. "I was reading a movie magazine last week and found out that Farrah Fawcett is one-eighth Choctaw Indian. Isn't that funny?"

"I didn't know that," said Wilson.

"Yeah," said Reggie. "That means she's got more Indian blood than you do. If you get to be an Indian, then Farrah gets to be Indian, too."

"If she wants to be."

"You really think that's how it works, don't you?" Reggie asked Wilson. Reggie was heating up. "You think you can be Indian just by saying it, enit?"

Wilson shrugged his shoulders.

"June 25, 1876," Reggie said.

"The Battle of Little Bighorn," said Wilson.

"No white people survived that, did they?"

"Nope, just a Cavalry horse named Comanche."

"Every horse is an Indian horse."

Wilson nodded.

"We might let you be an Indian for an hour if you buy us a drink."

Wilson bought the two Indians their drinks.

"Hey," asked Wilson, with little subtlety. "You guys been following that Indian Killer case?"

"What about it?" asked Reggie.

"They found another body," said Wilson.

Reggie looked at Ty, then back to Wilson.

"How do you know that?" Reggie asked Wilson.

"Well, I don't like to talk about it, but I'm an ex-cop."

"We know you're an ex-cop," said Reggie. "And you're a writer, too. Now, tell us something we don't know. You think we're so stupid. I was a goddamn history major. I've studied books you wouldn't know how to read. Jeez, you come in here always asking questions about how we live, what we eat, about our childhoods. Taking notes in your head. We know it. What do you do when you leave here? Dig up graves?"

Wilson was wide-eyed.

"Don't be so surprised, Casper. You white guys always think you're fooling us poor, dumb Injuns."

"Well, uh, I, ah," stuttered Wilson, trying to regain his composure. "I was down at the station. They found the body downtown. They think the Indian Killer did it."

"Every time they find a white guy, how come they think the Indian Killer did it?"

Reggie stared hard at Wilson. Ty took a step back. Wilson could feel the tension in the room. He could see Reggie's blue eyes darken with anger. As casually as possible, Wilson reached inside his coat, and kept his hand there. Wilson had known Reggie for a while, had sat with him, and had tolerated the insults. Wilson had thought it all in good fun, but now he wondered if he had been mistaken.

"You know an Indian guy named John Smith?" asked Wilson with just the slightest tremor in his voice.

Reggie shook his head. Ty made no response.

"I know him," said a woman.

All three men turned to look at Fawn, who had been watching the confrontation, along with everybody else in Big Heart's.

"Don't talk to him, Fawn," said Reggie. "He's full of shit."

Fawn ignored Reggie.

"I danced with John the other night," Fawn said to Wilson. "He was kind of weird. Good-looking. But off, you know?"

Wilson took the photograph out of his pocket and showed it to Fawn. Reggie stepped closer to Wilson.

"Yeah, that's him," said Fawn. "See what I mean? Good-looking. But goofy."

"You think he's dangerous?" Wilson asked.

"John? No way. Reggie's the dangerous one. Reggie and his dipshit sidekicks beat up John. Enit, Reggie?"

"Shut the fuck up," Reggie said. "He's a cop."

"An ex-cop," corrected Ty. Reggie silenced him with a rude hand gesture. Reggie took another step closer to Wilson, who reached further into his jacket. Reggie noticed and reached inside his jacket.

Nobody moved or said a word. Wilson looked around the room. The Indians stared at him with suspicion, bemusement, anger, and outright disgust. Wilson knew he had crossed some invisible boundary. His presence in the bar had been tolerated only because he had agreed to the terms of an unwritten treaty. Now he had broken the rules and smashed the treaty into pieces. Wilson could hear the alarms ringing in his head. He was not surprised that they sounded like drums. With his hand inside his jacket, he edged toward the door.

"You ain't being so friendly now, Casper," said Reggie, cutting off Wilson's path to the door. Wilson glanced at Ty, who took a few steps backward. Good, thought Wilson, he was not going to get involved. Yet Wilson still felt like an idiot. He knew he had taken everything for granted. He was all alone in a hostile place.

"You think you're so smart," said Reggie. "You come in here acting all Indian, thinking you fit in, thinking you belong. I got news for you, Casper. We only let you hang around because it was fun to pitch you shit. You just ate all of that shit up and swallowed it down. You just took our shit and bought us drinks. We've been playing you hard, Casper. You don't belong here, man, you never did."

"Reggie," said Wilson, searching for a way out. "I'm trying to decide if you've got a gun in your jacket. Maybe a blade instead. Or maybe you're bluffing. Maybe it's just your wallet. Or your comb. And I bet you're wondering what I have my hand on, aren't you? Do I have a knife, a pistol? I'm an ex-cop. I got to have a piece, right? Now, I was never Billy the Kid when I was working, and I've gotten older and slower, but I'm willing to bet that I'm fast enough to beat you. What do you think?"

With his hand inside his jacket, Reggie smiled at the mystery writer. Wilson was old and fat. He limped. He was going bald. Reggie smiled. Very slowly, he pulled his empty hand out of his jacket and showed it to Wilson.

"How, white man," said Reggie in a sternly cinematic Indian voice, which caused the whole bar to break into laughter. One small battle was over. Suddenly the victor because he had shamed Wilson, Reggie triumphantly stepped out of Wilson's way. With his hand still inside the jacket, Wilson edged toward the exit. He saw the smiling faces of the Indians as he backed out of the bar. Fawn was shaking her head. As the door closed behind him, Wilson heard the entire bar erupt into laughter.

19

Running

John ran until he could barely breathe. He ran down the alleys into the dark beneath the Alaskan Way Viaduct. He thought he might find safety there among the other Indians. But John could not find any Indians. He walked by the loading dock near Pioneer Square and found no Indians. From beneath the Viaduct, he peered north up toward the Union Gospel Mission and saw no Indians waiting to enter. No Indians in Occidental Park. No Indians among the homeless sleeping in cardboard houses down near the ferry docks. All the Indians had left the city and deserted John. He reeled with shock and fell to the ground. He pounded the pavement with his fists. He set his forehead against the damp cement and tried to quiet the noise in his head.

John was still prone on the ground when the 4Runner pulled up next to him. Aaron and Barry quickly climbed out of the pickup and jumped John, who curled into a fetal ball as protection. John could hear nothing now except the thud of boots against his body and the attackers' violent exhalations of breath. There were no voices, no music, no wind or rain. He heard neither the sudden screeching of brakes nor the shouted curses when Marie pulled up in her sandwich truck and confronted the white boys who were beating him.

"Hey, hey, get away from him!" shouted Marie. She held a butter knife in her left hand.

Aaron and Barry stopped beating John long enough to look at Marie. She was a tiny Indian woman holding a butter knife, for God's sake, and she was all alone.

"Get the fuck out of here," threatened Aaron. Then he recognized Marie from his brother's Native American literature class. "Oh, you fucking bitch. You're next, you're next."

Barry heard something new and more dangerous in Aaron's voice.

"You heard me," said Marie, her voice steady and strong. "Get away from him."

Aaron looked down at John, who was still curled into a ball. He looked back at Marie.

"Fuck you," Aaron said and took a step toward Marie. She held the butter knife out in front of her.

"That's all you got?" asked Aaron as he took another step closer to Marie.

Marie smiled.

"What you smiling at, bitch?"

She was still smiling when Boo opened the back door of the sandwich van and three Indian men and three Indian women stormed out. They were a ragtag bunch of homeless warriors in soiled clothes and useless shoes. But when John looked up from the ground, he saw those half-warriors attack the white boys. The Indians were weak from malnutrition and various diseases, but they kicked, scratched, and slapped with a collective rage. John wondered how those Indians could still fight after all they had been through. He had seen Indians like that before, sleeping in doorways, on heating vents outside city hall, in cardboard condominiums. He did not understand their courage, how they could keep fighting when all he wanted to do was close his eyes and fade into the pavement. The fight was quick and brutal. Two Indian men, clutching their stomachs, had fallen to the pavement. One Indian woman with a bloody mouth leaned against a car. Barry and Aaron fought their way through the remaining Indians and into their pickup.

"Get us out of here!" shouted Barry, who would notice his missing teeth later in jail. Aaron, who would notice the broken bones in his right hand when he fought the police officer who'd come to arrest him, dropped the car into gear and nearly ran over an Indian man as he careened off another car, jumped a curb, and drove away.

The Indians were celebrating their victory as Marie knelt beside John.

"Are you okay?" she asked.

John rolled over and looked up into Marie's eyes.

"John?" She was surprised. His face was battered and bruised.

He nodded his head.

"Are you okay?"

He nodded his head.

"Hey, help me out here," Marie called to the others. They carried John to the sandwich van and set him inside. The rest of the Indians climbed in and pulled the door shut behind them. The men were loudly celebrating, exchanging high fives and hugs. Boo, Indian-for-a-day, screamed triumphantly and pumped his fists into imaginary enemies, shadowboxing with his whole life. Marie sat in the driver's seat, resting her head on the steering wheel. She wanted to cry. She was shocked by her anger, and how much she had wanted to hurt those white boys. Nearly blind with her own rage, she had wanted to tear out their blue eyes and blind them.

"Did you see them run?" asked Crazy Robert. "They ran like Custer, cousins, they ran like Custer."

Joseph, holding his bruised belly in pain, laughed loudly.

"The Indians won again!" shouted King, forgetting that Indians had never won anything in the first place. The Indian men hugged one another, laughed into one another's faces, eyes brighter and wider than they had been in years.

Boo, who had been busy punching the shadows, now sat quietly in his chair. The Indian men had forgotten he was there. Boo looked down at his hands.

Agnes and Annie were tending to Kim's bloody mouth. Agnes held a handful of Kim's teeth.

"Hey!" Agnes shouted. "We got to get her to a hospital!"

Her green eyes electric with pain, Kim stared up at Agnes and Annie, and tried a toothless smile.

"We did it," said Kim.

"Did what?" asked Agnes.

There was no answer to that question.

"Marie!" shouted Annie. "We got to go!"

Marie sat up in the driver's seat, looked back at her passengers. John had struggled to a sitting position.

"John," said Marie. "You should lie down."

John looked at Marie. He saw the large eyes, the long, black hair, and those crooked teeth. He noticed that her glasses were missing. Probably knocked off her face during the fight. Scratch marks across her forehead and cheeks. The glasses were probably broken, lying on the street outside, in pieces and fragments.

"John?" asked Marie, wanting to ask a question, but unsure what she wanted to know.

The other Indian men had stopped celebrating to watch John. The Indian women watched him, too. John could see his face in their faces, the large noses and cheekbones, the dark eyes and skin, the thin mouth and prominent chin, white teeth. He looked into the faces of these Indians who had saved him.

King, the failed college student, who walked the shelves of the Elliott Bay Book Company, picked out a book at random, and read a few pages a day until he finished it. Joseph, the recluse, who always wore a pair of nonprescription sunglasses, kept a hand drum hidden in the brush near the freeway, and would still sing old tribal songs. The newspaper man, Crazy Robert, who was a reporter for the *Seattle Times* when he was twenty-five and homeless by the time he was thirty-five. Obese in his youth, Robert had become impossibly thin. And the women. Agnes, who kept a menagerie of stray dogs and scavenger birds, spoke in whispers. Green-eyed Kim, the angry one, the nurse who had spent ten years in prison for killing an abusive husband. Annie, with black hair that once flowed down to her knees, now knotted and tangled beyond repair. She used to sing standards in a Holiday Inn Lounge in Norman, Oklahoma.

John did not know any of these Indians, could know nothing of their backgrounds. He did not know why they had fallen apart or what small thread kept them tied together now. Despite all their pain and suffering, these Indians held together, held onto one another.

John looked into the eyes of those Indians. He looked into the eyes of Boo, the white man who had been forever damaged in a war. Boo and the Indians all had the same stare, as if they spent most of their day anticipating the sudden arrival of the bullet that was meant for them. John saw the bruises and blood. And wanted to talk, to finally speak. To tell them about Father Duncan and the desert, the dreams he had of his life on a reservation, and those rare moments when he had stood on tall buildings and seen clearly. But there was no language in which he could express himself.

John saw that Marie, the sandwich lady, was crying now, tears rolling down her face. Falling to the floor of the van, they would collect and fill up the world. He wanted to tell her everything. He wanted to get on his knees before her and confess all of his sins. He wanted to rest his head in her lap, feel her fingers combing through his hair, and hear her softly singing. *Hush, hush,* she would sing, *everything will be fine in the morning.* He wanted to tell her about the desert. He wanted to give her a gift for all that she had done.

"John," said Marie, wanting him to speak. She could see him standing at the protest powwow, not wanting to owl dance, but forced into it by tradition. She could see him, with golf club in hand, standing over Wilson and the cab driver, then curled into the smallest possible version of himself as those white boys punched and kicked him. John looked at her, through her. Marie felt a sudden rush of heat. She could smell smoke. She could see an empty landscape, golden sand, blue sky, a series of footprints leading toward the horizon. She could see the dark figure of a man in the distance. He grew smaller and smaller. No matter how far or fast she ran, Marie knew that she could never catch him.

"Hey, man," said Boo, trying to break the tension in the truck. The other Indians were silent and still.

John turned toward Boo, who could see the emptiness in the big Indian's eyes.

"Hey, come on," said Boo and offered John a sandwich. It was a small and ridiculous gesture.

John looked at the sandwich. He looked at the crippled white man, who had lost almost everything. He had lost his family, his home, his country, the use of his legs.

"Here," Boo said again and held the sandwich closer to John.

"John," said Marie, wanting John to accept Boo's gift.

John heard Marie's voice in the distance. He looked at the sandwich, that small offering. He closed his eyes and imagined his birth.

John hears the slight whine of machinery. He hears gunfire. Explosions. A bird cry. The machine closer now and louder. The *whomp-whomp* of blades as the helicopter descends. John hears it land on the pavement outside the van. John closes his eyes and sees the man in the white jumpsuit running across the pavement, holding a bundle of blankets in his arms. The white jumpsuit man wears a white helmet and visor that hides his face. Another white man and woman wait at the end of the street. They huddle together beneath a huge umbrella. The helicopter brings the rain. The man in the white jumpsuit holds the baby in his arms. Swaddled in blankets, the baby is warm and terrified. Beneath the umbrella, the man and woman wait. He is a handsome man, pale-skinned and thin. He grimaces, tries to smile, then grimaces again, awkwardly, as if the smile were somehow painful. She is a beautiful large-breasted woman with ivory skin and clear eyes. The man in the white jumpsuit runs to the man and woman beneath the umbrella, and offers them the baby swaddled in blankets. The baby is small, just days from birth, and brown-skinned, with a surprisingly full head of black hair. The white woman takes the baby and holds him to her empty breast. The baby suckles air. The white man pulls his wife closer beneath their shared umbrella. He tries to smile. The man in the white jumpsuit turns and runs back to the helicopter. He gives the pilot a thumbs-up and the chopper carefully ascends, avoiding power lines and telephone poles.

John opened his eyes and looked around the sandwich van. Everybody was quiet and still, waiting for him to speak or move. John, feeling unworthy and too ill to be healed, looked again at Boo's small offering. Bread, blood. John could hear the helicopter floating away.

John knew that the man in the white jumpsuit was to blame for everything that had gone wrong. Everything had gone wrong from the very beginning, when John was stolen from his Indian mother. That had caused the first internal wound and John had been bleeding ever since, slowly dying and drying, until he was just a husk drifting in a desert wind. John knew who was to blame. If it had been possible, John would have reached out, lifted the visor, and seen the face of that man in the white jumpsuit. John knew he would have recognized the curve of the jaw and the arrogant expression. John had seen it before.

Once more, Boo offered the sandwich to John, who this time shook his head at that smallest kindness. There was no time for kindness. John needed to be saved and John knew exactly which white man had to die for him. He moved to the back of the truck, opened the door, and stumbled to the pavement. He did not look back, afraid of what he might see, and nobody in the truck tried to stop him. Marie watched John go away. Her skin felt hot and dry. She wondered how it felt to kill a white man.

20

Radio Silence

Truck Schultz listened to the police radio scanner. Dozens of calls. Bar fights, domestic assaults, arson. The Seattle Urban Indian Health Center had been firebombed. Two police officers had been ambushed by rock-throwing Indians. Random gunfire. Police were looking for a truck full of white kids who were attacking homeless Indians. After he'd announced that the Indian Killer was responsible for Edward Letterman's death, all hell had broken loose. Worse than New Year's Eve. Worse than a full-moon Saturday night. Truck was in awe of his own power. He had to speak. He leaned toward the microphone.

"I don't think so," said Officer Randy Peone as he stepped into the studio. He pointed a finger at Truck. "You ain't got nothing else to say tonight. Not one damn thing."

21

How It Happened

Outside the Tulalip Tribal Casino, David Rogers was trembling. He was alone in the dark parking lot and was terrified. He had two thousand dollars in cash in his pocket and suddenly felt very vulnerable. As he tried to open his car door, he dropped his keys. He bent over to pick them up and he felt a hot pain at the back of his head, saw a bright white light, and then saw nothing at all.

When he woke, David was lying facedown on the back seat of an old Chevy Nova. Two white men, Spud and Lyle, first cousins, pulled David out of the Nova and dragged him through the woods to a clearing a hundred feet off the road. Still groggy, suffering from a severe concussion, David could barely focus on the two men. He looked down at the ground and saw a solitary flower. He wondered if it was a lily. He wondered if camas root grew there. He wondered how long it had been growing.

"He's awake," said Lyle.

"Holy crow," said Spud as he counted the money again. "Little bastard was rich."

"How much?"

"A lot, I think."

David looked up at the cousins. He tried to think clearly. He wanted to tell them something about Hemingway.

"He's seen our faces," said Lyle.

"Yeah, yeah," said Spud, thinking hard.

"You think anybody saw us take him?"

"Nah, those Indians can't see for shit."

Lyle and Spud laughed.

"What should we do with him?" asked Lyle.

"I don't know. I guess we should shoot him."

David tried to get to his feet. Spud pushed him backward and David sat down hard, his back against a fallen tree.

"He's just a kid," said Lyle.

"A rich kid."

"That'll be true."

Spud pulled out his pistol, a .38 Special, and aimed it at David's face. Lyle covered his face. Spud's hand was shaking. He closed his eyes and pulled the trigger. A startled owl lifted from a nearby tree.

"Holy crow," said Spud. "I killed him."

"Yeah, he looks like he's asleep."

"Well, what should we do now?"

"I say we get the hell out of here."

With that, Spud and Lyle climbed into their Chevy Nova, drove north through Canadian customs without incident, and into Vancouver. That same night, they lost the two thousand dollars in an illegal poker game, plus another thousand dollars in promises. When those promises couldn't be kept, Spud and Lyle were driven to a secluded spot by a river and forced to kneel in the mud. With their hands tied behind their backs. Spud and Lyle pleaded for their lives but only the river listened, and it didn't care.

Shot once in each eye, Spud and Lyle's bodies were found by a hiker later that summer. David Rogers's murder was never solved.

22

Testimony

"Could you tell us your name, for the record? And where you're from?"

"Uh, my name is Sean Ward. I'm a student at the University of Washington. I'm from Selkirk, um, Selkirk, Washington. I need to, uh, talk about some things."

"What do you need to tell us, Sean?"

"Well, this isn't about just me. Yeah. It's about my roommates, Aaron and Barry. Uh, that's Aaron Rogers and Barry Church."

"Yes?"

"Well, you see, we're the guys in the masks. The ones who've been beating up Indians. We're the baseball bats. Uh, yeah. We're the masks."

"Where are Aaron and Barry now?"

"They're still out there, I guess. I left them earlier. I tried to get them to stop, but they wouldn't."

"Is that why you have that bump on your head?"

"Yeah, Aaron punched me."

"Why are you telling us this?"

"I'm not sure, you know? I mean, I love those guys. Aaron and Barry. I mean, I think we started doing this for a good reason."

"A good reason?"

"Well, uh, maybe it's not a good reason. But people would understand, I think. You know that David Rogers? The guy who disappeared from the casino? He was our other roommate. I mean, David and Aaron were brothers. That's what started us in, you know. It was for, uh, revenge."

"How many people did you assault?"

"Well, there was the guy on the Burke-Gilman Trail. Then that couple on Queen Anne Hill. Then some homeless old guy earlier today. Uh, that makes it what, four people? Yeah, four."

"Three of those people are still in the hospital. You almost killed them."

"Yeah, I know. But, uh, I know you're not going to believe me. You shouldn't believe me. But I didn't hurt anybody. I carried a bat and stuff but I never used it. It was mostly Aaron. Barry, too. But it was mostly Aaron. I made them quit, you know? I made Aaron stop hitting people. If I hadn't been there, Aaron might have really killed somebody."

"You're in a lot of trouble, Sean."

"I know."

"Why'd you do this? What are you going to tell your parents? How are you going to explain this?"

"I don't know. I mean, uh, it's like this white-Indian thing has gotten out of control. And the thing with the blacks and Mexicans. Everybody blaming everybody. I mean, it's like white people get blamed for everything these days. I mean, I know we did some bad stuff. I know it. I know what me and Aaron and Barry did was wrong. But it was anger. Frustration, you know? David disappeared, and we, uh, just lost control. I mean, somebody had to pay for it. Somebody was to blame for it. I don't know what happened. I can't explain it all. Just look around at the world. Look at this country. Things just aren't like they used to be."

"Son, things have never been like how you think they used to be."

23

Dreaming

Wilson left Big Heart's after his encounter with Reggie and drove home to his apartment on Capitol Hill. He wondered how he was going to fix things with Reggie and Big Heart's. He had done so much for his fellow Indians. He had made the ultimate sacrifice. He wanted them to love him. He parked his pickup in front of the building, slowly trudged up the front walk, and checked his mail.

Isn't that how it happened?

He loved his mail. There was none, of course, but he checked anyway. Then he walked upstairs, opened his door, and turned on the light. His apartment was as neat as always. The small table. Two forks, two spoons, two knives, two plates. The black-and-white photograph of his birth parents on the dresser. The foldout couch. It was cold in the apartment because Wilson always turned down the heat before he went out. Seattle was cold at night during the summer and winter. He was slightly chilled and wanted to climb beneath the covers and sleep for days. First things first, though. He brushed and flossed his teeth, undressed, and tossed his dirty clothes into the hamper.

Isn't that how it happened?

Then he slipped into his favorite pajamas and settled into bed. He could hear his neighbors turning in for the night. Running water, flushing toilets, creaking bed springs. It was very quiet. One police siren, then another, and a third. Cars on the freeway ten blocks to the west. Muffled conversation between two men walking down the street in front of the building.

Isn't that how it happened?

In his bed, awake and wondering about the Indian Killer, about finishing the novel. He thought about John Smith, who, in Wilson's mind, remained as unfinished as the novel. In the dark, Wilson could still see the photograph of John at the construction site. John's fellow workers eat together, share a joke and common laughter, slap one another on the back. John sits back all by himself, his eyes dark and impenetrable. Wilson thought that a person driving down a road and coming upon a tunnel as dark as those eyes would stop, turn the car around, and go miles out of his way to avoid it. As it was, Wilson had tried to follow those eyes. Sitting with John's mother, he had felt it when something left her body. Something solid and substantial. Following John's eyes into Big Heart's, he saw Reggie's eyes, just as dark, but lit with a more volatile fire. Quicker to burn, easier to extinguish. Reggie was probably in Big Heart's telling stories and laughing right now, reliving his encounter with Wilson, turning a potentially fatal conflict into a series of comic escapades.

Isn't that how it happened?

Wilson was thinking about John Smith, then fell so quickly to sleep that he effortlessly slipped into a dream about Smith. He dreamed about Smith pushing that knife into the white man in the University District. He saw Smith slit the throat of the businessman. Then Smith was smiling as he lifted the young boy from his bed. Then Wilson saw himself with that knife. Wilson saw himself pushing the knife into one white body, then another, and another, until there were multitudes.

Isn't that how it happened?

Then the dream changed, and Wilson was pulling up in front of his apartment building again. A brown hand reached through the open window of the truck and smashed Wilson's head against the steering wheel. Stunned and barely conscious, Wilson slumped in his seat and somebody, a dark figure, reached inside Wilson's jacket and took his weapon. Then the dark figure opened the door and pushed him out of the way. With Wilson stuffed under the dashboard, the dark figure sat quietly at the steering wheel, waiting to see if the commotion had attracted any attention. A police siren in the distance, but nobody shouted out. No lights suddenly appeared in the apartment building. No cars passed by. The dark figure started the pickup and slowly drove down Capitol Hill.

24

Testimony

"Dr. Mather, I hear you know who the Indian Killer is."

"Well, Officer, I don't know who the Indian Killer is, but I have some information you may find useful in your investigation."

"And?"

"Well, it's about a former student of mine, a Spokane Indian named Reggie Polatkin."

"Any relation to Marie Polatkin?"

"Why, yes. They're cousins. How do you know her?"

"She's the Sandwich Lady."

"Excuse me?"

"She delivers sandwiches to the homeless."

"Really. I can't imagine her in such a role."

"What do you mean?"

"Well, she always seems so impulsive, so emotional. What's the word I'm searching for? So individualistic. Not tribal at all. I mean, she actually threatened me with physical violence earlier today."

"How did she threaten you?"

"She said she'd eat my heart."

"Really? Marie Polatkin said that?"

"Yes, she did. Of course, I had to drop her from my class. I'm thinking of pursuing more serious charges against her."

"Well, I wouldn't know anything about that. Tell me more about her cousin."

"Reggie? Well, as I said, Reggie is a former student of mine. We had a misunderstanding and he, well, he assaulted me."

"Sounds like you and the Polatkin family have a problem."

"I hardly find this amusing, Officer. I must protest your behavior."

"Protest noted."

"Officer, Reggie and I used to travel together. And we talked. Reggie had a very violent father. Very violent. A white man. I always worried that Reggie was going to hurt somebody."

"Why were you worried?"

"Because he said he dreamed about killing people."

25

The Last Skyscraper in Seattle

Slowly, Wilson woke and made several attempts to open his eyes. His head ached and he could taste blood. He tried to reach up and touch his face to see how badly he was hurt, but discovered that he was tied to a wall. He could not move his arms or legs. He tested the ropes, but they held tight. How had this happened? Wilson wondered if he was still dreaming.

But Wilson was tied to a wall. His head did ache and his mouth tasted of real blood. He couldn't move his arms or legs. He did test the ropes that held him. He stood eagle-armed, his wrists tightly secured to two-by-fours, his legs tied at the ankles to another two-by-four. All of the two-by-fours were part of a wall frame. Wilson looked around. By twisting his head, Wilson could see that he was tied to a wall frame in an upper floor of an unfinished downtown building. He could see the other frames that would hold the walls for the bathrooms and two large corner offices. He noticed frames for rows of smaller offices between corner offices. The elevators and shafts were finished, looked strange and out of place. Various saw-horses scattered here and there. A forgotten black metal lunch box near a power saw. An open metal door just north of Wilson. An unlit exit sign above it. Wilson tested the ropes. He could see through the wooden skeleton of the floor to the buildings that surrounded him. In one building, a janitor pushed a vacuum back and forth, back and forth. A police siren many floors below him. Then another siren, and a third, a fourth, blending into one long scream. Wilson could sense that somebody was standing behind him. Wilson knew that his shoulder holster was empty and that somebody behind him was holding the pistol.

"John?" asked Wilson.

"Yes," John answered. Wilson twisted his head violently from side to side in an effort to locate him.

"John? Where are you? Let me see you, okay? Let's talk, okay?" asked Wilson. John heard the fear in Wilson's voice, even as he tried to bury it beneath layers of professional calm.

"John?"

John inched closer to Wilson and touched his arm.

"Hey, John, you scared me there. Why don't you come out here where I can see you? We can talk, right? Why don't we talk?"

John remained silent.

"Hey, John, I met your mom tonight. She's a beautiful woman."

John saw his Indian mother on the delivery table. She reached for her Indian child.

"Olivia, right? She really loves you, man."

John saw Olivia, wearing only a towel, walking across a hard-wood floor. Her hair wet, her damp feet leaving slight prints on the wood.

"She wants you to come home. Don't you want to go home?"

Wilson waited as long as he could stand for a response. His voice broke.

"And what about your dad, John? What's his name?"

I don't have a father, John thought, but he saw Daniel dribbling a basketball in the driveway. *Like this*, Daniel was shouting, *like this*.

"Come on, John, talk to me. It's okay. We can talk about it. Everybody will understand. I'll make them understand. I'm a writer, John. What do you say?"

Silence. Wilson thought hard, trying to save his life.

"Listen, John, any Indian would kill a white guy if he thought he could get away with it. Which Indian wouldn't do it? I'm an Indian. I know. There are a million white men I'd kill if they'd let me. Talk to me, John. Indian to Indian. Real Indians. I'll understand."

John heard the fear in Wilson's voice now.

"Hey, remember up by my apartment? Remember when you had that golf club? Man, I thought you were going to beat my ass. Who were you with? That Indian woman, the one who hates me, right? Maria, Marie, Mary? What's her name?

"I knew an Indian woman named Mary. Beautiful Mary. Back when I was a rookie. She lived on the streets, man, and I looked out for her. Really, I did. I was the only Indian cop on the force. The only one. Can you believe that? There aren't many now, but I was the only one then. And I'll tell you. It was hard work. They always gave me the shit jobs. Called me Chief and Tonto and everything else. Man, it was awful. But I took care of the Indians, you know? All those Indians who lived downtown? Just like now, huh? Lots of them. And Beautiful Mary was my favorite. I mean, I never told anybody this before, but I loved her. I mean, really loved her. I kept thinking we were going to get married or something. I thought we'd have little Indian babies, you know? But then she was killed. Raped and killed. They stuffed her behind a Dumpster. I just wanted to die, you know?"

John stepped forward and pressed the pistol against the back of Wilson's head. Terrified, Wilson tried to think, not wanting the ultimate indignity of being killed by his own weapon.

"Please," Wilson said as he struggled against the ropes. He was afraid of the pistol. He was begging for his life from the man he knew was the Indian Killer.

"Don't hurt me," Wilson said to John. "I'm not a white man. I'm Indian. You don't kill Indians."

26

Testimony

"Mr. Williams, I'm sure you know why you're here, don't you?"

"Call me Ty. And yeah, I figure it's because of what we did to that white guy."

"And who is this 'we' you're referring to?"

"You know, Reggie and Harley and me."

"Reggie Polatkin, correct?"

"Yeah."

"And Harley?"

"Harley Tate, man, he's deaf. He's a Colville Indian."

"And where is Harley Tate now?"

"You mean you ain't got him? And Reggie, too? I figured you had us all nabbed."

"Nabbed for what, Ty?"

"For beating up that white guy on the football field. Well, I should say that Reggie really hurt him. Harley and I didn't know that was going to happen. What was that white guy's name. I read it in the papers, but I don't remember."

"Robert Harris."

"Yeah, that's it. Reggie took that guy's eyes. But he's doing okay, enit?"

"Mr. Harris is fine. But he says you tried to kill him."

"Hey, I don't know nothing about any murders. Yeah, I beat up on that white guy. But like I said, Reggie really hurt him. I didn't want no part of that. You got to talk to Reggie about that."

"You know where Reggie happens to be?"

"Nope."

"Where were you this evening about ten o'clock, Ty?"

"I was at Big Heart's, up on Aurora. I swear."

"And where were Reggie and Harley at ten?"

"I don't know, man. I mean, Reggie left after he almost got in a fight with Jack Wilson."

"The mystery writer, Jack Wilson? The cop?"

"Yeah, he hangs around the bar a lot. He's a Wannabe Indian."

"Wannabe?"

"Yeah, you know, wants to be Indian."

"I see, and what time did Reggie leave the bar?"

"I don't know. About nine or so, I guess."

"And you didn't go with him?"

"No, I swear. There's about a hundred Indians who'll tell you I was in that bar until closing."

"We'll check on that. How about Harley?"

"Harley took off this afternoon and I ain't seen him since. He and Reggie almost duked it out."

"Does Reggie own a knife?"

"A knife?"

"How many times has Reggie used this knife on someone?"

"I don't know anything about a knife. Hey, shit, this ain't about that Indian Killer, is it?"

"You tell us what this knife is about."

"Hey, man, you ain't going to pin that Indian Killer stuff on me. I didn't kill nobody. And Reggie didn't kill nobody, either. I know Reggie. He's smart. He went to college, you know?"

"We know. He beat up his professor. A great student."

"I don't know what that was about, man. Maybe Reggie was just trying to scare him. That professor put the whammy on him, you know? Got Reggie kicked out. Reggie was smart, man. I tell you. He didn't kill nobody. You go ahead and run your tests. Get all the witnesses you want. But I didn't kill nobody. Reggie didn't kill nobody."

"Do you own a knife?"

"Yeah, I got a Swiss Army knife, a butter knife, and a steak knife at home. Shit, yeah, I own knives. I have to eat, enit?"

"Did Reggie own a knife?"

"I don't know, man."

"And what about Harley Tate?"

"You'll have to ask him yourself."

"And where is he?"

"Only Harley knows where Harley is."

27

Decisions

"Don't hurt me," Wilson said to John. "I'm not a white man. I'm Indian. You don't kill Indians."

John wondered if Wilson knew the difference between dreaming and reality. How one could easily become the other.

In his dreams, John saw his Indian mother standing on the porch as he drove away from the reservation. It was cold and rainy, as it would be on a day such as that. Or on another day, in another dream, his Indian mother on the delivery table, in all the blood, too much blood. She has died during his birth. An evil child, he destroyed his mother's life as she gave him his.

Standing on the last skyscraper in Seattle, John was silent as the desert. The golden sand and blue sky. The long series of footprints leading to the horizon where that stand of palm trees waits. The wind beginning to blow. A storm approaching. Soon the sand would obscure the footprints and there would be no trace that anybody had come this way before.

John looked at the pistol in his hand and understood this was not the right thing to do. He dropped the pistol to the floor in front of Wilson, who was weeping. As Wilson continued to weep, the first ferry from Bainbridge Island docked at the wharf. Cars rolled off in orderly rows. Another jet passed by overhead, the nonstop from New York's Kennedy Airport. Indian lawyers were already in their offices. Indian doctors were sound asleep. Wilson wept. Mick, the bartender, sat alone at the bar in Big Heart's Soda and Juice Bar. He shuffled over to the jukebox, which was still playing songs that had been requested hours earlier, and pulled the plug. Olivia Smith stood quietly in the doorway of her husband's study. He was asleep, crumpled on the couch, a detailed map of the United States propped open on his chest. She curled up close to her husband on the small couch. In a downtown garage, the street sweepers had just finished their shift and were contemplating a long day of sleep. Fog. Rain. Wilson wept. Rescue helicopters landed at Harborview Medical Center a few blocks east of the last skyscraper in Seattle. Mark Jones stood silently at the foot of his parents' bed and watched them sleep. The ocean pounded against the shore. The alarm clocks were ringing, and workers, Indian and not, would soon fill the streets.

"What is it?" Wilson asked John. "What do you want?"

John stepped in front of Wilson. They stared at each other. John finally understood that Wilson was responsible for all that had gone wrong.

"You're the one," John said.

"What?"

"You're the one who's responsible."

"For what?"

John reached into his pocket and pulled out his knife. A thin blade. John didn't know if the blade would even cut Wilson. But if it worked, Wilson would bleed out all of his Indian blood, a few drops scattering in the cold wind. Then the rest of his blood, the white blood, would come in great bursts, one for each heartbeat, until there were no more heartbeats. John's former co-workers would find the body when they stepped from the elevator. The foreman's face would grow even more pale when he saw Wilson tied to the wall. The building would be haunted forever then. The foreman would finish the last skyscraper in the city and move on to his government job. He would be working on a freeway exit in the Cascade Mountains when he saw his first ghost. He would see Wilson, impossibly pale and bloodstained, walking down the freeway, his thumb out in hopes of a ride. Or John could cut Wilson's throat and then carry his body back down to the ground. He could drop his body into the cement mixer and fire the mixer up. He could bury Wilson in the foundation and nobody would ever find him. John knew that every building in Seattle contained the bones of fallen workers. Every building was a tomb. John pressed the dull knife hard against Wilson's throat.

"What is it?" Wilson asked. "What do you want from me?"

28

Leaving

Reggie Polatkin walked down the country highway. A hundred miles from Seattle, a thousand miles away, maybe more, maybe less. The sky was cloudy. It could have been night or day. Fields on either side of the road, though the crop was indiscernible. A cold breeze. Dead skunk smell saturated the air. So isolated. Reggie was startled when the car suddenly pulled up. A red truck, smelling of exhaust and farm animals. Reggie leaned into the open passenger window and saw the driver, an elderly white man. Gray hair, gray eyes, blue overalls. Chewing-tobacco stains on his large teeth. The old man smiled when he spoke.

"Hey, do you need a ride?" asked the old man.

Reggie nodded, climbed into the truck. He looked at the smiling farmer.

"Where you headed?" asked the old man.

"I'm running," said Reggie.

"I figured that."

"You ever hear of Captain Jack?"

"Can't say that I have. Was he a Navy guy?"

"Oh, no. He was a Modoc Indian. His real name was Kintpuash."

"Are you Modoc?"

"Nah, I'm Spokane. Little tribe that didn't do much fighting."

"Was Captain Jack a fighter?"

"Oh, yeah. He led about two hundred Modocs from a reservation in Oregon and set up camp in northern California, where they were supposed to be. Modocs aren't Oregon Indians. They're California Indians. Yeah, old Captain Jack had about eight warriors and the rest were women and children. Anyways, the Cavalry came after Jack. Captain Jack ran from them and hid in these lava beds, you know? Great hiding places. Miles and miles of tunnels and mazes. Captain Jack and his people fought off the Cavalry for months, man.

"Man, there was this one Modoc named Scarface Charlie who attacked a patrol of sixty-three soldiers and killed twenty-five of them. All by himself. You hear me? All by himself."

"He must have been quite the fighter."

"He was, he was. But they couldn't fight forever, I guess. They gave up. Captain Jack surrendered. I mean, he had all those women and children to worry about. So, Captain Jack surrendered and they hung him. They hung him, cut off his head, and shipped it off to the Smithsonian."

"The Smithsonian Museum?"

"Yeah, can you believe it? They displayed Jack's head like it was Judy Garland's red shoes or something. Like it was Archie Bunker's chair."

"That's a terrible story."

"Yeah, isn't it? And I'll tell you what. Captain Jack should never have surrendered. He should've kept fighting. He should've kept running and hiding. He could've done that forever."

"Is that why you're running, son?"

"That's right, old man, I'm not Captain Jack."

"So, where you running to?"

Reggie pointed up the highway, pointed north or south, east or west, pointed toward a new city, though he knew every city was a city of white men.

29

Flying

"What is it?" Wilson asked. "What do you want from me?"

"Please," John whispered. "Let me, let us have our own pain."

With a right hand made strong by years of construction work, with a blade that was much stronger than it looked, John slashed Wilson's face, from just above his right eye, down through the eye and cheekbone, past the shelf of the chin, and a few inches down the neck. Blood, bread.

"No matter where you go," John said to a screaming Wilson, "people will know you by that mark. They'll know what you did."

John touched Wilson's face with his left hand and then looked at the blood on his fingertips.

"You're not innocent," whispered John.

John dropped the knife, turned away from Wilson, quickly walked to the edge of the building, and looked down at the streets far below. He was not afraid of falling. John stepped off the last sky-scraper in Seattle.

John fell. Falling in the dark, John Smith thought, was different from falling in the sunlight. It took more time to fall forty floors in the dark. John's fall was slow and precise, often stalled in midair, as if some wind had risen from the ground to counteract the force of gravity. He had time to count the floors of the office tower across the street, ten, fifteen, thirty, forty. Time enough to look up and find the one bright window in a tower of dark glass across the street. A figure backlit in the window. Time enough to raise his arms above his head, his feet pointing down toward the street, falling that way. The figure moved in the window above him. He had time to wonder if the figure was dancing. Or shaking with fear. Or laughter. Or tears. He had time enough to watch the figure grow smaller as he fell. Falling, fallen, will fall, has fallen, fell. Falling. Because he finally and completely understood the voices in his head. Because he knew the heat and music left his body when he marked Wilson. John was calm. He was falling.

He was still watching the shadow in the fortieth-floor window when he hit the pavement. It was quiet at first. His eyes were closed, must have closed on impact. He listened to the silence, felt a heavy pressure in his spine, and opened his eyes. He was facedown on the pavement. Pushing himself up, he felt a tearing inside. He stood above the body embedded in the pavement, small fissures snaking away from the arms and legs. The body in blue jeans, red plaid shirt, brown work boots, long, black hair. A fine dust floating. An anonymous siren in the distance, on its way somewhere else. He looked up at the building across the street. The window on the fortieth floor was dark. He knelt down and touched the body embedded in the pavement. Still warm. He pulled the wallet from the body's blue jeans, found the photograph inside, and recognized the faces. He read the clipping about Father Duncan's disappearance. He pulled the cash out of the wallet, let the wind take it from his fingers, watched it float away. The streetlights flashed red, flashed red. He tucked the photograph and clipping inside the wallet, slid it back into the pocket of the fallen man. John looked down at himself and saw he was naked. Brown skin. Muscles tensed in anticipation of the long walk ahead of him. He studied the other body as it sank deeper into the pavement. John stood, stepped over that body, and strode into the desert. Dark now, the desert was a different place. Colder and safer. An Indian father was out there beyond the horizon. And maybe an Indian mother with a scar on her belly from a Cesarean birth. She could know John's real name. John wanted to find them both. He took one step, another, and then he was gone.

30

Testimony

"Ms. Polatkin, Marie, can you tell us something about John Smith?"

"He wasn't the Indian Killer."

"Why do you keep insisting on this? We have the murder weapon, we have Jack Wilson's sworn testimony. John Smith was the Indian Killer. Case closed."

"Jack Wilson is a liar."

"Have you seen Wilson's face? He looks like a car wreck. I hardly think he deserves to be called a liar. Have you even read his book about all of this?"

"No."

"You should. It's a very interesting portrait of John Smith. You'd like it. Wilson says that Indian children shouldn't be adopted by white parents. He says that those kids commit suicide way too often. You ask me, John's suicide was a good thing."

"Wilson doesn't know shit about Indians."

"Have you read Dr. Mather's book?"

"Absolutely not."

"Really? You're in it, you know? And it's not too flattering, I must say."

"So what."

"Mather thinks your cousin Reggie is the Indian Killer. He thinks you might have been a part of it, too."

"I hardly knew Reggie. And if I'd been a part of it, Mather wouldn't have enough fingers left to write a book."

"Are you threatening Dr. Mather?"

"No, I'm speaking metaphorically."

"Did you have anything to do with the killings?"

"No."

"Did you have anything to do with Reggie's assault of Robert Harris?"

"No."

"Do you know where Reggie is?"

"No."

"Do you know Harley Tate or Ty Williams?"

"No."

"Do you know where Harley Tate is?"

"No."

"Besides Wilson, you were the last one to see John Smith alive."

"Yeah. So?"

"What did you two talk about? Did you make plans for the future?"

"We didn't talk much at all. We were busy fighting off those white assholes."

"Barry Church and Aaron Rogers?"

"Yeah, why aren't you hassling them?"

"Barry and Aaron have their own troubles."

"Yeah, what did they get? Six months in county jail?"

"Weren't you in a class with Aaron's brother? The one who disappeared?"

"Yes."

"Aaron Rogers has indicated that you and David had a romantic relationship."

"That's a lie."

"My, my, Marie. Is every white man a liar?"

"Every one so far."

"So, what was the nature of your relationship with David Rogers?"

"We were in a class together. I talked to him a couple of times. He asked me out. I turned him down. He disappeared. They found his body. That's my relationship with David Rogers."

"I see. And did you know about the camas field on the Rogers's farm? Did you know about their land dispute with the Spokane Tribe?"

"The Spokanes have land disputes with most everybody. And no, I didn't know about David and the camas field."

"Did John Smith kill David Rogers?"

"No."

"How would you know that?"

"John Smith didn't kill anybody."

"Did you kill David Rogers?"

"No way."

"Did you and John Smith have a romantic relationship?"

"No. Listen to me. John Smith was screwed up. He was hurting. He didn't know up from down. He got screwed at birth. He had no chance. I don't care how nice his white parents were. John was dead from the start. And now you're killing him all over again. Can't you just leave him alone?"

"John Smith is all alone now. And he won't be hurting anybody ever again. It's all over."

"John never hurt anybody. And this isn't over."

"What makes you say that?"

"I just know."

"What else do you know?"

"I know that John Smith didn't kill anybody except himself. And if some Indian is killing white guys, then it's a credit to us that it took over five hundred years for it to happen. And there's more."

"Yes?"

"Indians are dancing now, and I don't think they're going to stop."

31

A Creation Story

A full moon. A cemetery on an Indian reservation. On this reservation or that reservation. Any reservation, a particular reservation. The killer wears a carved wooden mask. Cedar, or pine, or maple. The killer sits alone on a grave. The headstone is gray, its inscription illegible. There are many graves, rows of graves, rows of rows. The killer is softly singing a new song that sounds exactly like an old one. As the killer sings, an owl silently lands on a tree branch nearby. The owl shakes its feathers clean. It listens. The killer continues to sing, and another owl perches beside the first. Birds of prey, birds of prayer. The killer sings louder now, then stands. The killer's mouth is dry, tastes of blood and sweat. The killer carries a pack filled with a change of clothes, a few books, dozens of owl feathers, a scrapbook, and two bloody scalps in a plastic bag. Beneath the killer's jacket, the beautiful knife, with three turquoise gems inlaid in the handle, sits comfortably in its homemade sheath. The killer has no money, but feels no thirst or hunger. The killer finds bread and blood in other ways. The killer spins in circles and, with each revolution, another owl floats in from the darkness and takes its place in the tree. Dark blossom after dark blossom. The killer sings and dances for hours, days. Other Indians arrive and quickly learn the song. A dozen Indians, then hundreds, and more, all learning the same song, the exact dance. The killer dances and will not tire. The killer knows this dance is over five hundred years old. The killer believes in all masks, in this wooden mask. The killer gazes skyward and screeches. With this mask, with this mystery, the killer can dance forever. The killer plans on dancing forever. The killer never falls. The moon never falls. The tree grows heavy with owls.